The Rakess

"The rain always makes me feel . . . refulgent," Seraphina whispered. "Like my flesh is not large enough to possibly contain the things I feel and want. Like I am not constrained by rules or time."

The lightning struck again, setting the entire sky alight. It cast a glow upon the dreamy expression on her face. Adam imagined that face below him, rapt in pleasure, and shuddered.

"Will you be angry if I ravish you?" she whispered.

He looked up into her eyes, which were dark with desire.

"I'll be angry if you don't."

"Everything I want in a historical romance: smart, sexy, and feminist."

—Maya Rodale, *USA Today* bestselling author on *The Rakess*

"A new and soon to be iconic voice in the world of historical romance, Peckham distinguishes herself as a master of her craft."

—Liz Carlyle, *New York Times* and *USA Today* bestselling author on *The Rakess*

"*The Rakess* is a triumph, delicately written and unflinching in scope. The writing thrums with desire and conviction, and Seraphina and Adam will leave you aching for more of Peckham's passionate, progressive romances!"

—Sierra Simone, *USA Today* bestselling author

"An astonishingly good debut . . . The whole book is a breath of fresh air, both a complex, layered story and a soaring romance with two very real people at its heart."

—*New York Times Book Review* on *The Duke I Tempted*

BY SCARLETT PECKHAM

The Society of Sirens
THE RAKESS

The Secrets of Charlotte Street
THE DUKE I TEMPTED
THE EARL I RUINED
THE LORD I LEFT

SCARLETT PECKHAM

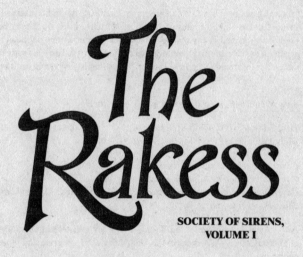

The Rakess

**SOCIETY OF SIRENS,
VOLUME I**

AVONBOOKS

An Imprint of HarperCollins*Publishers*

THE RAKESS. Copyright © 2020 by Scarlett Peckham. All rights reserved. Printed in the United States of America. No part of this book may be used or reproduced in any manner whatsoever without written permission except in the case of brief quotations embodied in critical articles and reviews. For information, address HarperCollins Publishers, 195 Broadway, New York, NY 10007.

First Avon Books mass market printing: May 2020

Print Edition ISBN: 978-0-06-293561-8
Digital Edition ISBN: 978-0-06-293562-5

Cover design by Patricia Barrow
Cover illustration by Alan Dingman
Cover photographs by Jeremy Bishop/Unsplash (storm); © Sabphoto/
Shutterstock (clouds)

Avon, Avon & logo, and Avon Books & logo are registered trademarks of HarperCollins Publishers in the United States of America and other countries.

HarperCollins is a registered trademark of HarperCollins Publishers in the United States of America and other countries.

FIRST EDITION

20 21 22 23 24   QGM   10 9 8 7 6 5 4 3 2 1

In memory of Mary Wollstonecraft, who is not a character in this book, but is the inspiration for it,

Fair readers, while this is a romance novel, it is a dark and stormy one. Here is a note on sensitive content, for those who like to know. (If you prefer to be surprised, skip this part!)

This book contains explicit sex; references to death of and abandonment by past romantic partners; trauma surrounding stillbirth, miscarriage and other aspects of 18th-century childbearing; sexual harassment, slut-shaming and misogyny; spousal coercion, kidnapping and control; and depictions of alcohol addiction and recovery.

Author's Note

Dear Reader,

I have devoured historical romance novels since I was a child. Which is why, perhaps, I am obsessed with rakes and ruin.

Growing up, it seemed like every other book I borrowed from the library was about a rake. You probably know him. He's the bone-meltingly handsome dissolute second son of a marquess or an earl. Charming but feckless. Seductive but empty. So good at sex it is like he studied it at University. And so devoted to practicing these amorous skills that you sometimes worry for his health.

We would often meet our rake in the arms of his mistress (one of many), whom he would dispassionately bring to the throes of ecstasy before ambling to his club for a desultory liquid lunch with his friends. His friends were also rakes—that is, unless we had met them in a previous book—in which case they were *reformed* rakes, who were now hopelessly besotted with their heavily pregnant wives.

This last part was key. The rake, I came to understand, was like a caterpillar, existing in a preliminary state. His sexual appetites were compulsive because he was emotionally undeveloped. His world was a swirl of wicked pleasures because he was trying to fill a larger chasm in his soul.

How delicious, to be the one to fill it. Because, as the saying goes, a reformed rake makes the best husband. After all, the devoted rake, transformed into the most doting of spouses, is still handsome, charming, virile, and so good at sex that it is frightening. But he is also madly in love with you. You have made him whole.

The fantasy of the rake is powerful. But it is always interesting to turn a fantasy on its head, shake it a few times, and see what topples out. When I thought of changing the traditional gender identity of a rake from a man to a woman, it occurred to me that there is already a feminized version of the rake trope in romance. We call her the ruined woman.

You know who I mean. The well-born daughter with a past. Perhaps she has had a lover, or perhaps there have only been whispers of one. But regardless, it has colored the world's understanding of her character and value. She is no longer marriageable, but she has been raised to *only* be marriageable. She must therefore either be rescued by a man willing to save her honor, or strike out in defiance on her own.

When the ruined woman falls in love, as she inevitably will, it will be with someone who sees past her damaged reputation to the wonderful person beneath. Often, she gets justice as well as love, winding up at the top of the society that tried to devalue her. Hers is a fantasy of redemption and vindication. And it is also delicious.

But her formative years are less appealing. For, unlike the rake, with his unrepentant wickedness and zest for erotic excess, the ruined woman is rarely living a life of pleasure. Perhaps she had a lover, who died before they married, or tricked her. But often, she did not even have a love affair—but has had her life destroyed by the mere suggestion of it. This is not a reflection of romance so much as a reflection of a double standard that persists in western culture: men who sleep around are admired for their virility, whereas women who sleep around are shamed for it, or worse.

And so it occurred to me that perhaps an interesting way to write a lady rake book was to combine the tropes of the rake and the ruined woman into one character. To make the heroine a woman who is blisteringly angry that she has been cast as ruined for a youthful affair, while her lover gets to be a rake. What happens if she objects to the very notion of ruin, and claims rakedom for herself?

And what happens when she falls in love? For in romance, neither rakedom nor ruin is ever the end of the story—it's the beginning.

While cogitating on all this (eighty percent of romance writing is cogitating, sadly), I happened to pick up the book *Romantic Outlaws* by Charlotte Gordon, a dual biography of Mary Wollstonecraft and her daughter, Mary Shelley. I read it in a few feverish sittings and came away with a burning, passionate love for Mary Wollstonecraft. This woman, I thought, was so like a romance heroine.

Among the things that she did in her life: founded a school; supported herself as a critic, philosopher, and novelist; conducted several intensely dramatic love affairs outside of marriage; embedded herself in Paris as a reporter on the French Revolution; traveled to Scandinavia alone with a baby to search for her lover's lost treasure; gave birth to the author of *Frankenstein*; and had the singular posthumous experience of said daughter losing her virginity on her gravestone.

Oh, and she wrote a seminal work of proto-feminist philosophy, *A Vindication of the Rights of Women*, which called for a radical change in the way that women were educated, and argued that women were as capable of reason and independence as men.

Wollstonecraft believed fiercely in these things in part because she had watched her own female loved ones suffer from their limited career options. She watched dear friends marry to support their extended families, only to become trapped in abusive relationships or die in childbirth. She herself struggled to find ways to support herself and her sisters without the ability her brothers had to inherit family money or enter a more lucrative trade than the low-paying teaching and governess positions that were available to her.

And while she was certainly not a freewheeling rake, she lived life outside of society's conventions. She disavowed marriage due to the way it proscribed a woman's rights, and loved passionately and had a child anyway. None of these things came without a cost. She battled depression for most of her life, and twice attempted suicide after the father of her child left her. She survived, recovered, and continued seeking justice, career success, and love.

When she did eventually marry, in order to prevent her second child from facing the stigma of illegitimacy, she struggled with creating an equitable distribution of domestic labor in her home, so that she and her husband could both continue their professional work. But then, just when she was finally settling into a loving and equal partnership, finding joy in motherhood and also in the book she was writing—a gothic novel called *Maria* set in an asylum where the protagonist's husband has entrapped her for defying him—she died from complications of childbirth.

Rather than celebrate her as the revolutionary thinker she was, her critics used the details of her life to paint her as an immoral woman, and dismiss her ideas. History has since corrected itself, thank goodness, and today her work is enshrined in feminist and historical scholarship.

But I am not a scholar. I am a romance novelist. I wanted to give her *my* kind of happy ending.

Because in Wollstonecraft's story, what I saw were rakes, and ruin, and a woman who used every tool at her disposal to call out injustice and live her life as she saw fit. A woman who suffered for her ideals during her lifetime, and was slut-shamed upon her death. A heroine who deserved to get exactly what she wanted.

Seraphina Arden is not a direct fictionalization of Mary Wollstonecraft. But her opinions owe a large debt to Wollstonecraft's ferocious intellect, fighting spirit, tumultuous emotions, and capacity for passionate love.

As a book critic, Wollstonecraft had many scathing criticisms of romantic novels. I have no idea if she would think this one is sentimental drivel by yet another scribbling woman. But I hope some part of her would have read Seraphina Arden's story and found it, well, delicious.

And I hope you enjoy it, too!

Love,
Scarlett

"Men, some to Business, some to pleasure take;
   But ev'ry Woman is at heart a Rake."

—Alexander Pope

Part One

———— ❧ ————

Contrary to the legend, the night we formed the Society of Sirens did not begin as a revolt.

It began, ironically, with French champagne chilling in a silver bucket.

With me, wearing a new dress of scarlet silk and feeling my pulse beating in my throat as I applied the scent of bergamot to the hollows of my neck and thought, Tonight will mark the era of our vindication.

I remember swishing down the hall in that red gown, feeling like a dancer about to pirouette onstage after a lifetime of rigorous rehearsal. I stopped to pick up Jack Willow's paper, so I could brandish it triumphantly as I greeted my three friends. I had rehearsed the words I would say to them in greeting, holding up our essay:

Relish it, my darlings. Look how far we've come.

So many years had passed since Lady Elinor Bell had first introduced us. Back then, we had been three lost, fallen girls, landing in Elinor's parlor from disparate corners of society with only our low morals in common. I was the Cornish miner's ruined daughter, correcting Jack Willow's circular by day and bedding philosophers by night. Cornelia was Elinor's niece, cast out by her aristocratic family when her relations with her painting tutor proved more than educational. And Thaïs was a lady of the night who had come to Elinor seeking donations to start a charity for girls forced into prostitution.

Elinor made daughters of us. She taught us that family could be hewn from love rather than blood. She showered us with guidance, introductions, and bequests, insisting that the misfortunes of our lives had been shaped not by any failing in our characters but by the concessions, injustices, and heartaches that made womanhood a kind of penalty.

She insisted on a principle that our biographies had theretofore contested: that we mattered. That girls—even so-called ruined ones—were not a thing that could be thrown away.

She'd saved us.

And now, with the publication of this essay, we were going to save others.

The article called for pledges to build a philanthropic institute that would work for the advancement and education of the female sex. We'd all had a hand in crafting the proposal, but only Elinor had signed it. We'd thought this was a clever act of subterfuge. The Crown increasingly saw the faintest whisper of equality as sedition—to stamp such a proposal with the names of disgraced women would certainly raise ire.

We reasoned that the faultless reputation of a proper matron like Lady Bell could disguise the radicalism of our ideas enough to demand a hearing.

We assumed that Elinor—a matriarch, a wife, a viscountess—was safe.

But we were wrong.

For when I answered the door that night, Elinor was not with Cornelia and Thaïs.

Instead, they clutched Jack Willow between them—hunched and bleeding, with two black eyes. Thaïs was breathing shallowly. Cornelia, who never cried, was weeping.

"What's happened?" I asked, rushing them inside. "Where's Elinor?"

"He's taken her," Thaïs whispered. "Lord Bell. Says she's gone radical and destroyed his good name."

"Taken her?" I sputtered, still not understanding. "But where?"

Jack leaned against the wall. "He won't say."

Cornelia gestured at Jack's swollen face. "He ransacked Jack's shop. Said he's going to the papers to expose Jack and Elinor as Jacobins and adulterers. Threatened to sue Jack for criminal conversation, shut down the whole press."

Elinor had always dismissed her husband's jealousy over her friendship with Jack as amusing proof that Lord Bell, beneath his bluster, loved her.

But Bell's possessive streak had been a symptom of ownership, not affection. And Elinor, despite her greater intellect, her larger fortune, and her kinder heart, was her husband's minion under law.

And he wanted her to know it.

We realized, that night, that we'd miscalculated; Elinor had never been safe. And if she wasn't, no woman was.

And if no woman was safe, what was the point of being cautious?

If the finest lady any of us knew could be abducted from her home by the man to whom she'd dutifully borne two children, then what did adherence to the codes of feminine respectability protect?

Perhaps there was more freedom in being the kind of

woman who was not respectable. For such women have little left to take away.

As infamous, unmarried ladies branded harridans and whores in the endless gossip about us in the papers, did we not possess a kind of power? Bad women, after all, are the subject of endless fascination to the sex that wants to subjugate us. We were accustomed to our misdeeds being chronicled in headlines, discussed in village squares.

Why not attach our ideas to this notoriety? Why not raise money for our cause by waging a war of shock and scandal?

It was only then that we opened the champagne. We raised our glasses not in a toast but in a vow: to create a place that would make the world more safe for women like Lady Bell. For women like ourselves. For all womankind.

And to get Elinor her freedom from Lord Bell.

Which is all to clarify the rumor that the night we formed the Society of Sirens had been planned as a rebellion all along.

It wasn't.

Sirens, you see, are not born thirsting for justice.

Sirens are made.

Chapter One

Thirty years earlier
Kestrel Bay, Cornwall
June 1797

At the ungodly hour of half past two on a sun-braced afternoon, Seraphina Arden stood before her looking glass in her flimsiest chemise, squinting against the glare coming off the ocean as she removed pins, one by one, from her coiffure.

She unspooled a long curl from above her temple and arranged it to trail over her left breast, drawing the eye to the hint of pink one could just barely make out through her thin lawn shift. She untucked another tendril from her nape, letting it unfurl down the middle of her back. The effect was louche, as though she had been grabbed in a passionate embrace.

Perfect.

She was the very image of an utterly ruined woman.

Henri enjoyed that kind of thing, if she recalled.

It had been years since their last encounter, but the memory of those nights in Paris still made her breath catch. Even mediocre painters had a facility with their hands that elevated the purely carnal to an art form—and Henri's work was celebrated on three continents.

She draped a cloak around her shift and set off down the coastal path toward the abandoned belvedere at the border of her property and Jory Tregereth's. As weather-wizened as a ruin, perched precariously among the cliffs, the old folly afforded a magnificent view of Kestrel Bay, if one didn't mind steps overgrown with tufts of purple fumitory weeds and winds that nearly knocked you over as you climbed.

The air smelled like her childhood—like brine and sand and pollen. A heady, salty scent that made her ill at ease. She had come here to remember how that era of her life had ended, but now that she was here, every memory of it smarted.

Henri would be good for her. He would remind her who she had become, and distract from the relics of what she'd lost.

She ascended the steps carefully, wincing against the bright, flat glare off the Kestrel. At this time of day, the light hit the cliffs in such a blinding arc it was difficult to parse the sky from the sea.

But she only had eyes for Henri.

He'd come early. He was leaning against the balustrade with his back to her, absorbed in sketching cliffs. Oh, but he was picturesque. Like a chiaroscuro, with his dark clothes and hair cutting against the misty vista of the ocean. She'd forgotten precisely how well formed he was: long and lean with those broad shoulders and strong arms and clever artist's hands. She couldn't make out his face, but in silhouette his jaw was better made than she remembered. The two years since their last assignation had agreed with him.

Something inside her lit, in a way it hadn't since that night six weeks ago, when Elinor had disappeared and all the pleasant parts of life had faded into numbness.

"Henri," she said.

He didn't turn, unable to hear her over the roar of the violent, salty air whipping off the ocean. Which gave her a delicious idea.

She draped her cloak over the rail of the belvedere, toed off her shoes, and crept forward, silent, silent, across the floor until she was just behind him. She placed a single finger at the bottom of his neck, below the knot of satin ribbon holding his raffish hair into a queue. That spot that lit up all the other spots that wanted touching.

No man could resist it.

She would know.

"Henri," she whispered in his ear.

He leapt, arching his back toward a marble column behind him as though she was a cutpurse who'd assailed him rather than the woman whose bed he'd traveled hours to make use of. His sketchpad clattered to the floor. His face was obscured by the shadow of the column, but his hand caught her wrist and dragged her forward, toward the light.

She bit her lip at the pang of anticipation. He remembered how she liked it: rough.

"What in Christ's name?" he growled in the low, clipped vowels of a Scot.

A Scot?

He stepped forward into the light, and his face was as harshly handsome as it was completely unfamiliar.

Who was he?

She wrenched her arm out of his grip and stepped back, clutching herself to block his view of her . . . her *everything* . . . through the filmy fabric of her shift.

She glanced up into his face, trying to place him, hating herself for worrying that he was someone from her past, someone who might say something cruel or reach out and—

Her bare foot landed on the page of his discarded sketchpad. She glanced down. It was not the cliffs he'd been drawing.

It was the jointed beams beneath the belvedere.

She glanced back up and caught him staring at her.

And there was such a terrible hunger in his eyes that they could have been her own.

ADAM ANDERSON TORE his gaze away from the woman who had nearly sent him toppling over the low stone balustrade and shrugged his coat from his shoulders, holding it out to her so that she might use it to cover herself.

"I beg your pardon, madam. Here, take this."

She had been clutching her barely shrouded body protectively, as though he—not she—had been the one to pounce.

It was not an effective means of restoring her modesty. Standing as she was in that fierce shaft of light, her thin gown was transparent, swirling luminous around long, finely made legs that rose into lavishly flared hips and a dark thatch of—*Christ*.

She held his glance for a long moment. And then she dropped her self-protective posture, something like amusement blooming in her eyes, and padded calmly back across the stone floor in her bare feet, ignoring his attempt at chivalry.

"Who are you?" she asked idly.

Her gait was defiant, the shadow of her buttocks swishing from side to side beneath her gown in bored, unhurried time.

He felt a flash of irritation at himself for continuing to ogle her.

But that gown. The way it swirled around those legs beneath it.

Stop.

"I'm Adam Anderson," he said to her back. "Mr. Tregereth's architect. Forgive me if I've disturbed you. He did not mention this building was in use."

The woman reached for a cloak she'd left tossed against the railing. She arranged it around her shoulders and glanced back at him, her expression wry. "And I imagine he would not approve of it had he known."

Her face was arresting. Slanted black brows, an elegant slash of a nose, green eyes smudged with heavy lashes. It was a face he could have made a feast of drawing, in the days when he still drew women and not window fixtures.

"Tregereth is not demolishing the belvedere?" she asked. "That would be a shame. It makes a pleasant little ruin and I enjoy looking at it from my window." She pointed up to the weathered but grand house that stood a half mile up the coastal path, at the promontory of the cliffs.

He'd been told the place was abandoned.

He gestured at a cracked piece of the stone floor that had begun to list, sloping down toward the cliff's edge. "This foundation needs rebuilding. It's not steady. You should be careful, coming here alone."

"Did you think, Mr. Anderson," she asked, widening her eyes, "that I intended to be alone?"

His sketchpad caught the wind and threatened to sail over the ledge. She stopped it with the toe of her bare foot, then bent down and handed it back to him.

For a brief moment, their fingers touched. The hairs on his forearms stood, as though she'd sent a current through him.

He wrenched his hand away, and she watched him do it, abrupt, a touch delayed.

Something knowing rippled through her eyes and the corners of her mouth turned up. "If a gentleman should appear here in search of me, send him up to my house. And if you would be so kind, don't mention this to Tregereth. He has never approved of my visits."

She winked, turned around, and strode up the steps in her bare feet, holding her slippers in her hand.

"Forgive me, madam, I didn't catch your name," he called after her.

She turned back. "Seraphina Arden," she said with a low, theatrical bow and laughter in her eyes. Laughter that implied, *Of course that's who I am, you dullard*.

Belatedly, he recognized her angular silhouette from the woodcuts sold in stalls along the Strand etched with the words *The Rakess*.

The woman climbing back up the cliff in a state of scandalous undress laughed at him because she should need no introduction; she was one of the most infamous women in all of England.

Chapter Two

When men indulge themselves in worldly pleasures outside the sanctity of marriage, they are called rake-hells and admired for their virility. They may marry, profit, and even rule this country with no spot upon their character. But if a genteel woman so much as walks out alone, it is whispered she is compromised. Why should a single rumor doom a woman for the same sin from which men are excused?

—*An Essay in Defense of Ruined Women*
by Seraphina Arden, 1793

❖

Seraphina awoke to the flotsam of the previous night's revelry scattered around her bed and the body of a Frenchman wrapped around her person.

Henri stirred beside her. "*Cherie*," he murmured, half asleep, trying to rub her nose with his handsome, stubbled cheek.

She dodged and rose from bed.

Last night, Henri had tragically revealed himself to be that most unwelcome of creatures: a cuddler. One of many undesirable traits she had not recalled from their days in Paris.

He'd arrived with an alarming number of trunks, an avowed intention to spend the summer "making love" to her in the sunlight off the Kestrel, and most disturbing,

the news that since their last parting he'd carried *a lock
of her hair in his coat.*

She shuddered.

She had not yet had the heart to tell him that her idea
of a blissful summer *affaire de coeur* was a rousing
romp in bed followed by fond promises to repeat the
adventure in another two years' time when they parted
in the morning.

Henri was sweet, but men were best left to administer-
ing boudoir pleasures and lifting things a woman oughtn't.
For finer intimacies, they only disappointed.

She'd invited Henri here to distract her from her
memories of Kestrel Bay and the sickly feeling they
lodged in her chest—not to enhance her unease with
new anxieties.

She dreaded lovers who coupled bedsport with emotion. Nothing made her feel unsteady like a man who
wasn't leaving in the morning.

Besides, she'd spent most of her evening with Henri re-
calling the architect from the belvedere, and the way he'd
sucked in his breath at her touch, like she'd stung him.

That's what she needed—a stranger. The rush of pure
seduction.

Which did not lessen the awkwardness of extricating
herself from this misunderstanding with Henri, and his
tender gaze, and his lock of stolen hair.

"Darling?" She poked his shoulder.

"Mmmmm." He rolled over in her bed.

Oh, her pounding head. She had been far too liberal with
the spirits last night, for wine was her most proven antidote
to worry. She had hoped enough of it might rouse in her
the courage to inform Henri he was a temporary guest.
Or, failing that, at least alleviate the constant thrumming
of her worries—Elinor, the book, the memories.

It hadn't worked on any of them.

She bent down to gather the butt of a cheroot from a saucer on the floor and yelped as something sharp bit into her foot. Shards of last night's wineglass twinkled from a puncture in her heel. She bent and plucked them out, wincing at the pain.

"*Poupée*," Henri murmured, rolling over at the sound of her distress. He winced at the sight of her blood. "*Mon dieu, ton pied!*"

"Just a cut."

"Come, let me kiss it better." He reached out and grabbed her shin. She backed away and jammed her smarting foot into her slipper, safe from the dubious healing powers of his lips.

"Come back to bed," he pouted.

"I'm afraid I have to write. Take your time. I'll have Maria send up breakfast so that you are well fed for your journey."

There was a sudden heavy silence in the room.

"My journey?"

She grudgingly met his eye. "My dear, you are so kind to offer to keep me company here. But you see, I'm woefully behind in my work, and with you here to tempt me, I'll be too distracted to write. There's a boardinghouse in Penzance if you wish to stay on. Excellent light."

"Penzance," he repeated, as skeptically as if she'd said "Hades."

"It's only an hour's ride away—if I finish my book, I'll come and see you at midsummer. Now be good and I'll send your man up to make you handsome before luncheon."

She limped downstairs without waiting for a reply. Her secretary, Tompkins, was in the parlor, collecting more of the evidence of last night's indiscretions.

What were her stockings doing discarded beside the sofa? Was that really *another* empty bottle of Château Margaux? Thank goodness Tompkins was constitutionally incapable of shock.

"Oh, Tompkins. What a scene."

This precise scene—the empty bottles, the unwanted man, the aching temples—was becoming far too common. She was not known for temperance with spirits but lately she could be accused of being . . . injudicious. What had begun as a distraction from her concern for Elinor was in danger of settling into something more like a way of life. She kept meaning to retrench and be good. But the dread she felt every time she attempted to work on her memoirs made the desire to loosen the coil of her thoughts with a sturdy drink seem justified.

She'd be good later, when this was over.

Tompkins plucked a crystal decanter from inside the open belly of Seraphina's late mother's pianoforte and gave her the kind of smile that withheld judgment without exactly covering concern.

"There's coffee for you in the study."

"Thank you. You are a saint. And I have the kind of headache due to the worst of sinners. I don't suppose we have a headache powder?"

"Waiting with the coffee. And I left your correspondence. You've had a letter from Miss Ludgate."

At last. She itched for news from London. She had left it in a state of upheaval, all the papers whispering of Elinor's sudden disappearance, and the announcement of Seraphina's coming memoirs.

"Bless you. And might I ask another favor? Please have Monsieur Lapierre's servants see that his conveyance is ready to depart after luncheon. And give them the direction for the inn at Chapel Street."

Tompkins wrinkled her brow. "Certainly. Though, it was my understanding he planned to stay through July."

Seraphina picked up the Frenchman's discarded cravat with two fingers. "Yes. That's just the trouble, isn't it?"

Tompkins granted her a wry smile. "I see. I'll take care of it."

"You always do. Thank you."

Seraphina walked into the small parlor she had adopted as her study. It held a view of the ocean, a table she'd repurposed as a desk, and little else. In her childhood, it had been the sewing room, where she had whiled away her days under her stepmother's exacting observation, making useless embroidered handkerchiefs for a father too coarse to bother using them.

She had chosen this room to write her memoirs just to be perverse.

But perhaps the true victim of the irony was her. Her parents, after all, were dead. Whereas *she* was alive, and this room brought back her fury at them without precisely inspiring her to turn it into gripping prose.

She picked up the letter from Cornelia.

Sera darling,

I hope that the ocean is agreeing with you. Thaïs and I yearn for your return but we are contenting ourselves with rebellious plotting and fine wine in your absence. Write us and tell us how you are, for if you don't, we will be forced to come after you to reassure ourselves you are rusticating in tranquility and not glowering into the cliffs and beating your breast thinking of Him. If you are tempted to do the latter, even briefly, please let this note be your reminder He is not worth it.

JW is avoiding letters as Bell's solicitors are following him and he suspects they read his post, but he visited me yesterday with news from his investigator. Prepare yourself for this next sentence, love, for it's not a happy one: we think that bastard Bell has E locked in an asylum. JW's man believes the place is somewhere near Bell's holdings in the South, but has not yet been able to confirm the whereabouts. I'll write as soon as I know more.

Don't despair, dear. We'll find her, and we'll bloody free her if we have to storm the castle keep ourselves.

Thaïs has just arrived and she sends her love as well and says WRITE US, WENCH.

With love,
Cornelia (and Thaïs)

Lady Elinor Bell in an *asylum*.

They had assumed Bell was holding Elinor in one of his Northern properties—perhaps his shooting estate in Scotland. This was so much worse.

What corrupt institution would accept an able-bodied, perfectly sane woman as a lunatic, regardless of what lies her husband claimed about her fidelity? Was the suggestion that women would benefit from education, apprenticeships, and independence so incredible that a physician would believe it was symptomatic of insanity?

She felt the anger she had come here to remember, yes.

But she also felt the vulnerability that came with bold transgression. It was one thing to be defiant in the company of people who agreed with you. It was quite another to do so in the world of men who saw your actions as the early symptoms of a coming plague.

They must be careful.

She must be careful.

Nonsense. Don't let them make you timid. That's exactly what they want.

She needed something to calm her nerves.

Out the window, she noticed the architect in the distance, walking from Tregereth's toward the empty drover's cottage up the downs. He must be staying at the cottage while he did the renovation.

He really was a striking man, with that sun-tanned skin and lustrous hair and excellent, broad shoulders. The memory of his fingers biting into her wrist had been the most exciting part of her entire evening with Henri.

She wondered if Mr. Anderson was as skilled at his trade as he was at staring soulfully out to sea. If so, he would have to be a genius, for she had not seen a man look quite so appealing in an age—and she was not in the habit of leaving appealing men unnoticed.

She could find uses for such a person.

She, Thaïs, and Cornelia had made a pact to build a handsome, dignified building in the middle of London for their institute. The kind of building that would assert by its sheer heft the worth of women like themselves, and rebuke by its elegance the notion that a certain kind of lady had no claim on decency, let alone the rights of men.

They had come up with a goal of raising fifty thousand pounds, on the basis of that number sounding large and impressive. But it would help to have a sense of how much the building they imagined might actually cost.

Perhaps she could ask Mr. Anderson's advice, as a favor.

It would be a serviceable prelude to gleaning his enthusiasm for providing *other* sorts of favors.

She dashed off a note.

"Tompkins," she called. "Would you mind another errand?"

ADAM LIFTED HIS face to the humid wind blowing off the cliffs as he made his way back up the path toward the cottage he'd let for the summer. Cornwall in June was a sultry, sticky business, and he paused to remove his waistcoat and unknot his cravat, letting the breeze filter through his linen shirt.

He heard a clacking in the distance and looked up to see he was passing by Miss Arden's house. A shutter on her terrace window was loose, blowing in the wind. He had the strangest urge to walk up the steps to her property and offer to fix it.

But that would be perverse, as he'd spent most of the previous evening fighting off distracting thoughts of her knowing smile when she'd caught him looking at her. Had there been an invitation in it?

It didn't matter. He was not here to think of women.

He averted his eyes from her house and walked more quickly.

The glare of Cornish summer was a welcome respite from the gray light of Cheapside, even if the work he'd taken on for Tregereth was the kind that left him ir-ritated at the necessary frivolity of renovating yet another country pile when he itched for work of real distinction.

But distinction was a privilege for the rich. He needed to do well by this commission, for in a stroke of luck, Tregereth's house happened to be directly down the coach road from Alsonair, the principal holding of the Marquess of Pendrake, who helmed the Board of Works. Pendrake was said to be on the cusp of commissioning a new naval armory, the Crown's largest public building in decades. It was Adam's fondest hope that Pendrake might be moved by the graceful signature of Anderson Mayhew, Architects, as he passed by Tregereth's.

Perhaps Adam could even secure an introduction.

He'd been waiting for such an opportunity for half his life. The firm he had founded with his brother-in-law's backing was moderately successful, but the patronage of baronets requiring additions to their modest manors was not going to lead him to the kind of commissions that would fulfill the promise he'd made to his wife's family when they'd allowed their daughter to marry so far beneath her station.

Mayhew had invested in Adam's firm believing him capable of great works, with great return on capital. Bridges. Aqueducts. Public institutions. He owed the Mayhews far too much to continue building fripperies for country squires year after year.

Particularly given what he'd already cost them: their daughter.

He could not make up for the loss of Catriona. But he would feel better if he could at least repay his share of the six thousand pounds in capital Mayhew had invested when they'd moved the business to London.

"Papa," a small voice cried from the distance.

He looked up to see his children gamboling down the hill. He was shocked by how transformed they looked after a fortnight here, as though they'd breathed in happiness with the seaside air. Perhaps they'd inhaled too much of his own melancholy with the dreary London fog these last three years. Here, they seemed lighter.

Adeline rushed toward him as he rounded up the path. He grinned at his grass-stained, spritely daughter even as his heart lurched to see her smile like that—at only four, she was already the very image of her mother.

"Papa! We saw a lamb. He came right up to me," Addie told him, breathless.

Adam scooped her up into his arms, enjoying the peal of laughter this provoked. "What lamb could resist the lovely Adeline?" he asked her.

"It was a sheep," Jasper corrected, intent that his sister should know the difference. "Three white sheep and one black one."

Adam reached down and ruffled his boy's hair, wondering if there had ever been such a solemn seven-year-old. "Then I hope you apologized to the lot of them on behalf of your sister. Grown sheep detest being called lambs."

Adam's own sister chuckled from the blanket where she was tucked under an enormous straw bonnet against the sun, reading a book. "We took a walk up the downs this morning. Jasper made the acquaintance of the shepherd and Adeline engaged in a barking competition with his dog."

Adeline gave a sharp bark into his ear to demonstrate. "Arrruff! Arrrrrrruff!"

Adam lowered her to the grass. "Run and play," he said, scooting her off to join her brother, who had already lost interest in the adults and was constructing a fortress out of the shards of Cornish shale that pebbled the grasses and tufts of gorse along the cliff tops.

He glanced down at the cover of his sister's book. *An Essay in Defense of Ruined Women*. Seraphina Arden's signature work.

He stiffened.

He had not mentioned his encounter with its author to Marianne. It embarrassed him to think about his reaction to Miss Arden. The way he'd been unable not to notice the limning of her body through that sheer, wind-whipped gown.

"A little dry reading?" he asked, pointing at the book.

Marianne laughed sheepishly and tucked it under the edge of her blanket. "I know she's controversial, but Miss Arden is Kestrel Bay's most famous resident, and I thought it might be interesting to form my own view of her arguments after hearing so many complaints about them at the market."

He smiled. "And what is your assessment?"

"You know, Miss Arden is not nearly as shocking as the rumors suggest. One would think the book was bawdy, the way they shout about her fallen state, but it's mostly about laws and education."

"It's not just Miss Arden's fallen state they shout about. It's her ideas."

"Ideas that I cannot say I disagree with. I find her rather clear-eyed."

He didn't disagree either. His wife had made him read the book in its first printing and he'd thought Miss Arden skillfully made a case for a more equitable state between the sexes. Had he not been so disordered by her near-nudity when she'd said her name, he would have told her so.

He wished he had.

"I heard that Miss Arden lives just up the path," Marianne said. "Apparently she's here for the first time since her girlhood. The women at the market seemed less than pleased about it. They believe she's stirring up some kind of trouble."

Adam sat down beside her on the blanket. "As it happens, I met her."

Marianne's eyes lit with interest. "And you said nothing! How did you manage such an intriguing introduction?"

"I didn't. She happened upon me in Tregereth's belvedere when I was inspecting the foundation."

His sister widened her eyes in delight. "Was she as terrifying as they say?"

He debated saying nothing, out of respect for Miss Arden's privacy, but the incident had been so singular he was relieved to have someone to share it with. "She was, shall we say, indisposed. To put it delicately."

Marianne clapped a hand over her mouth and laughed. "Oh, Adam. You poor man. Imagine *you* and an indisposed woman."

If only she knew.

He blushed and looked away. "I think she found the encounter amusing."

Marianne patted his arm. "Well, at least Miss Arden lives up to her legend."

"Right." He gazed out at the ocean. The swells breaking along Kestrel Bay were mighty today. He picked up his sketchbook and fished a piece of charcoal from his pocket. The upside to his mindless work for Tregereth was the chance to enjoy this view.

"Papa!" his daughter shouted. "A horse."

He looked up and saw, indeed, a rider approaching from the direction of Miss Arden's house.

"Mr. Anderson?" the rider called, drawing near. She was a severe woman with handsome features, no hat, and a confident way of sitting on her mare.

He stood. "Yes?"

"I'm Miss Tompkins, Miss Arden's secretary." She held out a note. "She asked I deliver this to you and wait for your reply."

He reached up and took the folded paper from the woman's hand.

Mr. Anderson—It was a pleasure to make your acquaintance yesterday. That my esteemed neighbor Mr. Tregereth has not yet come to me demanding satisfaction for trespassing on his land attests to your kind discretion. I wonder if I could request another favor: I am considering commissioning a substantial building and have need for the opinion of an architect. Might I prevail on you for a brief audience? I am entirely at your disposal.

Seraphina Arden

She wanted to see him.

Was it possible that their encounter had stuck with her the way it had with him?

Miss Tompkins looked at him expectantly, awaiting an answer.

He hesitated. Back in London, he had seen mentions of Miss Arden's name in relation to some scandal among the peerage—something about a noblewoman who had run off with a radical. Affiliation with such talk would do him no favors, given his ambitions. The type of men on whom his fate relied had little tolerance for Jacobins.

And yet, he thought of Seraphina Arden's crooked smile—the amusement in her eyes, when she'd looked back at him, like she knew she had something he was terrified of wanting—and felt himself nodding at her servant.

"Tell Miss Arden I will call on her tomorrow on my way home from Mr. Tregereth's. She can expect me at half past four."

Chapter Three

To take a lover outside the bounds of wedlock always invites risk, but the burden is not shared equally. If both sinners' souls are imperiled in the next life for their transgressions, why should women alone pay the price in this one?

—An Essay in Defense of Ruined Women
by Seraphina Arden, 1793

───────────────❧───────────────

Writing was not ameliorated by a fine appearance, and yet Seraphina lingered over her toilette, brushing her hair until it gleamed and choosing a low-cut azure gown that did nothing for her prose but flattered her complexion and made a feast of her bosom.

One did not lengthen one's manuscript by staring out the window, but as soon as the clock struck four, she found her gaze drifting from her work to the coastal path, hoping for a glimpse of a tall figure.

She rolled her eyes at herself, and wished Thaïs or Cornelia were here to laugh at her for allowing her urgent work to be distracted by thoughts of a Scotsman's shoulders. But by half past four, she had abandoned the pretense of work entirely and assumed a vigil.

She'd been surprised when the architect had so readily agreed to call on her, but perhaps he'd agreed only out of politeness and had now reconsidered. He would not be the first man who had judged an association with her too great a risk. He would be the latest in a long and boring line of them. A point of pride on most days.

So there was no explaining this maidenish staring out the window and certainly no excusing the way her skin became too hot when a figure bearing Mr. Anderson's proportions came walking up the coastal path.

She returned to her desk, smoothing her hair and making every appearance to seem unconcerned and lost in thought when Tompkins knocked on the door to announce her visitor.

The man who entered the room was dressed more formally than the windblown version she'd encountered in the belvedere. He had the kind of build that tailoring was made for, and though his coat bore the dust of a day's work in the Kestrel breezes, he wore it like he was in a ballroom. She could only imagine the dazzling figure he would cut at a London soiree in a fine topcoat.

She was glad she'd worn this gown today. She'd make good use of it.

"Mr. Anderson," she said, rising in a way that showed off her figure, "thank you so much for the call."

He held himself stiffly, formal, looking polite and affable but a touch unsure about the eyes. She noticed he kept them trained on her face, as though perhaps they wanted to venture lower.

"My pleasure, Miss Arden," he said.

"Please, have a seat." She indicated the chair before her desk and he drew it back, making space for his long legs. He placed the small, tidy leather satchel that he carried on the floor. Despite his politeness, he had the attitude of being comfortable in his own skin. He knew himself. She could always tell.

Which meant his unease was about her.

"Are you familiar with my work, Mr. Anderson?"

This question was a test, as a certain kind of man would leer in response or make a joke of her.

But he only nodded, serious, if guarded. "I am."

So he was not a libertine. She would start with business and move on to more carnal propositions once she had a better sense of him.

She gave him her most fetching smile. "Then perhaps you already know that I am an advocate for female education. I am here in Cornwall working on a manuscript calling for subscription pledges to build an institute for women devoted to education, and female training. I hoped that you might help me understand the cost of the project, such that my goals don't exceed the likely expenses."

He leaned back, seeming satisfied with this explanation.

"I see. I'm happy to provide whatever knowledge I can. What exactly do you wish to build?"

"A handsome structure in London—perhaps in one of the new squares to the north of the city. It would need to include dormitories, a grand lecture hall, and five or six workshops to prepare ladies for apprenticeships."

His brow furrowed. "Apprenticeships for ladies? Do you mean needlework and service and the like?"

She smiled. "Apothecary, smithery, joinery. Any trade at which one can make a living."

He inclined his head, though not with any challenge. "Ah."

If Mr. Anderson had heard of the scandal the origination of this plan had caused, he did not let on. Though, she supposed the public outrage that had gripped London in the weeks since Elinor's abduction was more about Bell's claims of her adultery than about the essay that had provoked him to accuse her of it.

This was why they needed to wed their mission to secure funds with scandal. In the quest for public notice, gossip won over philosophy every time.

"The building must be gracious and comfortable," she said. "Not some penal place to learn drudgery like one of those oppressive Magdalen houses. I'm imagining a home where a lady might cultivate her mind and spirit. With a bit of a garden and plenty of light and air and places to enjoy conversation."

A light in his eyes bloomed, and he leaned forward. He seemed intrigued by the idea. This was not the usual male response to her proposed plans, which tended to fall between objection and outright derision.

"How many women would you wish to accommodate in residence?" he asked.

"At least a hundred at a time. And the facility must have a nursery for any with young children."

He tapped his chin, musing. "Have you any paper?"

She rummaged in her desk for a leaf of paper and handed it to him, along with a pencil. He bent over the pages, a lock of his chestnut hair falling over his forehead. His fingers were long and square and agile and he projected such a sense of certainty—of calm, efficient skill—that she found herself transfixed by the sight of his swift sketching.

A quarter of an hour passed as he drew, pausing to ask her questions about the need for faculty accommodation, visiting lecturers, and stables.

He was intelligent and thorough—exactly the type of person with whom she preferred to work. Besides, competence, self-assurance, and dexterous fingers were all favorable qualities for the other role she had in mind for him.

"There," he said, handing the page over to her.

In a few economical lines, he had sketched out a building that rose up proudly from an open square, with a neoclassical symmetry and a graceful elevation.

"I'd suggest a horseshoe structure across four levels, opening onto an interior courtyard lined with outbuildings for the workshops off a mews. It allows for the central facade to be quite grand, while creating a more intimate feeling in the residence off to the wings."

She marveled at the drawing. It was practical but fanciful. Exactly what she wanted. "How much would it take to construct something like this?"

He paused, thinking. "Anywhere from three to six thousand guineas. Plus the land, furnishings, and labor."

She looked up in surprise. "That's quite a range."

"Much of the expense will depend on your taste. The rest depends on your architect."

His eyes were brown and warm and did not dodge hers. "Oh?"

"Aye. A good one can keep material and labor costs low without sacrificing the quality of the construction and design."

She could not ignore such an opening falling so neatly into her lap. She smiled into Mr. Anderson's nice eyes. "I see. And are you one of these *good* architects, Mr. Anderson?"

If he heard the invitation in her voice, he did not acknowledge it. Instead, he chuckled. "I fancy myself something of a talent. But we Scots are famously vain creatures."

"So I've been told," she purred.

He leaned back from her desk. "I can send you a list of reputable firms if you plan to invite proposals."

She leaned forward, in a way she knew would press her breasts up against her stays so they swelled invitingly. "I'd be grateful."

His eyes, damn them, remained on her face.

His expression was still warm, but it was difficult to gauge whether he had perceived that her interest in him was not entirely professional.

Where had that hungry gaze gone? Had she imagined he had wanted her?

There was only one way to find out.

She rose and gave him a meaningful smile. "Mr. Anderson, I was just about to go out to the terrace for some air before you arrived. Would you join me? I think you will find the view of the Kestrel extraordinary from this elevation, and the light is so good at this time of day."

ADAM FLINCHED AT the condition of Miss Arden's house as she led him to her terrace. It was as airy as he'd imagined when he'd seen it from a distance, but in far worse repair. The walls shook and rattled with the moaning wind, and he wondered if she suffered from the drafts coming off the ocean. If he'd had more time, he would offer to inspect the building.

Walls shouldn't rattle the way hers did.

But she didn't seem to mind. She sauntered gracefully through the room as though the floorboards didn't groan beneath their feet. Something about the way she moved was at once sumptuous and authoritative, like a panther.

Watching her made his pulse quicken.

"Do you spend much time here?" he asked, so as not to become too fixated on his rather rude desire to stare at her. For a moment, in her study, he'd had the odd sensation that her manner was flirtatious. But surely he had simply imagined it. For why would such an exotic, feline creature as Seraphina Arden take more than a cursory interest in *him*?

"I haven't been here since I was a girl," she answered. "I inherited it two years ago, after my stepmother died."

A peal of wind caused a shutter to clap against the house. Seraphina winked at him. "That's no doubt her ghost. Trying to drive me out by haunting me."

It was actually the ravages of salt air, rusting the hinges. But he sensed she was amused by the idea of a bitter spirit pounding at the windows to unsettle her.

"I could send a man to come replace the hinges if it bothers you."

She waved the offer away. "Oh, not worth the labor. I'll only be here for a month. I came to write my memoirs of my youth. The decrepit state of the place adds atmosphere, don't you think?"

He nodded and followed her out the door to a small table overlooking the sea. Her house was nearly a hundred feet above Tregereth's. The view was stunning.

As was Miss Arden, standing in the sunlight. With her strong features, she was as striking to behold as the purple clouds behind her.

It had been years since he'd been so taken by a woman's looks. It was not so much that she was beautiful—her face was more striking than pretty—but the fascinating way she caught the light.

And, of course, that bloody sheer chemise she'd been wearing when he met her, which his thoughts kept drifting to at odd hours of the day.

"You do have a gorgeous view," he said. "If I could find time, I'd love to paint it."

Or paint her. He had not painted a woman since Catriona's death.

"You paint landscapes?"

He cleared his throat, not wishing for the conversation to turn too personal.

"I did once. Now I must content myself with sketching houses."

Miss Arden gestured for him to join her at the table. "You're welcome to make use of my terrace if you wish to resume the occupation. It's so nice to be friendly with one's neighbors."

He glanced at her. Something in her tone was breathy, like she meant more than she said and wanted him to know it.

Was that some other kind of invitation, or was he imagining it? His skill at parsing flirtation from polite conversation had gone dull from underuse. Since Catriona's death, he'd spent most of his time working or with the children, declining introductions to eligible widows and invitations to parties where mixed company was expected.

He felt clumsy.

In any case, it did not matter, for he suspected that her building project was one at which his connections would be alarmed. There could be no future in fostering a friendship with a radical, as much as he might enjoy the frank style of her conversation and her amusing manner.

He hoped he conveyed his genuine regret when he shook his head. "I'm afraid between my work and my family I will not likely find the time."

She stretched back, as if to feel the sunlight on her shoulders. Her movements set off the profile of her figure in the light, and she glanced at him out of the corner of her eye, as if to see whether he noticed.

He did.

He should leave.

"I saw two children playing on the path this morning," she said. "Are they yours?"

"Yes. As I must be here for the summer, I thought to bring them with me. Get them out of the London murk to take in a bit of seaside air."

"Your wife must enjoy the holiday as well."

She said this with a pointed tone that made him almost certain she was asking something else.

"My sister cares for my children. I'm a widower."

Her face furrowed. "Oh, I'm very sorry."

He shook his head, not wishing to dwell on this topic of conversation, which never became easier. "It was years ago."

Three years and seven months, to be exact.

"And yet not so very far away," she said, catching a glimpse of something in his face, which to his chagrin had never had the usual Scottish talent for opacity. "It never is, you know."

She gave him a small, sad smile, and he was grateful for the appearance of a servant, saving him from having to say more.

The maid placed a carafe of wine and two glasses between them. She filled Miss Arden's glass with claret, then moved to fill his own. He pressed his hand over the rim. "No, thank you. It doesn't agree with me."

Miss Arden cocked her head at him. "Château Rauzan-Ségla does not *agree* with you?"

In truth, he wouldn't know, as he had never tried a drop. Not after watching the effect spirits had had on his father.

She swirled her own glass and inhaled, closing her eyes with pleasure. "That, Mr. Anderson, is very unfortunate for you indeed." She drank a sip, an arch expression in her eyes. If that look was designed to draw his interest, it was effective.

But not necessary.

One did not need wine or bold conversation to be struck by Miss Arden. It was all he could do not to betray the fact that the sight of her exposed collarbone was as compelling as the view of the bay behind her.

"I should be going," he said, half rising.

"Oh, stay," she said, in such a way that he instantly sat back down. "You must let me give you some refreshment to thank you for your wise counsel."

She smiled at him and turned to her servant. "Bring Mr. Anderson some tea. And perhaps some of those honey biscuits from London. If we cannot ply him with spirits, we shall ply him with something sweeter."

She winked at her maid. Perhaps he'd been wrong to think her half-laughing, half-seductive air was directed at him. Perhaps she used it on everyone. She turned back to him.

"I must say, Mr. Anderson, I was not sure if you would be willing to come here after our rather . . . *unexpected* meeting. I hope I didn't shock you. And please accept my apology for the interruption to your work."

"No apology is necessary, Miss Arden. I have forgotten the matter entirely."

He had not forgotten it. He had dreamt about it two nights running.

He most definitely needed to leave.

She smiled, as if she could sense the lie. "Tell me, what was it you were sketching when I interrupted you?"

"A bulwark to protect the belvedere against erosion."

She tapped a finger to her lip. "And did you like what you saw, Mr. Anderson?"

At what he was imagining in her tone, his heart beat faster. He frantically scanned his mind for a reason to cut the conversation short.

"It will take some clever engineering but new beams beneath the old foundation should do the trick."

Her lips quirked up beneath her finger. Wolfish. "I was not asking your opinion of the *belvedere*, Mr. Anderson."

His heart briefly stopped beating altogether.

Before he could respond, the servant returned with his tea, and he waited in silence as she arranged a plate of biscuits before him for what felt like ages.

"I don't purchase sugar, I'm afraid," Miss Arden said.

He suspected as much. She was associated with the printer Jack Willow and his league calling for abolition, equal voting rights, and the end of monarchy.

"Neither do I," he said. He supported the cause in principle, though he'd not done as much as he'd like to further it himself.

Miss Arden reached across the table and stole a biscuit from his plate, a gesture that displayed her bosom to such a shocking effect that he had to force his eyes above her shoulder to remain a gentleman.

When he dared look back down, she met his gaze with a challenge in her eyes, a smile playing across her generous mouth.

"You can look. I told you the view was all yours to admire."

He nearly choked on his biscuit.

"I see I've shocked you," she said. "Again." She smiled in what could only be described as sympathy.

He had never been spoken to so boldly in all his life. His instinct was to jolt up from the chair and leap over the railing to the safety of the coastal path.

But something about the way she was looking at him, measuring his response, made him stay. She acted the way he'd always rather wished to: as if there were no consequences to what she said or did or thought.

She was daring him to meet her in her boldness.

He had two children, a sister who depended on him, a fortune to make so that they might have the secure future he alone could give them. He could not afford to take risks.

But with her eyes on him like that, he thirsted to be reckless.

Just for a minute.

Just to remind himself that he had not always been this kind of man.

That he had once been a person who did not shy from innuendo, who did not deflect advances, who did not recoil at the sight of a loose strand of a woman's hair gleaming, as hers did now, just so in the sunlight.

He leaned over the table and met her eye. "I'm not easily shocked, Miss Arden."

"No?" she asked.

"No." Then he *did* allow his eyes to linger on her. "If you mean to shock me, you'll have to try harder than that."

She laughed. "Shall I presume, then, you are aware of my reputation?"

"I doubt a soul in England is unaware of your reputation."

She smiled, delighted. "I hope not. I work so hard to be notorious."

"Then let me congratulate you on your success."

"Success is a relative term, Mr. Anderson." She leaned in and whispered, as though confiding a secret, "I am a rather unpopular figure in most circles."

That was such a dramatic understatement that she seemed almost demure. He laughed. "I'm aware of some controversy over your views, yes."

"Oh, the trouble is not simply my *views*, Mr. Anderson— it is the fact that I live up to them that is the real scandal."

"Live up to them? You mean you *do* corrupt susceptible girls and tempt them to a life of sin, like they claim in the papers?"

"No. But I could be called guilty of inviting nice archi- tects to advise me on building costs when advice is not the only thing I'm after."

This was the moment at which, if he were the decent man he strove to be, he would excuse himself and go running toward the Kestrel.

Instead, he merely tapped his finger on his chin and widened his eyes guilelessly, meeting her pose of inno- cence. "I see. And what else, precisely, is it that you're after?"

She leaned forward and smiled the smile of a cat who has cornered a canary. "The same thing I was after when you discovered me undressed in the belvedere."

He leaned toward her. "And what was that, Miss Arden?" he said, lowering his voice so it was barely louder than a whisper.

"I was expecting a lover. And I mistook *you* for *him*."

He had always been grateful he did not have a com- plexion built for the rosy flush that stole across the faces of flustered Englishmen in times of embarrassment. Now he realized he had simply never been flustered enough to test it. He felt himself going positively pink.

Pink and also . . . He was grateful for the table, shield- ing his lap from view.

She rose up from her chair and moved toward him, continuing to talk in a low, throaty voice. "You see, the man I was expecting wasn't quite up to the task of entertaining me. He was too . . . attached. Disappointing, as I was hoping for congenial company these next few weeks while I'm in Cornwall."

Did she mean—

She paused and smiled wryly, like they were both above embarrassment in such a moment. "Yes. I mean in bed."

His throat went completely dry.

"I was wondering if you might wish to join me there," she added. For a moment her frankness slipped, just a bit, her voice lilting into a telltale softness that revealed this request was not made as flippantly as she implied.

She looked down at her hands, almost as if she felt shy, because she hoped he would say yes. Would be *disappointed* if he did not say yes.

He felt a sudden wave of tenderness for her—for possessing the bravery to reveal what she wanted so candidly. It made him want to draw her toward him, take her in his arms.

It made him long for some other life in which his answer could be anything but what it must be now.

No.

She must have seen both the hunger and the hesitation written on his face, for her eyes lingered on his, probing. "Ah," she sighed. "I see. You want to, but you won't."

She smiled, as if she knew him, or people like him, and found them cowardly and disappointing. He winced at being recognized for what he was. He found himself disappointing, too.

"You needn't fear I have designs on you, Mr. Anderson," she said briskly. "I have no interest in your affections or your purse strings, to be clear, and if it's my reputation that you fear, please trust that I can be discreet. I'm not looking for a love affair. Just a little bodily amusement with a stranger while we're both in this forlorn place. No strings. No hearts. No future."

She ran her eyes from his face down to his shoulders, and then the rest of him, examining his body so precisely that it may as well have been her fingers that ran up and down the length of him.

He felt a surge of desire so sharp to be looked at in this way that he wanted to grab her and place her hands where her eyes trailed, to feel another person's skin on flesh that had not been touched since—

Since Catriona.

Since his world had fallen apart.

Since he'd bloody let it, indulging just this kind of risk.

Be careful, no more children, she won't survive it, the physician had warned them.

They hadn't listened. They'd wanted each other more than they'd wanted to be careful. It had been the greatest mistake he'd ever made.

The reality of his circumstances came surging back.

The two sweet children who were no doubt sitting at home, wondering why he was late for supper.

Their mother, who he'd helped put in her grave.

The armory commission he would never have a chance at winning if the Tories thought he was the type to fraternize with radicals.

A life he could not allow to fall to pieces once again.

He rose abruptly, jostling the table in his rush to get away from here. His voice was ragged when he found it.

"No, Miss Arden. I'm sorry, but no."

If fear alone could save us from love, we would all be safe, for the perils are manifold: conception; childbed fever; bastardy; disease; shame; ignominy; exile; destitution; heartbreak.

But is it not human to covet those things that come at the dearest cost?

—*An Essay in Defense of Ruined Women*
by Seraphina Arden, **1793**

———————◆◆————————

"ardon?" Seraphina said to the large, handsome man scurrying away from her with the alacrity of a crab that had just realized she intended to boil it for supper.

"I'm afraid we have misunderstood each other," Mr. Anderson said, discomfort straining his features and turning his sculpted cheeks pink. "I cannot do what you suggest."

Had she misunderstood him? Given the voracious way he'd looked at her a moment ago, she'd assumed he would accede to her suggestion with the same amused smile he had worn in parrying her double entendres.

Few men turned down offers of unattached coupling. Especially with *her*.

And yet his face was frozen in a rictus of dismay.

She could not help but be mildly offended by the degree of his apparent horror.

She rolled her eyes. "You needn't act like I proposed to torture you, Mr. Anderson. A simple 'no' will do."

The glint of alarm in his face softened slightly. Unfortunately, it did not give way to the heat of unrepentant lust. He still held his lovely, broad-shouldered body erect, no doubt poised to leap off the railing and into the overgrown Cornish heath below should she approach him again.

Not that she would. She *did* have dignity, when she chose to exercise it.

She sat down on a settee and wrapped her shawl around her shoulders. There was no use in looking bare and seductive if he was not interested in amatory company, and it was chilly in the breeze. She shivered, feeling rather low.

Perhaps she had been too quick to dismiss Henri. It was going to be a boring, restless summer after all.

At her retreat, Mr. Anderson's shoulders slumped. He let out a breath that was half sigh, half rueful laugh. "It seems I am capable of being shocked after all."

Well, at least he could see the absurdity of the situation. She allowed him his levity. "Indeed."

"I apologize, Miss Arden. I assure you I mean no insult."

She waved this off but he continued to stare at her, frowning a bit.

"Truly," he said, lowering his voice.

Oh, now he thought he had shattered her tender feelings. How very tedious.

"Not at all. I'll have forgotten it by breakfast. It was no doubt wrong of me to ask. You are a solemn widower and I am a loose and terrifying woman. It would not do to corrupt you."

It wouldn't, clearly, and yet she could not help feeling annoyed by the vehemence of his rejection. It did not help that he was now gaping at her with perplexed dismay, as though he saw a magic square with mismatched sums rather than a woman. That stare made her feel like the caricatures of her in the papers—that rapacious beanpole giantess with the hooked nose and insatiable appetite for men. She fed the rumors, yes, but she did not appreciate seeing them reflected in the eyes of people who actually knew her.

She hoped he could not perceive her thoughts, but she gathered that he could, and that was why he lingered with that concerned expression on his face.

In any case, it was time for him to leave, so she could nurse her bruised vanity in the time-tested balm of excellent French burgundy.

"I should bid you good day, Mr. Anderson. I am most grateful for your architectural advice."

Instead of leaving, he pulled up a chair from the table and sat down beside her.

"I fear my response just now lacked gallantry. If my circumstances were different, Miss Arden, I would be flattered. You only took me by surprise." He bit his lip. "Again."

Was that a trace of a mordant smile? At least he had a sense of humor.

She inhaled, gathering her face into the impenetrable smirk she had rehearsed so many times in the mirror. She had spent a decade fashioning herself into a woman of restrained emotion. That she was even slightly flustered by his response to her proposal was a sign that Cornwall was wearing on her nerves.

"Thank you, Mr. Anderson. No need for flattery. I asked, you answered, and now the sordid matter is behind us."

But he continued staring at her with that pitying expression.

"You were candid with me, so allow me to be candid in return," he said. "My responsibilities are such I cannot risk entanglements, however tempting."

"Entanglements? I was not proposing marriage, Mr. Anderson. Merely inconsequential fucking."

His brown eyes met hers. "Fucking is rarely inconsequential."

How odd. She thought she'd shocked him with her frankness but now he spoke without embarrassment of matters most men avoided entirely.

"Yes. If you have read my book, you might have gathered I insist on a number of precautions against such consequences. After all, I can assure you from experience that they would be far more inconvenient for *me*."

Not that it was any of Mr. Anderson's concern. She had no idea why she was saying this. The burgundy, most likely. She reached for the gold cheroot case Henri had left behind and busied herself lighting the tobacco paper. She inhaled and let the smoke fan out around her, to shroud her in her own disreputability. She had given up tobacco in support of the cause of abolition, but tonight she craved the fortifying buzz of fire in her lungs.

And she wanted to blow smoke at Mr. Anderson, like a dragon.

She was not above a touch of theatre.

"It is a shame that anyone must suffer for such tempting pleasures as you offer," Mr. Anderson said.

She narrowed her eyes at him. "But men *don't* suffer. Women do."

He laughed bitterly. "Don't we?"

She looked at him, waiting for him to say more, but he was silent. She smoked and listened to the waves crash against the cliffs below, waiting for him to leave.

He reached over to the table, where he had left his satchel. From it, he produced a thin bound volume. It was a copy of her first book: *An Essay in Defense of Ruined Women.* Well-worn, with frayed binding.

"If you mean to quote me on the risks of fornication, I will spare you the trouble. I wrote the book on it, you see."

He gave her a sheepish grin that made him once again seem boyish. "It's my sister's. She wondered if I might charm you into signing it for her. Since it is clear to both of us my charms are rather lacking, perhaps I could prevail on your pity?"

Unfairly, he was even more handsome when he made jokes.

She took the book. "What would you have me write?"

He let out a sigh that made her shiver. "How about, *To Marianne Anderson, whose brother wishes he could be a different sort of man.*"

THAT COAXED A smile from her.

Finally.

He could see from her tart, bruised manner that he had injured Miss Arden's pride by rejecting her offer. He was not sure why it felt so vitally important to convey to this woman he barely knew that he wanted her, even if he couldn't have her.

Perhaps because it had been so long since he'd been cognizant of wanting *anything* outside of architectural commissions. He was grateful to remember that this part of him still lived, even if he could not let it be a part that he indulged.

It was his mind that shied from her offer, not his body. His body was increasingly regretful.

"Your sister truly requested my signature?" Miss Arden asked.

He smiled. "She did. She's an admirer of your work. As was my wife."

Miss Arden raised a brow. "You allowed her to read it?"

He snorted at the thought of "allowing" Catriona to do anything. "She read what she liked."

She smiled. "So you're the clever sort."

He laughed, pleased at this assessment from the infamous philosopher.

Or perhaps just pleased at this chance to have a conversation with a woman other than his sister. Being here reminded him of the long discussions he used to have with Catriona, talks that veered to such strange and honest places they often shocked each other and themselves with the words they had uttered in the dark. He rarely spoke that way now to anyone.

He missed it.

He was so lonely.

And he hadn't even been aware of it.

Miss Arden took the book from him and scrawled a few words on the title page.

To Miss Anderson, in solidarity with womankind. Best wishes, Seraphina Arden

She handed it back to him and reabsorbed herself in her cheroot. Curled up in her shawl on the settee, her legs tucked beneath her gown, exhaling smoke into the wind, she was not the temptress he had met the day before, nor even the provocateur who had propositioned him a quarter of an hour ago. She looked tired, perhaps adrift in thought.

He could so easily lean over now, kiss that weary expression from her mouth.

He wanted to.

But there was little to be gained by indulging such desires. That, perhaps, was the truth behind Miss Arden's sadness. Where did the thrills she suggested ever lead but a kind of devastation, even if it was just a quiet, private one?

Better to abstain.

A lesson he relearned every morning when he woke up in bed, alone.

Adam took the book and rose. "Well, Miss Arden, I must be going."

He bowed and turned to retreat down the terrace steps.

She reached out and touched his arm. It was just the faintest touch, but it went through him like she'd grabbed him by the waist.

He turned toward her, trying not to betray in his face the effect that mere whisper of a touch had had on him.

"I did mean what I said, Mr. Anderson. Tomorrow, should we encounter one another, we will forget this evening ever happened. I will be a woman who once asked you a question about architecture, and you will be a man who was kind enough to answer it. Mere neighbors."

He nodded. "I look forward to being neighborly."

"Then perhaps you might consider introducing me to your sister, if I am not too scandalous for her acquaintance," she said faintly. "It's quite difficult to find stimulating company here, unless one enjoys being shouted at in the public house."

She said this over-casually, as though it was an afterthought.

He smiled at her one last time. "I'll extend the invitation. She'll be pleased. Good night, Miss Arden."

As he walked down the steps to the coastal path, he wondered if Miss Arden had summoned him here because she was as lonely as he was.

He could not afford the risk of joining her in bed. But he might, discreetly, venture the smaller one of calling her a friend.

God knew that he could use one, too.

Chapter Five

The only proven antidote to conception is chastity, yet like any virtue, chastity is easier to praise than to uphold. If only the efforts spent condemning carnal vice could be diverted to understanding how best to avoid its consequences. If lust is a sin, then human beings will always sin. But with more knowledge, they might ask God's forgiveness privately and be spared the damning judgment of their fellow men.

—An Essay in Defense of Ruined Women
by Seraphina Arden, 1793

———————— ✑ ————————

Seraphina awoke to an ache along the tops of her thighs. A familiar feeling, like her flesh wished to come loose from the bone.

Oh, thank God.

She fumbled for the small, leather-bound diary among the stacks of books and papers at her bedside and fanned through it for her log. She penciled a tick next to the date. Soon the discomfort in her breasts would start.

And then, God willing, she would bleed.

She surveyed the marks and lines hatched across the page where she tracked her monthly courses. In the sixteen years since the incident, she'd made a study of the way her body presaged the tidings of the curse. It had been twenty-seven days since her last menses. During that time, there was an X for intercourse on the twelfth of the previous month—that would have been the handsome abolitionist she'd taken home from Jack Willow's monthly Equalist Society supper above the printing shop—and then, of course, her evening with Henri.

She was always scrupulous. The drawers of her dressing table were stuffed not with cosmetic balms and pleasant fragrances but jars of sheepskin condoms packed in oil and bags of herbs said to reduce fecundity. She'd made a kind of science of it, interviewing midwives and physicians for their theories on conception so that she might share them in her pamphlets. But the truth was there was little true consensus marking science from the stuff of witchcraft.

She'd been fortunate. There'd been no further incidents. But whether it was the armors or the vinegar or the bitter teas or pure blind luck that kept her barren, she could not say.

In truth, so many years and lovers had passed without conception, it was most logical to assume that she could not conceive at all. Given the grim scene those many years ago and the gravity of her illness afterward, a barren womb would not come as a surprise.

But she would not think of that. As a rule, she *never* thought of that.

It made her impossibly sad.

Instead, she limited her lovers to men amenable to her precautions. She drank the tinctures, made the hatch marks in her journal. And every month, around this time, the fear set in that the bleeding wouldn't come. Her life became a vigil for the symptoms of menstruation.

Given the grip that this anxiety had on her, to partake in intercourse at all was a kind of mental torture. As much as she enjoyed the act, every lover was a finger poised along the blade of a knife sharp enough to cut her.

She sometimes looked at women holding babies and wondered if she did it because she wanted to be cut.

She closed the journal, stood, and shivered in the morning air. This house was freezing. A fortnight here and she couldn't wait to leave.

She washed her face and ignored the plain day dress Maria had laid out the night before, eschewing it for a striking gown the color of a golden egg yolk. It was one of her favorite pieces, a saturated saffron hue that contrasted with her pale skin and dark hair, cut to emphasize her flaring hips and narrow waist. She surveyed the effect in the mirror. Dashing.

She added an amethyst necklace and matching ear bobs. She looked like she was going to a soiree in Mayfair rather than a drafty sewing room to write, but the attire did its job. In it she felt more like Seraphina Arden. Less like little Sera, who'd hated living in this house even before she'd been cast out of it, and hated being back.

If only Mr. Anderson had proven more interesting company, perhaps she might not need to take her creature comforts from her wardrobe. She was not angry that he had turned down her proposal the previous evening, but she could not look at her reflection in the yellow dress without imagining him seeing it and thinking to herself, *So there.*

She passed through the kitchen and made herself a cup of tea, then sat down at her table in the sewing room and collected the pages that amounted to the draft of her next book. She smoothed out a blank page and picked up her quill.

As had been the case for the last week, no words came to mind.

Nothing.

Only a cramping in her abdomen, the kind she got when she was anxious and trying not to notice.

It was far too quiet here. She had hoped the silence would be more conducive to her writing than the commotion that clattered in through the windows of her house in London, but instead it made her agitated.

She was running out of time.

Her manuscript was due to be published in two installments in early August, which meant the pages would be needed at her printer's for the proofs and typesetting by the beginning of July.

She had three weeks to write the tale of her undoing.

Usually she wrote quickly and precisely, rarely laboring over drafts. But this time the words had proven slower to arrive and murkier in meaning when she put them down.

The argument that closed the book—the call for funds to build the institute—was finished. But the story that must preface it for her to win the publicity and sympathy she needed to convert readers to philanthropists eluded her.

Her friendship with the Methodists and the antislavery agitators who formed the Equalist Society of which she was a member had taught her a useful truth: people were won over by their hearts, not their faculty of reason. Arguments about injustice did not move them to action. Sad stories did.

And there was a marked appetite for hers. Speculation had been whispered for years over what exactly had turned a ruined Cornish mining heiress with little education into a notorious London authoress and, in time, a divisive advocate for female rights.

She had eschewed the trend of fallen women writing the sordid accounts of their seduction, choosing to write philosophically rather than to reveal the details of her past. But if she was to raise the money they required, she needed fame and sympathy on her side.

Thus, the month before she had announced a forthcoming work: *The Memoirs of a Rakess.* She would, she made it known, spare no detail, and no person, in her story.

The logic of the plan was simple: the scandal of her story, and the august reputations of the villains she would name in it, would create a fervor for the manuscript. People would buy it for the gossip. Those who hated her already would hate her more, but others would perceive the moral of the tale: the unfairness of her losing everything while the men who'd had an equal hand in her disgrace rose to ever greater prominence, unscathed.

She would harness outrage at this injustice by using the final pages of her book to call for donations for the institute.

She would turn sympathy into the capital to help the plight of women.

All she needed were the words.

But the words failed her, given all the years she'd spent making a point of never speaking them. Even Thaïs and Cornelia only knew the barest outline of what had happened.

This was not because she was discreet. It was because she couldn't stand to think about it.

Even when it had been happening, she'd tried to push the reality away, convinced if she just refused to feel the pain it could not be real.

She had hoped that the view of Kestrel Bay would help the memories come more easily. But sitting here, in the very room where she had made that first, horrible confession that cold October morning, watching her step-mother's unmoving face and rapidly flickering fingers, unceasing in their sewing—froze her.

It was too still. Too quiet. Too much like those endless, tense days of her childhood, embroidering in silence.

She opened a window, hoping the roar of the waves crashing against the rocks would ease the feeling of still-ness, but it was unusually calm this morning. The air was warmer outside than inside—balmy and soft. Perhaps she would write out of doors.

She took her papers and the ink and quill and went outside into the sunshine.

"Toss the line!" someone shouted in the distance.

She looked out in the direction of the voice and saw that Mr. Anderson was standing at the foot of Tre-gereth's property, conferring with a group of builders. Beyond them, another group of men worked at erecting some sort of pulley from the roof to the tent where they had assembled construction supplies at the bottom of the house.

The noise soothed her, even if the sight of the architect brought back a rush of longing for what she wanted from him and could not have.

She wished she could resent him for it, but the frank-ness with which he explained his reasons for refusing made her like him more, not less.

Perhaps it would serve her, to long for him; to long for a man in this house brought back a flood of memories.

She spread out a fresh page. Dipped her quill in ink.

She closed her eyes and let the briny air wash over her and tried to recall this feeling the way she'd experienced it as a girl.

It began as these things do. He was a neighbor.

He took an interest in me and I bloomed in it. Before him, I was nothing. Soon, his gaze on me was the only thing that made me breathe.

I was a homely, bookish girl, prone to flights of fancy and fits of temper. He was handsome and amusing.

Why he loved me I could not have told you then, for it was my miracle, my mystery.

Now I'm certain that he didn't.

What drew him to me was something else. A flicker at my core I was not yet aware of.

He saw it before I did: my hunger.

And something else: my vulnerability.

To him I was an opportunity.

But to me, he was a god. I loved him with a kind of religiosity. How could I not?

He, who could have anyone, had chosen me.

I would have died for him.

And in a way, I did.

A child's wail broke through her thoughts.

A child?

She stood and peered out beyond the terrace. A small, red-haired girl was sprawled on her stomach on the path that ran a few meters below the terrace steps, crying out in pain.

She looked like the little girl Sera'd seen walking with Adam Anderson. His daughter.

Seraphina rose and darted down the steps to help her.

ADAM LOOKED UP from his building plans when he heard a shrill wail.

He had a parent's preternatural recognition of his children's noises of distress, and that sound was his daughter's distinctive cry of pain.

He scanned the horizon and saw Addie splayed out a few hundred yards away, just below Miss Arden's terrace steps. A woman in a vivid yellow gown was crouched down beside her in the dust.

It was Miss Arden.

He dropped his plans and began to run.

Miss Arden lifted Addie to her feet and said something to his daughter that made her laugh.

Thank God. If she could laugh, she was not too badly injured.

"What happened?" he asked, dropping to his knees to inspect his daughter, breathless from running.

Addie beamed at him, pleased to be the center of attention.

"It seems Miss Adeline Anderson here took a spill on this very unfriendly chunk of rock," Miss Arden said, gesturing at a stone.

He felt such a surge of gratitude to her for easing Addie's tears that he had to restrain himself from clutching them both to his chest.

Nonsense. Focus on your injured daughter.

He knelt down and gripped Addie tightly, shuddering a bit at the thought of what might have happened if she had slid a foot closer to the edge of the path.

Addie tolerated his embrace for just a moment before holding up her hand to show him where a bit of gravel had dug into the flesh, leaving it mottled and scraped.

"Miss Arden says that I may throw the rock off the cliff," she informed him cheerfully, the drying tears forgotten. "To punish it for its abuse of me."

"An eye for an eye," Miss Arden said, very serious. "It's only what the rock deserves."

Addie picked up the stone in her uninjured hand. He reached out to stop her, lest she go over the edge in her attempt to toss it, but Miss Arden had already taken her gently by the shoulder to steady her.

"Careful, darling," she said. "Not too close to the cliff."

He took Addie by the other shoulder and leaned her toward him, so he could look into her eyes. "Addie, you mustn't ever get too close to the edge, do you understand? And you mustn't run on the path."

His voice was gruffer than he liked, and Addie's top lip began to quiver.

"I didn't mean to," she said plaintively to Miss Arden. "I tripped."

"Your papa isn't angry, only frightened," Miss Arden said conspiratorially. "Promise him you will be very, very cautious whenever you are on this path."

Addie looked at him. "I promise."

He kissed her forehead. "Thank you, lass."

Miss Arden winked at him, in a way that made it obvious she could see how upset he was and that he needn't worry. It was a look Catriona used to give him, to reassure him when he was anxious about the children. The memory knocked the wind out of him.

Miss Arden turned her attention back to Addie. "Now then, stand straight."

Keeping the girl at several feet's distance from the ledge, Miss Arden helped her swing back her arm to throw the stone. "There we are. Let it go."

The small rock plunged down the hill. Jasper and Marianne reached them just in time to see it smash onto the rocks below. Addie whooped with delight.

"May I throw one?" Jasper asked.

Miss Arden bent down and produced another stone, holding it out to Adam's son. "A favor in exchange for your name, sir."

He bowed very seriously. "My name is Jasper Anderson, ma'am."

"Well, young Mr. Anderson, you will wish to hold this rock at about your ear, clamp your feet down on the ground, and throw it over-head. I have always found using two hands rewards one with the most satisfying splash. But be careful not to get too close to the edge."

"Like this?" Jasper concentrated on perfecting his posture, letting Miss Arden adjust his arms just so.

He launched the rock and turned around to grin at Adam and Marianne, who was whispering breathy apologies in Adam's ear for letting Adeline evade her. Adam patted his sister on the back. They had to do something about Addie. Lately she was always testing what she could get away with, and she put herself in danger.

"Did you see, Papa?" Jasper called.

Adam belatedly turned his attention to his boy. "Well done, lad," he said.

"You have quite an arm," Miss Arden added, in a tone that made Jasper plump with pride.

Adam stole a glance at her. He could scarcely believe that this kind, maternal person was the same woman who had invited him into her bed the night before.

And yet they *were* the same—the same wry humor, the same air of self-assurance, the same habit of looking out the corners of her eyes at him and smiling, as if a secondary understanding ran between them beneath what was being said.

"Addie, let's go back to the house and tend to your hand," Marianne said. "Thank Miss Arden for her kindness."

"Nonsense," Miss Arden said. "Come right upstairs. We'll get her cleaned and bandaged so that she doesn't bleed on her pretty dress."

Adam hesitated, not relishing the idea of his children in Miss Arden's house, with its uneven floorboards and infamous proprietress, but his sister stepped forward before he could think of a polite way to object. "Thank you, Miss Arden, that's very kind."

"You must be Miss Anderson," Miss Arden said. "Of the excellent taste in books."

Marianne grinned. "The very same. Thank you for your dedication. I shall cherish it."

Miss Arden led them up the stairs to her house and through the door to the kitchen, where her maid was puttering with chipped plates. "Have we any lemonade, Maria?"

Maria nodded and set about preparing a pitcher and glasses as Miss Arden fetched a cloth and water for Marianne, who ministered to Addie's hand.

He hung back by the door with Jasper, both of them watching the efficient movements of the ladies. Addie, meanwhile, was allowing her aunt to dress her wound while staring raptly at Miss Arden's yellow gown.

He couldn't blame her. He wanted to stare, too.

"That's better," Marianne said as she finished wrapping Addie's hand.

"Thank Miss Arden for her help," Adam instructed.

"Thank you, Miss Arden," Addie lisped obediently.

"My pleasure. Miss Adeline, I implore you to tread carefully when you walk outside. Our Cornish footpaths can be treacherous."

"The views are beautiful though," Marianne said. "You grew up here?"

"Yes. It was a lovely place to be a child. I spent my summers wading in the rock pools. Swimming in the sea. But my favorite thing was Golowan."

"Galljalong?" Addie giggled, delighted to hear an adult say such a silly-sounding word.

Miss Arden smiled. "*Golowan*. It's the Cornish celebration of midsummer. The whole town prepares for it every June, and on the Eve of St. John, there is a procession with torches and bonfires and dancing and delicious foods and festive dress."

"Festive dress!" Addie breathed, big-eyed with delight. She loved pretty clothes.

"Might *we* go?" Jasper asked, turning to Adam.

"Oh yes, I want to go, too!" Addie said immediately. "May we, Papa? May we?"

He grimaced, thinking of his small children in a throng of rural villagers with torches. "We'll see."

"If you go, you'll need costumes, of course," Miss Arden told them. "A Celtic kilt would suit you, Jasper, and Adeline would look lovely as a druid sprite."

"But we don't *have* costumes," Jasper said, looking worriedly at Adam. "All our things are in London."

"I imagine all my old costumes are upstairs in the attic," Miss Arden said. "I'm sure we could fashion something for you."

She paused and looked at Adam, as if belatedly remembering he was in the room. "That is, if your papa agrees." She shot him a look as if to say *sorry*.

"Papa will say it's too dangerous," Jasper groaned. "He says everything is too dangerous."

Adam gave his son a look. "Not everything. But bonfires and torches, perhaps."

"It is the job of fathers to keep their children safe," Miss Arden said to Jasper. She looked over his head at Adam and smiled. "And you, I'm afraid, seem to be blessed with a good one."

Her praise made him unsuitably happy, though he was not entirely sure she was correct about the merits of his parenting, given that in this moment he was considering consenting to let his children borrow costumes from this woman for a paganish procession just so he might find himself in her midst again.

"Well, Miss Arden," he said, "it is time we return your kitchen to peace."

He felt her eyes on him as he said the words. She made him intensely aware of his own presence. He could feel his shirt brushing the skin of his back. His fingertips, grazing the table a few feet from Miss Arden's own.

"Indeed," Marianne agreed. "'Tis past time these young people returned home for their lessons."

Adeline popped out her lower lip in distress. "Lessons! We did lessons *yesterday.*"

Miss Arden knelt to address the girl seriously. "One must do lessons every day if one wants to learn, Miss Anderson. This is very important for young ladies. The more lessons, the better off you will be when you're grown. Insist on extra lessons, I say."

Adam smiled, enjoying the way Miss Arden adjusted her philosophical positions to suit the understanding of a child. She was good with children. It was perhaps unfair of him, but he had not imagined a woman of her reputation might take genuine interest in bairns. He was touched.

"Hear that, Addie?" he said. "Miss Arden is a wise woman. You'd be best to listen to her. Now say farewell."

The children said their farewells and his sister shuttled them out the door. He turned to follow but Miss Arden tapped him lightly on the shoulder. She may as well have hit him with a hammer, for he felt her touch reverberate straight down to his hips.

Every time she touched him, the same bloody effect, like he was a schoolboy.

He wondered if she knew—if she could see it.

"Mr. Anderson, I'm sorry," she said in a low voice. "I should not have mentioned the festival without consulting you. I didn't think before I spoke."

She looked sincerely regretful. He was again surprised by this. Her kindness.

He decided to be honest. "You meant no harm. It's only that I try to make sure they don't go anywhere I'm not familiar with, or where Scots might be unwelcome. After their mother's death . . . it's my superstition but I like to do what I can to keep them safe."

Marianne thought he over-sheltered the children. For months after Catriona's death, he had barely been able to bring himself to leave for work in the mornings, not wanting to let what remained of his family out of his sight.

Miss Arden looked at him with sympathy. "Of course. I see. I should hope you would not find unfriendly people here. Golowan is a cheerful celebration and welcoming to visitors. I do think your children would enjoy it."

"I'll consider it. Will you attend?"

Her mouth opened, as if in surprise, and then she laughed, shaking her head. "No. Unlike you I am *not* a stranger here, and I suspect most people would prefer that I make myself one."

"Ah. I'm sorry." His own mother had faced the disapproval of the town where he'd been raised, having borne two children to an English lord who kept her as his mistress in a house near his shooting estate. Adam knew how the whispers and looks had pained her, though she'd always pretended that they hadn't.

"Oh, that's quite all right," Miss Arden said. Her expression hardened into something like that detached gaze she'd worn when he'd disappointed her on her terrace. "I take comfort from the fact that the dislike is mutual."

He didn't quite believe her. It had been clear enough to him last night that she acted more impervious than she really was. And he couldn't blame her. No one liked to wear their pain openly.

Before he could say anything more, Miss Tompkins walked through the kitchen door, carrying a basket.

"You're back," Miss Arden said. "How was the village?"

Tompkins grimaced and held up a piece of paper. "This was posted by the gates to the house," she said acidly. "The fence is covered in them."

Miss Arden's face went pale. "They wasted little time."

Adam leaned over to inspect the paper. It bore Miss Arden's image, but whoever had drawn it had made her face hawkish and her figure a grotesquerie of swollen hips and breasts spilling from a low-cut gown. "Kestrel Wants No Hussies" was printed below in smudged ink.

Poor lass. What a bloody thing to read about oneself.

"Ignorant brutes," Tompkins muttered. "If I catch them at it, I'll bash them with a broomstick."

"Oh, they just want a reaction," Miss Arden said. "Best to ignore it."

She said this with conviction, but she looked shaken.

He was inclined to agree with Miss Tompkins. Given the mocking whispers his own mother had endured throughout his childhood, he would happily throttle any man who was capable of spewing such filth.

"May I have that?" he asked Tompkins.

Both she and Miss Arden looked at him in surprise. "You would like a souvenir?" Miss Arden asked.

He was not entirely sure if she was joking.

"No." He took the paper, rolled it up, and tucked it inside his waistcoat. "I want to see to it that my men remove these from your gate right away. We'll look into who might have posted them."

Miss Arden seemed like she wanted to protest, but Miss Tompkins gave her a loaded look and smiled at him. "Thank you, Mr. Anderson. You are kind to offer help."

Miss Arden met his eye. "I'm sure he will say he is merely neighborly," she said to Tompkins, without breaking his gaze. Her expression danced with something playful. Something like the way she had looked at him as her sheer dress had whipped around her ankles in the belvedere.

God, to be looked at like that.

"Not merely," he said. He heard a whisper of regret in his own voice. From the way she paused, he knew she heard it, too.

He was glad.

Glad? Christ. Stop this.

He lowered his eyes so she would not be able to look upon the desire in them and patted the poster. "I must return to Tregereth's. I'll see about these vile things."

He turned to leave but paused, for it had to be said even if he knew his throat would become raspy with emotion. "And Miss Arden?"

"Yes?"

"Thank you for attending to my daughter. I shudder to think what might have happened had you not been close by."

She glanced up at his tone, which was indeed more graveled than he liked. And then she smiled at him, utterly without irony.

And with that smile, in her butter-yellow dress and purple ear bobs with the sun shining off her lustrous hair, she looked nothing like that woodcut. She looked like a stained glass window or an illuminated manuscript. Like the woman who kept appearing in his dreams.

"Of course, Mr. Anderson," she said. "Merely being neighborly."

He nodded and stepped out the door into the sunshine, wondering why it was that every time he was in Miss Arden's presence his heart ended up in his kneecaps.

Chapter Six

Miss Arden models herself a reformer when she is nothing but a temptress, a fallen Jezebel whose fine speech belies a mission to turn England's virtuous females into unrepentant whores. Her announcement of her memoirs should not be met with anticipation, but disgust. The only place her words belong is in the fire.

—*The Town Mercury*, 1797

❧

It wasn't so much a noise as a prickle on her spine that woke Seraphina in the early light of dawn.

She froze, listening.

A pebble hit her window.

Someone was outside. On the terrace below her bedchamber.

"Tompkins?" she hissed. "Maria? Is that you?"

Silence.

She angled her ear toward the window. Footsteps?

It's nothing. Go back to sleep.

She heard another pebble.

She bolted out of bed and crouched on the floor, rummaging for a dressing gown and regretting that in the heat she had chosen to sleep nude.

She threw the garment over her shoulders and clutched it tight around herself as though it might protect her from whatever was outside.

Prowlers, no doubt. Just like when she'd been seven-teen.

She'd willed herself to forget those visits in the dead of night. Never violent, never loud enough to wake her father. Just intrusive enough to make her know that she was being watched.

Well, she was no longer seventeen, and she didn't intend to scurry on the floorboards being terrified in silence.

She took a pitcher of water off her dressing table and rose onto her knees, creeping to the window to peer just above the sill in case whoever was afoot below was armed with heavier rocks.

She'd douse them with cold water. Teach them that she was no longer a person to be stalked.

But there was no one on the terrace.

It was not a person, but a bird.

A kingfisher. Splayed on its back, its turquoise wings outstretched like an opened lady's fan, and its wheat-gold breast sliced open.

She gasped and clutched the window ledge, fighting a wave of sickness.

The bird moved one wing and with a terrible certainty she realized the poor creature was not yet dead.

Oh no. Oh please, no.

She ran down the stairs and to the terrace doors, scrab-bling with the lock. She burst outside and knelt before the tiny, bleeding bird. It made a low, wretched noise—a sound of suffering. She felt a sob rise from her throat. "Oh, you poor darling. Poor darling."

She wanted to soothe it, to clutch it to her chest. But that would only hurt it.

That old, frantic feeling—making her lungs tight and hot, like she'd dragged too long on a cheroot—starved her of air. *Something small she couldn't save.*

She looked desperately about the terrace for someone who might help, but she was alone. What could she *do*? The creature would not live. The only mercy was to end its suffering, but how?

No. No, please.

She had no choice. She closed her eyes. Her hands shook as she picked it up. Its tiny body trembled, warm and soft.

"Sweet thing, I'm so sorry. So sorry," she whispered. "You don't deserve this."

Her fingers remembered the gesture from when she'd helped the cook with chickens as a girl. A brisk, gruesome pivot of the wrist was all it took to snap the neck.

She released the sob she had been holding and the poor, beautiful bird went still.

Sera sat there for a moment, crouched on her knees, shaking.

She had kept kingfishers as a child, in a cage. Her father had trapped them by the river that ran at the border of her property and he'd given her one as a gift when she was eight. When she'd worried it was lonely, he'd caught a mate. She'd loved those birds. She still thought of them when she wore bright colors. It was one of the few memories from her girlhood that was not tinged with loss.

Until now.

Who would do this? Who could be so depraved?

She looked around again, below the terrace, to the empty coastal path. To the hedges alongside it.

"Who's there?" she shouted in a voice she hated. "What do you want?"

No one answered.

But she could not stop herself from continuing to scream. "Am I such a threat to you? Me? Why? Why are you so frightened by the mere presence of this *woman* that you'd kill a helpless bird?"

She fell to her knees, panting.

There was no answer. Of course there wasn't.

Why had they ever threatened her? Persecuted her? What had the people of Kestrel Bay ever thought they were protecting by making her a figure of contempt?

The answer, of course, was everything and nothing, and so it was appropriate that there was no response to her cry, save the low crashing of the waves down beneath the cliffs.

She stood up and took a cleansing breath. If someone was still watching her, they would only be gratified to see she was disturbed by this.

Better to shake it off.

She would find a box, and bury the bird on the beach at low tide. She turned and walked back to the terrace doors.

A piece of paper fluttered above the doorframe, suspended by a single nail.

It was another woodcut. The same awful image she had winced at in her kitchen. The vile caricature Mr. Anderson's kind apprentice had removed from her gateposts morning after morning for a week.

The only difference was that this one had a note scrawled crudely at the bottom of the page.

Birds of paradise aren't wanted here. Beware.

THE WOMAN BATHED amidst the breakers at the bottom of the cliffs, salty spray splashing her delicate white gown until it strained tight and transparent against her flesh. Her dark hair dripped and swirled around her shoulders, falling to her hips like a mermaid's. Her wet dress clung to her rounded form as tightly as scales to a fish.

She looked at him as she raised one leg above the surf, her toes dancing in the foam atop the breakers, and peeled her dress up higher, to her thighs. *Come to me*, she beckoned with her eyes.

Adam wanted to so badly he felt it in his chest.

He walked forward, wading through warm water, slick rocks beneath his feet. She lifted her gown higher, peeling it up over her thighs and then, slowly, over the dark thicket above them. Upward, upward the soaked fabric rose, over her gently rounded belly and the hard, pink nipples of her breasts. She pulled it over her head and let it fall into the surf. Nude, she raised her hands up to the sky and leaned back into the sunlight, her hair blowing in the sultry ocean breeze, tangling in the wind.

He finally reached her. She took his hands and drew them toward her breasts, so that her nipples grazed his palms. Her dress caught around his ankle, floating in the shallows.

He pressed his skin to hers. She was all wet heat. He dragged his hands down around her generous hips to take her buttocks and draw her to his groin.

"Adam," she whispered.

Yes, yes, yes, his body answered. The sun grew brighter and they were hot and wet where they were joined and pleasure shot up through his legs, slick and salty, churning like the hot turquoise of the sea.

"Adam."

His eyes shot open.

The room was white with the morning light streaming off the Kestrel, but he was not cavorting in the shallows with a mermaid who bore the exact dimensions of Seraphina Arden.

He was in his bed, in his cottage, and his sister was knocking at the door.

Fuck.

He reached out for a homespun towel by his shaving stand.

"Yes, Marianne?" he called through the door, praying she would not somehow hear the evidence of his shameful state in his voice.

"It's nearly seven."

"Thank you."

He never slept this late. He certainly did not laze in the sunshine, frotting his own sheets until he was late to meet his foreman.

He cut his chin with hurried, irritable shaving, not enjoying the sight of his own reflection in the looking glass, guilt oozing from his eyes like cherries from the lattice of a tart.

His appetites had always had too strong a hold on him, the legacy of his father.

He'd once thought he could indulge them sensibly—responsibly, within the bounds of marriage—but when his lust had cost him Catriona, he'd sworn he'd never in his life bend to such temptation again.

He was a widower. A father. An architect.

That other part of himself, that awful, weak, and wanting part, had no place amidst this life: the ever-mounting building costs and delinquent payments and the endless need to produce a folio of better work to secure himself and Mayhew a place in London's cutthroat world. To secure a future for the children he'd left motherless. To prove himself better than his father, despite his humbler birth.

His father had chosen weaknesses over his responsibilities—died young, leaving a trail of bastards, Adam and Marianne included, and a bankrupt estate that had passed to some unlucky distant cousin. All

Adam had inherited from his father was his propensity for lust and chestnut hair.

But vices thrived in regularity and died out from starvation. One could feel their presence without caving to them. After all, he had his mother's people's blood in him as well. The grandfather who'd taught him to hold his head up high and do right by his family no matter what. The mother who'd fought for his education and refused to be cowed by shame.

His father's yen for pleasure could be contained, if he was strong enough. And after losing Catriona, he'd been so numb, so guilty, that the urge to exercise it almost fell away.

But apparently it had not fallen away entirely.

For Miss Arden, and her sheer gown and her mussed hair and her knowing stare, had awakened that old, persistent hunger.

I'm afraid we have misunderstood each other, he'd told her when she'd invited him to bed.

He was treacherous, a hypocrite. She hadn't misunderstood a thing.

It had been a week since then, and he was still dreaming of her. His desire for her beat behind his every thought, like an ever-present second pulse.

He was like a schoolboy. It was unbecoming. He had to take control of himself. Read his Bible. Draw porticos and colonnades until the thought of a woman's curves no longer plagued his mind.

He splashed water on his face until the guilty expression left his eyes.

Dressed, he ventured to the main room of the cottage. Marianne was frying eggs in a heavy pan and the table was piled with toasted bread and her homemade berry jam.

"Thank you for waking me," he said in a low voice.

She shrugged. "Unlike you to oversleep."

"I was up late reading." Rereading, really, for he'd borrowed Marianne's copy of Seraphina Arden's book. Its grim assessment of inequality between the sexes had not lessened his desire for the woman herself, but it had reminded him how penetrating her intelligence was.

Which only made him want her more.

Marianne held out a letter. "This came for you while you were asleep. Delivered by a footman from the Marquess of Pendrake."

Adam froze. "Pendrake. You must be mistaken."

She laughed. "I'm not. You should have seen his livery. Prettier than a princess. Adeline was sick with envy."

Adam tore the letter open.

Mr. Anderson,

I requested your name from Mr. Tregereth after noting the speed of the work you've done on his renovation. Lord Pendrake is seeking an architect to build a small temple in the garden here at Alsonair. I wondered if you would be so kind as to meet with me to discuss the matter tomorrow at two o'clock.

Regards,
Jeremiah Lotham, Estate Secretary to
the Marquess of Pendrake, Alsonair

Wordlessly, he handed the letter to Marianne.

She read it quickly, then looked at him, her eyes shining with excitement. "Adam! I can't believe it. You must write to Mayhew and tell him—he'll fall over."

He shook his head, scarcely able to believe it himself. "I'll write back this morning."

This was exactly what he needed. Something to push wistful distractions out of his head and remind him he had a purpose here that had nothing to do with Seraphina Arden.

"Did you get good news, Papa?" Jasper asked.

Adam's heart clenched, for Jasper was always so carefully attuned to his moods, quick to absorb his father's worries like a sponge.

"I did indeed. And I have a mind to celebrate. How would you and Addie like to have luncheon at an inn today? We can taste some Cornish delicacies."

His children looked up in delighted surprise.

"Yes, Papa," Jasper said.

"Yes! Yes!" Addie cried.

Marianne beamed at him. He was rarely available to the children during daytime even on Sundays, the demands of his work being what they were. It would be a special treat to have an outing together as a family, and do them all good.

"I'll come to collect you at midday," he said.

And he would think of this, when his mind wandered. An outing with his children and his sister. A meeting that could propel his ambitions and help him dig his way out of debt.

Not a woman splashing in the surf.

Chapter Seven

The news that Viscountess Bell has been accused of adultery with the notorious publisher Jack Willow is the latest proof that seditionist tendencies are a corruptive plague that blackens not just the politics but the very moral fiber of the kingdom. If a noble wife and mother can succumb to such moral rot, no one is safe from the depraving influence of rogues like Willow and their thirst for chaos. The scourge must be stopped before the weakest among us—our women and our children and the poor—lose their characters, and the very fabric of society descends into unrest. Lady Bell and Willow should face the harshest punishment. They deserve whatever hell awaits them.

—*The London Caller*, 1797

❧

It was difficult to write when one's mind was filled with bird corpses.

Seraphina did not believe in the superstitions that had ruled her stepmother's life, with every yowling cat or crescent moon heralding a sign of some misfortune. But the delicate little kingfisher had been an ominous way to begin the day, and then the post had arrived, still without any news of Elinor or word at all from Cornelia. The silence from her friends only added to her sense that darkness was trying to close around her. For the first time, she wondered if it was a mistake to come back here.

She'd hoped that coming to Kestrel Bay would help retrieve the memories she'd pushed back into the recesses of her mind. Remembering what had happened here was crucial to writing with the animating rage she must to fulfill the purpose of her book.

She and her friends had christened themselves the Society of Sirens because, like the sirens of myth, they wanted to avenge themselves against the forces and people who had constrained their lives. The trouble was that she had spent the last sixteen years affecting measured distance to insulate herself from just that kind of anger.

She'd come here for exactly the awakening she'd received this morning. But she'd forgotten that with the anger came despair. Words had always been her shield, but words could not protect her from whoever left dead creatures on her terrace.

Outside, she heard children's voices. She'd forgotten she'd invited Marianne Anderson to bring her niece and nephew over to look through her old costume box.

Delightful. She needed something light and innocent to becalm her mind. It would steady her for an afternoon of writing.

She heard Tompkins greeting them and found the Andersons in the parlor, where the children were seated politely with their aunt, wearing spotless clothes she suspected were their Sunday finest.

Adeline was visibly bursting with the strain of this display of manners, wriggling in her pretty dress. Sera hid a laugh. The little girl's fine spirit put her in a brighter mood.

Stay that way, you gorgeous creature, she wanted to tell her. *Don't let the world diminish you.*

"Good afternoon, children, Miss Anderson," she greeted them. "Don't you look lovely."

"Papa's taking us to the village today," Jasper said.

Sera smiled at the earnest little boy. "Is he? What fun."

It lifted her mood to think of Mr. Anderson leaving his construction site to accompany his brood for a festive lunch in town.

"We're going to eat a pie with our hands," Adeline said, sounding as if she had not quite decided whether she found this idea enticing or revolting.

"Pasties," Marianne clarified. "The children are very excited to taste a Cornish pasty."

"Well then, you must build up a good appetite. A pasty is a hearty meal that tastes the best when one is famished."

"What's famished?" Adeline asked.

"So hungry you could eat an entire hog," Sera said.

Adeline shivered. "I don't want to eat a hog."

Jasper leaned in to whisper in his sister's ear. "That's pork. You like pork. You had rashers for breakfast."

Sera felt a pang at his sweetness—wanting to correct his sister without embarrassing her. A good boy. Wholesome. Like his father.

The presence of these children was just what she needed. It was comforting to be around people who had no opinion on her moral standing. Who merely looked at her as a woman who could furnish them with playthings.

"Rashers are pigs?" Adeline wailed. "No one told me they are pigs!"

"A town-bred child," Sera said dryly to Marianne, who was trying not to laugh.

"I'm afraid so," Marianne agreed.

Sera bent down to the distressed girl. "Never mind the poor pigs, Miss Adeline. Every creature is some other creature's supper, I'm afraid."

"I'm not a creature's supper!" Adeline said, indignant.

"You are if wolves eat you," Jasper said solemnly.

Adeline's face crumpled at the thought.

Seraphina picked her up before she had a chance to cry. "Aren't we lucky there are no wolves in Cornwall? Come, Jasper, on to the matters of the day. Your costumes for Golowan. I believe our dear Miss Tompkins found an entire box of them."

She led them to the old trunk of her stepmother's, which Tompkins had lugged down from the attic.

"Jasper, the men wear tunics and carry torches, and the boys accompany them with wooden staffs wrapped up in burlap and trim." She pulled out an old garment her stepmother had sewn for her father. "This will be too large for you, but perhaps your aunt can mend it so it fits."

"Of course," Marianne said.

"And for Miss Adeline, the little girls wear white frocks and string flowers in their hair." She pulled a dress that had been hers as a child from the trunk. "This will do nicely."

Adeline giggled at the old-fashioned garment.

"Do you know how to thread a flower garland?" Seraphina asked Marianne.

"I'm not sure I do. Perhaps you could show us. If you have the time. We wouldn't want to impose."

She'd rather do anything than write, so she rummaged in the box for scissors, needles, and a spindle of twine. "Let's go outside and pick our flowers."

She spent the next hour with Marianne and the children in the sunshine, wandering the garden beside the house, until they had collected far more wildflowers than were needed and a tall branch that could serve as Jasper's pole.

Once they had a full basket, they returned to the terrace, where Seraphina spread out their bounty and showed the children how to pierce the center of a flower with a needle and attach it to thread to make a crown. Maria brought them lemonade sweetened with honey and by the time the sun was overhead, the four of them were laughing like old friends.

Sera always forgot how much she liked children. Their amusing antics and strange observations were such a soothing distraction from her dread of the work awaiting her that she lost track of the time. She was surprised when a man shouted a greeting from the distance.

It was Adam Anderson, walking up the coastal path.

God, he was handsome. It should be a crime to look like that.

The breeze blew his hair in the wind, and he'd become more tan, no doubt from working out of doors. He was so different from the pale men she knew in London, who had the crouched posture and narrow shoulders that came with a life toiling over words. Adam looked natural against the backdrop of the cliffs, full of rugged health and vigor. She wanted to go up to him and breathe him in. He'd probably smell like sweat and earth.

"Papa!" Adeline cried, running to greet him with a large bunch of flowers. "Look, we're druids!"

He glanced at Sera briefly over his daughter's head, his eyes flashing with something sharp and aware. Was that excitement to see her, or alarm at the sight of his children learning pagan rites under the tutelage of a loose woman?

She willed his eyes to linger on her with abject arousal or unrequited longing, or at least some sign that in the week since she'd last seen him he'd thought of her with anything like the frequency she'd thought of him. But he turned his attention to the children.

"I was on my way to the cottage to collect you," he told them. "Are you ready for our voyage?"

"Yes!" cried Jasper.

"No!" Adeline objected. "I want to stay with Miss Arden."

Sera repressed a smile. At least dear *Adeline* was suitably enamored with her.

"Perhaps Miss Arden would like to join us," Marianne suggested, turning to Sera with a warm, genuine smile. "It is time for luncheon, after all, and we have worked up enough of an appetite to eat at least one pasty each."

Seraphina shook her head without even considering it. It was not her place to intrude upon a family outing. And she did not wish to go into the town, where she might see people she had once known. "Oh, thank you, but I must return to work."

Adeline looked at her with huge, beseeching eyes. "Oh, please, Miss Arden, come and watch me eat the pie!"

"I'm sure it will be quite a thing to watch," Sera laughed. "Our pasties are the size of your wee head."

Adeline wrinkled her nose. "My head isn't wee."

"Yes, it is," Jasper informed his sister, after a brief assessment.

"Are you certain, Miss Arden?" Adam asked, looking her way with more intensity than was warranted by an offhand invitation. "We'd all love the company."

The way he said it, low and warm, sent a flutter through her.

He had thought of her. She knew it. She could feel it, running between them. Piercing her. Still, she searched his eyes, wondering why he would want her company. She detected a slight note of challenge in the way he held his shoulders. Whether he issued the challenge to her or to himself, she was not sure.

Adeline flew into a rapture at her father's encouragement. "Yes, come with us!" she pleaded, dancing about at Sera's feet.

Perhaps she would.

After all, hiding in her crumbling house was not the way to signal her defiance to whoever wished to drive her out of town. Sharing a meal with a wholesome family would prove to anyone watching her that she was neither scared nor ashamed.

And it had been ages since she'd eaten good pasties.

Good pasties were her bloody birthright.

Sera smiled down at Adeline. "Very well, luncheon it is."

Out of the corner of her eye she noticed Adam smile and look down at his feet. It made her want to smile back.

ADAM FOCUSED ON his children's every word as they made the voyage to the inn. In part because it was nice to spend an afternoon with them, and in part because focusing on their chatter helped him not to lose his wits over the nearness of Seraphina Arden.

It had been a perverse impulse to encourage her to join this outing, given that he'd conceived of the trip to distract himself from his thoughts of her. And though it was ungracious to dwell on it, there was a risk to being seen out with her in public, when word of their acquaintance could filter out to the village and fall upon the wrong ears. He was certain Pendrake, who led a faction of Conservatives, would not approve of Miss Arden's sort.

But when his sister had invited her, it had seemed rude not to second the invitation, given she'd spent the morning entertaining his small children.

But really, he'd just wanted her to come.

And now that she was walking a few feet from him, he was a mess of nerves. It was a peculiarly specific feeling—the desire not to betray how nervous one was in the presence of a woman one could not stop thinking about. He was grateful for her ease with the children; listening to her make light conversation with them gave him something to focus on besides worrying that he seemed too eager, or wondering how he looked, or trying to discern whether she was watching him.

He had not felt this way since he was a much younger man. He wondered what she would think if she knew the stir she caused in him.

She would probably think he was painfully inexperienced.

But that wasn't it. He did not react this way to women. He reacted this way exclusively to *her.*

He focused on the journey to steady his nerves. The Old Well in Curno was the closest inn to Miss Arden's land—miles nearer than the alehouses in the larger town of Penzance—but getting there required a short ferry ride across the River Senn and a walk along the shore to the village, which looked out across the beach to the fishermen's day boats.

Adeline insisted on wearing her garlands, inspiring Jasper to entertain her along the way with a story of a fairy princess name Lady Adelina who could sail the seas floating on a raft of wildflowers.

To Adeline's delight, Miss Arden helped his son spin this tale of enchantment, pausing every so often to embellish the tale with some fact about the mystical powers of the Cornish flora. She was so good with the children that he half forgot she was the infamous Rakess.

But that was uncharitable. Catriona had been hungry in their bed, and a doting mother. The two qualities were not in opposition.

"Shall we walk along the beach instead of along the road?" Miss Arden asked, when the ferry deposited them on the far side of the river. "I know a tidal pool where we might find the most unusual spiny creatures."

"Spiny creatures?" both children shrieked, Jasper with delight and Adeline with horror.

Miss Arden winked. "Don't worry. Nothing we can't outrun."

Adam swallowed back a chuckle.

He tried to catch her eye, to smile at her and show his gratitude for being kind to his children. But she so assiduously failed to look at him he could only assume she did so on purpose.

He wondered if perhaps some of the fluttery feeling of awareness in his belly was not his alone. If she, too, was moving as if in a haze, half focused on the world around her and half focused on how she might appear to him.

He hoped so.

He knew he shouldn't, but still, he hoped so.

She led them up the narrow cliffside path that veered toward Curno's yellow stretch of sand until they reached a jetty, beneath which was a shallow rock pool. Miss Arden showed the children bright yellow seaweed that speckled the rocks and pointed out sponges and tiny crabs that lived in the shallows.

As the children played, she picked up a length of thick, brown seaweed. "Laver," she said to Marianne. "They make a bread with it in these parts. Have you tried it?"

"No," his sister said, bending in to smell the leaf. She inclined her head quizzically and took a tiny bite. "Oh, I see. Quite savory. Perhaps I will collect some on the way back and try a recipe with it at home."

Miss Arden pointed out other local edibles: samphire, delicious boiled and served with butter alongside a piece of fish; and thick, luscious tangles of sea beet, which she told Marianne her cook used to love to serve in winter, when the garden greens had long gone brown and dead.

She was quite pointedly not talking to him, so he tried to imagine her as a child, spending her summers wading these shores. Nowadays her accent bore no trace of Cornwall and her brisk ways were of the London salons where she was known to be a fixture. He marveled at the transformation.

She'd said she was writing her memoirs. He'd be curious to read them. He wanted to know her better.

When they reached the fishing boats, they turned off the beach and walked up to the village. The air around the old public house was redolent of fried fish, reminding him of the inns along the banks of the Thames at home.

The inn was nearly empty. Marianne settled the children at a table while he went up to the bar to order food. Miss Arden came and stood beside him. He could smell her fragrant, flowery perfume cutting through the greasy air as she waited for him to order enough food for a small feast.

"And five half pints of elderflower cordial," she added, when he'd finished.

"It's the special here," she confided, when the publican turned away.

Finally, she spoke just to him. He was so pleased he wanted to dance a jig, but instead he only smiled at her. "Ah, I knew it would be good to have a local lass about."

She smiled back. "You were kind to invite me."

"Thank you for spending time with the children. Addie's enchanted by you." Not unlike her father.

"Not at all," Miss Arden said. "Your family makes very pleasant company. Far more so than a quill and paper."

"I look forward to reading your new book, when it's published."

She smiled again, but differently. This was a womanly smile, one he felt directly in his throat. "Oh, I don't know about that, Mr. Anderson. It will no doubt be far too scandalous for the likes of you."

He angled his head down and spoke lower. "I'm not so delicate."

She cocked her head at him and ran her eyes up his torso, lingering on his arms. "No. Perhaps not."

Gooseflesh prickled on his forearms. He could think of nothing to say in response.

She pursed her lips, like she saw the effect she had and was pleased by it.

Fortunately for him, the publican brought their tray of drinks and handed it to Seraphina, who took it capably and sauntered back to the table.

Adam took a moment to steady himself against the bar.

Wouldn't do to swoon in front of his family.

"Taste," Miss Arden was instructing Marianne and the children by the time he reached the table. She leaned over to help Adeline with her cup.

His daughter carefully slurped up a sip, then beamed. "It tastes like flowers!"

"Perfect for Lady Adelina," Miss Arden laughed. She seemed years younger when she laughed like that, her face crinkling up in joy. "The fairy queen's elixir."

"What's an elister?" Addie asked.

"A potent brew from which to draw strength. 'Tis important for young ladies to be mighty."

Marianne bit her lip and shot a look at Adam that clearly meant *I love this woman.*

He gave her a measured smile back, not wanting to convey too much enthusiasm, lest she see his boyish fascination with Miss Arden and worry he might do something rash.

He would not do something rash.

He couldn't.

"Will we try pasties?" Jasper asked.

"Indeed," Adam said. "As well as fish and Cornish crab."

"Crab?" Adeline repeated, looking horrified. "Eat a crab? Like the one on the beach? I liked that little crab. I shan't eat him."

"Oh but, Adeline, he is so delicious stewed in butter," Marianne said, provoking a lively debate on the potential pleasures of dining on sea creatures, a conversation that was as horrifying to Adeline's mind as it was delightful to Jasper's.

A maid came from the kitchen with two steaming platters and a basket of golden fish on a pile of paper to sop up the grease.

The children were delighted with the repast, and their cheer, with the shining sun, his family all around him, the merry presence of Miss Arden, made him feel a moment of gratitude, as well as sadness. They had not been so happy in quite some time.

It tugged at him, that he'd let life become so somber.

And it tugged at him that Catriona would miss all this. All the happy little moments as their two babies became people and tried drinks that tasted of flowers and met fascinating people and ate pies with their hands.

Jasper plucked a piece of fish from the steaming pile and craned his neck down to inspect the paper.

"Look!" he said excitedly. "It's Miss Arden, in this paper. That's you, isn't it?"

Seraphina took the paper from the boy's outstretched hand. It was a crude drawing in heavy, smeared ink, but it was unmistakably meant to be her likeness. The artist had made her tall frame weedy and reproduced her patrician nose as a hook, topping off the likeness with a witchy snarl of hair.

"What does it say?" Jasper asked, trying to make out the words through the blotches of grease. Adam squinted.

Vice and Sin Ahead for Kestrel, the headline ran. *Notorious Rakess Brings Disease of Mind and Body Like.*

Chapter Eight

Seraphina looked in panic at Adam, but he calmly took the paper and held it just out of Jasper's view.

"Kestrel Bay is pleased to welcome home Miss Seraphina Arden, the famous authoress," he pretended to read.

She felt such a surge of gratitude to Adam that she had to pick up a crab claw and begin cracking it apart so he wouldn't see that she was touched.

"You're *famous*?" Jasper uttered, staring at her. "What for?"

She tried not to choke on her crab. "Oh, I'm not," she said quickly.

Adam laughed and shook his head at his son. "Miss Arden is being modest, but she is quite famous. She writes books that help people understand how to make the world more fair, and she and her friends raise money to gain support for changes that will help. Your mama loved to read her books."

She blushed, for she could not remember a single time she had ever been described by a man so favorably. Nor could she remember the last time a person from outside her carefully selected circle of sympathetic people had been so kind to her. She felt this kindness shoring her up, washing away the lingering doubts from her dreadful morning.

She glanced out the window to disguise her eyes, shy to be so emotional with the whole Anderson family's eyes on her. Unexpectedly, a woman stared back at her through the other side of the glass.

Tamsin Rowe.

Every last bit of equanimity washed out of her. She wanted to look away. To crawl beneath the table, or to run out the back door of the inn.

Instead, she held her neck rigid and placed her palms flat on the table, refusing to avert her eyes. She forced her lips into a smile.

Tamsin dodged her glance and quickly walked away.

Sera exhaled a shaky breath. Of course Tamsin would flee. Tamsin had revealed her true nature long ago.

"Someone you know?" Adam asked.

Before Sera could answer, Tamsin reappeared at the front door. She walked toward their table.

"Seraphina," she said, her voice trembling. "I can't believe it. I thought I'd never see you again so long as I lived."

"I expect not," Sera said softly. She held herself very still, shocked that her old friend—if *friend* was indeed the word—had the boldness to confront her face-to-face. It felt important to seem utterly serene and confident before Tamsin. To be Seraphina Arden, Rakess and founding member of the Society of Sirens, not the little miner's daughter who'd had her life destroyed and been betrayed by all those she'd loved best.

"I've heard about your . . . your life," Tamsin said, choosing her words carefully, clearly mindful of the presence of the children. "They say you are building a . . . a movement of some sort, is that right?"

"Of a sort." Seraphina smiled. She was as shaken as Tamsin looked, but she'd rather die than betray her nerves. Tamsin would no doubt tell others she had seen Seraphina, and she wanted them to hear she had looked self-assured and *happy*.

Tamsin, for all the polish she'd always had, seemed at a loss for more to say.

Sera could not resist issuing a challenge. "You should call on me. I'll tell you about it." She met Tamsin's eye for a long, tense moment. "We could always use supporters for the cause. And it would be good to become reacquainted, after all these years."

Tamsin blushed. "You know I couldn't." Noticing the perplexed looks from the Andersons, she blushed harder and stepped back. "Excuse me, I have interrupted your meal. Sera, I'm pleased . . . to see that you're so well."

Her voice sounded almost tearful. Even the children hung on her every word, so obvious was it that she meant something more than she was saying. Seraphina fought the urge to roll her eyes. The years had not diminished Tamsin's ability to put on an appearance of sentimental attachment that did not extend to her true feelings.

"Thank you," Sera said, with false graciousness. "It's good to see you. My best wishes to your family."

Tamsin's eyes flashed. She nodded and walked away, her head bowed low.

Seraphina felt the blood that had rushed to her head cool. She had behaved exactly as she should, whereas Tamsin had been obviously uneasy. If the interaction had been a battle of a sort, she was exceedingly proud of herself for coming out victorious.

"Who was that?" Jasper asked her.

"An old friend," she said.

Adam cleared his throat, obviously trying to spare her his curious children's questions. "Shall we order pudding?"

Seraphina smiled. "If I recall, they do a delicious saffron bun."

While the children discussed the merits of pastries versus trifles with Marianne, Adam touched Seraphina's hand beneath the table. She started at the unexpected, illicit presence of his fingers on her knuckle, warm and firm.

"Are you all right?" he asked in a low voice.

She was certainly better now that he was petting her.

She put her free hand on top of his and patted it. "Yes. It's just that this place is filled with ghosts."

He nodded like he understood and hesitated just a moment. And then he squeezed her hand before moving his away.

ADAM WILLED HIMSELF not to focus on Miss Arden, but his hand burned beneath the table all through dessert.

She made an obvious effort to be cheerful with the children as they finished their sweets, but Adam noticed that on the journey home she was silent. She made no further mention of the woman who had startled her at the public house, but he sensed she was shaken from the encounter.

He wondered who the woman was to her.

When they reached the cottage, Adam told the children to thank Miss Arden for her generosity.

"Thank you, Miss Arden, for our costumes," Jasper said.

"You are most welcome. I hope you have a wonderful time at Golowan."

"Will you come with us, Miss Arden? To G'wan?" Adeline asked.

"Oh yes, please?" Jasper echoed. "That way we will be sure to know what to do. I hate to look foolish."

Miss Arden's mouth opened in mute surprise. She shot Adam a look, seemingly apologizing for having involved herself too deeply.

The cautious man in him wished to make excuses—for he knew that making a habit of being seen in Seraphina Arden's company might spur rumors, and those could follow him back to London or to Pendrake. Besides, Miss Arden herself had made clear there was no love lost between her and her former neighbors.

But the way she had reacted to that woman in the tavern—taking such pains to be gracious despite the woman's obvious unease with her—made him feel protective. If Miss Arden was not welcome in this town where she had been a little girl, she was, at least, welcome with his family.

Reputation was important, but decency was more so.

He would leave it up to her.

"Yes, Miss Arden," he said, "we'd be honored to have you as our guide. Though, of course, we will understand if your work keeps you too busy."

There, that seemed right. If she would like to come she should feel welcome, but if it was a burden, she should feel no obligation to accept.

"Very well," she said after a pause. "Thank you. I would be delighted to join you. We can take my carriage into town, in fine style."

"How lovely, Miss Arden," Marianne said. "We shall all look forward to it."

"As will I. Farewell, then." She gave them a smile—not entirely a happy one, he thought—and turned back to the coastal path toward her house, hugging herself against the wind as she walked.

He had the impulse to catch up with her—escort her as far as her terrace—but that would be too eager. And what was there to gain, by furthering his attraction to her?

He needed to cool his interest, not nourish it with intimate seaside walks.

He made his own way back to Tregereth's, where he had arranged to meet with his foreman to discuss the progress of the morning. Graveson was already there, along with his son Dabbie.

The lad, a gawky boy of sixteen, smiled shyly. This was to be his first job in his role as builder's apprentice, and he looked about as fit for it as Jasper.

Adam looked over the map of the grounds and nodded as Graveson pointed out where the crews were deployed and the state of the various projects.

"We're going to be able to start the masonry next week," Adam said. "I've a meeting with a local quarryman to arrange the delivery of the slate."

"If the foundations hold, that is," Graveson said. "The fishermen say a squall's coming. Could lose the afternoon, maybe two days if it's a bad one."

Adam scoffed. The sun shone down, hot and bright. "Two days? I'd like to see it."

"Ye've not yet seen the Kestrel weather," a local man named Tegan piped up. "Comes from nowhere. Can knock a grown man flat."

Another member of the crew nodded. "Aye. Keep yer wee ones from the cliff's edge—it's topsy-turvy after winds. Slabs wash right off the ledge."

He winced. He would speak to Marianne.

"How does the demolition stand?" he asked. Graveson walked him through the various projects for another quarter hour.

He was pleased. The work was well ahead of schedule. He wanted this to get back to Pendrake's man.

"Keep at it," he said. "I'm going to see the joiners. We'll speak this afternoon."

"One more thing," Graveson said. "You asked about the posters at the neighbor woman's. Dabbie here caught a man hanging one last night."

Adam looked at Graveson's son. "Did you?"

"Aye. I rode out to the tavern with some of the lads," the boy admitted, coloring slightly. "On the way back we saw a man at her gate. We shouted at him till he went runnin'. Jarvis said his name is Nancarrow, and he works as groundskeeper for Baron Trewlnany at Gwennol Bluff."

Adam smiled at the boy. "Excellent, lad. But don't spend all your nights at the tavern, aye?"

Adam walked off to find the joiners, committing the names Nancarrow and Trewlnany to memory. He doubted there was any real danger to Seraphina here in her home village—she was no doubt accustomed to much more potent threats given the stirs she made in London—but it was best to make sure she had no reason to fear them.

He would visit her on his way home to sound a warning.

And if his stomach knotted at the idea of seeing her again so soon, he would ignore it.

If his hand still throbbed in an echo of her touch, he would ignore that, too.

To pass on this information was not an indulgence of his weaker self. It was merely being neighborly.

Chapter Nine

And here it was, as clear and haunting as Tamsin Rowe's pale eyes staring at her through the window of a seaside inn: the past.

Sera's quill flew across the page as she tried to translate her memories into words.

First it was only a habit of drawing me out when others weren't attentive. A whisper at the refreshments queue. A chance meeting at the market. A tour of the conservatory while the others danced.

I could not be near him without blushing. I could not look upon him and not hope. Every time he spoke to me, I went breathless. I'd go home and write his words in my diary and read them until the ink was smeared, feasting on those pleasantries like nourishment.

Meet me by the bridge, he told me, *pressing a note into my hand. A slip of paper with no words, only a time and date. I wore it in my locket then. To this day, I have that note. The only one I ever received in his hand.*

No one noticed my long walks. If I came back damp or mussed, it was because we were from Cornwall, and the wind whipped off the sea.

Who would think a girl like me—tall as a man

*at fifteen, harsh-featured and undistinguished—
would find any trouble to get into?*

*Who would think that beneath that bridge he
would awaken a part of me I'd never known I had?*

She stopped, her hands shaking. Ridiculous, to let this
unnerve her. Ridiculous, that the sight of Tamsin should
reduce her to the child she'd once been. A child she
had abandoned long ago and to whom she'd bade good
riddance.

Just Sera then. Plain, lonely Sera, who had been so
grateful for the friendship of a girl so much lovelier than
herself. Tamsin was *still* lovely. Hair glossy black, nearly
violet, not a single strand of gray. Those big blue eyes
and widespread mouth. The small brown mark along her
cheekbone, that little imperfection that seemed to call
attention to the delicacy and regularity of her features.

She had crow's feet at the corners of her eyes now and
was more substantial about the bust and hips. That made
sense. Tamsin had children. Four, she'd heard.

She wouldn't think of that.

She cracked her knuckles and returned to her pages.

*Perhaps, that first time, he truly did just wish to
walk across the bridge with me and watch the
ocean.*

Perhaps he meant to leave me whole.

*He was not innocent, but perhaps I took him by
surprise.*

*For before I was alone with him, I had not
known what it was to want. I had not imagined I
could possess such yearning.*

*Could he have known? Could he have sensed it
in me, lying dormant?*

*For all that I endured as consequence, I would
not trade those moments. Two years, we visited
that bridge.*

It was never the bridge that I regretted.

She rose, stretched out her back, then walked into the
parlor. This would be easier to remember with a glass
of wine. Half a bottle remained in the decanter from
last night's supper, when she'd exercised restraint. She
snatched it from atop the sideboard and returned to the
sewing room. She filled a glass, drank half of it down
quickly, and felt the warmth sitting in her stomach.

That was better.

He'd taught her to enjoy this, too, the gentle lift from
spirits. A flask in his pocket on chilly afternoons, a
mouthful of sweet cider brandy. Never enough to make
her drunk. Just enough to make her giggly and yielding.

Now she rarely laughed when she drank.

*During this time, his future—the one ordained by
the gentlemen who decide this kind of thing, not the
one unfolding between our bodies—was set. An
understanding between families a decade in the
making became a public courtship, one I could
observe on Sundays at church and at balls held
by neighbors. And still, we met at the bridge. We
met until finally his betrothal was announced in a
room where I stood ten feet away, applauding as
though it did not slice me open.*

*Up until the banns were read, I believed him
when he said he was waiting for the time to tell
his father the truth about us. That he would, of
course, marry me and make it right.*

That he loved me.

That this was all a terrible mistake.
But, of course, you know this part.
He didn't.

She drained the rest of the wine from her glass and considered refilling it.

Too much and she might be tempted to indulge in more accounting than she ought. The story sitting on the pages of her desk was a story of loss. At the time she had assumed the loss of *him* would be the painful one, but looking back, it barely stung. It was the others that were more difficult to bear, when tallied. Tamsin. Her stepmother. Her father. This place, and all the people she had known. The girl she'd been. The woman she'd imagined she'd grow into.

She'd never meant to become Seraphina Arden.

It had been thrust upon her. The best of the fates that remained when the other, more obvious endings had been taken.

She stood and looked out the window.

A storm was coming.

You could always sense it in the air before the clouds rolled in. She remembered the feeling from her youth. The way the light went sickly. The thickening of the air.

This afternoon the ocean had been flat as glass. Now the chop of the Kestrel was shucking up around itself. Soon it would turn into breakers.

A gust of wind smacked that rickety wooden shutter against the windowpane so suddenly she yelped.

"Are you all right?" Tompkins called, rushing into the room.

Sera clutched her heart. "I—yes."

"You don't look it," Tompkins observed, taking in her mess of papers, her ashen face.

Sera relaxed her shoulders. "I am perfectly well. I cannot be blamed if the shutters knock against the house with the subtlety of a murderer."

Tompkins pursed her lips, and Seraphina wished she had not been so responsible as to hire a woman of great perception and ability as her secretary. Such people sometimes saw more than one liked.

"Mr. Anderson is here," Tompkins said. "He hoped for a word, if you have time."

Mr. Anderson? But what could he want from her, when they'd parted not three hours ago? Would it be too wicked to hope he'd been so beguiled by her facility with picking apart a crab that he'd reconsidered her offer of carnal abandon?

Doubtful. Still, a distraction from her thoughts was most welcome, whatever he was here for.

"Yes, show him in," she told Tompkins.

"He's waiting in the parlor."

"I'll join him there."

Another gust of wind rattled the doors off the terrace as she entered the room.

Mr. Anderson stood looking out the window. She should not torture herself lingering over his physique, which was so perfect as to be a kind of punishment, but with his back to her, he was in the very pose he had assumed when she had first seen him in the belvedere.

The memory made her breath quicken. She cleared her throat.

"Mr. Anderson. Good evening."

He turned and smiled at her. He had such a *nice* smile.

"I hope I'm not disturbing you."

"No. I was just going over budgets. Never my favorite task." She didn't know why she lied about what she had been doing, but she felt protective of him. Like if she spoke of her work, its sadness would infect him.

"Ah, accounting." He winced in sympathy. "I share your lack of enthusiasm for that particular chore."

She noticed that more of a Scottish brogue had entered his speech. His accent seemed to ebb with his sense of formality. Clipped and nearly English when he was focused, lapsing into a decidedly Celtic lilt when he seemed more at ease.

She could not help but think that in the throes of passion he must sound like a right highlander. She bit back a laugh at the direction of her thoughts and arranged her dress neatly over the settee, sitting nice and prim like a lady who did not receive injured birds as symbols of her unsuitability.

Stop it.

"I hope your men are prepared for a bout of bad weather," she said, gesturing outside. "We are due for an impressive storm."

"Aye, the builders predicted it hours ago. Said they could feel it in the air. I gave them grief. Thought perhaps they were looking for an afternoon's leave to sunbathe."

"Anyone who grows up in Cornwall knows not to trust the sun. I could sense it coming, too. It's the heaviness, you know. And the smell. Can't you feel it, that premonition in the air? It makes my skin prickle." She shivered.

He paused, and she could tell he was trying to feel the weather. He nodded, slowly. "Perhaps I can. It almost gives one gooseflesh."

Oh, the thought of him with *gooseflesh*.

She really must stop. "You wished to speak to me about something?"

His face turned grim. He had the kind of face that looked good when it was grim, for the lines became more pronounced and brought out the character in it. She wondered how old he was. Younger than her, she thought, but not by much.

"Yes. One of my apprentices was returning from the tavern last night with a few of the local boys and caught your vandal in the act." He pulled a poster out of his satchel and handed it to her.

She inspected it. The same unsettling design she'd found above her door this morning.

She wanted to clutch herself against the uneasiness that once again went through her at the knowledge that people were coming here, to her own home, intent on scaring her. But it would not do to fret in the presence of Mr. Anderson. Men were for displaying wit and cleavage to, not emotions.

"How unoriginal," she said dryly. "Trust defenders of decency to fall short when it comes to creativity."

He frowned. "Apparently the man who hung it is a groundskeeper at Gwennol Bluff. Do you know the place?"

Her insides wrenched.

She knew it well.

She tried to find her voice but suddenly it seemed she did not have one.

Mr. Anderson watched her closely. "Are you all right, Miss Arden?"

She took a deep breath. "Quite. Yes."

"I thought I might go and have a word with this fellow Baron Trewlnany, the owner. Let him know his man is stirring up trouble."

Christ, that was all she needed. "Oh, please don't. I'll see to it myself."

And by see to it, she meant ignore it. If Trewlnany was behind this, she would not give him the satisfaction.

Mr. Anderson wrinkled his brow. "If there's local trouble, it's best to smother it immediately. Get the magistrate involved if need be. An unprotected property is vulnerable at night."

Please. As though the magistrate would care.

As though her *property* was the thing in danger.

It was not the rotting beams and timber that would be perceived as a threat. It was her presence here. She hoped she was mistaken, but between the bird, and Gwennol Bluff—

Stop. Don't think of it.

She sat forward, recovering her composure. "I've years of experience in dealing with exactly this kind of pest, Mr. Anderson. It's the fight they're after—the satisfaction they've distressed me. Acknowledging them only gives them what they want."

He looked unconvinced. "I'm going to ask the men to keep a closer eye on your gates. Call it a surfeit of caution."

What was she, the princess in Jasper's fairy story?

She wanted to object. She *should* object, for these posters were not his concern.

But she thought of the kingfisher, and she only nodded. "That is kind of you."

All at once, the last traces of light went black outside and rain began to fall down in heavy beads, pelting sideways at the windows. She jumped.

Mr. Anderson grimaced. "Augh, I didn't time it right. Thought I had a spell more time. I should leave before it becomes impossible to make it home."

"Nonsense," she said. "The cliffs are prone to land-slips in the rain. Stay and dine with me. Hopefully it will quiet in an hour or two."

His posture said he would decline this offer, which depressed her, for she did not wish to be alone. Rain made her unsteady at the best of times, and in this low mood she was liable to drink too much and write letters to Cornelia and Thaïs that were so maudlin and self-piteous that her friends would come here to save her from herself, and she would never finish her book before the deadline.

Or maybe she just wanted him to stay.

Why had she sent Henri away? Could she not have suffered a few weeks of over-exuberant emotion if it came with the proven opiate of sex? Erotic entertainment was like a trapdoor from one's worries. She longed to slide out of her mind and into bed.

A rumble of thunder shook the house.

Mr. Anderson's shoulders dropped, as though in defeat. "Well, I suppose there's no getting home in this. Very well, yes, I will dine if it's no trouble to you."

She smiled, and for once was grateful to Cornwall for its dramatic weather. "Splendid."

MISS ARDEN SEEMED on edge. Adam could see her striving for her usual insouciance but beneath it she looked uneasy. Lines he had not noticed before pinched around her mouth.

Maria had set out supper for them in the dining room. The meal was humble. Monkfish, potatoes, creamed greens, and bread.

"Had I known I would have company I would have asked for something heartier," Miss Arden said. "Will you be hungry?"

She took a generous sip of wine and seemed to be asking this question on behalf of his shoulders, which she kept stealing glances at in a way that made him pleased and shy.

"It's delicious, thank you," he said. "I've been enjoying the Cornish fare. Fresher fish than one gets in London."

"Yes, one of the few tempting attributes of my patrimony. Where are you from?"

"Scotland," he quipped, emphasizing his brogue.

She gave him an astringent look. "Yes, that much is clear. I meant whereabouts there."

"Near Edinburgh."

"Ah, Edinburgh is a fine place. You attended the university there?"

"Aye."

"And how did you come to architecture? The family business?"

"My wife's. Her father built half of Edinburgh. He was friendly with my grandfather, and when I showed an interest in drawing as a boy he took me under his wing. Paid for my schooling."

"That was kind of him," Seraphina said.

It had been, though there was more to it than simple charity. When Adam had showed an interest in Catriona—and she in him—the elder Mayhew had thought it better that Adam learn a trade more profitable than art. Giving up painting had been the price of courting Catriona. One he'd gladly paid.

"Aye. He did it for Catriona. My wife."

Miss Arden's eyes widened in interest. "You knew her as so young a man?"

He nodded. "Since I was a boy, really. We were neighbors."

"A childhood amour," Miss Arden smiled. "How sweet. What was she like as a girl?"

"A right terror," he said before he could think better of it.

Miss Arden laughed with genuine appreciation. "Oh, my favorite type."

He grinned. "As a boy I thought she was a pesky lass, always trailing after James. There wasn't a school for girls, so she'd make us teach her our lessons."

Miss Arden's eyes lit up. "She sounds like a fine woman."

"She was." He speared a hunk of fish and chewed on it determinedly, eyes on his plate.

Miss Arden watched him. "You miss her," she said quietly.

He sighed. He was tired of holding the memories in silence. "Every day. I was thinking of her today, at luncheon. How much she would have loved watching the children eat strange foods, chase crabs."

"What happened to her," Miss Arden asked in a soft voice. "If you don't mind my asking?"

"Died in childbed." He would spare her the grim details.

Even without them, Miss Arden sat very still, as if trying to hold back emotion. "I'm so sorry."

He could tell her words were heartfelt, and it deepened his discomfort. "Thank you. I was blessed to have a happy marriage, and I'm grateful I have the children to remember her by."

She nodded, pushing her food around on her plate but not eating it. He decided to bring up a happier topic.

"Have you ever considered marrying?" he asked.

Her demeanor changed from melancholy to amusement at once. "Me!"

He grinned at her. "Yes, you."

"Heavens no," she pronounced with seeming relish. "I oppose the institution."

He paused. He had never heard of such a thing. "You oppose *marriage*?"

She nodded blandly. "I've yet to publish my arguments against it for one must be cautious about such things, but in private, yes, I find it deprives women of their meager autonomy and what few pitiful rights they are granted under law. I would as soon cut off my own legs as marry."

"Surely it's not as bad as that," he said. "Besides, you have very fine legs. 'Twould be a pity to lose them."

Oh Christ, he'd really said that. He nearly choked on his water.

But instead of volleying back some outrageous flirtation, as he expected, Miss Arden looked at him intently.

"A dear friend of mine has recently been locked in a lunatic asylum by her husband because he objects to her ideas. And he is within his legal rights as her husband to imprison her. So, yes. I think it is as bad as that."

He stopped chewing. "I'm sorry," he said.

She waved away his sympathy. "I only mention it to illustrate my point. That the majority of women have marriages that do not end in their literal imprisonment does not change the pernicious fact that the law makes such abuses possible. Husbands should not have such power over wives. And until they don't, any sensible woman wouldn't marry, if she had the choice."

He thought of his father, who had not married his mother but had abused her anyway. "Perhaps the larger principle is that those with power should behave decently."

"Ah, Mr. Anderson," she said, widening her eyes in challenge. "I hadn't figured you for a philosopher."

He was not sure if she was flirting with him, insulting him, or both. He leaned in closer to her across the table. "Call me Adam, if we're speaking of dismembered limbs and lunatic asylums. And you ignored my point."

The corners of her mouth turned up, as if he had correctly answered a question she hadn't asked. "Well, Adam, I don't disagree with you. But that doesn't fix the injustice of marriage. If a system relies on one party's decency—if that decency is the only failsafe protecting the weaker party—it is broken."

He liked that she'd decided he was worthy of debating. But he liked it even more that she'd said his given name. He wanted to say hers.

Seraphina.

It would feel delicious rolling off his tongue, with all those slinking syllables.

Instead he said, "Could one not grant women more protection, rather than condemning the whole institution? I see your point, but I enjoyed my marriage."

She refilled her glass. "What about it?"

Every single thing.

"Companionship. A pleasant home. Our family."

"And don't you think your wife might have enjoyed these things more if she were granted the same freedom you were to choose them?"

He couldn't remember Catriona ever doing a single thing she didn't choose. But he supposed no one had ever asked her to. Neither he nor her father was the type to make demands. Perhaps if he had made more demands, demanded caution and—

He stabbed another piece of fish and chewed, grinding it beneath his molars.

"Perhaps she might have liked to be something in addition to a wife and mother?" Seraphina pressed.

He wasn't sure. He'd never asked her.

Seraphina was continuing to stare at him, waiting for an answer. So he gave her the most honest one he could.

"I don't wish to speak of Catriona."

Her face softened at the gruffness in his words. "No. I'm sorry. I didn't mean to interrogate your marriage in particular." She looked into his eyes, and her gaze was kind. "You must stop me when I become a pest."

He decided to change the subject once again. "I gather you do not care for this place. May I ask why you've come back?"

She settled lower in her chair. "Did I not already say? To write my sordid history."

"Who says it's sordid?" he asked.

She took a sip of wine and swallowed it, then gave him that tart smile. "My enemies."

He laughed at her puckish pronouncement. "Do you have many?"

She smirked. "You've seen the posters."

He nodded, feeling less amused. "Aye."

"Kestrel Bay is the least of it. You should see the London papers. Apparently I am the French Revolution Incarnate. Not to mention a loose woman of low morals and rapacious appetites. Always that."

He burst out laughing at her dry summation of her reputation. "I suppose I have heard a bit. Though, perhaps not as much as you assume. Lately I find I have time to read little that isn't related to slate prices and building commissions."

"I'm raising money to build the institute I mentioned, with two friends. One is a disgraced aristocrat who paints portraits of those abandoned by society and the other is a courtesan. We've made a little pact to become even more notorious in the interest of the common good. We aim to raise fifty thousand pounds."

He could not begin to imagine how he should react to this.

Seraphina laughed at his dismay. "Oh, I've shocked you with my wickedness. Well, don't worry. It's quite relaxing to be exactly as wicked as people think you are. Relieves the tensions in one's neck."

She took another sip of wine. The woman could drink a sailor under the table. She didn't seem drunk, however, only detached. Like the painful things she spoke of had no effect on her. As though she was a character in some ironic story.

But he'd seen her careful plans for her institute, seen her care and kindness with his children, seen her face blanche at the poster mocking her. He didn't believe she was as impervious to criticism as her manner would lead one to believe. He wondered why she felt compelled to perform for him, here in her own home.

"Actually, you don't strike me as particularly wicked," he said softly.

Her eyes flicked up to his and held his gaze.

"Oh, Adam. But I am."

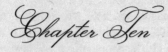

Chapter Ten

Adam looked away at the hint of sensuality in her words.

Good.

She had not cared for the way that he had been regarding her. Like *she* was an injured bird. Pity ranked on her personal hierarchy of desirable qualities in a male dinner partner only slightly below a will to dominate.

Though perhaps she could use his sympathy to extract a favor. "Actually, on the subject of the institute, perhaps you could be of use to me."

He smiled. "Oh?"

"I'm collecting pledges from businesses who will take on female apprentices in trades women are not typically trained in. We could use an architect to train a woman in whatever it is you do. Drawing pictures of houses? Ordering . . . nails?"

He snorted. "I am flattered you hold my vocation in such high esteem."

"No one said ordering nails is *easy*. I am all admiration." She winked.

"I suppose a woman could do the work of a draftsman, with proper training," he allowed.

"A woman can do any work she is taught, I assure you. She has a mind, you see, and hands." She widened her eyes as though this was a shocking assertion.

He laughed. "Very well. You may count on my firm."

A great crack of lightning lit up the sky across the cove, turning the cliffs a vibrant shade of greenish yellow.

Adam stared out at the image, rapt.

"It's breathtaking, isn't it?" she asked. "As a girl I loved the storms. I used to climb out onto the balcony off the attic and watch them. It's high enough that you can see all of Kestrel Bay."

"I imagine it's a sight to behold."

"Would you like to see it? I'll take you up."

"I don't want to interrupt your meal," he said, pointing at her barely nibbled fish.

"I find I lack an appetite. Come."

She nodded for him to follow her and made for the staircase. It was dark and eerie with the house shaking and the rattle of the rain. He followed behind her at a fair distance. She could not resist twitching her hips just a bit more than necessary as she climbed. She had promised herself not to continue her attempts to seduce him, but after enduring the maddening sight of his shoulders all through supper, she could not resist an opportunity to make him regret what he'd declined.

Besides. She had begun to wonder if he'd changed his mind.

The room at the top of the house had been hers as a child, and it still held her things. In the dim light she could make out the narrow bed she'd slept in, her collection of seashells on the shelf. The room was clean—Maria had been scrupulous about tidying the house before their visit—but the items were so exactly as she'd left them sixteen years ago that they may as well have been covered in dust, or frozen in amber, like fossils.

"This is your room?" Adam asked.

"It was. I took over the marriage bed. Irony, you know."

She kept her tone light, but the state of her old bed-chamber disturbed her. She had not been in this room since returning home. Had her father and stepmother never moved a thing? How strange, to preserve a shrine to a daughter you'd made clear was as good as dead to you.

She unlocked the door leading to the balcony and looked over her shoulder at Adam.

"It's just out here." She reached up to the shelf beside the door and found the stack of oilcloths she used to keep there for just this purpose. She took one down and draped it over her hair like a cloak, then stepped outside onto the ledge, beckoning for Adam to follow her.

Instantly, despite the cloth, rain smacked her face. She buried herself deeper under the cloth and shivered. From this height, you could see the dark gray slashes of rain descending from the sky in columns, see the breakers crashing fifteen or twenty feet up the edges of the cove.

It was violent, but it was beautiful.

She held up the corner of the oilcloth so Adam could join her. He ducked beside her, holding the cloth up with his taller frame. He did not touch her but she was conscious of her hair blowing in the wind, coming loose from her pins and whipping against his neck.

She didn't care.

Perhaps it was the wine, but the rain and wind felt cleansing. She took her free hand and held it out into the downpour.

It battered her hand with such force that she yelped and snatched her fingers back. She heard a low rumble beside her. Adam, laughing.

She glanced up at him, to see if the beauty of the storm moved him the way that it moved her. There was a smile in his eyes and on his lips. It made her want to stand on her toes and kiss him.

A gust of wind sent a bale of rain directly at them, drenching her. Adam turned toward her, using his body to protect her from the wind.

"You're cold. Let's go inside," he said. He had to shout to be heard above the storm.

A stronger gale whipped at them. She shivered again. "No, let's just stand here a moment longer."

Up here, looking at the world lit up with the squall, she felt apart from the concerns that weighed on her. The posters, the bird, Elinor, her damned unwritten book.

She tipped back her head to feel the rain ripping across her face. It felt so good, so cold and pure, like it could abrade her of the sick dread that had taken root around her liver.

She dropped her side of the oilcloth and stepped out into the rain.

Cold, hard drops beat down upon her face and hair, blinding her.

She lifted up her arms and let herself be taken by it, by the darkness, by the roar.

It felt bracing.

Like being, for just a moment, fully and vividly alive.

ADAM WATCHED AS Seraphina Arden stepped into the storm and became the image from his dreams.

Drenched gown, hair whipping in wet tendrils, head thrown back, arms held aloft to the sky. She looked like a goddess awaiting anointment from the heavens.

A streak of lightning cut across the cliffs behind her, slashing the horizon into fifty purple tendrils. Seraphina looked beautiful against the flashing sky, and he had a weakness for beauty.

But that was not a good enough reason to let her be killed in a storm.

"Come in, you'll be struck."

She only lifted her arms higher and threw back her head.

As another crack of lightning burst through the sky, he pulled her toward the shelter of the eaves. She twirled around to look at him, her face lit up in a smile that transformed her. She laughed, so purely and happily that it was catching, and he laughed, too. He placed a hand on her back to guide her under the shelter of the eaves. Her foot slipped as she moved near him. He reached out to catch her. Suddenly they were both falling toward the open door behind them. His hand slid over the wood as he tried to catch the frame, but he missed, and then they were in a heap, tangled, half inside, half out, her body pressed on top of his.

She was shaking with laughter. Her entire body quaked with it.

Normally he would be horrified to be pressed so intimately against a woman, but the chaos of them falling in the rain like children was so absurd he found himself chuckling as well.

"Oh, I'm sorry," she gasped. She wriggled, trying to right herself, but tangled beside him in the narrow doorway, she had to wedge her knee in between his thighs for purchase.

Suddenly it was not funny.

He could tell she felt it the same moment he did. The moment a childish pratfall became neither humorous nor juvenile, but something unmistakably adult.

They both stayed completely still, and if either of them breathed, he could not feel it.

The only thing he could feel was his own arousal, swelling to attention.

God damn it.

He leaned back on his forearm to unwed himself from her but her hand came down and stopped him.

"Stay, if you like," she whispered.

It was insanity not to put himself to rights immediately. And yet, his cock was asserting its own version of what was rational, and Miss Arden was twitching her generous, generous hips along its dimensions, as if to help plead its case.

He didn't move.

"The rain always makes me feel . . . refulgent," Seraphina whispered. "Like my flesh is not large enough to possibly contain the things I feel and want. Like I am not constrained by rules or time."

The lightning struck again, setting the entire sky alight. It cast a glow upon the dreamy expression on her face. He imagined that face below him, rapt in pleasure, and shuddered.

"Will you be angry if I ravish you?" she whispered.

He looked up into her eyes, which were dark with desire.

"I'll be angry if you don't."

Immediately her mouth came down on his.

Her lips were cold and wet with rain. He caught her chin, held her still, and kissed away the droplets. She tasted tart, of wine. Her fingers moved up, wending through his hair. She untied his queue, smoothed his hair, and deepened the closeness of her mouth to his.

He plunged his tongue into her mouth and her hand went to his cock, which was as hard as he could remember it ever being, straining obscenely through the wet fabric of his breeches.

"Oh, but you are splendid, aren't you?" she said, rubbing the dimensions of it slowly, expertly, in a way that caused heat and friction. He sucked in his breath, too

overcome with the erotic pleasure of it to be embarrassed by the naked need of his reaction.

Her hand climbed up and snaked inside his breeches,
unhooking the falls. "Why, Mr. Anderson," she said.

She was not a dainty woman but even still the size of
his straining erection looked brutish in her hand. She
didn't seem to mind. She was smiling like a cat. "What
a lovely surprise," she whispered, rubbing him in a way
that made his vision go black.

He could feel her desire, feel her body melting into his.
He should do something, get up, but her hands rubbing
places where he had not been touched in years was making him insensible. He groaned and buried his head in
the hollow of her neck.

"Oh yes, darling," she whispered. "Oh yes, you do
want this. I thought so."

Her hand found a steady, competent rhythm around
his prick—brisk, no girlish tease to it. She touched him
the way he might touch himself. He felt tremors rising
in his thighs—he was going to come with a few more
strokes.

"Sera—" he gasped, not even able to get out her full
name.

"I know," she whispered. Her hand stopped but did
not release him. He throbbed in her grip, his entire lower
body rippling at the sudden loss of that exquisite motion.
Perhaps she had come to her senses, since he had proven
himself incapable of it.

But no, she wriggled lower, moving down his chest,
letting her breasts rub down his stomach and over his
cock until her mouth was poised above his thighs and
her lips were—*fuck*.

Her tongue swirled, laving his cock from underside to
tip. Thunder exploded behind them and her hand found

the place behind his bollocks that made him mad and stroked there with a kind of upward pressure, igniting a flood of feeling so intense that he was going to—no, he *was* coming.

He shouted and spilled into her velvet blessed mouth.

"Fuck, I'm sorry," he moaned, as she released him.

"No, darling, don't apologize," she said, leaning in to wipe her lips against the fabric of his shirtsleeve. "I told you I was wicked."

Chapter Eleven

God, she'd needed that.

Sex always made Sera feel more like herself.

Even in her earliest days, meeting a boy on a bridge, she'd been seduced by the way touch could make you mighty. Short of opium, she could not think of a headier intoxicant than watching a man slap his fist against the ground, panting and cursing at the spell she'd cast over his whole being.

She'd enjoyed watching Adam tremble.

It was only when he straightened up into a sitting position, his gaze fixed on her face, that the thrill began to fade.

The whites of his eyes glinted in the moonlight, and some turbulent emotion glimmered in them. She suspected she knew what came next.

She had been with enough serious, responsible types—solicitors, reformers, preachers—to know that the more conscience your lover professed to have in advance of fornication, the less he tended to be able to look you in the eyes after he came.

"Come here," he said, in that twirling burr. He opened his arms. He wanted her to sit against him, between his thighs.

Cautiously, she did as he asked, though she wished for tenderness as avidly as she wished for recriminations. When she did not immediately relax, he drew her in by the waist, pulling her closer, and his chin came to rest near her shoulder. His hands found hers and played with them, rubbing back and forth along her knuckles.

"Thank you," he said quietly.

There it was. She said nothing, waiting for the inevitable pivot: thank you, *but*.

"Calling you Miss Arden just now seems inappropriate," he said. "May I call you Seraphina?"

"Sera."

"Sera," he repeated. His breath fell in a steady rhythm on her neck. "Gorgeous Sera."

She froze. *Who?*

"I woke up to a dream of you this morning. You were bathing in the sea. In a white dress that I could see through. Your hair flying all around you, wild."

His fingers came up and softly combed through her hair, teasing out the knots that had formed between the wind and rain and all their squirming on the floor. It felt heavenly, but she was not yet sure where this was going, so she fought the urge to close her eyes and enjoy it.

"What were you doing in the dream?" she asked.

His chest rumbled with laughter beneath her shoulder blades.

He moved his hands up, over her breasts. "This."

He had large hands, and she had small breasts. The effect of this disproportion was that he could . . . *yes*. She closed her eyes as his thumbs and fingers roamed over her nipples, toying with them until they were so hard they hurt in a way that was indistinguishable from pleasure.

His mouth came down on her neck, and he placed a soft, hot kiss where it met her shoulder.

She leaned into the warm and nervy tingling as his lips climbed to the hollow beneath her ear. She gasped.

"Oh, Sera," he whispered. "May I touch you?"

She nodded. Touching was fine. The problem was going to be if he stopped.

His hands, working in parallel, slid firmly down her sternum and over her waist. He spread his long fingers out over the swell of her hips, tracing her contours. "I love how you're shaped. Someday, if you'd let me, I'd love to draw you."

She did not love this mawkish sentiment but his hands felt so good that she kept silent. His cock had begun to stir again and its throbbing at the base of her buttocks, where she sat against him, added to the pleasures of his hands on her belly, his mouth working its slow way over every last inch of her neck.

He found the hem of her dress and slowly pulled it up over her thighs. He arranged it around her waist and kept one hand pinned there, above her belly, as his other hand moved to her mons.

His fingers grazed her at the slit, finding the wetness that had pooled there as she pleasured him. He knew what he was doing and the surprise of that was a pleasure of its own. She gasped, and his cock responded with a jerk that she could feel. She opened her thighs wider, inviting him to take whatever liberties he wished.

His fingers found the small, tight bundle of nerves at her center. She said a silent prayer of thanks for men who did not need to be instructed.

He'd said his marriage had been pleasant. She nearly believed this pleasure had been mutual.

"*Yes.*"

He had her. She sank back against his chest and floated on the pleasure, her mind emptying like water sluicing down a drain.

She cried out softly, trembling.

Then they were both still.

In the minutes that had passed, the rain had grown less violent, and the wind no longer howled.

She closed her eyes and sat there, conscious of allowing him to hold her for longer than she had permitted anyone in some time. At the height of her arousal it had felt utterly erotic but now that she was spent—and also increasingly conscious of being soaked through and cold and somewhat sore from being pinned inside the door—it felt rather uncomfortable.

She wriggled away from him and struggled to her feet. "We should dry off or we'll be ill. Come, I'll see you to my bedchamber so you may neaten yourself."

He rose to his feet as well. But as she was opening the door to the stairwell he said, "Sera."

She turned back. "Yes?"

"Thank you. I haven't been with a woman since—" He paused. "In quite some time. I hope—"

She had been wrong about him. He was not the kind of man who became ashamed after sex. He was the kind who became *moved*.

Much, much worse.

She shook her head and put a single finger over his very fine lips. "No need for speeches, Adam."

His eyes widened. "Speeches?"

She sighed, because he was a nice person and her neighbor, and she would likely be of a mood to do this again some other time, so it would not do to injure his feelings if she could help it.

"Adam, I enjoyed that. But I ask nothing personal of my lovers, so you need not worry about assuaging my emotions with some kind of declaration."

His eyes flashed. "I was not intending to assuage your emotions, only to express my appreciation for what we just shared. Which I found quite personal."

His tone rebuked her.

"Of course," she allowed. "Literally speaking, it was personal. What I mean is, we are neighbors. We won't become more. You need not worry, or form expectations, on that account."

His bearing went stiff. He did not like what she was saying.

Well, that was fine. Better to endure a bit of discomfort in the beginning than reap recriminations later on.

"I understand," he said. "You can trust I will attempt not to overburden you with declarations of attachment, Miss Arden."

His tone was light—almost amused—but his eyes gave away the fact that she had offended him.

She looked away. "I'm glad we agree. Now come downstairs. You're soaked."

SERA—MISS ARDEN?—HE WAS no longer sure what to call her now that she had given him her lecture on the impersonal nature of wild, rain-soaked lovemaking—led him down the stairs to her bedchamber, where someone had lit a fire and the lamps.

Her room was piled with books and papers and jars of herbs and expensive gowns. He imagined this was how Addie would keep her room, if he would let her. Well, aside from the corked bottle of wine sitting on the windowsill. Sera reached for it and poured herself a glass.

"You can dry your clothes by the fire, if you like."

Her cool manner should have been a relief, given that what he had done with her had been a lapse of all his finest judgments, but instead it made him feel oddly more tender toward her. He gathered this was the opposite of her intended effect.

She was trying to push him away, but something about this messy room made her seem more human, less brittle.

He *liked* her. He had not met a person he liked so much in quite some time.

Her frankness reminded him of his mother's people, and her appetites reminded him of himself. The tension between her forward manners and her distant demeanor reminded him of no one he had ever met, and made him want to know her better.

To understand her.

Still, if she wanted him to keep his distance, he would not tarry here. They would be in Cornwall for weeks. He had time.

"The rain has slowed," he said. "Thank you for the offer of dry clothes, but I'll walk home now while I have the chance."

If he was not mistaken, she was relieved to see him go. "Yes, of course. Take the inland route along the carriage road. You will not want to risk losing your footing on the coastal path."

She turned and busied her hands with some pots on her bureau. He got the distinct impression she was fiddling with them so as to appear too busy to properly say farewell to him. But to leave with no further acknowledgment of what had happened would make it seem unreal, or shameful, and he did not want to color it with negative emotions.

If it was meaningless to her, it was not meaningless to him.

"Sera?" he said to her back.

She turned to look at him over her shoulder, her face carefully blank.

He moved behind her and smoothed an errant strand of hair behind her ear. He ran his thumb down her neck. He hadn't left marks. Good. He kissed the top of her head. "Be well, aye?"

She said nothing.

He turned to leave, but something made him pause at the door and turn back to look at her one last time.

"That meant the world to me," he said quietly. "Thank you."

She turned around, frowning, her fingers twisting together as though in distress. "Adam, don't get romantic notions about me. Truly. I don't know how else to say it. I won't be good for you."

He touched the sides of her bedroom door. "This frame should not shake like this even in a strong wind. I'll send my joiner to fix it in the morning. As befits a neighbor."

She nodded, still blank.

"And Sera?"

"Yes?"

"I decide what's good for me."

Chapter Twelve

The cottage was dark by the time Adam made it soggily back home. A candle burned beneath Marianne's door and the children were asleep. He'd missed putting them to bed. He had not meant to stay so long at Seraphina's.

There was much he had not *meant* to do at Seraphina's.

He'd welcomed it in the moment—been grateful for it, desperate for it—but the further he'd walked from Seraphina's house along the muddy road, the more he'd felt like he had failed himself.

He had his meeting at Alsonair tomorrow morning, after all. He had a family who'd been waiting for him.

But was it that? Guilt at choosing pleasure over his responsibilities?

Or was it that he had not liked the way the night had ended?

His thoughts kept returning to the coldness that came over Seraphina after their coupling was over. The sense that he could have been anyone, standing awkwardly in her room—that he was just a body that had served its purpose and must be tolerated until its owner realized he was supposed to leave.

At the sound of his entry, Marianne came out of her room in a night-rail. "Oh, thank God. I was so worried. I expected you back hours ago."

"I'm sorry. I got caught in the storm on my walk. Took shelter at Miss Arden's house."

She gave him a long, solemn assessment, making him acutely aware of how wet and rumpled he was.

"Adam, the children were in a fit thinking something happened to you in the rain. Jasper could not fall asleep. You must be more careful. You are the clock they set their small lives by."

He slumped into a chair to remove his boots, feeling like an utterly bad father. "I know it. I'm sorry. I'll pay more mind to the weather."

"Was that all it was?" she asked softly. "Weather?"

He had never been able to hide anything from his sister. They were a year apart, each other's only family, and they'd spent their entire lives under the same roof. They did not communicate so much in words as in bone-deep knowledge that made talk beside the point of understanding.

So he didn't bother to deny it.

"It was not . . . entirely the weather. No."

He and Marianne exchanged a look. His, somewhat embarrassed. Hers, concerned.

"Adam, I admire Miss Arden. But if you plan to court her, there are complications we should consider. Things we'll have to explain to the children."

Court her. He could imagine Seraphina's face rippling with horror at that notion.

"It's not like that, Marianne," he said quickly. "She's made it clear any lingering attachment would be most unwelcome. We are merely . . ."

He paused, feeling excruciatingly uncomfortable at this acknowledgment that he had begun an amorous affair. It seemed selfish and reckless even in his own imagining. It would seem worse in his sister's. And he was not even certain it was true.

Would Seraphina wish to repeat their encounter? And if she did, would he?

He certainly did not want *this* feeling.

"It's foolish," he said, deciding. "I'll end it."

Marianne sat down beside him and patted his hand. "Oh, Adam, that's not what I meant. It's all right, you know, to want companionship. I know that you're lonely."

He took her hand. "We're both lonely, aren't we."

"Aye," she said, staring glumly at the fire.

They'd all been muddy with grief when they'd arrived in London, so shortly after Catriona's death. Him, Marianne, Mayhew, the children—Cat had been the center of all their lives. By the time the shock of her death had begun to lift, Marianne was absorbed in caring for the children on her own, and Adam was preoccupied with the business. Mayhew had made a life for himself in London, on the basis of his family's connections, but with a few exceptions, Adam and Marianne kept mostly to each other.

"Have you heard from Mrs. Cason?" he asked her.

"Heard what?" she asked dismissively.

He tsked lightly, for she could keep nothing from him either. They had not talked openly of the loss Marianne had suffered shortly before they'd left London, but he'd been aware of it. He'd felt her sadness.

"She wrote," she said, keeping her voice light. "They'll marry in Bath at the end of the month."

He squeezed his sister's hand. For the last two years she had enjoyed a friendship with a young widow who lived in their building in London. A friendship of the sort that Marianne's evening visits to Harriet Cason's rooms sometimes did not conclude until early in the morning, when she came home just as Adam was rising. She'd been serenely happy on those mornings—as content as he'd ever seen her. But in the last few months Mrs. Cason had begun accepting the overtures of a navy captain, and Marianne's visits to the widow's rooms had become more brief, and then ceased altogether.

"I'm sorry, Mari," he said.

She shrugged. "'Twas only a matter of time, I suppose. She wants children."

"And you?"

She smiled. "I have yours."

They both stared at the fire, silent.

Adam sighed. "Aren't we a joyful pair."

"Adam, truly, don't misunderstand me. There's no harm in seeking company. You *should* seek company—between your work and Mayhew and the children, you'll go mad if you continue as you have been. Just try not to disappear without warning, so they don't fret after you."

She was being kind, but he wondered if she was too charitable. Jasper had taken the loss of his mother so hard. He'd been a bubbly baby, but after her death he hadn't spoken for nearly a year. Adam remembered well how large adult worries could loom in a boy's small heart, and he did not want his son to feel as he had felt, like he must monitor every current in the air of his family home, lest the whole precarious balance crumble when he let down his watch.

He rose. "I'm going to go look in on them."

Marianne nodded. "Aye. Good night."

He quietly opened the door of the children's room, stepping lightly in his stocking feet so as not to wake them. Jasper was sleeping as he always did, straight beneath his covers on his back. Adam kissed his son's forehead.

Across the room, Addie stirred.

"Papa?" she whispered. She was her brother's opposite, turning her sheets and pillows into a nest she burrowed into like a gopher.

"Aye, love," he said, sitting down at the edge of her bed and straightening out the counterpane.

"I had a nightmare," she said. "Will you hold me?"

He leaned back and put his arms around her. "You're safe, my darlin'. Close your eyes."

He stroked her hair as she snuggled against his shoulder. His chest felt tight at the thought of these two tiny people unable to sleep, worrying after him. It was his driving desire in life that they should not worry. That their comfort and their sweet little souls and their futures were well attended to.

That they did not need to be told that they were safe.

Protecting them was more important than his loneliness.

He would do well to remember it the next time a stirring woman told him she was not good for him.

He would do well not to repeat tonight's mistake.

SERAPHINA AWOKE IN a warm shaft of sunlight with the memory of Adam Anderson on her skin, and smiled.

She'd been hard on Kestrel Bay, allowing her unhappy memories to make her ill disposed toward the place where she'd grown up. But with the promise of a man like Adam to amuse her, and a gentle breeze blowing on her naked skin, she felt rather sentimental about the attractions of this place. The salt air was warm and sticky after the storm, redolent of sex. The driftwood that washed up on the bleached shores reminded her of bodies on a bed after a rousing toss within the sheets.

She had yet to have Adam in her sheets.

She was impatient to correct that.

She dressed quickly, scrawled a note for him, and set off toward his cottage to deliver it. It was early yet; perhaps he would still be there.

She did not make it fifty yards before she spotted him making his way up the path toward Tregereth's.

The morning agreed with him. He looked vigorous and fresh, clean-shaven with dampened hair. She waved. She hoped he would be daring and embrace her, so she could smell his shaving oil.

He smiled at her but did not quicken his pace to reach her, nor touch her.

She tried not to take this as a bad sign.

"Good morning," he said, with a half bow.

A bow? Surely they were past the stage of public bowing. Did he expect her to curtsy?

She gave him a coy smile instead. "Good morning. I was just on my way to find you." She took the note from her pocket and held it out to him.

He glanced down at his name on the folded paper. "Should I read it now?"

Was that reluctance? Had she been too firm with him last night? Made him guarded?

"It will save you a reply," she said, trying to be charming.

He didn't smile. His face remained impassive as he read her note. *I enjoyed last night. It left me wanting more. Come see me after nine o'clock.*

He stared at it for far longer than it took to read three sentences. Her hands began to sweat as she realized what this pause meant: no.

No?

"It's only an invitation," she said quickly, hearing a sharpness in her voice that slightly humiliated her. She cleared her throat. "You needn't accept, if you did not enjoy our evening," she added in a more measured tone.

He lifted his gaze from the note and up into her eyes.

"I did enjoy it," he said softly, raking his fingers in his hair. His brown eyes seemed darker, almost black. "Perhaps too much."

"Forgive me if I do not grasp your meaning," she said.

He smiled sadly. "Last night was such a pleasure, Sera. But I left wondering if we both regretted it."

"Regretted it?" she found herself sputtering. "Me? What makes you say that?"

He raised a brow. "You seemed eager for me to leave."

Well, she had been. What did he expect, an invitation to gaze into her eyes whispering sweet nothings? It was *sex*. Very *good* sex.

She found it difficult to believe that he would give her up altogether just because she'd told him not to lose his head. He was a man, after all. She was not a sentimental lover, but she knew her way around a cock.

"I simply wanted to make sure you did not get the wrong impression," she said.

He looked out at the waves, then dragged his eyes back to hers. "And what impression is that, Sera?"

She did not like being looked at so directly in the harsh light of the morning. "That you must . . . make a show of affection or attachment after sex."

He twitched up the corner of his lip. "If you believed that is what I thought you wanted, you must find me quite dull-witted."

Despite herself, she chuckled. "Am I so obvious?"

"You are honest about what you want. And if I were to match your honesty, I would say that I can't give you what you desire. I think about you too frequently to pretend that I can come to you lightly."

Oh.

Was that . . . was that not quite a fine compliment?

Granted, one she did not want, as it meant she could not have more of him. But it left her oddly flattered. Somewhat breathless.

He seemed to sense that she was flustered. He smiled kindly.

"In truth it is ill-advised of me to indulge myself in pleasures when I have so many other considerations, so you've saved me a great deal of self-reproach." He paused, and his smile became rueful. "Most . . . regrettably."

He shrugged, as if it was obvious that he could not help but do the sensible thing.

God, she sometimes wished she had that instinct.

He frowned. "You aren't . . . cross with me?"

She was, actually, but the fact that he cared softened the blow. She smiled at him. "Adam, it's quite all right."

And perhaps it was. Last night, she'd been worried she would hurt him. Now, she wouldn't have to.

"I'm disappointed, certainly. But I think you're wise."

He sighed. "I'd rather not be wise. I hope you know that."

He really was the good sort. But she could not resist leaving him a little bruised.

"'Tis a pity, you know," she said softly. "I rather liked you."

His eyes flashed. "Aye?"

She reached out and swept away an eyelash that was resting on his cheekbone. "Aye."

The words had the effect she'd hoped for.

He caught her hand and dragged it to his lips, pressing her knuckles to his nose like he was breathing in her skin.

Finally, he released her. "Be well, Sera."

With one last sad expression, he bowed and walked past her, continuing on his way to Tregereth's.

She stood still for quite some time, watching him go, and wishing he'd responded differently.

Wishing she did not feel so very low.

Wishing she could recapture, just for a moment, the sense of hope and peace she'd had when she'd first opened her eyes and thought of him.

Wishing, at the very least, that it was not much too early for wine.

Chapter Thirteen

It was a miracle that Adam did not walk straight off the path and into the sea on his way Tregereth's, because he trudged along by instinct, in a blur, with four words ringing through his head.

I rather liked you.

Past tense.

Surely, if he had made the right decision, he would not now feel so frantic with regret.

She had *liked* him.

It was a rather bland sentiment to be so gutted by, but he could not shake the feeling that the words expressed more tenderness coming from her than they would from anyone else.

Perhaps she'd only said them because he'd demonstrated himself to be detached enough to sever their connection. But regardless, they still touched him.

He was so shaken by that exchange that he felt lightheaded.

Which was unfortunate, given he was due at Alsonair within the hour. There was no time to pity himself. Ending things was for the better.

He walked more quickly and pushed Seraphina from his mind, forcing himself to think of architecture.

He stopped to borrow a horse from his construction crew at Tregereth's and rode the several miles north along the coast to Pendrake's, distracting himself from his low mood by rehearsing the salient parts of his pitch in his head.

He rode through impressive iron gates and up a wide path graveled in Cornish shale that twinkled pale blue and dusty pink in the sunlight. The drive was lined with elaborately manicured gardens bearing more resemblance to Paris than the English countryside. So Pendrake had a taste for Continental grandeur. Good to know.

Adam followed a servant up a footpath from the stables to the house, a grand, four-storied structure that sat perched atop the ocean.

"Wait here," the footman said, pointing at a sofa in a sumptuous receiving room. "I'll tell Mr. Lotham you've arrived."

Adam walked over to the window as he waited. It faced the sea. In the distance, he could just make out Seraphina's house on the promontory over the cove.

Don't think of her.

"Mr. Anderson," a voice said from behind.

He turned around.

"I'm Mr. Lotham," said a man in spectacles. "And this is Lord Pendrake."

"Of course," Adam murmured, already falling into a low bow, for he had recognized Pendrake's angular build, sharp jaw and jet black hair from illustrations in the papers. "His lordship needs no introduction. It's an honor."

Pendrake stalked over to a chair and lowered himself into it, kicking his legs out in front of him so that they spanned half the room. "Lotham mentioned he was meeting you and I recalled your name. Lord Howard was raving over the renovation you did for him in Kent."

"Ah yes. A beautiful house. Lord Howard has exceedingly distinguished taste."

Adam's words sounded obsequious to his own ears, but the marquess only smiled. "Yes, quite," he said, steepling his fingers.

"Have a seat, Mr. Anderson," Lotham said, gesturing at a sofa.

Adam did, arranging his folio on his lap. "I brought a book of ornamental designs I've done in gardens. I think something of the French style would suit your grounds. I was admiring the elegant design as I drove in."

Pendrake waved his hand dismissively. "Leave that here for Lotham to show my wife. It's her idea. Wants a temple or some such folly. You know ladies. Tiresome." He rolled his eyes.

Adam nodded as though he shared this low opinion of female taste. He felt the glares of Marianne, Catriona, and Seraphina in his mind's eye as he did so.

"I thought I might solicit your interest on a larger project for the Royal Board of Works. Confidentially, we'll soon be commissioning a new naval armory. A substantial project, highly complex."

Adam's heart beat faster. "I did hear mention of the possibility," he said, trying not to seem too eager.

"Yes, my dear colleague Lord Falconer wants the commission to go to his nephew, Richard Folke, and thought giving Folke advance word would seal it. Folke, of course, cannot resist prattling around town about the fortune he stands to make, and now every architect in London is at my door begging for their chance. You know him? Folke?"

Richard Folke was the most prominent architect in London. That he was already being considered for the commission was not good news for Adam.

"Mr. Folke's work is—"

"Bloody expensive," Pendrake said drily. "He ran up a surfeit of eighty thousand guineas on the Bank of Manchester and the project took four years longer than expected. Scandalous. Thinks he's the best so he can get away with it. But I have the treasurer breathing down my shirt and I need a man who can think in budgets rather than frilling every surface with cupids and cherubim to line his own pockets."

Adam smiled, agreeing with Pendrake on this point. "My lord, it is my philosophy that efficiency of design is the test of an architect's skill. An armory should be a handsome, dignified building, as befits the Royal Navy. And such a thing can be designed with great economy, particularly if one is attentive to the flow of labor."

Pendrake smiled. "Exactly. Howard said you were the best he's ever seen at managing costs and you finished the job ahead of schedule. Unofficially, I'd like to invite you to submit a proposal for the work. Lotham here can send you the specifics. We are publicly considering the other proposals, but between us, it's Folke's race to lose given his connections, and I'd like to have a man of my own in the game."

A man of my own. Oh Christ. To be Pendrake's man. The opportunities.

"My lord, thank you. It would be an honor to propose a design for such a project. I'm immensely flattered to be considered."

"Fine. Lotham, send Mr. Anderson what he needs promptly, as I'll need the proposal in six weeks."

Adam tried not to flinch. Six weeks would barely be enough time to complete the drawings if he devoted his every working hour to it at his studio in London. But he was needed here to oversee this phase of Tregereth's renovation for at least another three, which would mean—it would mean he wouldn't sleep.

He simply would not sleep.

"Of course, my lord."

Pendrake nodded. His purpose here settled, the marquess leaned back. "Lotham tells me you're doing fine work at Tregereth's. How are you getting on?"

"Very well. It's a beautiful part of the country."

"Tregereth obsesses over trifles. Always has, his father was the same. Don't let him bog you down in this and that. More important work to be done."

Pendrake gave Adam a stern look, making sure Adam took his meaning. *I am to be your priority.*

"Not at all, my lord," he said, hoping his words conveyed cooperativeness without necessarily agreement. He did not wish to seem dismissive of his existing customer any more than he wished to offend his potential benefactor.

Pendrake reminded him so much of his father—asserting his opinions on anything and everything with no consideration for tact and every expectation he would be agreed with. The arrogance of it made Adam ill at ease.

"And mind his neighbor, the Arden girl," Pendrake said. "Beastly woman. Radical. Can't fathom what's brought her back here."

Adam was startled by the fact that Pendrake was aware of Seraphina's temporary presence here.

He thought of her, not an hour before, her hair blowing in the wind. *I rather liked you.*

His mouth went dry. What could he say? He couldn't openly defy a man like Pendrake, who was offering him everything he'd worked for. Fortunately, Pendrake was already rising, clearly not inviting a response.

Adam rose, too, and bowed, feeling more like a coward with every inch his torso moved closer to the floor.

After a brief conferral with Lotham over the garden folly, he was back on his way south. He should be elated that this opportunity had fallen in his lap, but he wasn't. He felt queasy.

Was this who he'd become?

Some head-bobbing, eager-to-please sycophant who ignored insults to his friends to curry favor and made decisions out of fear?

He looked out at the ocean. Wild and roiling in the aftermath of last night's storm and utterly contemptuous of the rocks it crashed against. He wished he could be one of those swells, hurtling toward a mightier edifice with no thought to the risk of impact.

He wanted to build an armory. He wanted to pay his debt to Mayhew. He wanted to provide a secure future for his children.

But not at the cost of his self-respect.

He thought of Pendrake's words—*beastly woman*—and recalled Seraphina's expression when he'd declined her invitation. For just a moment, her face had collapsed, like Adam had called her a cruel name.

She was not remotely beastly. She was a person, who could be hurt, like any other.

And he was an architect. He knew enough about terrain to understand that when waves crashed into rocks, it was the rocks that suffered, not the waves. Cliffs were formed by the slow, persistent wearing down of stone by tidal swells.

Perhaps that was the meaning of his dreams of water: that he should cast his lot with the churning of the ocean, rather than trust the deceptive solidity of rock.

SERAPHINA WAS IN a rotten mood.

After her deflating conversation with Adam Anderson this morning, the day had gone on interminably, sad and dull, with nothing to look forward to, nothing to break the dread of the blank pages that awaited her, and no word from her friends.

She had written eight times to Thaïs and Cornelia since she'd received Cornelia's letter about Elinor, and received nothing back. Even accounting for the distance between Cornwall and London, *something* should have reached her by now.

Did they not know she would be in agony, worrying?

The sparing correspondence was not so unusual in Thaïs, who had not learned to write more than her name until Elinor had taught her at the age of twenty-two. But Cornelia was a famously prompt and prolific correspondent.

Sera poured herself a glass of wine—her third—and paced about her parlor, imagining dreadful things.

A knock sounded at the terrace door.

She froze. Who would be visiting at this time of night, and why would they come to her back door?

She held herself still, conscious she was alone. Tompkins had already gone upstairs to sleep, and Maria and the cook were in the kitchen. Whoever was outside would see her in the candlelit room, but she could not see out.

She thought of the kingfisher. Had it been a warning of some greater violence?

"Sera," a low, Scottish voice called through the glass.

It was *Adam*.

She clutched her hand to her chest and threw open the door.

"What are you doing sneaking around like a thief? I thought you were a prowler." Her voice was shrill.

Adam darted inside, rain dripping from his hat, and looked stricken when he saw her clutching her heart. "I beg your pardon. I'm so sorry. I didn't consider I might scare you. It's just the terrace doors are closer to the path, and it's raining again."

She tried to calm her breathing because she disliked the idea he would see her as some silly, easily spooked woman. But this did nothing to chasten her temper.

"What are you *doing* here?" she snapped. She did not need a man who'd already severed their ties scaring her half to death at ten o'clock.

He rummaged in his coat pocket and held up the note she'd given him this morning.

"I was hoping it was not too late to accept your invitation."

She huffed and gave him a sour look. She had spent all day mourning him. And now he'd *changed his mind*?

Certainly, she wanted him back in her bed. But if she allowed him there, would he have another flare of conscience in the morning, keeping her in a state of endless agitation as to whether she was an undue risk?

She did not appreciate being toyed with.

"I thought you'd deemed me hazardous to your well-being," she said, not bothering to keep her frustration out of her voice. "What changed your mind?"

He looked at her intently. "I realized I was being cowardly."

"In what way?" she pressed.

"Denying I want you. I do."

A fortifying thought. But a bit too late.

"Are you going to be one of those men who want me when the sun goes down and remembers I'm a liability in the morning? Because I have had those types, Adam, and they are tedious."

His jaw twitched. She'd hit a nerve.

"I don't do things like this," he said finally. "I lost my nerve. But it seems I've found it. If you'll still have me."

She sank down on the sofa, feeling weary. "Oh, very well," she grumbled. "Stay if you wish."

His eyes scanned over her face, narrowing with concern.

Oh dear. She hadn't thought of how she looked. Her chapped lips were no doubt stained red from wine, and she'd been crying about Elinor, so her skin would be blotchy.

She fervently hoped he wouldn't think she'd been crying over *him*.

"You look like you could use a friend," he said softly.

Something inside her pinged like a mallet on an over-tightened spring at his tender tone of voice. Tenderness was not a currency accepted here, especially from someone who had made a speech about his unwelcome feelings this morning.

She should not have told him that she liked him. She'd only said that because he'd ended their affair. He'd tricked her into being more earnest than she ought.

Females were chided for their vulnerable hearts but in her experience the human male was equally susceptible to mistaking desire with that stickier kind of ardor: *love*.

They were not the same thing. Indulging the body led to release. Indulging the emotions led to its opposite: entanglement. A condition that could not be prevented with a sheepskin condom.

There was a name for a man who fell in love with you: a bloody nuisance.

She set her wineglass down and stood up, to match his height.

"Yes, well you see, my friend is locked away in an asylum, and my other friends are ignoring my letters, so actually, I would quite like something more reliable on the spirits. Like a fuck. If that is, indeed, why you've come."

His mouth pursed. He leaned back against the wall, looking at her as though he was a naturalist trying to classify a rare kind of spider. "I suppose I did, to put it crudely. But if you would like to talk about whatever's troubling you—"

She raised a hand to stop him. She would not allow him to treat this like something it was not. "Adam, I am a woman rich in friends. I adore my friends. But I *never, ever* sleep with them. So please choose which it is you wish to be to me. A friend? Or a lover?"

He continued to hold her gaze, no change in the expression on his face. "I fail to see what harm there is in being both. I would like to be both."

She smiled tightly and rose to her feet. "And I would not. So make the choice."

He walked toward her until they were nearly touching. And then he stepped closer, into her space. She stepped back toward the fire and he followed her, maintaining the distance between them until her back was pressed into the mantelpiece and there was nowhere else for her to go.

He was large, and he could overpower her, and his cock was hard.

Her anger melted into lust. *This* was the man who had grabbed her in the belvedere. This was the one she'd wanted all along.

"Seraphina," he said flatly.

She looked up at the grim set of his face, acutely aware of his larger presence looming over her. "Yes?"

"I won't insist on being friends if you don't wish to. But if we're going to be lovers, don't speak to me that way."

She widened her eyes. "Like what?"

"Like I will take more than you are offering."

She smiled tightly. "Very good, Mr. Anderson. You're learning."

"Actually," he said, sliding his body against hers, "I suspect there is very little about what we're about to do that I don't already know."

This show of arrogance pleased her.

"Mmm," she breathed. "So stern tonight. What am I going to do with such a demanding man?"

He reached out and gripped the mantelpiece behind her, his forearms bracing around her shoulders. "I would suggest you begin by taking me to bed."

His erection pressed into her belly. She nearly lost her breath.

"Take me to your bed," he repeated, in a way she felt directly in her cunt.

She took him by the hand and led him to the stairs.

As soon as they were in the dimness of the stairwell, away from any windows or passing servants, he grabbed her from behind and pressed himself into her. He lifted the hair at her neck and kissed her roughly at her nape, using his teeth, until she gasped in pleasure. She arched to give him better access to her skin, wanting him to feast on her, to leave her marked.

"Go," he said into her ear. "Quickly. I wilna take you on the staircase."

She liked that raspy, unschooled brogue. It was the sound of a man who was losing his grip on control.

As soon as the door was open to her room, he nudged her toward the bed, not stopping to light the lamps or remove his coat. He pressed her roughly back against the counterpane until her back was flat with the mattress. He sank to his knees and lifted up her skirts.

"This is what I've been imagining since I left here." His fingers locked around her thighs and spread them wider. She felt his breath on her cunt.

She closed her eyes as his whiskers grazed against the outer down.

Animalistic.

Delightful.

He teased her there, nuzzling her folds apart, his fingers gripping her thighs. His grasp wasn't painful, but he applied just enough pressure to remind her that she was in his control. She whimpered and opened her legs wider, urging him to give her more.

He pulled her closer to his face and flickered his tongue across her clitoris.

She gasped.

Most men, in her not inconsiderable experience, had to be instructed to find that particular place.

"You are quite schooled at this," she gasped out.

Something about him was different tonight. Like he'd been hoarding a part of his personality away and had decided to unleash it. Deliciously. On her cunt.

He looked up at her, his mouth twisted in amusement and the unmistakable sheen of pride. "I think you will find I did not come here for an education."

She wanted to laugh at the wicked gleam in his eye but instead she extended her hand and pressed his head back down to her quim. "Now, now. Let's save the boasts for—"

She gasped again as he used his mouth and tongue and the slight stubble of his whiskers to reduce her to a puddle of desires. She urged him against herself, moaning out inarticulate cries of lust, until she broke into a violent shudder, shouting out some pleasure-twisted version of his name.

As she lay spent and panting, unable to so much as move, he stood, shoved off his overcoat, and perched beside her.

"Worthy of a boast?"

"I am willing to admit I might have underestimated your talents," she said breathlessly.

He smiled and traced his finger over her nose. "Yes. You did."

"Do you have others you'd like to demonstrate?" she asked.

He chuckled as he idly scooped her breasts out of the top of her neckline and turned his attention to her nipples. She closed her eyes and let herself be the object of his explorations, first his fingers, then his lips.

She stretched out beneath his ministrations. "Are you open to suggestions?" she asked, opening one eye.

"Whatever the lady wishes," he murmured.

"Rub my tits with your cock."

She wondered if this would shock him, but he just raised a brow, leaned away from her to rid himself of his remaining clothing, and straddled her.

He was quite the sight without his shirt. She had never been with a man so finely sculpted or so large. His prick was dark and wanting at the tip.

"Oh, you are delectable. Come here." She took him by his buttocks and urged him to drag the head of his cock between her breasts. He sucked in as she took his length in her hands and began to play with him, rubbing the glistening evidence of his desire in the shallow between her ribs.

"How scandalized will you be if I want you to come on my breasts?" she asked.

His eyes lit up with the recognition that only some-times awakened with a new lover—the appreciation of likeminded taste in deviance. He gave her a wicked smile and pushed her shoulders back into her pillows, yanked down her bodice to fully expose her, then stood above her on his knees.

"As long as you let me watch."

She held his cock by the base and squeezed as she stroked him with her other hand, and when he came, it was in warm spasms on her skin. He threw back his head and cursed, then sank back down beside her.

He rubbed a finger through the splatter of his seed on her chest. "I've made a mess of you, lass."

"I know. I'm fond of it." She reached for the edge of the sheet to clean herself off, but he took it from her hands and did the job for her, then pulled her on top of him and kissed her on the lips.

"You are a pleasure," he murmured.

That was self-evident, so she bit his lower lip. "You promised not to get emotional about me, Mr. Anderson."

"How would you like me to get, Miss Arden?"

She snaked her hand down to his cock, which had fallen to half-mast. "Hard again."

He smiled wickedly. "Let's get you out of this gown." He helped her with her bodice and stays, but when she was down to her chemise, he stopped her, pulling the straps back up over her shoulders. "No, that stays on, I think. I've been thinking about that shift ever since I saw you in the belvedere."

"Oh?" she asked, tremendously pleased. "What were you thinking?"

He took her by the hips and lifted her rather effortlessly onto the mattress, then climbed on top of her, so that his revivified erection pressed into her lower belly. "How it would feel against my prick."

"Lower, please," she said, urging his cock to brush

against her cunt. He returned his lips to her mouth and kissed her hungrily as he rubbed his erection directly where she wanted it. She moaned absently and bucked beneath him, trying to frot her way into another crisis, but the shift between them, soaked with her arousal though it was, made her hungry for more than simple friction. She wanted—needed—to feel him against her skin.

She reached for the hem and pulled it up. He stilled and lifted his hips so she could remove it, but when she pulled him back down and said, "Continue, please," he paused.

"Rub it against me," she said, taking his cock in her hand and sliding it over the lips of her puss, so it brushed her clitoris. She gasped. "Yes. Get it nice and wet."

He groaned, dipping himself just in the channel of her cunt, then dragging it up and teasing her with it. Heaven, heaven, but not precisely what she wanted.

She stilled.

"Adam."

"Yes?"

"Fuck me."

Chapter Fourteen

At the crudity of her words, he paused, gasping for breath.

"Fuck me," she repeated.

He wanted to do what she asked. He was *dying* to do what she asked.

The thought of sliding himself into her cunt made his throat clench. Christ, it had been so long since he'd been inside a woman. He could scarcely remember what it felt like, only that there was nothing like it.

And he liked how her eyes lit up whenever he threw comportment aside and acted like his most bestial self. She wanted him to be carnal and he enjoyed the reaction indulging her elicited.

But fucking—actual fucking—was entirely too dangerous.

There were risks, and then there were stupid bloody risks.

He leaned down and kissed her forehead, still teasing her with his erection. "Not that, lass. Come here. I'll fill you with my fingers."

He scooped her up and put her on his lap, so his erection poked between her thighs, and put two fingers inside her. Her cunt was so tight and wet and hot that feeling it with his hands and not his penis was offensive to his very being. Oh, to be a more unreasonable man.

"How's that?" he whispered, adding another finger.

She groaned in pleasure. "I wish you would let me ride you. But this will do quite nicely if you won't."

"Fuck, I like your filthy little mouth. Make me feel good."

She gripped his cock and jerked it, and they formed a kind of dance, fucking each other with their hands in a frantic, inelegant clench until they came within moments of each other, his seed spilling over her thighs as she shook around his fingers and then collapsed against his chest.

He cleaned them both off with the sheet she'd used earlier, so that none of his seed found its way inside her, then pulled her up against him. She snuggled up without objection.

For a few minutes they stayed like that, both breathing. He had missed the agreeably boneless feeling of a satisfied woman against his bare chest.

"Thank you, lass."

She sighed, lazing her fingers down the side of his abdomen in a way that made his skin jump. "I'd like to do this again," she said.

"If you keep doing that, we'll be liable to be doing it again in a few minutes."

She chuckled. "Randy fellow, for a proper Scot."

"You have no idea."

"I think I'm beginning to have one. I was quite dreading boredom over the next few weeks but perhaps there is hope after all. 'Tis good to have accommodating neighbors."

He pressed his fingers over her lips, which were wide and flared outward from her face in a way that his artist's eye was drawn to. She had *such* a remarkable face. "Aye."

She rose up on one elbow. "May I ask you a question?"

"You may."

"Why don't you wish to fuck me?"

He paused. Speaking of the reasons was an intimate, personal matter. He did not wish to discuss the situation with Catriona. How the physician had warned them that another child could damage her health. How they'd been careful, but not careful enough.

How the physician had been right.

So he gave the easier answer. "It's not that I don't wish to. But I'm a bastard. And I've done well enough, but it's not a fate I'd wish on a child of my own. And you've made clear you're not in the market for collecting husbands."

"No," she drew out. "Most definitely not. But I do have my methods for preventing such misfortunes. They've worked for years, and not for lack of opportunity, should you find you can be persuaded on this point."

"How?" he asked, out of morbid curiosity.

She wriggled out from under him and went rummaging in the drawer of her beauty table. He took the opportunity to admire her figure. She had wide, womanly hips and a narrow waist that tapered into proud, broad shoulders. A musical physique.

When she came back she held a jar. "An armor," she said. "You tie it around your prick to catch the seed. Whores use them to prevent disease, but my physician believes they help to prevent conception as well. Though, you must also withdraw before spending, to decrease the chance of seed entering the womb."

He leaned closer to the jar of shriveled, translucent husks suspended in oily murk. Not a bloody chance.

He looked into her eyes. "Don't mistake me, Sera. I'd love to make love to you properly. I just can't."

She looked annoyed, but after a brief pause, shrugged. "I suppose we will have to make do with being extremely perverse."

He smiled. "What perversities do you fancy?"

"I like it rough. Men find me quite frightening, you see. It's refreshing to be tossed around."

That he could accommodate. He stood and lifted her over his shoulder. "Like this, wench?"

"Mmmm."

He sat her bare arse'd atop a bureau against the wall, pressed her shoulders back into the plaster, and kissed her in a way that would have been intolerably brutish if she hadn't asked for just such forcefulness. Her enthusiasm was instantly clear—she wrapped her legs around his torso and dug her nails into his arms and devoured him.

He wrapped his fingers in her hair and tugged, and she moaned, and he did it more forcefully and she moaned even louder, and they were lost in it again, until a commotion floating up from downstairs caught his attention above her cries of pleasure. "What's that noise?"

She froze, craning her neck to hear.

"Oh no," she whispered.

He remembered how frightened she'd looked when he'd surprised her on her terrace. How she'd tried to hide it, but her hands had trembled when she'd opened the door.

She was terrorized. It made him want to murder the people who were scaring her.

"It better not be those louts with the damned posters," he growled, abandoning her on the bureau to find his discarded clothing. She jumped down and began to find her own, and when he looked over at her, she was white with fear.

It made his heart clench. Poor lass. She didn't deserve this.

"Sera," Tompkins's voice called.

"Who the bloody hell is here?" Seraphina cried in a thin voice.

"Thaïs, Cornelia, and Jack."

"Who?" Adam asked, but Sera was too busy throwing on her dressing gown to take the time to explain that her friends had either gone mad or something terrible had happened.

"What in the name of holy Eden are they doing traveling in a bloody storm?" she called through the door to Tompkins.

"Tell Miss Arden we don't control the weather," Cornelia's voice called from downstairs. She did not sound upset in the least.

"Sera, come down and welcome your half drowned friends," Thaïs shouted.

They were standing at the bottom of the staircase grinning, looking like they'd washed in on a raft.

"Darlings!" she laughed, racing toward them. "I would think you were apparitions except your ghosts would never appear so ill kempt."

She opened her arms and Thaïs and Cornelia ran into them. They were damp.

Thaïs stepped back and lifted her nose up in the air, a devilish glint in her enormous blue eyes. "She smells of sex," Thaïs said.

"You would know," Cornelia drawled.

"Sex with a *man*," Thaïs pronounced definitively, sniffing her.

Such pleasantries were the reason Sera adored her friends.

Jack stood in the doorway, watching this reunion with an expression of wry amusement.

Sera took his hand, kissed it, and ushered the lot of them into the parlor. "What are you *doing* here? Sit by the fire and warm up, you all look like river creatures."

"What has happened to you? You look like you've lost a stone," Cornelia said, yanking Sera back to examine her from head to toe.

"Oh, just the toll of unearthing my tragic history," she said airily. "I am living on wine, tobacco, and malaise."

Speaking of wine, this called for celebration. "Tompkins," she called over her shoulder. "Find us some wine, would you? And perhaps a few morsels from the kitchen?"

Cornelia turned around. "Lots of morsels, please. Some of us cannot subsist on malaise alone." She paused, and her voice turned into a purr. "Oh. Good evening."

Adam stood awkwardly in the landing of the staircase, looking like someone trying to dissolve into thin air.

Thaïs cackled. "I knew it."

"And here we thought you were wasting away in tragic isolation," Cornelia said to Sera, not without an admiring tone.

Thaïs sashayed across the room to Adam, her wet hair and soaked attire doing nothing to diminish her exquisite beauty nor her aura of sexual knowing.

"Thaïs Magdalene," she said, discarding her natural Seven Dial's accent for her sonorous courtesan's voice and extending her hand to be kissed.

Either because he recognized her name, he had heard their chatter, he saw how invitingly Thaïs was looking at him, or all three, Adam flushed like a boy. Apparently, his smoldering rogue routine only extended to the bedroom.

"Adam Anderson," he said gruffly. "Pleasure."

Cornelia stalked over, her brown skin glowing in the candlelight. Her aristocratic posture was as exactingly elegant as Thaïs's was louche and she looked, as she was *wont*, splendidly amused. "I am Cornelia Ludgate," she said. "And that fellow is Jack Willow."

Jack gave a friendly nod from his shivering crouch above the fire.

"Seraphina did not mention she had made friends," Cornelia said to Adam.

"We're hardly friends," Seraphina said. "And Mr. Anderson was just leaving."

"Charmed to make your acquaintance," he said, sparing Sera a grateful glance at the excuse to cut this bald examination short.

"You'll be all right in the drizzle?" Sera asked.

"Aye. I'm made of sturdy stuff," he said, bowing again.

"*Indeed*," Thaïs remarked, sucking in his proportions appreciatively with her eyes.

As soon as Adam was out the door, Thaïs and Cornelia were upon her, twin pictures of intrigue.

"Where did you find such a *strapping* caller?" Cornelia asked.

Sera sat down on the sofa. "He's an architect doing renovations nearby. I inveigled him to help me pass the time."

Her friends draped their wet forms down on either side of her, as if to extract gossip by smothering her in dripping cold muslin. She tried to squirm away, but Cornelia poked her in the ribs. "Is he good?"

"At architecture?" Sera asked blandly.

"I believe this is my cue to use the necessary," Jack said. He flashed them a knowing, if slightly long-suffering, grin as he left the room.

They all collapsed into laughter. Oh, it felt so good to laugh with them.

"At least tell us if he is as comely beneath his linens as he looks!" Thaïs demanded.

"Better," Sera said. "And he's shockingly . . . *adept*." She winked, enjoying it as their eyes widened in appreciation.

Thaïs rubbed her hands together gleefully. "She fancies him!" she cackled to Cornelia.

"Oh, nothing like that!" Sera protested. "He's a bit too nice for my taste. But I'm rather enjoying him for now."

Oddly, saying it stirred up a touch of melancholy. It was true of course, that she'd have to end things before long. But now that she'd had another taste of Adam in her bed, she didn't want to give him up.

"Oh, indeed," Cornelia said, nodding gravely. "Handsome, adept, and nice? Dreadful stuff. You *must* dispense with him."

"May I have him when you're done?" Thaïs asked prettily, fluttering her lashes.

She decided to change the subject before the thought of retiring Adam from her bed made her forlorn.

"Oh, loves, I've missed you," Sera said, wrapping her arms around them. "But what could possibly have possessed you to journey all the way here without writing?"

Jack peeked back into the room, as if he'd been waiting in the hall for the subject to change from the subject of copulation. Normally he looked like a bulldog crossed with a prizefighter, but his stocky bearing held none of its usual vigor, and his face was hollowed out. He was a scarecrow version of the man he'd been two months ago.

Thaïs pointed at him. "We couldn't write because Jack thinks Bell might try to intercept our letters."

The feeling of warmth and comfort that had washed over Sera in the presence of her friends went decidedly icy at Bell's name.

"We discovered where he's keeping Elinor," Jack said, rubbing his eyes. "A place called Willowgate, a few hours from here."

"Dear God," Sera breathed. "Cornelia wrote that you suspected, but . . . All this time, I don't think I really believed he was capable of it."

Cornelia crossed her arms over her chest. "Luckily, the bastard doesn't know what *we're* capable of."

"Damned right," Thaïs said, rising. She slung an arm around Jack's shoulders. "Bell always said Elinor kept tavern company, and he wasn't wrong, was he, Jackie?"

Jack opened up a satchel and produced a map. "No. And we lowlife bastards are going to get her out."

Chapter Fifteen

"I was expecting an asylum to be more forbidding," Cornelia mused the following morning, looking out the carriage window at the pleasant, manicured lawn of a handsome manor house.

"The forbidding thing is the fact that Elinor is locked inside it," Seraphina muttered, eyeing its impressive iron gates.

"I only meant," Cornelia said loftily, "that it is not precisely Bedlam." Her aristocratic accent was at odds with the drab dress, white apron, and spinsterish lace cap she wore in her effort to disguise herself as a nurse.

"Do not match wits, you harridans, my head can't bear it," Thaïs groaned.

They had stayed up late into the night fortifying themselves with brandy while Jack demonstrated such arts as picking locks and felling a man with a quick jab to the kidneys. Now, Jack was hiding in wait in the forest like a common highwayman, and Sera and the girls were dressed as matrons, with picks and scissors sewn into the linings of their gowns.

It was all rather gothic for Seraphina's taste.

"Now remember," Thaïs said. "We talk our way in, I stir up a mighty clatter, you two find Elinor. If we can get her outside to Jack we have a fightin' chance."

That was it. That, and a flimsy story about a sick aunt, was their plan.

"I still have a bad feeling about this," Sera muttered. "If we spent a little more time planning, I'm sure we could come up with something—"

"We don't have time," Cornelia said quietly. "If Bell learns we left London he will suspect we've found her, and move her before we have a chance to get her out."

Thaïs rolled her eyes at them. "You both worry too much. Jack's man got all the information we need. No bars on her window, only two attendants. We'll be toasting with Elinor by supper."

"Not all of us count petty crime among our chief accomplishments," Sera said.

Cornelia shushed them. "Someone's coming," she murmured, gesturing at a tall man in a long black coat approaching the gate.

Thaïs gave Sera and Cornelia a blinding smile. "That must be the doctor. Let's be villains, girls."

With a wink, she threw open the door and stepped outside.

"Good day, sir," she called in a well-bred accent, curtsying. She'd worn a modest yellow dress sprigged with roses and a girlish bonnet over her red curls. If the large amount of wine she'd consumed the night before and the inverse quantity of time she'd had to sleep it off were having an effect on her health, it did not show in her appearance. She was so dazzling that the doctor audibly gasped at the sight of her.

She smiled at him beneath her lacy bonnet. "Sir, I'm looking for Willowgate Asylum. Have I come to the right place?"

"Indeed, miss. I'm Dr. Hogue. May I help you?"

"I do hope so. My name is Miss Elspeth. Forgive me for not writing in advance, but I am desperate. My elderly aunt has gone mad, and I am looking for a place where she might seek treatment."

The doctor looked delighted. "How dreadful for you and your family," he said in a concerned tone that did not travel to his eyes. "I would be happy to take her."

Sera gaped at Cornelia. "He acts like a piece of bullion just fell from the sky," she whispered. "It's bloody mercenary."

"Hush," Cornelia whispered back, pinching her wrist.

"Allow me to show you inside to make arrangements," the doctor said in an oozing voice, resting his hand on the small of Thaïs's back.

Sera's skin crawled in sympathy.

Thaïs glanced back at the carriage. "I've asked my friends to accompany me, if you wouldn't mind. My aunt's condition is so upsetting I am liable to forget the details."

"Of course," the doctor said. He removed his hand from Thaïs's posterior, conscious of being watched.

Cornelia inhaled like she was about to dive into the ocean from a cliff top, took Sera's hand, and stepped out the door of the carriage.

"This is Miss Best, my aunt's nurse," Thaïs said, gesturing at Cornelia. "And my lady's companion, Mrs. Lowell."

Sera curtsied, bracing under the doctor's eelish gaze. She had worn old mourning garments of her stepmother's, stuffed at the bosom, in an effort to look as unlike herself as possible. If any of them were recognized, their mission would be over before they even got inside.

But the physician barely bowed to them, quickly turning his eyes back to feast on Thaïs's sumptuous proportions. "Follow me, Miss Elspeth."

"What a beautiful place," Thaïs enthused as they approached the house.

It was, indeed, much lovelier than Sera had been expecting, given what Jack had learned about the medieval-sounding treatments it was known for. But a pretty prison was still a prison.

"Lovely grounds help soothe our patients' spirits," the doctor said. "Though they are not allowed, of course, to go outside."

"Oh, I should hope not," Thaïs agreed. "Fresh air is so perilous for a fragile constitution."

"Especially for ladies," the doctor said. "And we only treat ladies." He led them inside and showed them to an expensively appointed parlor, where a young woman sat at a desk writing. She looked up when they entered.

"Miss Smith, these ladies are here to inquire about treatment for a lunatic," the doctor said. "Would you bring us a pot of tea?"

Miss Smith smiled at the doctor pleasantly and rose, but her expression faltered when her gaze fell upon Seraphina. She adjusted her spectacles, as though trying to place Sera's face.

Sera ducked her head beneath her stepmother's hideous hat and looked out the window, holding her breath.

"Miss Smith?" the doctor urged.

"Of course," the girl finally said, her eyes still fixed on Sera.

Please, Sera prayed silently. *Please don't let her realize who I am.*

The girl turned around and briskly left the room. Sera let out a breath.

Dr. Hogue gestured at a sofa, and the three of them sat down. "Now then. What is the nature of your aunt's malady, Miss Elspeth?"

Thaïs launched into a litany of outlandish symptoms— conversations with the laying hens, an appetite for beetles, delusions of being the king. Sera wondered if she was being too dramatic to be credible, but the doctor listened raptly, nodding.

When Thaïs had exhausted her imagination's supply of ailments, he smiled. "Your aunt will do very well here. Now, where shall I send the bill?"

"Before we discuss the arrangements, Dr. Hogue, perhaps you would give us a tour?" Thaïs asked. "My aunt is a dear woman, when she is not dancing through the gardens in the nude. I want to be sure she will be comfortable here."

The doctor hesitated. "I'm afraid we don't take guests inside the asylum. The presence of new faces can be overly exciting for our patients."

"We shall be very quiet and discreet," Thaïs assured him.

"No doubt, Miss Elspeth, but I'm afraid I can't permit it."

Sera's pulse began to race. If he would not let them beyond this sitting room, what could they do to evade his supervision?

"I've long said your aunt is in better hands with me, at home," Cornelia sniffed to Thaïs. "You know how travel upsets her. She'll likely get worse in a place like this."

Sera nodded to Thaïs. "I agree, Miss Elspeth. At least at home we can be sure she is in a sympathetic atmosphere."

Thaïs nodded, making as if to rise. "Perhaps you're right, ladies. Doctor, thank you for your time, but I think—"

Dr. Hogue shot to his feet. "Oh, I daresay treating a patient in such a condition as your aunt at home may worsen her health. But your concern for her comfort is touching. Miss Elspeth, if your friends would not mind waiting here, I suppose a brief tour will do no harm."

"How kind, Doctor," Thaïs chirped.

The doctor gave Cornelia a smug smile, like he had just stolen her lunch. "Follow me, Miss Elspeth. Ladies, Miss Smith will be in shortly with your tea."

As soon as they left, Sera gripped Cornelia's hand. "Clever thinking."

"Oh, I don't like this," Cornelia sighed. "Do you think he believes her?"

"Yes," Sera said. "Thank God for blinding beauty."

"I trust she will use it to wreak havoc. Let's go look for Elinor."

But before they could even rise, Miss Smith returned carrying a tea tray.

Blast. They needed to get rid of her.

Sera glanced at Cornelia, unsure what to do.

Cornelia's eyes traveled to Miss Smith's teacup. A silent signal. *Laudanum.*

Cornelia clutched her stomach. "Miss Smith, forgive the indelicacy but I find the travel here did not agree with me. Would you show me to the necessary?"

Miss Smith hesitated, glancing at Sera. "Of course. Come with me."

"I will prepare us tea," Sera said. "Miss Smith, do you take milk and sugar?"

"Yes, please."

As soon as they were out the door, Sera strained the tea into three cups. Into Miss Smith's she poured a hefty amount of milk, two lumps of sugar, and enough laudanum to send a small woman into a blissful doze.

Miss Smith returned, alone, and Sera held out the cup, feeling queasy. She had been accused of many crimes during her life, but she had never actually been guilty of committing one. She preferred to fight with words, not poisoned chalices.

It's for Elinor. Muscle up.

Miss Smith took the tea, but set it down on the table without taking a sip. Sera took a sip of her own tea encouragingly.

Drink it. Drink it.

"I recognized you immediately," Miss Smith whispered. "You are Seraphina Arden."

Sera's hand spasmed, sending hot tea splashing over the rim of her cup. "Oh, no, you must be mistaking me for someone else," she said lightly, trying not to spill more of the scalding liquid on her hands.

Miss Smith smiled, and offered Sera a serviette to wipe the tea from her hands. "I suppose you must think the doctor would not take your friend's aunt if he knew who you are, but you needn't worry. I won't tell him. I'm an admirer."

An admirer! They could use this.

The girl reached down to pick up her tea. Sera kicked the table leg, causing the tea cup to overturn onto the carpet.

"So very sorry!" Sera exclaimed. "How clumsy of me."

She knelt to mop up the spilled tea. Miss Smith also knelt, and Sera took the opportunity to whisper in her ear. "Thank you for being so discreet. The truth is that I learned of this place because my friend Lady Bell is being treated here."

"Ah, yes," Miss Smith said. "She is lovely."

Sera looked into the girl's eyes. "She is a dear friend. I'd love a chance to visit with her while we are here. Perhaps you could take me to see her?"

Miss Smith shook her head sadly. "The doctor does not allow visitors. But you need not worry. Lady Bell does not seem the slightest bit mad. I believe she is just here for rest."

"Then surely a short visit would do no harm. Just for a few minutes. Please."

"What's the matter!" Cornelia cried, returning to the room to see her and Miss Smith crouched on the floor.

"Miss Smith here is a supporter of the cause," Sera explained in a low voice. "And she has given me the most soothing news. It seems that Lady Bell is not mad."

Miss Smith's face had gone taut with worry, as if she was reconsidering the wisdom of having shared this information. "Yes, but nevertheless—"

Sera took the girl's hand. "That makes her a *captive*, dear. Nothing but a captive."

Miss Smith's face contorted, as if she had not considered this.

"Please, take us to see her," Sera said, squeezing Miss Smith's fingers. "We have been so worried. You can't imagine."

Miss Smith inhaled, then slowly nodded. "Very well. But we must go quickly, and you must be brief. The doctor will be furious if he learns that I've allowed it."

Blessed child.

"Thank you. I cannot tell you how much this means to us."

Miss Smith stood and gestured for them to follow her out of the room and into a corridor that divided the public and private wings of the house. She paused, checking for anyone within view, then opened the door into a far less pleasant hallway that smelled of stale urine. It was lined with identical doors, each a few feet apart.

Cells. *Poor Elinor.*

Miss Smith paused in front of one and took a key from a ring at her waist. "She's in here," she whispered. "One of our best rooms."

The quiet in the hall was broken by a cry in the distance. "Oh, help me, Doctor!"

Thaïs, wailing.

"Oh dear," Miss Smith said. "I must go help Dr. Hogue. I'll knock in a few minutes when it's time to say farewell. Quick, in with you."

She opened the door to a dreary room and gestured them inside it, locking the door behind them.

Elinor was sitting in a chair with her back to them, facing the wall. She turned her head at the sound of the door, and her face broke into a shocked smile.

"My darlings, is that truly you?" she breathed. She seemed dazed, as if she wasn't sure if they were real.

Sera crouched down before Elinor and spoke in a low, urgent whisper. "We're here. And we've come to get you out."

The trouble was how. They had not anticipated being locked *inside* the room.

The tiny room was dark, with a single small window near the ceiling allowing a wan shaft of gray light to filter in. It was less a window than a port-hole. Sera looked about the small room for ideas. It held nothing but a single wooden chair and a narrow bed.

And attached to each corner: shackles.

She had been cowardly to hesitate in coming here. They *would not* leave without Elinor.

Cornelia was already dragging a chair beneath the window. "Does this open?" she asked.

Elinor looked alarmed. "Darling, Bell will have you arrested if he knows you've come for me. You are kind but you must not risk it."

"He can only do that if we are caught," Sera said.

Elinor shook her head. "He is angry enough to do anything. You must not risk his ire. For both our sakes."

Cornelia turned around with murder in her eyes. "Aunt. He has already locked you away. He has kept you from your children. What else is there to take?"

"You," Elinor said. "I won't let him hurt my girls."

"We would rather live with the consequences than bear another day knowing you are locked up," Cornelia said. "We are all sick with it."

Elinor sighed and looked down at her wrists. "Then I hope you brought a knife."

Belatedly, Sera realized Elinor's arms were locked to the chair by a pair of thick leather cuffs cinched tight against her sleeves with padlocks.

"Only the doctor has the key. Hogue is convinced I'm a threat to my own life."

"That bloody bastard," Cornelia hissed.

"Well, I did threaten to starve myself if he dunked me in his ice bath one more time," Elinor said with the barest hint of a smile.

Seraphina was mildly relieved that their friend had at least not lost her mordant sense of humor. She pulled up the hem of her dress and removed a pair of heavy shears secured in the lining with thread. Kneeling over Elinor, she slowly inched the metal blade beneath the leather.

Elinor sucked in her breath. The cuffs were so tight that there was barely room to edge in the blade.

"Be very still," Sera whispered. "I don't want to cut your wrists."

As Sera slowly sawed through the thick leather, Cornelia began toiling with the window, grunting.

"Do you see Jack outside?" Sera asked.

Elinor looked up sharply. "Jack is here?"

"Yes," Cornelia said. "He's dressed as a gardener. He's even stolen himself a wheelbarrow." She knocked on the window to alert him to their location, waving, then went back to struggling with the windowpane to force it open.

"It won't budge. It's been sealed with paint." She fished a knife out of her own hemline and set about chipping at it as Sera finished cutting through the cuff.

This was taking far too long. Miss Smith would be back any minute, and if she discovered the cuff had been damaged, Elinor would no doubt suffer the consequences.

The thought was chilling.

"There we are, that's one," she said, freeing Elinor's arm.

She paused and stood to press her ear against the door, listening for signs of Miss Smith. It was quiet.

"Hurry, Cornelia. I can't hear any more commotion," Sera said as she bent to work on Elinor's other cuff. "Thaïs must have run out of distractions."

Cornelia scoffed. "Not yet. She'll have fainted dead away now and have them crowded around, trying to revive her. Here, I think I've got it. Come help me lift."

Sera handed the shears to Elinor, who used her free hand to continue gnawing through the leather.

Sera and Cornelia gripped the windowpane, counted to three, and heaved. It still would not budge.

"Oh dear God. All of this to be thwarted by a window?" Sera murmured.

They could see Jack below, pretending to pull weeds. Cornelia pounded to get his attention. He looked up. She gestured desperately, indicating it wouldn't open.

He looked around for passersby, then turned his wheelbarrow over and stood up on it between the wheels. He took a steel pick and a hammer from his leather belt and set to work prying it open from the outside.

Sera felt her spirits lift as the glass began to rise, creaking in protest.

Until she heard footsteps coming down the corridor.

"Someone's coming," she hissed. "We must get her out. Now."

Cornelia took Elinor's hand. "Stand on the chair, dear, and we will lift you."

Sera rushed back to the chair and took one of Elinor's feet as Cornelia took the other and Elinor hoisted herself up by her arms.

"Cornelia, one more push," Sera grunted, summoning every ounce of strength she possessed.

"I've got her," Jack called. "Just a little higher."

With a final gasp, Elinor went over the sill and tumbled toward the ground.

She and Jack fell into the shrubs. For a sickening moment, neither of them moved.

Get up. Get up. Please get up.

Jack stirred first, turning to help Elinor. The look that passed between them as he set her down on the grass took Sera's breath away. She knew the rumors of adultery were unfounded, but the affection between the two of them was so obvious she almost sympathized with Bell for deeming it a threat.

It made her think, momentarily, of the way Adam's eyes had darkened when he'd said, *You look like you could use a friend.*

Absurd, thinking of Adam at a time like this.

"We must run, as fast as you can," Jack said, taking Elinor's hand. "Are you ready?"

Elinor looked up at Seraphina and Cornelia through the window. "Yes. Goodbye, my loves. And *be careful.*"

Miss Smith knocked at the door. "Ladies. I'm afraid it's time." They heard her key turning in the lock.

Christ. If they had been a half a minute longer, they would have been caught in the act.

Sera leaned out the door before Miss Smith had fully opened it. She put a finger to her lips, urging quiet.

"She fell asleep, poor thing," Sera whispered. "Exhausted from her tears."

Cornelia gingerly closed the door behind them, making a show of doing it quietly so as not to wake the patient inside, while blocking Miss Smith's view inside the room.

"Thank you," Seraphina said to Miss Smith. "I think the visit did much to lift her spirits."

Miss Smith smiled. "She is lucky to have you. Shall I show you out? Your friend had a bit of a fright, and she is waiting for you in the parlor."

"Thank you." Seraphina took the girl's hand, regretting that this kind young woman might lose her position as a result of their actions. "Should the doctor discover we saw Elinor, please don't tell him my name. But if you encounter any difficulty, write to me in care of my publisher. I can always find a position for a brave young woman."

"You can count on my discretion," Miss Smith promised.

Back in the study, Thaïs was prone on the couch, with Dr. Hogue fussing over her.

"Oh, Nurse Best," she murmured weakly to Cornelia. "I've had one of my spells." She looked up sweetly at the doctor. "Nurse always knows what to do."

Cornelia knelt over Thaïs and put a hand to her brow, clucking. "We must get you home to your bed, dear, lest the megrim set in."

Sera wanted to stall, in case Elinor and Jack were still in view of the house. "Doctor, do you have a chair we could use to take Miss Elspeth to the carriage? She is so unsteady after her fits."

"I'll get one," Miss Smith said, disappearing.

"Thank you for your kind attendance, Doctor," Thaïs crooned to him. "I know my aunt will be in good hands with you."

The man looked like he did not know what he wished for more—the beautiful woman's adoring smile, or her money.

By the time they met their waiting carriage, there was no sign of Jack and Elinor, save for an overturned wheelbarrow near the edge of the woods.

None of them dared to so much as breathe until they were half a mile from the asylum's gates.

"I saw the baths," Thaïs whispered, once they were safely down the road. "The treatment rooms are on the second floor. So they can't escape." She paused, her fingers screwed up into contorted fists, like an arthritic crone's. "None of the ladies he showed me seemed mad. Not one of them."

Cornelia lowered her head into her lap.

Sera only closed her eyes, depleted.

Sometimes the grim realities of womanhood, and the danger of addressing them when one lacked power beyond rage, were so heavy it silenced all discussion. One did not need to name the feeling. One simply felt the weight.

The ride back was somber.

They kept quiet, listening for signs of pursuit. But the wooded road was mostly empty. All they could do was hope that enough time would pass to give Jack a head start before Elinor's absence was discovered.

When they arrived in the late afternoon at Seraphina's house, Cornelia looked at both of them in shock. "I'm beginning to think we got away with it."

A weak ray of hope rose up in Seraphina. "With any luck, they'll be here soon. Let's go out to the terrace and celebrate with a drink."

Cornelia pulled open the terrace doors and stepped outside. "What's this?" she asked, leaning down to look at something.

She screamed.

Sera rushed to see what she was looking at.

It was a basket.

And inside—

ADAM PACED ANXIOUSLY up and down the coastal path, trying to clear his head.

He had a stone problem.

The slate he'd ordered from Newquay had not arrived when it was due, and a message sent to the quarryman had been returned with a scattered letter saying it was not expected for a month. A delay like this would cascade down the flow of work, adding hundreds in labor costs while Adam's crew waited with nothing to do.

He could not afford mistakes like this.

He could not afford Pendrake hearing rumors about delays and excess costs.

A muffled sound from the distance caught his attention. He craned his neck to hear, praying it was not one of his children.

A second, louder sound pierced the air. A shriek.

It was coming from Seraphina's house.

He turned toward that awful sound and ran, ghastly visions floating through his mind.

If they bloody hurt her—

He found Seraphina and two of her friends standing at her terrace doors gaping at a woven basket. He tried to get a glimpse inside, but their skirts blocked his view.

"Is everything all right?" he called to them.

They were all oddly dressed. The freckled, red-headed woman who had introduced herself as Miss Magdalene the night before was wearing a maidenish muslin dress that contrasted vividly with the daringly low-cut gown she'd had on when she'd sauntered across the room to introduce herself. The elegant, dark-skinned lady, Miss Ludgate, who had been dressed regally the night before in fabrics and jewels even Adam had realized were expensive, wore a drab homespun gown and a cap over her hair. Sera was in a gown made for a more curvaceous woman, and had stuffed the bosom to make it fit.

She whirled around clutching her unnaturally swollen chest, startled by his voice. Her face was drained of color and her eyes were fixed beyond him, blank.

He quickened his pace to reach her.

"What's happened?" he asked, placing a hand on her shoulder. He wanted to do more—sweep her into his arms and hug away that terrified expression—but he sensed she would not wish for it.

Tompkins crouched down and lifted up the basket. Inside, four wee blue birds with their chests sliced open, lying on a bloodied poster of Seraphina Arden's face.

"Bloody Christ," he snarled.

Miss Magdalene clutched herself, murmuring about "murdered bloody budgies."

"They're kingfishers," Sera corrected her in a shaky voice.

"I don't care if they are parrots from the jungle. Someone is leaving them dead on your doorstep. You are coming back to London with us."

"No, I'm not," Sera said wearily. "I will not be run out of my own home."

"Your home is St. Martin's Bleedin' Lane," Miss Magdalene shot back. "Tell her, Cornelia."

Sera held up her hand to silence them. "This is just *harassment*, Thaïs. Provocation. And I will not delight the people wishing to scare me by showing them it's worked."

Adam shook his head. This had gone too far. "I'm going for my horse and will have words with Trewlnany about his man. This will be stopped."

"No, you will *not*," Seraphina uttered, eyes flashing. "Understand me, Adam. Not. One. Word."

She held his gaze intently. He'd never seen her look so fierce.

He paused, his pulse beating in his throat. "*Why not*, Sera?"

"Because I know the people here. I have known them all my life. If they want a battle, I know exactly how to win it, I assure you. And it's by calmly finishing my book."

He dropped his shoulders, realizing they were pinned up by his ears with tension. "Fine. But, Sera, I'd like to send a man here, up to your home to keep watch. You have no male servants and the presence of a burly fellow can send a powerful message to those who like to harm wee helpless things. Aye?"

She screwed up her face distastefully.

"Yes, Mr. Anderson," Tompkins said. "I agree that such a step is prudent." She shot a glance at Seraphina. "If you don't want it for yourself, think of your defenseless servants."

"Oh, very well," Sera muttered.

And then she turned to her house and kicked the wall so hard bits of plaster sprayed out from beneath her boot heel. "It makes me so bloody *angry*. Why can't they leave me well enough alone?"

She kicked the wall twice more.

"Sera, love, stop," Miss Magdalene cried hoarsely. "You'll injure yourself."

But she didn't stop. She kicked the wall with such force that she fell back onto her rear in the grass. She cursed, then let out a wail of pure frustration.

She reminded Adam of Adeline when the world had spun out of her control, and all she could do was rage at it.

So he did what he did for Addie in such times. He crouched down beside her and gently touched her shoulder. "You're upset, love, aye?" he asked in his softest voice.

"Yes, I am upset," she shouted. "I have every right to be upset. My friend was made a prisoner by her own husband. My neighbors are killing birds to threaten me. And yet *I* am the one considered dangerous to the social order? What have I done? What on earth have *I* done?" She pounded the grass with her palms.

He wrapped her in his arms and squeezed her tight.

He expected Sera to push him off, but instead she stilled.

"Just take a breath," he whispered.

She inhaled deeply. Her fingers found his waist and clutched at him. He stroked her hair. Over her shoulder, he saw her friends looking on at them, perplexed.

"I'm just so bloody angry," she whispered, as if needing an excuse to let herself seek comfort.

"I know it, Sera," he murmured. And it was not a noble feeling, but a part of him was pleased that she was letting him hold her. The part of him that flared in indignation when she protested that they were not friends knew she needed kindness. He wanted to show her she could take it from him safely, without worrying he'd lose his head and propose marriage on the spot.

Slowly, the tension in her body relaxed. She pulled away and brushed off her skirts.

"I'm sorry," she said, rising to her feet. "Every so often a woman must indulge in a hysterical outburst, lest the things they say about our precarious sanity seem unfounded."

Her friends only stared at her warily.

"Come back to London with us," Miss Ludgate said in a voice scarcely louder than a whisper.

He did not wish to see Seraphina go. But if someone would do this, who knew what else they might do. He'd rather see her go than see her hurt.

"It might be wise, Sera," he said.

She shook her head vehemently. "No. No, I'm fine. I came here for a reason—to remember, so that I can write my book. And I will tell you this. It's working. I remember all too well."

Adam pulled out his timepiece. It was nearly six o'clock. He was reluctant to leave but he could not worry his children again.

"I have to return home. I'll come back tonight to check on you and bring a man to keep watch outside."

Seraphina's friends nodded. "Thank you," Miss Ludgate said. "I would not have believed Sera had made a friend here of all places, but I'm glad she has."

He waited for Seraphina to object that they were not friends.

But she said nothing. Only stared off at the ocean, as if she hadn't heard.

Chapter Sixteen

Most of the time it was a pleasure to have a friend who always knew the precise make of one's character. Sera and Cornelia were so alike that it sometimes made Thaïs, who was less critical and sharp-tongued and had been raised in an altogether different sort of world, protest that they were like one head with different bodies.

But sometimes one did not wish to be known quite so well.

Which was why Sera scowled at Cornelia as her friend watched Adam Anderson walk away, a small smile playing at her lips.

"Don't," Seraphina warned.

"What?" Cornelia asked innocently.

"That," Seraphina said, pointing to Cornelia's upturned lips.

Cornelia looked at her like she was a fool. "Forgive me, dear Sera, for displaying emotion. But *that*," she said, pointing to Adam's silhouette walking toward his cottage, "is a man who *cares* for you. And it's nice to see."

Seraphina rolled her eyes, refusing to discuss such things. "An unremarkable response to an eminently likable woman such as myself."

Thaïs guffawed and Sera turned her glare to her. "Don't laugh, you wretch."

Thaïs crossed her arms and smiled. "Seraphina Arden, you have a brain the size of a pumpkin. Hips like the curve of an angel's harp. But no one works as hard as you to be unlikable."

"*You* like me," Sera pointed out darkly.

"Yes," Cornelia said drily. "But Thaïs is known across the continent for her perverse tastes."

Thaïs's gaze softened. "Of course you are likable, love. I only mean that he's nice, and you are usually quite peevish to anyone who's nice to you."

Seraphina rolled her eyes, feeling uncomfortably exposed. "That must be why I so dearly love the pair of *you*," she grumbled.

"I'm right, and she knows it," Thaïs said to Cornelia. "She can fuss all she likes."

Well, yes, of course they were right. She *did* feel more at ease with people who were distant and reserved than those who wore their emotions openly.

But this was not a flaw in character.

It was a prejudice for people like herself.

She preferred talk of feelings to be safely ensconced within the realm of theory, especially when it came to men. The men she favored were the kind who did not wish to linger. Who shared a taste for the kind of relationship that did not take root beneath the skin.

It was important, this rule, as the kingfishers attested. Only two men had ever known of her love for kingfishers, and one of them had cast her from his house and the other, she increasingly suspected, was leaving their corpses as gifts. Terrorizing her in a way that said if she remembered, he remembered, too.

This was why it was inadvisable to share the contents of one's heart. When the warm feelings curdled, the knowledge of those tender places remained like a map of where to twist the knife.

And yet, her body still vibrated from the warmth of Adam's hug.

She'd enjoyed that hug.

She'd enjoyed it *far* too much.

She needed to draw a firmer line with Adam. His kindness was admirable, but it would not lead to anything she wished to entertain.

"I will say this for Mr. Anderson," she said, plastering a puckish smile on her lips. "He is not nice *in bed*."

She had been hoping for a laugh to break the tension, but instead Thaïs's eyes went reflective.

"'Tis a well-known fact that I'm nice in bed," she mused. "But I don't give my lovers hugs like that outside of it."

Sera groaned. "What is your point, dear?"

"That the two things are not related."

Cornelia waved their attention to the road. "Stop quarreling. Elinor's here."

ADAM WAITED UNTIL the children were in their beds to collect Tegan and make the trip back to Seraphina's. A small party was seated on her terrace, and the air tinkled with their laughter.

It relieved him that their mood was light. And yet, he wondered what harassment Seraphina and her friends must be accustomed to if they could recover from such a dreadful scene so quickly.

He was still rattled. He had returned home so ashen that Marianne had inquired if he was feeling ill.

Seraphina was lying flat on her back on a settee, staring up at the sky as she smoked a cheroot. An empty bottle of wine was beside her on the floor. Miss Magdalene was uncorking another.

Miss Ludgate was talking with Mr. Willow and an older woman Adam hadn't met.

"Your nice man is here," he heard one of the ladies say in a wine-loosened voice.

Sera rolled over on one arm and waved her fingers at him. "Why, Mr. Anderson. My guardian angel has returned."

Her tone arrested him. It was wry, almost like he was a joke to her.

It prickled at him, given the tender moment they'd shared not three hours ago.

"And who is this?" Sera added, gesturing at Tegan.

"This is Mr. Tegan. He'll keep watch till midnight, then trade with another man. They'll stay until you wake up in the morning."

"I'll get a chair and some refreshments to make you comfortable, Mr. Tegan," Tompkins said, leading Tegan away.

The unfamiliar woman rose, smiling at him in a way that reached her eyes. She had blonde hair that had begun to fade to silver, and a remarkably gentle face. "You must be Mr. Anderson. The girls were telling me what a kind friend you have been to Seraphina during her sojourn here. I'm Lady Bell. I'm so pleased to meet you."

Lady Bell? Was this not the woman Seraphina had said was locked away?

"A pleasure," he said, trying not to seem confused.

"Don't look so shocked," Sera called merrily. "We broke her out of gaol."

Her voice was loose. He wondered how much of the empty bottle she'd drunk on her own.

Miss Ludgate leaned toward him. "We must ask for your discretion in this matter, Mr. Anderson. We do not wish for it to be known that Lady Bell was here. Can we count on you not to mention it?"

"Of course. If all is well, I'll leave you to enjoy your evening," Adam said. He did not wish to interrupt them, and he had misgivings about knowing too much of the whereabouts of a missing viscountess.

"Oh, don't go just yet. Stay and have a drink," Miss Ludgate said, patting the empty chair beside her. Her speech, he noticed, was like that of an earl's—exceedingly fine. Marianne had clued him in to who she was—a well-known portraitist. There had been a hefty scandal when a series of portraits of the Black Poor she'd painted in the style of generals and aristocrats had been revealed to be her work. Despite the scandal, the series had won her acclaim. In the world of the arts, she was considered a talent, if a controversial one.

He glanced at Seraphina for a clue as to whether this invitation was welcomed, and she smiled languidly. "Yes, don't go just yet."

He felt conflicted. Her blousy mood unsettled him. And yet when she looked at him like that, he could not imagine leaving.

"But," she said, poking her finger in the air, "we have made a solemn vow not to discuss our troubles, for we only have one night together. So if you stay, you must promise to amuse us."

He smiled. "A high order. But I'll try my best."

Mr. Willow winked, perhaps offering him a bit of sympathy at being thrust into this crowd. Adam shot him a look as if to say, *Wish me luck. I'll no doubt need it.*

Lady Bell reached across the table and touched his arm. "Seraphina tells us you're an architect, Mr. Anderson?"

"Adam builds those pretty little Greek revivals all your husband's people like," Sera said.

This was an accurate description of his work but he wanted to explain to these people, who were so accomplished, that it was not the sum of his ambition.

"Neoclassical additions to their houses are what people will pay me to design, and I'm happy for the work," he said. "But I have a mind to do more than houses, someday."

Sera raised a brow. "Like what?"

"Bridges, aqueducts. I'd prefer to work on a grand scale. Damned follies for the rich drive me mad, if I'm honest."

She seemed to approve of this, which pleased him.

"You should show designs for such work in an artistic exhibition," Miss Ludgate suggested. "It might help raise interest."

"I've been working on a new folio," he admitted.

She rummaged in her pocket and produced a card. "Write to me," she said, holding it out. "I would be happy to help you have it shown."

He smiled. "Thank you. I appreciate that."

"How is Tregereth treating you?" Seraphina asked. "He was always . . . punctilious, if I recall." She wrinkled her nose.

"Still is," Adam said, flattered that she had asked. "You should have seen him this morning when I told him I couldn't get the slate he wants. You'd have thought I shot his dog."

Sera turned and looked at Miss Ludgate with an arch expression. "Ah, slate troubles. To have the concerns of a man."

He was no doubt being overly sensitive, but he felt rather wounded by her tone. "I'll happily trade you the slate troubles to write books all day," he drawled. "Sounds far easier on one's back."

"You aren't qualified, I'm afraid," she retorted. "Only supremely ill-used women earn such privileges."

She looked offended by his quip, and he instantly regretted making it. He was being a bit sensitive, because he craved her respect and could sense he didn't have it.

"I'm sorry, you're right," he said sincerely. "I didn't mean to dismiss your work."

"You wouldn't be the first."

All the more reason to be better. "Is that what your book is about?" he asked softly. "Being ill-used?"

He hoped she might confide in him. Tell him a bit about her past.

"Yes," she said, a touch too cheerfully. "'Tis very grim. You shall weep when you read it."

"I hope not," he said.

"If you fail to weep," Miss Ludgate drawled, "she has failed."

Miss Magdalene rolled her eyes. "Ignore them, Mr. Anderson. No one tickles our dear Seraphina and Cornelia like themselves, especially once they've got wine in them. Tell us, how does the slate trouble you? I've never understood how architecture works." She paused and gave him a brilliant smile. "I'm a whore, you see."

Adam nearly choked.

Seraphina did, too, though with laughter. "Oh, Thaïs, you mustn't. He is a *nice* man, remember? It is not kind to shock him."

"Oh, I'm not shocked," he said evenly, though, of course, he was. "It's a dull tale. I ordered a special local variety a month ago, cut to my measurements, and the quarryman lost track of it."

He looked at his nails, feeling self-conscious that these people would be bored by his work. But Seraphina sat up and looked at him with interest.

"Have you spoken to Paul Bolitho?" she asked.

The name meant nothing to Adam. "Not acquainted."

"He's a mason a few villages away. He may have what you need. I can take you tomorrow if you'd like."

He was unduly touched by this offer. "I would appreciate that. Thank you."

"'Tis the least I could do, after you have provided a centurion to guard us," she said, waving his gratitude away.

"You should feel safe in your own home," he said.

She glanced away. He sighed. He was beginning to tire of her brittle mood tonight. He should go.

Miss Magdalene yawned. "We should sleep, my friends. We have to leave at the virgin's slit of dawn." She peeked out at Adam under her extraordinary lashes, as if to check whether he was offended.

She had clearly never cursed with a Scotsman.

He just winked, and she smiled back approvingly.

Cornelia rose. "Sera, give us kisses now so we needn't wake you in the morning."

Adam watched them embrace each other long and hard. He was glad that Sera had such friends. He was, in fact, a touch envious.

"How did you become acquainted with Miss Ludgate?" he asked, when they had gone. "Marianne told me she is quite a celebrated artist."

"Lady Bell introduced all of us. Cornelia is her niece."

"Oh?" They did not share a family resemblance. Lady Bell was so pale and blonde she might be Swedish, while Miss Ludgate was Black.

"Cornelia's mother was Demeter Folie, a famous courtesan in her day, from Barbados. Her father was the youngest son of the previous Duke of Rosemere—a painter who made the family crazed with his politics and the company he kept. He painted Demeter and they fell in love, as the story goes, and had Cornelia. But they died when she was just a baby, in a carriage accident. Rosemere's heir took Cornelia in and raised her. Never had a natural child of his own. But they fell out when she came of age, owing to a scandal over her painting tutor. They don't speak."

Adam winced. He was well aware of the silences and secrets that haunted aristocratic families. He could only imagine what Seraphina left unsaid. "And what of Miss Magdalene?"

Sera snorted. "You really haven't heard of her?"

He shook his head.

"So innocent, our Mr. Anderson," she chuckled. "She is the most expensive Cyprian in all of London. Never sees a lover more than once, and only entertains one man a month. She entered the trade under quite dreadful circumstances but managed to extricate herself from the bawd who procured her, and made a name for herself on her beauty and cleverness. She came to Lady Bell looking for funding to start a charity for girls like her. And Lady Bell introduced the three of us."

He could hear her pleasure in recounting her friends' histories. Her pride in their stories. "And how did you meet Lady Bell?"

She grinned. "Jack. When I left Cornwall, I lived with an aunt in London who was a bit of a Bluestocking. She was friendly with Jack and found me work in his printing shop. Jack was a friend of Cornelia's father, who introduced him to Elinor. She would visit the shop and encouraged me to take up writing. I don't know what might have happened to me if it weren't for her. My aunt died a few years after I moved, and Elinor introduced me to the girls, helped me when I was short of money. She was like a mother, really."

She yawned, and he realized she had likely gone so soft in her demeanor because she was exhausted. He stood up to leave.

Seraphina caught his hand. "Don't go."

He smiled at her apologetically. "I'm tired, lass. And so are you."

"But I have an inquiry," she said, as though this was portentous news. He had never seen her display the signs of drink so obviously. It made him uneasy, drunkenness. And she always seemed to be drinking.

"I shall grant you one question," he allowed.

"Why, if you don't enjoy your work, do you do it?"

He shrugged. "Same reason anyone does. Money."

"But if you want to design bridges and aqueducts, why don't you?"

"Have to be hired first. Competition is fierce for such work. But I'm working on a proposal for a substantial commission now. Hoping it will put Mayhew and I on the map." He felt a twinge of guilt for not disclosing who the project was for, given the foul things Pendrake had said about Seraphina. He hoped she wouldn't ask.

"Who is Mayhew?" she asked instead.

He could have sworn they'd already discussed this. Had she forgotten? "My brother-in-law. James. He runs the other side of the business. The connections and charm and whatnot. Proper gentleman. Unlike myself."

Seraphina gazed at him. "You seem like a proper gentleman to me."

"I'm a decent mimic—" he began to explain.

"Except in bed," she interrupted.

His mouth fell open. "Oh. I—"

Fuck. What had he done? Was that the reason for her strange, edgy mood? Had he been too aggressive the previous evening, misjudged her appetite for such games, and—

"That was a compliment, Adam," she whispered.

He let out a breath. He did not know what to say.

Her lower lip went out. "Oh, poor dear. I didn't mean to imply you were anything other than exactly what I wanted." She got up, stretched up her arms in a manner that could only be described as *erotic*, and walked over to him.

He looked up at her, feeling rather vulnerable. He wanted her affection, after all this tension. He craved it.

But her mood was making him decidedly nervous.

"Have I done something to upset you?" he asked. "I hoped to please you."

"Oh, Adam," she sighed, a sad smile on her face. "I know." She held out her hand. "Come upstairs and I will show you just how much you do."

He took her hand and kissed it. "Another night. You're in your cups."

She laughed wryly. "I'm afraid you will struggle to find a night when I am not in my cups, Mr. Anderson."

He frowned at her. This assertion did not strike him as the least bit humorous.

Seeing that he was not amused, she stood up straighter. "Just a little joke, Adam. I'm not fuddled. Just a bit tipsy. And do you know what I like to do when I'm a bit tipsy?" She fluttered her eyelashes at him and smiled.

"What?" he asked.

"Fuck," she said, with an air of mock gravity.

"I see," he said.

She inclined her head at him, desire glowing in her eyes. "You don't want to?"

He did want to, damn him.

He knew he shouldn't, but the night air was soft and her gown clung to her in such a way that he could tell she was not wearing stays beneath it and he was, to use his sister's word, lonely.

Always lonely.

"It's not that. I don't want you to wake up in the morning and reconsider when it's too late."

She put her fingers in his hair, and began to rub his head lightly, brushing up the strands, grazing his scalp very delicately with the tips of her nails. "I won't reconsider. My attraction to you is not confined to a bottle of wine. I've been thinking about this all night."

He closed his eyes. "Me, too, Sera."

He pulled her toward him, opening his thighs so she could stand inside his legs, and hooked his feet around the backs of hers. He let his arms droop around her waist.

"I want you," she whispered. "Come upstairs or I shall have to throw you over the balustrade and ravish you."

"I'm the one who will be doing the ravishing tonight, lass."

"Then I hope you will get on with it."

She pulled him up and led him inside and up to her room, doing that thing with her hips he'd noticed the night before. Magnificent hips, this woman. So magnificent he reached out, put his hands on them, and stopped her. "Come here."

He pinned her against the wall and kissed her long and hard. She gasped lustily and wrapped her leg around his. Her hand went to his buttocks, pressing him against her.

"You're so hard."

"Looking at you makes me hard. You're a hazard to decency."

"It's true," she said, lifting up her skirts. She propped her foot up on the banister behind him. She was wearing nothing beneath her gown.

He did not need to ask to understand the meaning of this invitation. He put a hand across her slit. She was wet for him. He dragged his fingers over the seam, then to the bobbin that made her squirm. He pressed his prick into her thigh, wondering if he might come just from the heat of her wet cunt on his fingers.

"Bed," he rasped out. "Now."

As soon as they were in her room, she was taking off her gown. He kicked off his boots and worked at his breeches. She turned around, watching him, a hand to her cunny.

"Christ, that *cock*. I *love it*."

She stepped forward and took it in her hand, squeezing at the base. "Fat and hungry and upset," she said. She ran a finger over the ooze at the head, which was indeed an angry shade of purple. "So upset," she murmured. "I know just the treatment."

She reached across to her night table to a jar of oil and produced a condom.

He squinted, trying to see the contraption. It looked like hollowed innards, with a red string attached to the opening. "Sera, we talked about this."

"I know, but I want you inside me. Don't you?" Her eyes were on his penis, and her voice was throaty, hungry.

He wanted to throw her on the bed and take her without another word.

"It's not that I don't want to. It's what can happen afterward."

"Nothing will happen," she laughed. "Here, I'll show you how it works, and you can decide for yourself." She bent down and rolled the thing over his appendage. He did enjoy that, her fitting the tube around him, tying it snugly with string.

"See," she said, admiring her handiwork.

Christ on the cross, with her hands on his prick, adjusting the ties to her satisfaction, he wanted to believe her.

"Be careful to withdraw before you spend. Afterward I'll drink an herb that helps to clear the womb. The combination has never failed me. I would not do it if I felt there was a risk."

He believed her. Or perhaps he just wanted to be inside her so badly he would believe anything.

One time, he reasoned.

Just to remember what it felt like.

Just to have this, once, with her.

"On the bed," he ordered. She smiled and obeyed him.

He lay down beside her and pulled her on top of him. "Last night, you said you wanted to ride me. This morning I spent in my sheets thinking of it."

Her thighs opened at the tip of his cock. He cried out as slowly, slowly, she sank down around him. She paused, arched her back, and let out a ravaged moan.

For a moment, he held her by her waist as she writhed up and down his cock, each time dragging herself lower to take more of him.

When he couldn't stand it, he guided her off of him. "On your hands and knees," he ground out, so aroused he was nearly past the point of sentient speech. She did as he instructed and he held her thighs as he sank into her from behind, slow and hard. She threw back her head and arched her back. He put his hand over her folds and rubbed her swollen wetness as his body remembered why this act had once been his favorite thing on earth.

He drove in and out and she met his rhythm, squeezing his prick with her muscles in a way that made his vision wobble. He felt her building to a peak and abandoned himself to the rhythm of her pleasure, stroking her as he fucked her, listening to her fill the room with the sound of his name. She began to shiver under his hands and he knew his own time was not far off and braced himself for a few good strokes before he would slide out and then it was *happening*, already, too soon, and he reared back and out of her but he was already spilling by the time his full length was free. Seed dripped down his hand.

"Fuck," he murmured.

"What?" she gasped, still shaking.

"It came off."

She cursed.

Before he'd even gathered his wits enough to find a cloth on which to clean his hands, she was off the bed and walking nude across the room.

"Maria, bring up tubs of water," she called out the door. "I need a bath."

She pulled a dressing gown from a hook beside the door, wrapped it around herself, and went barefoot to her dressing table, where she began to pull glass bottles from the drawers and measure out bits of herbs into a mortar, skilled as an apothecary.

Lecherous bloody bastard. What were you doing inside a woman when you know what you're like? Why don't you ever learn?

"I'm sorry, Seraphina," he said.

He was.

More than she could know.

His gut clenched with guilt, for he had succumbed to that old weakness knowing he lacked the strength. Had always lacked the strength. Had always given in to it, let desire occlude his senses, his knowledge of what was right.

She breathed in through her nose. "Never mind. A bath in warm vinegar and a pennyroyal tea will reduce the chances. It is no great crisis."

Damn him for trusting their fates to some innards tied around his prick with twine. Damn him for letting his desire for a woman convince him of something he knew better than to do.

Damn. Just damn.

"You can go, Adam. Maria will be up soon and I'd just as soon she not encounter you undressed."

She said it flatly, the voice that had trembled with passion a minute before now devoid of feeling. He had not bathed himself in glory, but could they not at least discuss the particulars of this unfortunate circumstance with the basic cordiality of neighbors, if not the intimacy of lovers?

He dressed as she busied herself with her potions, fingers nimble as a sorceress brewing the fixings for a spell.

He wondered if beneath this silent ritual, she was as distressed as he was.

He came behind her and pressed his fingers over the bony protrusion of her shoulder blade. "Sera, were anything to happen, I will do the honorable thing."

She whirled around and barked out a laugh. "Adam. *Please.* Don't be absurd." She shook her head and turned back to her herbs.

He'd had enough brittleness from her. They'd just bloody *made love*. "What is absurd about my desire to do the right thing by you?"

She let out a sound that implied the answer, as far as she was concerned, was *everything*. "Adam, how can I make it clearer that what is between us is not the kind of thing that ends in a march to the altar?"

"You needn't speak so snidely. I'm only saying that I wish to be a decent man. We needn't be friends if you find it so distasteful but I don't deserve to be treated like your enemy."

"Oh, I have plenty of enemies," she said quietly. "I know the difference. Did you not see the dead birds they left as gifts?"

The memory of it still made him want to retch. "I did, and you didn't bloody deserve that."

"Of course I didn't deserve it," she said calmly.

He wanted to shout in frustration. "I sometimes wonder if for all your grand ideas you think you do. You deserve kindness, pleasure, *niceness*—"

She held up her palm, her face a symphony of anger. "How dare you assume you know what I think?"

"I only mean—"

"Enough. Just because you fuck a woman doesn't mean you understand her. Go. You have outstayed your usefulness tonight."

Outstayed my usefulness. My God.

He turned and strode to the door. "Happily."

Chapter Seventeen

Seraphina Arden did not traffic in regrets.

Regrets were for people who lacked conviction in their actions. People with pulpy, overswollen hearts. Her heart was as sharp as Cornish shale.

So why couldn't she sleep?

She rose from her bed to her looking glass and observed herself.

You should not have fucked a man like that, her eyes flashed at her, reproachful.

And why not? she retorted, pinning up her hair in a defiant swoop that made her even taller than she was. *No calamity will come of it.*

The calamity is that you hurt him, her eyes responded.

'Tis not my responsibility to protect his tender feelings, she rejoined, anchoring the swoop with pins in a way that made her scalp sting. *He. Was. Warned.*

The woman in the mirror was not impressed. *Leave him alone.*

"Of course I will leave him alone," she said aloud. "He'll want no more of me anyway."

A knock sounded at her door. "Sera? Are you awake?"

It was Elinor.

She rose and opened the door. "I'm sorry, I was talking to my reflection, who is being pugnacious. Did I wake you?"

"No," Elinor said in an unsteady voice. "I had a nightmare and I saw a light in your room."

It was difficult to see her most redoubtable friend look so shaken. Sera reached out and drew Elinor to her breast. "Don't fret. It will get better from here."

Elinor looked unconvinced. "I thought I would make myself a cup of tea to soothe myself. Join me?"

Sera took her lamp and followed Elinor down the stairs to the kitchen.

"Tea will keep you up," she said, rummaging in the cupboard. "Let's have wine instead."

"Darling, you cannot live on wine alone."

"Nor can I live without it," Sera rejoined, pouring two glasses.

Elinor accepted the wine, but with a frown. "I wish you would take care. You are looking dreadfully thin."

The motherly concern in her tone made Sera's throat ache. She would not accept such fuss from Thaïs or Cornelia, but Elinor brought out something softer in her.

Sera put her arms around her friend and rested her head on her shoulder. "I know. I will. It's just that I've been so worried about you."

Elinor kissed her cheek. "I'll be all right, you know. Don't cry."

Sera had not realized she was crying. Oh, how childish. She wiped away the moisture from her eyes.

"We haven't had much time to talk," Sera said, pulling herself together. Now was not the proper time to burden her friend with her turbulent emotions. "Did you have any word from Bell at the asylum?"

"He came a week after he took me there. Offered to let me out if I promised to retract my essay and avow his claims about Jack as true. He was furious when I refused. I've heard nothing since."

Seraphina considered this. "I suspect he and his cronies want Jack's press shut down. Think it will silence the lot of us."

"He does. But he also wants to punish me. The night we fought, before he took me, he said my loyalties are to Jack and not my family, that I'm a moral danger to our children, that I've ruined their chances in society with my radicalism. Usually I pat his brow and assuage him when he gets into one of his tempers but I was so angry that I couldn't bring myself to soothe him. At which point . . ." She shuddered.

A chill went down Seraphina's spine. "Did he *hurt* you?"

Elinor shook her head. "No. He would never deign to lift a hand to me. Such displays are beneath him, in his estimation. He left, and I hoped he would simply becalm himself at one of his clubs, but instead he came back with his solicitor and announced he intended to sue Jack for criminal conversation. I told them there was nothing between us besides intellectual sympathy and friendship, but of course they found the notion of my supposed intellect as suspect as Jack's innocence. They bound my hands and carried me while I fought them, until my son heard the commotion and came upstairs. And then I walked to the carriage willingly, because I could not bear for him to see his mother as a hostage."

Elinor released a quavering sigh.

Sera clutched her hands tightly. "Oh, E. I'm so sorry."

"I can only think of how the children are faring. What they must think of me. What he's told them. For my own sake I can withstand a bloody asylum but when I think of them—"

Sera took her hand. "They love you."

Elinor just shook her head. "I can't believe it's come to this with Bell. We were never a great love match but I did care for him, when we married. But ever since the revolution he's become so irascible, so suspicious and convinced the kingdom is about to topple underneath his feet. There's no reasoning with him. And his friends— Pendrake and Carlton and the like—they only rile him further."

"I'm so sorry, my darling," Sera repeated. It felt silly to say it again, but what else was there to say?

Elinor shook her head. "Don't be sorry, Sera. *Use* it. We must use my story, all of us. This is why the law must change. If he can do this to me, there is no hope for women with fewer friends or resources."

Sera smiled. If she could make one promise, she could make this one: "Don't worry, my dear. We are going to make him regret this."

Elinor took a sip of wine. "You know, for all my anger I can't acquit myself of the feeling that I caused this. He's always been suspicious of my friendship with Jack and truthfully . . . while there is no affair, perhaps I am guilty of harboring more affection for him than is right of a married woman. Perhaps in my heart . . ." She shook her head.

Seraphina leaned down and kissed her friend's temple. "If harboring affection for a gentle man when one's husband is a tyrant is a crime, it's the law that's reprehensible, not the woman. You have done nothing wrong. You must not blame yourself for this."

Elinor bit her lip. They were quiet for a moment.

"I liked your Mr. Anderson," Elinor said. "He seems to care for you."

Sera slumped, still feeling rather sick over the way their evening had ended. "Yes. He persists despite my attempts to disabuse him of the notion that that's wise."

Elinor frowned at her. "Would it truly be so bad, after all this time, to try with someone? Before you push them away?"

She kept remembering Adam's face, looking up at her softly in the moonlight, whispering, *I want to please you.* She put her forehead on the table. "He has two children. A business. He couldn't be with me, even if I wanted him."

Elinor reached across the table and lifted up her chin. "I'm not saying it must be this man, right now. But wouldn't it be such a wild revenge, Sera? If you fell blissfully in love with someone who adored you?"

She would not state the obvious: *No one adores me for long.*

Elinor yawned, which Sera seized as an excuse to end this conversation. She leaned up and kissed Elinor's cheek. "Try to get a little sleep."

ADAM SAT UP and worked on the armory plans, determined not to think of Seraphina. If she did not want to factor into his thoughts as anything other than a body, he would bloody grant her bloody wish.

He let out a sigh of pure disgust.

Fuck.

What had he been doing?

Fuck.

The sun was beginning to break through the night sky and his hands were cramping by the time exhaustion overcame the circling of his thoughts.

He scribbled a note to Marianne not to wake him up, left it on the kitchen table, and climbed into bed, relishing the fact that one could not think when one was sleeping.

He dreamt of violent churning water and ominous cliffs, craggy with the promise of a fall. He dreamt of gales and storms and shipwrecked vessels crashing against breakers.

Of whirlpools.

Of drowning.

But then the water calmed and the sun rose over it in a startling pink glow, and on the beach was Seraphina in her gauzy gown, walking toward the shore.

As she walked, her body swelled, until her breasts strained against her shift. Her stomach was round in a way that was unmistakable and made him ache. She paused and smiled and let the water soak her dress as she walked toward him, the white chemise becoming sheer and clinging to her roundness. His cock and nipples and the filaments of skin along his spine all rose because she was so full and beautiful and he had made her that way.

"Adam," she said, her voice unfamiliar with joy. The same joy that fluttered in him, for they had made a child who would someday splash in the shallows of this cove.

He moved toward her, this magnificent, earthly creature, his Seraphina. He cradled the promise of their family in his heart as he finally reached her and pulled her toward his body, and she was warm and soft, her skin heated by the sun and dripping from the spray. He kissed her, and she tasted of salt and of the sea. Her belly brushed against him and he feasted on her, carnal and possessive and a beast.

Waves rose around them and lifted her dress into a swirl above the water and he grabbed her hips so he could join with her, fill her up with his hunger and his love.

"Adam," she whispered.

"Sera," he murmured, closing his eyes, lost to all but feeling, and he drove up to find his way deeper inside her, when a wave came crashing from behind and sent them tumbling below the surf. He felt her move away as he struggled to lift his head above the cresting sea. Her shift floated just beyond his reach. His nose and lungs and eyes all burnt with salt but he dove back, but he could not find her, and when he came up for breath, the sky had gone a purpled green. The air was cold, and she was nowhere in the churning water.

"Sera!" he shouted.

"Ser—" Another wave knocked into him and he was at the bottom of the ocean, a hundred feet below, and he saw a glimmer of her dress above him, and he swam, fighting to reach the surface, and when he got there, choking, he could not see—

"Adam!"

Oh, thank God.

"Adam!"

He opened his eyes and it was bright again, light streaming through the windows of his Cornwall cottage.

His sister was standing over him, saying his name.

"Adam, you were shouting," Marianne cried. "What is the matter?"

Fuck.

Chapter Eighteen

Seraphina fell asleep at her kitchen table next to a half-empty bottle of wine, like a joke about a bitter woman who'd someday die alone and be eaten by her dogs.

"Dear God, Tompkins, why didn't you rouse me?" she yelped, when she discovered this unhappy circumstance.

Tompkins looked at her without amusement. "I tried. Three times."

"I feel awful." More precisely, she felt like she was made of stiff linen creased by a blistering-hot iron, then crumpled into a drawer by a vengeful maid.

Tompkins ignored her groan, plucking the wine bottle with distaste from the table.

"Oh stop," Seraphina muttered at her. "I know, I know."

Tompkins turned around. "Do you? Because I've pulled you from the floor more often than I care to recall in the last month. You're making yourself ill."

"How fortunate I don't pay you to look after my health."

Tompkins crossed her arms. "I am worried about you."

Sera softened. She walked across the kitchen and draped her arm over Tompkins's shoulder. "I know. I'm going to be better. Now that Elinor is free, there is less to worry me."

Tompkins sighed. "Mr. Anderson is here to see you."

"What?" Sera hissed.

Tompkins gave her a glinting, somewhat evil smile. "He's waiting in the parlor."

God help her. She'd hoped their disagreement would be the kind that faded away from inattention. She did not want to have to look at his face while the memory of her rotten words was still fresh enough to recall verbatim.

"Can you give him tea to distract him while I try to make myself look like someone who did not sleep on her kitchen table?"

"I should tell him exactly where you slept. He'd give you a blistering lecture, I suspect."

"Yes, Tompkins. Luckily, I have already received one from you."

She went up to her room to make herself presentable as best she could, though she looked haggard in a way that could not be disguised by pretty dresses. She could not remember the last time she'd slept more than a few hours in a night.

Well, why bother trying to hide it? Surely he was only here to tell her in the light of day that he no longer wished to see her. She did not need to look like a dew-damp milkmaid beauty for that.

She threw on a drab old brown dress that hardly fit her anymore and went downstairs to face him.

"Sera," Adam said, turning toward her at the sound of her feet on the stairs.

He clutched a handful of flowers. A bunch of spring squill and sheep's-bit and sea pinks, the kind that grew along the coastal path.

He had obviously picked them himself.

He silently held them out to her, his face solemn.

Oh hell and damnation but the sight of him moved her. *Bloody why?*

What kind of foolish woman, knowing what she knew, knowing who she was, knowing the realities and possibilities of the world as well as she did, would see a man like him clutching a bouquet of handpicked wildflowers and feel a surge of anything other than pure dread?

What was this heart, that never stopped fluttering at things it had learned long ago only brought despair?

"Adam," she sighed, staring warily at the flowers but not reaching for them, "thank you, but I'm not—"

"The kind of lady men bring flowers to?" he supplied, lifting up the corner of his mouth.

It both flattered and exasperated her that he knew what she was going to say. "Am I so predictable?"

He leaned back against the kitchen door and looked her up and down. "I don't know what you are, Seraphina Arden. I just know I'm sorry for last night, and I wanted to apologize for storming out of here."

Stop beating like that, she commanded her heart. *Slow down*.

She took the flowers, if only to give herself something to do with her hands.

"You had every right to storm off," she said, trying to affect the tone of a woman who was not melting. "I was being most unpleasant, if I recall."

The intensity of his gaze did not lighten with the breeziness of her tone. "And I should have stayed until we reached an understanding of why we both became so upset," he said patiently.

But she *knew* why she had been upset: she had let things go too far with a man who was not willing to observe her required degree of detachment. Understanding this did not require a conversation; it required an ending.

She played with the bouquet, trying to determine how best to tell him this.

But the flowers pulled at her. They were so helplessly sweet, still warm from his hands. She fussed about for an empty glass to put them in, her fingers oddly clumsy. She opened the wrong cupboard, cursed, found a suitable jar on a shelf, nearly dropped it, all the while feeling his eyes fixed on her in a way that made her nervous, and not knowing what to say.

She tucked the flowers into the jar, and thought of Elinor's words the night before. *Would it truly be so bad, after all this time, to try with someone?*

But how would she even . . . She sighed, stopped fussing with the flowers, and made herself look at Adam directly in the eye. "Perhaps the one who should apologize is me."

He crossed his arms over his chest, waiting for her to explain. It was excruciating to be looked at so closely. She imagined he could see every line in her skin, every red vein around her nose, every drop of shame at how she had behaved.

She looked down at her hands. "I was unfair to you last night. I do not usually trifle with men who care about such things as honor. I'm sorry that I urged you to do something I knew very well you would likely regret."

He came toward her, put his hands on her twisting fingers, and brought them to his lips. "Lass, I wanted it, too. You're not to blame."

Oh God, he was so *kind*.

"I'm sorry," she whispered. "I lost my head. You unnerve me, you see."

He drew her closer, into an embrace.

No. Her pulse beat in frantic time. *No! No! No!*

She could not be trusted with him. Flinty hearts like hers endangered softer ones like his. She cleared her throat. "Adam, I think it's best we not . . ."

His arms loosened around her and he looked down at her face, waiting for her to finish the thought. Her heart beat at double pace. Every instinct she possessed was in turmoil.

Flee, her body ordered. *Try*, her mind insisted.

"Did you still wish to see Paul Bolitho?" she squeaked out in a voice she barely recognized. "I can take you, if you like."

He opened his mouth, paused, then laughed softly, like he was relieved. "Yes. If you wouldn't mind the errand."

"Would you like to go this morning?" she said quickly, before she lost her nerve. "I'm not in the mood to write."

He searched her eyes, not speaking. "Aye, if you have time," he finally said, looking utterly confused.

"I do!" She gave him her most enthusiastic smile and shoved her shaking hands into the pockets of her gown.

"I'm relieved." He shook his head, and slowly led. "For a moment I thought you were about to send me away for good."

Try, she kept repeating in her head. *Try*.

She walked across the kitchen, took his chin in her hand, and gave him a short, sweet kiss. "No, Adam. I'm glad you came back."

"Me, too." He lingered in her grip for a minute, like he was soaking in affection. Finally, he pulled away. "Let me fetch my cart from Tregereth's. I'll return for you in half an hour."

When he left, she slumped against the counter, feeling like she'd just climbed to the summit of a cliff.

Tompkins walked in, took in the sight of her hunched over the butter, and shook her head. "Sent him away? Pity. I liked him more than your usual lot."

"Well, don't be too despondent," Sera sighed. "He'll be back in a few minutes."

Tompkins slowly lifted one eyebrow. "Oh?"

Sera could not fault her secretary for seeming incredulous. She scarcely believed it herself.

"We're going to buy slate." She tried saying this as though it was normal behavior.

"Ah," Tompkins said, nodding in mock comprehension. "Slate. Of course. You have always been so fiercely interested in minerals."

Sera plucked a flower from the noseguy and tossed it at Tompkins's gray head. "You are insufferable. Can a woman conduct a summer affair without harassment from her secretary?"

Tompkins shook her head. "A summer affair," she mused to the kitchen walls. "Next she'll tell me she's joined the Tories."

Sera rolled her eyes. "Maria?" she called. "Come and make your mistress comely."

Sera tried not to think of anything beyond her reflection as Maria twisted up her hair and helped her with her stays. Instead she applied bergamot oil to her neck and salve to her lips and smiled serenely despite the way her stomach dropped when Tompkins came to the door to announce her "suitor" had returned.

"Thank you, Tompkins," she said, flouncing past her.

"Enjoy your outing," her secretary added, smiling rather sentimentally, in a way Seraphina did not like.

"I shall *try*," Sera muttered. But in truth, she felt oddly giddy about the prospect of a morning drive along the country roads with Adam.

She walked out into the morning and smiled at Adam. In his horse cart he looked like a handsome farmer come to collect a maiden he was courting.

How exotic.

He gestured to the road beyond her gate. "Are you expecting someone?"

"No." She shaded her eyes to see what he was looking at.

A stately carriage was traveling up the road at breakneck speed, throwing up dust behind it.

A laugh bubbled up from her chest, deep and bitter, as she recognized the colors of the coachman's livery.

HAD HE IMAGINED that just for a moment, Seraphina had smiled at him like an excited maiden? Had she ever looked at him like that before—like she was girlishly pleased to see him?

Now she was laughing grimly as she observed the carriage pulling through her gates.

"Who is it?" Adam asked.

"Lord Bell," she muttered, striding to greet the vehicle.

It came to a stop and an egg-shaped man with a bald pate stepped out, not waiting for his coachman to open the door.

"Lord Bell, I thought that was you," Sera said pleasantly.

"Where is she?" he barked at her, belligerent from his expression to his tone. Adam jumped to his feet and watched the man closely, poised to get between him and Seraphina if need be. But Sera paid no attention.

"Pardon? Who do you mean?" she asked Lord Bell, cocking up her head to one side.

"My wife," he snarled.

Sera pretended to be taken aback. "I'd love to know the answer myself, my lord."

Adam marveled at her demeanor in the face of Bell's barely checked fury. She did not seem the slightest bit afraid.

Bell walked toward her with his fists clenched so tightly they were red at the knuckles. "Don't waste my time, Miss Arden." He glared angrily over his shoulder at the coach, where a second, thinner man was climbing down with obvious trepidation. "Hogue!"

Hogue cowered at the booming of Bell's voice, but his demeanor changed when he caught sight of Seraphina. "That's one of them," he cried. "That's one of the ladies responsible for the abduction."

Sera looked upon him blankly. "Apologies, but I've never seen this man before in my life."

Bell stepped toward her until his barrel chest nearly touched her breasts. She was taller than him, but his aggression belied his stature. Adam stepped closer to her side, just in case she needed someone to lunge for the man's throat.

"My lord, perhaps I can help," he said, keeping his tone polite enough, but using his body to communicate that by "help" he meant wallop Bell if he moved any closer to Seraphina.

Bell ignored him, pointing his finger so close to Seraphina's face she could no doubt smell his breakfast.

"I know you took Elinor. Produce her or I will go inside and drag her out myself."

Sera stepped back distastefully. "You are welcome to come inside. Though I haven't the slightest idea what you're raving about." She turned around and opened the door to her house. "Tompkins," she called, "we have an unexpected guest. Our old friend Lord Bell is here. It seems he has misplaced his wife. Do show him around."

She held open the door and stared down Bell. "Go on. I'll be right here. Make yourself entirely at home."

With a string of curses, Bell stormed past her, dragging his man behind him.

Hogue paused and narrowed his eyes at Seraphina. "You are a liar, madam. You most certainly were at my hospital yesterday."

She smiled at him sadly. "Sir, I believe you are suffering hallucinations. Perhaps you should have your sanity checked."

His mouth dropped in outrage and he scurried after Bell inside the house.

Sera sat down calmly on a bench, as though nothing in the world was wrong. Not knowing what else to do, Adam sat down beside her.

The sounds of clattering footsteps and colorful invectives streamed from the open windows of the house.

"Are you all right?" he asked in a low voice.

She leaned back contentedly and gazed at the clouds floating in the sky. "Of course. It's such a pretty morning. Quite clear for summer."

He snorted. "Yes, Sera. Beautiful weather we're having."

In her position, he would be terrified that Bell might find some trace of his wife's presence and go straight to the magistrates. But Sera seemed utterly at ease. Almost pleased.

Perhaps this was a trait one needed to become a creature like Seraphina Arden: the ability to feast on threats and turn them into strength.

She peeked at him from the corner of her eye and smirked as more clattering boomed up from the second floor. "Please excuse my guests. So entitled, the nobility."

"Very rude," he agreed.

She tapped her fingers on her knee like she was bored. "He'll likely take his time. What shall we do to amuse ourselves?"

When she looked so playful, with mischief dancing in her eyes, all he wanted was to lean over and kiss her. But he couldn't do that with Bell about.

So instead, he pulled out the sketchpad and charcoal he always kept in his pocket. "I haven't had my chance to draw you."

She arched her neck and stretched to set off her bosom attractively. "Shall I pose for you?"

He laughed. "No, just sit and be yourself."

He lowered himself onto the grass in front of the bench, facing her, and began to sketch. First the firm lines of her brows and jaw. Then her elegant long neck. Her complicated nose.

Christ, he loved her face.

She became restless with his eyes flickering over her and started playing with her hair.

"Don't fidget," he ordered.

She grimaced. "I don't do well with boredom, Adam."

"Where the bloody hell is she?" Bell's voice rang out from above.

"You find this boring?" Adam asked, wincing at the noise.

She rolled her eyes. "He's the worst kind of bore. I can't fathom why Elinor married him."

Adam pretended to consider this. "Oh, I don't know. I found him rather charming."

She snorted. "Clearly you have very eccentric taste." She gestured at herself dramatically. "But then, I suppose we knew that about you."

He shook his head. "My taste for you should not be classed as an eccentricity, Miss Arden. You are very pleasing to the eye."

She blushed bright pink. He grinned down at his pad. He had not expected she was the type to swoon at compliments. It made him want to pin her down and tell her in excruciating detail how much he loved her nose, and hips, and height, and wild hair, until she squirmed about in mortification. He chuckled to himself at the notion of it, and she pursed her lips.

"What?"

He grinned. "Just imagining what I am going to do to you later, when Bell isn't poking about."

She smiled. "You are quite skillful at that."

He gave her his most sinful leer. "Just wait."

She widened her eyes in mock outrage. "I meant at drawing, Mr. Anderson."

"Pity," he said, returning to his sketch.

She snorted. "Do you do it often?"

He lifted his eyes to let them laze over her breasts. "Every day, if I can."

She reached out and tapped his knee with her boot. "You are a pest. I am trying to ask about your art. Do you still paint?"

He dropped his attempts at banter, rather flattered that she wanted to know about him. "Not often. I had to give it up to begin my apprenticeship. It felt . . . like I was deluding myself. But I enjoy sketching."

Her eyes darkened. "It's not too late, Adam."

He was touched and altogether embarrassed by this statement. "Oh, it is. Don't spare my feelings, I'm quite at peace with my lot."

He glanced down and added some final bits to the shading around her eyes. "There," he said. "All done."

He hoped she liked it. He felt a bit self-conscious, making a show of his artistic skill when she was so often surrounded by *real* artists.

She scooted down from the bench and reached for the sketch. "Oh, I'm nervous. I hope you haven't done me as a witch. Let me see."

Her face went slack when he handed it to her.

Oh dear. She didn't like it, and she was trying not to be unkind about his skill.

"I'm just an amateur," he said quickly, blushing. "I hope I didn't exaggerate my talents."

"No . . . it's very skillful, it's just . . ." She held the sketch up, confused. "You made me beautiful."

He was surprised by this assertion. He had not meant to flatter her with an especially pretty likeness. He shrugged. "I only drew you as you are."

A ghost of a smile played on her lips, before she squeezed them together. "Well. I must question the accuracy of your eye. But I am very pleased."

Her voice on that last word was so soft and flushed with simple happiness that all the restraint flooded out of him. He leaned toward her, and she looked up into his eyes, and he reached out—

"I'm going to have you bloody well arrested as soon as I find her!" Bell shouted, crashing out of the front door. "You, Willow, the whole conspiring lot of you."

Sera turned away, startled, and Adam dropped his hand and they both leapt to their feet.

Hogue scurried after Bell, looking like a terrier who'd been caught shitting in his owner's shoes.

"I wish you the best of luck in finding her," Sera called brightly to Bell's back.

Bell whirled around. "You are an utter disgrace." His gaze turned to Adam. "And *you*, sir, should be more careful who you consort with, whoever you are."

With that, the two men climbed into the carriage and drove off.

It was only then that it occurred to Adam that Lord Bell may very well know Lord Pendrake. And if he did, this day could come to haunt him.

"Now then," Sera said cheerfully. "Stone?"

Chapter Nineteen

*F*or having so recently been accused of abducting a viscountess and threatened with the magistrates, Seraphina was in rather high spirits as they drove to Paul Bolitho's.

It was easy to enjoy Adam's handsome presence and dry wit, now that she had resolved to *try*.

"How long do you intend to stay in Cornwall?" she asked as he steered the cart down the narrow, gorse-lined road. She hoped he would not leave before she did.

"Depends on how quickly I can procure the stone and finish the structural work. After that I'll leave the joiners and painters to it. I need to be back in London in six weeks at the latest."

"Ah, you will outlast me here. What will you do without my company?"

He lifted the corner of his mouth. "Waste away in despair."

She smiled. "I should hope so."

"In truth, I have quite a lot of work to do. New plans for a project Mayhew and I are proposing."

They passed a pile of torches in the center of the village square. She clapped her hand to her mouth. "Golowan. Oh, the procession is tonight! I nearly forgot."

"The children haven't. Adeline has insisted on wearing her costume all day." Adam hesitated. "I wasn't sure if I should mention it, given the threats you've received, but they are still hoping you will join us." He looked over at her, his eyes hooded. "If you'd rather not, I understand."

She could tell he wanted her to go. She *should* go. She'd adored the procession as a girl. Why should she let threats and posters keep her from enjoying herself? "I won't disappoint your children. Of course I'll come. Besides, I can't leave them to make the journey to town in your horse cart."

"They like my horse cart," was all he said. But he was smiling in a way that made her stomach resume that fluttery feeling, so she refrained from speaking except to direct him to Paul Bolitho's workshop.

And yet, now that the promise of an evening out in town hung over her, her light mood began to drain away. Would dressing in festive attire disguise her identity enough to celebrate unnoticed? What would Adam's children think, if she was jeered? And what would he think, seeing her as an object of derision? It was one thing to know about her reputation. It was quite another to endure the worst of the harassment. She was hardened to the abuse, but the Andersons would feel the sting and flinch from it—or from her.

She cleared her throat. "It's just to the left."

Adam turned the cart. "Just here?" he asked.

"Yes, with the sign."

"Are you all right?" he asked quietly. "You look pale."

She was not sure. At the sight of the mason's snug stone building, she regretted coming. She'd often visited here with her father, and it was exactly as she remembered it.

But *she* wasn't. She was Seraphina Arden now.

And Paul Bolitho had been *her father's* friend, not hers.

"Sera?" Adam reached over to offer her help stepping down.

She snatched her hand away so quickly he looked like he'd been burned.

"Aren't you coming?" he asked.

She shook her head. She could no longer fathom why she'd felt it would be a good idea to accompany him here. She did not want to see Paul Bolitho. Or rather, she did not want to subject herself to how Paul Bolitho might react to seeing her.

"I'll wait here, if you don't mind," she said.

"It's getting hot. Won't you be uncomfortable in the sun?"

"No, it's pleasant in the breeze."

There was no breeze.

Adam gave her a long, searching look. "Sera, if you don't wish to see him, why did you come with me?"

She was taken aback by the directness of his question. She did not wish to confess that a specific kind of fear was curling up around her lungs. One she'd first felt sixteen years ago, when the rumors had begun to spread. When things she'd only told her lover suddenly became a kind of village lore, and people stopped meeting her eye in the square.

She decided there was no use making an excuse. Her behavior *was* odd, given that this outing had been her suggestion. "Paul was a close friend of my father's, and I have not seen him since we became estranged. I'd rather not come in just to be tossed out. Please don't mention me to him."

"Lass," Adam said softly, looking at her like she was an orphan selling cloth scraps in the street.

"Go on." She waved him away rather truculently and shaded her eyes from the sun to keep him from continuing to look upon her with that unsettling pity. She was relieved when he finally went inside.

It made her irritable to be observed acting in a way that could only seem pathetic. Adam couldn't know what it felt like to be cast out of a place. How you never knew who might welcome you and who might curse you and who might leave repulsive threats on your terrace in the night. How it was easier to stay away and not have to learn the answers.

She could not account for why she kept risking chance encounters when she knew the town was littered with memories and people like traps strung up in the forest. She must stop this.

"Why, Seraphina Arden!" a warm voice called.

Paul Bolitho strolled out of his workshop with Adam, grinning at her like she was his own daughter. "I'd heard a rumor you were back in town and didn't believe it until Mr. Anderson said you'd recommended this place."

"Mr. Bolitho mentioned he'd like to see you," Adam called. "I gave him the convenient news you were a few yards outside his door."

She cut Adam a dark look for his perfidy. "I . . . yes, here I am."

"Come down and let me look at you, child," Paul said, holding out his gnarled laborer's hand to help her.

She took it, and he drew her to himself in an embrace. "'Tis good to see you, Sera. You look well." He stepped back. "So tall, just like your papa."

She ignored this comparison and focused on Paul's kindness. "How is your family, Paul?" she asked.

"Oh, well enough. Harold's gone to the navy and Small will take over the shop one of these days. I'd bring him out to greet you but he's in town with his sons, preparing for the procession."

She smiled. "Give him my regards."

He nodded. "Are you staying at the old house?"

"I am."

Paul grinned. "Your papa would be pleased. Briony wanted to sell the place and move nearer to her family in Penzance, but he wouldn't let her. Said he wanted you to be able to find him whenever you decided to come home."

She stared at him, unsure if she had correctly followed what he said. "Papa said *what*?"

Paul nodded, his eyes misted with nostalgia. "He missed you something dreadful, child. Never was the same after you left. Walked around like one of his lungs was missing."

She felt like she might float away. Like nothing held her to this earth.

She forced her face to remain in a semblance of a smile. "It is good to see you, Paul. Adam, if you are finished here, I must return home."

She permitted Paul to give her one more hug—overly tight—and joined Adam in the horse cart. She stared straight ahead until they were out of sight of the workshop.

Adam smiled at her. "He thinks the world of you, Sera. He was so pleased when I mentioned you."

"Why did you do that?" she hissed. "I asked you not to."

He flinched, worrying the reins in his hands. "I thought I'd mention your name and see whether he seemed kind. And he did, so I told him you were here."

She glared out at the tall hedgerows that lined the road, feeling trapped by them.

"You're upset," Adam said.

"Yes, I *am* upset."

He bit his lip. "I would never deliberately put you in a difficult position," he said softly. "I suppose I thought it odd that you spent an hour driving out to this place, to see a man you clearly have a high opinion of, just to sit outside. I thought maybe you lost your nerve."

"Lost my nerve!" she exploded. "I broke a woman out of an asylum yesterday and defied her husband this morning without breaking a sweat. You think I'd cower before the village stone mason?"

"No, Sera. I know you are courageous. I just thought that it might be nice to see someone who welcomed you. An old friend. I'm sorry if I misjudged that."

Dear God. This was why she did not *try*.

"*I* make my decisions, Adam. I do not need a man to make them for me out of his supposedly better judgment. Do not act against my wishes again."

"Understood," he said. "And I'm sorry."

She sat silently, still seething. Her father's face, contorted in rage, kept flashing through her mind.

"I can't believe he said that," she muttered. She didn't really want to talk to Adam after his betrayal, but twisting the sentiment around in her head was causing her to feel like she might combust.

"Said what?" Adam asked.

"That my father thought I would return."

How could he think she would believe herself welcome? And why had he never written? She was not hard to find.

"You didn't think your pa might miss you?" Adam said softly.

She snorted. "Certainly not."

And it was just as well she hadn't known. If she had, she might have been tempted to forgive him out of sentimentality. And her opinions on sentimentality were no warmer than her opinions on regret.

Adam was staring off ahead at the dusty road. "I'm sure he did, Sera. Perhaps if you had a child, you'd think differently. It's a tragic thing, to lose one."

She went very, very still. "Yes."

He glanced at her, and she contorted her mouth into a blank line so that he would not see how his words made her want to slap him, and said, "I suspect Mr. Bolitho exaggerates. My father could have found me easily, if he wanted to. He was alive when my book was published."

Adam considered this. "Sometimes it's hard to face people that you've hurt, even if you long to make amends. He might have been afraid. Or ashamed."

Oh, poor dear man who cast his daughter out. What a pity. She smiled tightly. "One can avoid such difficulty by not hurting people in the first place."

Adam frowned. "I'm so sorry that he hurt you."

"Don't be," she snapped. This conversation was growing entirely too damp. "It made me what I am. Soft treatment makes soft people."

It made her feel better to say that. It was true, and she would do well to remember it next time she lost her wits over a bunch of wildflowers.

He looked at her from the corner of his eye. "Is softness such a crime?"

She chose to treat the question as rhetorical. She did not answer questions that incriminated her.

They lapsed into an uncomfortable silence.

She began to feel badly for speaking harshly to Adam. It *had* been nice to see Paul Bolitho, she supposed. Adam had meant to be kind.

But she could not admit that now.

"This heat is unbearable," she said, offering him the comment like a token of peace.

Adam wiped his own brow. "'Tis muggy indeed. Unpleasant weather here in Cornwall."

"Like the people," she muttered.

He laughed at this harder than the quip deserved, like he was eager to restore their previous good humor. "Shall we stop somewhere for lemonade?" he asked.

"You know, there used to be a woman who sold ices on Golowan day at the market. I wonder if she is still there. Turn here, by the square."

The town was full of people buying festive foods and making preparations. She spotted several people she remembered—the vicar and the butcher and Abby Halliwell, who had married Tom Maben. She pulled her hat down over her eyes, lest she be recognized, but no one paid her any mind.

The woman with the ices stood in front of the post office, exactly where she'd always been. Sera hopped down, leaving Adam with the horses, and walked across the street to buy two sweets. She licked the edge of hers quickly so it wouldn't melt, walking briskly back to deliver Adam's to him before it was a puddle in her hand. In her rush, she stumbled on a loose paving stone and her hat came off her head.

She knelt on the paving stones to pick it up, juggling the ices in one hand.

When she stood up, Baron Trewlnany was staring at her from across the square, his face contorted in disgust.

SERAPHINA LOOKED LIKE she might faint.

Adam followed her gaze to see what had alarmed her. She was looking at a handsome, well-dressed man with auburn hair who stood regarding her with a dark expression on his face. He was flanked by a group of ginger-headed children.

The littlest child pulled his arm, and this seemed to break him from his trance. He turned to his family and ushered them away into a waiting carriage.

The woman Sera had greeted at the inn came walking out of the haberdasher with a package and climbed into the carriage after them.

Seraphina remained fixed where she stood, watching the carriage drive away as nectar from the melting ices dripped down her fingers. Her face was like a dead woman's.

"Sera?" he called, walking toward her.

She started, as if she had forgotten he was waiting.

Slowly, she made plodding steps back to the cart. He took the ices so she could climb up. She did so without a word.

"What's wrong?" he asked.

"Nothing," she said absently.

"You look like you've seen a ghost."

"Just old friends," she said faintly. "People I haven't thought of in some time."

She did not eat her ice. She held it out over the edge of the buggy as they drove and let it fly out of her hand. Her distress was so obvious that he could not in good conscience eat sweets, and he threw his out, too.

He hated to see how much this place had hurt her. How it had the power to diminish her.

He wished he had not encouraged her to make this drive.

"Sera," he said slowly, "perhaps it would be best for you not to come tonight. You're welcome, of course. But if it's too painful to be here, you needn't come for our sake. The children will understand."

She shook her head. "Nonsense. Of course I'll come. I'm quite all right."

It was obvious she wasn't. She worked her fingers together in her lap with such agitation that he wanted to take her hands in his to calm them. But when he tried to touch her—just a gentle pat over her knuckle—she pulled her hand out of reach.

They drove back to her house in silence.

"I'll collect you in my carriage at seven," she said when they arrived. "Have the children wear gloves as the torches can be hot."

"You're sure you wish to come?"

She sighed, like he was trying her last nerve. "I wouldn't miss it, Adam."

He was not reassured. He wanted to follow her inside and discuss the matter further, but she was already walking toward her door, and her posture did not suggest she would welcome being followed.

"We'll look forward to it," he called after her uneasily.

She nodded without turning back around, and went inside.

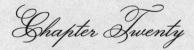

First she resolved not to think about it.

It was nothing. The fact that Trewlnany had a family was not new information. That her hands had not stopped shaking since she'd seen him was ridiculous.

When another quarter hour passed and still she could not think of anything save the sight of Trewlnany with four red-headed children, she decided to pour herself a dram of brandy to calm her nerves.

One dram was not going to do the trick, it seemed. She poured another.

The spirits, as spirits did, reduced the gnawing sharpness of the present.

Which left her with the past.

She had come here to stare it down but she had not found the fortitude to hold the memories squarely in the foreground of her mind. She'd yelled at Adam for doubting her bravery but he was exactly right: she was a coward.

She had to stumble upon Trewlnany to force the past fully into focus.

But now she felt it.

All of it.

It was so bright and hot it burned her belly, sent acid rising to her throat.

She prepared a fresh quill and resolved to write down whatever came into her head.

Damn Paul Bolitho, but what came to her was her father.

Every daughter wants her father's good opinion, she scrawled.

> *Even if she does not like him, even if no love is lost between them, she desires the affection of her parent. Mine was not fond of me. I was a tall and solemn-looking girl responsible by way of cursed birth for the death of his wife, for which neither of us could entirely forgive me.*
> *When my courses stopped, I knew that I would lose what little esteem he had ever had for me.*
> *But I also knew that he would save me.*

She paused, closed her eyes. Took another sip.

> *For there's another truth about girls and fathers. A daughter never doubts her father's power. We are raised to believe he is omnipotent, second only to our Maker.*
> *And so I confessed my sins. I told him of my lover, of the promises he'd made. I thought my father could take these things and transform them into that glimmering solution: marriage.*
> *As I told him my secret, I saw hatred cross his features.*
> *Not disappointment. Hatred.*

The nib of her quill caught against the paper and discharged a spray of ink. She paused to mop it up with her sleeve. The ink bled into the papery lines at her wrist.

He hated me because he knew what was and was not possible. He knew what his powers were, and he knew their limits. I made him see the exact size of his influence.

Some things, once done, cannot be fixed by fathers.

That was when I understood what it meant to be a wealthy tradesman's daughter.

I was not the kind of girl whose honor would be redeemed by an inconvenient marriage.

I was the kind of girl who's offered money, not redemption.

She thought of the kingfishers. She thought of how she'd been paralyzed at Paul Bolitho's, sitting hot and rancid in the sun, remembering the taunts and jeers that had greeted her once whenever she'd gone outside.

The stories about me began to spread. Whispers of my wantonness. My lusts. People who'd known me since I was a baby saw me on the street and moved away, like I might infect them with disease.

I wanted to believe my lover had not spread these whispers, but only him, his father, and my own parent knew of my condition.

He made my private passion a public perversion.

She did not elaborate on his reasons. That there were things he'd told her, things she knew that could damn him. They were not part of this story. She'd promised him she'd never tell, and if she did, she was no better than he was. Besides, the point remained:

He destroyed my name to spare his own.

Perhaps I let him.

After all, who would believe me, if I had named him? Who would believe me, if I said he'd professed love, promised marriage?

Why would a man like him say such a thing to a girl like me?

And so I went from a fallen girl to a ruined woman.

She read over what she'd written, trying to collect herself by focusing on the words.

The prose was overly florid, but then, that was the effect of the brandy. She'd revise the pages later. She checked the clock. Five. She had time still. Better to write while the words beckoned. Then she'd sober up with bitter tea and go to collect the Andersons.

The solution was marriage to a man forty years my senior, a cousin of my father's. I would travel to his plantation in Barbados and become mistress of his home, where three previous wives had died in childbirth or illness. An aunt whispered to me of the state in which he kept his slaves. Of the brutality, the heat, the maladies, the desperate air of madness.

When he arrived to claim me, he was crass and ignorant and looked on me in a way that made my skin crawl.

It woke me from the stupor of my broken heart.

To save myself, I announced the truth of my condition at our engagement supper.

She could feel them, her family, looking at her. The shock. Her father, pretending she was joking.

Her insistence: *I am with child.*
The planter leaving in a rage, yelling he'd been duped.

My father locked me in my bedchamber and seethed
so volubly the house shook.
    My aunt offered me a room in London and pas-
sage on a mail coach and I took it.
    The day I left was the last time I saw my father
alive.

She was trembling, her writing scarcely legible, but
she could not stop now.
There was only one thing to do. Finish it.
Tell the end of the damned story. The part she'd barely
acknowledged to herself in years.
She needed more brandy.
She emptied the rest of the bottle into her glass.

The blood appeared on my linen three months
before the child's term was due.
    The child. That was how I thought of her.
    I resented her for springing up inside of me, a liv-
ing embodiment of my shame who kicked my ribs
and swelled my stomach, growing like a tumor as my
guilt became more evident to all who looked on me.

Oh, she couldn't write this down. It was sickening and
shameful.
But was that not the purpose of this book? To give
testament to the cost? To make them feel what it was
like? How they made you doubt yourself, hate yourself,
believe you were at fault. That it got inside you, until
the things you said about yourself were crueler than the
whispers on the street.

Her hand kept scrawling, flinging ink.

When I saw the blood matted on my thighs, I felt a surge of vindication. "It wasn't meant to be."

The moment she appeared, I knew she wouldn't live. She was so, so very small, scarcely larger than a pilchard. I knew she wouldn't live and I knew equally that I must save her.

The midwife and my aunt tried to take her from me and I fought them off and barred the door with a strength I should not have possessed but somehow did. I pressed her to my skin and tried to transfer life to her from me by contact. I tried to will it to her, through some alchemy of love and prayer and mother's milk and desperation.

Perhaps it worked.

She lived for two hours.

Sera got up and paced the room. Her desk looked like the wreckage of an abandoned printing shop, pages draped over every surface drying, dotted here and there with blots of ink and fingerprints and spilled brandy.

She wanted to rip the pages up and throw them in the sea.

She sat back down, replaced the nib in her quill.

They told me it was a blessing that she passed peacefully.

But I knew it was a second punishment. Not for my original crime of wanting him, but for my second crime, forever unforgivable, of not wanting her until it was too late. Until I got my wish.

The rest of the story has been told before and I will not repeat it here.

> *But I will add one postscript, as illustration.*
> *For there were two parties that made my daughter and wrote the story of my ruin. One whose life was splintered by it, who lost everything. And one who married, had a family, sits in the House of Commons, and who will one day inherit a fortune and claim his place in the House of Lords.*

She scribbled out his name as the clock struck seven.

WHEN SEVEN O'CLOCK came and Seraphina did not arrive, Adam was relieved, as the children had fussed over their costumes and were not yet ready to depart.

When a quarter past seven arrived and still there was no sign of her, he began to worry.

When the clock struck half past, and Jasper stared, long-faced out the window, fretting they would miss the procession, Adam began to be quite irritated.

He was just about to set out for her house to inquire when Jasper, peering out the window, cried, "I see the carriage!"

Thank God. He'd been contemplating disappointed children and a difficult conversation with Seraphina.

He and Marianne ushered the children out the door as the carriage approached the house. However, it was not Seraphina who greeted them.

"Good evening, Mr. Anderson," Tompkins said through the open window. "I'm afraid Miss Arden has fallen ill. She sends her apologies and asked me to accompany you and the children to Golowan in her stead. I am from Penzance, so I am quite familiar with the customs."

"Fallen ill? How dreadful," Marianne said. "Perhaps I should go and keep her company, since she will miss the festivities."

A strained look passed over Tompkins's face.

Sera had not fallen ill.

"No, she would hate to think of you missing the procession on her account," Tompkins said. "She sends her regards."

Damn her. She'd tossed them aside without so much as the courtesy to write.

As much as he sympathized with Seraphina's reluctance to go out in public, he would not tolerate her trifling with his children's emotions. He'd given her the chance to beg off well in advance, and she had insisted on raising their hopes instead.

His children looked up at him. "We are to go *without* Miss Arden?" Adeline asked. She had lately developed the habit of repeating unpleasant facts as questions, as though by framing the unwanted thought as a query she might find the substance of it miraculously changed.

He shook off his frustration. He did not want his gripe with Seraphina to cast a pall on his children's adventure. "Yes, but we'll have a wonderful time with Miss Tompkins," he assured Adeline.

He took her hand and helped her climb inside the carriage. Jasper was next, then Marianne.

"I'll ride up with the coachman," he said. He wanted to be able to see what they were approaching before arriving. If the festival was as fiery as Seraphina had suggested, he did not want to put his children in the thick of it.

The roads were crowded with merrymakers and the coach fell into a queue. As they approached the square, they heard the drums and flutes of Celtic tunes.

His anxiety eased as they came in sight of the square. The streets were filled with families and many of the revelers were dressed in costumes like the ones Sera had given to Jasper and Addie.

"Shall I let you out here, sir?" the coachman asked.

"Yes, in front of the milliner's shop."

He tried to pay attention to his children's exclamations over various curiosities and revelers—women dancing, men wearing hoods like dragon's heads—but he could not shake his discomfort over Seraphina's sudden absence. The children kept asking after her, a sign that they were more disappointed than they'd let on. Jasper insisted they buy her a Celtic amulet sold by a man dressed as a wizard at one of the market stalls, so that she would have something of the night when she had recovered her health.

As they moved away from the square and along the procession route that lined the street to the ocean, he felt worse. The air smelled like gunpowder from the torches carried by the parading throngs, and the firecrackers that the boys and men sparked in the streets.

"What's that?" Addie asked, pointing in the distance to a large dummy of a crowned man hoisted in the air on a throne held above the heads of marchers in the procession.

"An effigy," Tompkins told her.

"What's an effigy?"

"It's the likeness of a person people wish to mock. An old custom," she explained.

"Who is it supposed to be?" Jasper asked.

Tompkins squinted. "Looks like King Louis of France."

The children were distracted by a group of dancers passing by. Tompkins showed Adeline and Marianne how to do the steps. As the marchers holding effigies drew nearer, the crowd grew more raucous, by turns cheering, hissing, and waving torches high above their heads. Adam squinted to make out the other figures. There was General George Washington, who'd bested the Crown in the colonies. Someone who must be a local politician, whose likeness Adam didn't recognize.

Marianne pointed in the distance. "It's Miss Arden," she whispered in his ear. "In the procession. An effigy."

Christ.

Sure enough, a giant dummy of her made from sticks and straw stuffed into a crimson dress, loomed in the distance. It had long, tangled clumps of seaweed for hair and the word *harlot* painted on its chest.

"Jezebel!" a voice shouted.

Someone threw a piece of fruit, and it hit the dummy in the face.

To Adam's horror, someone threw a torch. The effigy's hair caught fire. The marchers stopped and beat the dummy on the ground to put out the blaze.

The violence of it—the gleeful hatred—made him want to retch.

He was glad Sera had not come. He would hate to see her watching this. The last of his anger melted, replaced by a fierce desire to go to her.

"It's getting late," he told the children. "Let's buy pasties and take them back to the carriage so we can be home in time to see the fireworks."

"No!" Addie protested. "I want to see the end of the procession."

But he did not want his children to connect the flaming woman being beaten to the approving profane hisses of the crowd with the lady who had been a friend to them.

It took an age to procure food and find the carriage and by the time they did the pasties had gone cold and the children were crabbish at being made to leave. When they reached his house, he helped Marianne and the children down but did not go inside.

"I'm going with Tompkins to Miss Arden's to check in on her," he told Marianne. "Let them watch the fireworks."

Tompkins did not look pleased to hear this. "Sir, I'm not sure Miss Arden would welcome company tonight. She's likely asleep."

"If she is, I won't disturb her."

They traveled the short distance up the road in silence. Finally Tompkins spoke. "Mr. Anderson, Miss Arden won't like me saying this, but she isn't ill. She sometimes has . . . spells of turbulent emotion. She's wont to drink more than she ought. I don't think she would wish for you to see her when she's in that state."

"Too late," he said, his gaze fixed on the silhouette of a tall woman who stood far too close to the precipice of the cliff, her hair whipping in the howling wind.

"Hell," Tompkins muttered.

He thumped on the carriage roof to signal to the driver to stop.

"You take the carriage home," he told Tompkins. "I'll bring her inside."

He called Seraphina's name as he stepped out into the night.

She looked up at him but did not wave or smile. She merely turned her head back to the horizon and listlessly lifted a bottle of wine straight to her lips, like some bawd from a Hogarth etching.

The closer he came, the more he could see she was not herself.

"Sera," he called. "Step back from there."

"Don't be a bother," she slurred.

He reached out and took the bottle from her. She reached after it unsteadily, making some incomprehensible sound of protest. It was nearly empty. Had she drunk a liter of wine herself?

He moved it out of her reach and pulled her forward. She shrugged him off and sat down on the rocky ground. He sat down beside her, using his body as a barrier between her and more of the alcohol she had clearly had too much of.

She reached across him to grab the bottle. "Go away."

"Sera, love, why are you doing this?"

"Doing what?"

"Drinking yourself ill. Alone."

She made a sound of derision. "Go."

"It's not safe for you to be out here like this. Let me take you home, at least."

She stood up angrily, but she was unsteady getting to her feet and stumbled backward, closer to the ledge. In the distance, the fireworks began, booming like an eruption of artillery. The fire in the sky flashed in Sera's eyes, making her look possessed. He grabbed her and pulled her toward him.

"Stop it," she said angrily. "Leave me be."

"Seraphina, you are going to hurt yourself." He pulled her to more solid ground. Perhaps with too much vigor, for she nearly fell on top of him.

"If you're going to be rough with me, at least make it enjoyable." She ran her hand down his shirtfront with a leer.

He drew a breath. This was how his father had behaved to his mother when Adam had witnessed his visits as a boy. Defiant and lecherous and grasping, breathing clouds of boozy air.

The stinking sour smell of wine on her was enough to

make him sick. The sky crackled with gunpowder. He felt like he was in Hell.

"Let's get you to bed," he said.

She reached for him. "Only if you'll join me there."

"Not tonight," he said, dodging her. "You need to sleep."

Her hands went for his shoulders. He edged away, but she clutched him closer, fumbling at his neckcloth.

He grabbed her wrists more tightly to get her attention. "No, Sera."

She stopped trying to kiss him and inhaled with a sharp breath. "Yes. Hurt me, just like that."

He dropped her wrists, feeling scalded.

"Don't stop," she rasped. "Throw me on the ground and fuck me."

She stood with her hip cocked out, arms crossed. He could tell she was not trying to seduce him so much as to shock him into leaving her alone.

He wanted to.

His every impulse was to abandon her to her drunken tantrum.

But he could not stand to leave her to take her chances with the cliff's edge. He put his arm around her back and began marching toward her house. "Come inside. You will regret this in the morning. The sooner you sleep, the sooner you can get started."

"Don't you dare insult me," she hissed.

He turned around. "Insult you? What have I said that isn't true? You disappointed my children after making a promise, and here I find you are not ill but bloody soused."

She narrowed her eyes into slits. "Oh, maybe if I had a *child*, I'd understand? This again?"

"That is not what I mean. I know you have not had an easy life, Sera, but I have seen what becomes of people who would rather drink their unhappiness away than face it, and I assure you it is not a pleasant end."

"What do you know of my unhappiness?" she whispered. "You know nothing. *Nothing.*"

Not for lack of bloody trying. How many times had he asked about her past, only to be given dismissive answers about a tragic tale? She did not want a confidant. She wanted a witness to her self-destruction.

He was tired of playing the part.

"I have known plenty of my own unhappiness without needing to borrow yours," he said.

She stuck out her lower lip, petulant like a child. "You're *nice*, I thought. Be *nice* to me."

He'd done that. It hadn't taken.

He tried to keep his tone gentle. "The nicest thing that I can give you right now is honesty. I admire you, Seraphina. But seeing you in this state is hard to bear."

"Then leave," she said.

She staggered past him and marched back toward the precipice. She plucked her abandoned wine bottle off a rock and brought it to her lips, imbibing with all the elegance of a sack-sopped seaman. She marched back toward him but tripped on a rock and fell down, landing on her elbow with a foot dangling off the cliff.

He heard gravel falling down and crashing on the rocks below. Panic, pure and feral, sent him running.

"My God, stop it," he shouted. He slung his arm heavily around her waist, dragging her up six paces away from the precipice. "Do you wish to fall to your bloody death?" he screamed.

She muttered something that sounded like "what business is it of yours?"

"That's it. Come with me up to your house or I will carry you."

She wrenched away from him and stalked off up the hill to the path, but was so unsteady she fell forward to her knees, yelping in outrage.

Pitifully, she began to weep.

He couldn't watch.

He should not have to watch.

He hated this. He hated this so much.

This was every terrible moment of his childhood. His dread of visits from the man their mother called their "uncle," which began with lavish gifts and devolved within days into drunken scenes. Outraged remarks slurred through sour breath. His mother pleading with the stumbling drunkard who would not acknowledge the fear he'd caused them in the morning.

Adam wanted to run as fast as he could away from here.

But Seraphina was right. He was too bloody *nice*. Too nice to let her stomp her way right off a cliff.

He let out a deep sigh and did the only thing there was to do. He picked her up and slung her over his shoulder and carried her up the hill to her terrace.

She cried brokenly onto his shoulder as he walked the paces to the house. Her tears falling on him made him angrier, but he let her cry. He opened the terrace doors and took her inside. Tompkins was waiting.

Tompkins stared at Sera, then at him, with a quiet kind of anguish. "I was worried it might come to this. I hid the wine before I left but she always finds it."

He nodded wordlessly. It chilled him how Tompkins's tone held no surprise. It reminded him of his mother: *I dumped out all the spirits, but he found more.*

"It's all right," he said. "I'll take her upstairs to her bed."

Chapter Twenty-One

Sera cried bitterly as Adam cleaned gravel from her palms.

After hours outside in the wind, the house was too warm, and an unpleasant flush stung her cheeks.

"Ow!" she cried as he rubbed none too tenderly at a cut. She enjoyed making her face accusatory. He was tending her to make a point about how good he was, as if to prove that she was bad. His very presence made her angry.

She'd never claimed she was good.

She'd tried to warn him.

She just wanted him to leave.

She shimmied away to evade his grip but succeeded only in falling against the dressing table, which lodged into her hip and made her entire body ring with pain.

"Damnation!" Tears overtook her again and she collapsed onto the floor, burying her face in the bedskirts.

"Sera, you're scaring me," Adam said quietly. "You're going to hurt yourself. I want you to take off that dirty gown and then I'm putting you in bed."

"No," she moaned. "Go away."

She hated for him to see her this way and yet part of her wanted him to see. Now he would know without question that his affection was wasted on her.

She was like a dead cockle washed up on the shore. Hard and spiny and gleaming on the outside, but hiding a soft and rotting creature that splashed foul-smelling ooze on those brave enough to pick it up.

"Sera," he said, with desolation in his voice. "Come here."

He pulled her to himself and hugged her. She cried harder, that he was sweet even through his anger.

His kindness only made her more despairing, because she could see it plainly in his eyes that he was done with her. This was why she didn't *try*. You let people closer and it hurt worse when they saw who you really were. When you bared your soul to them and they said, "You're just drunk, go to bed."

She knew how this would end. He would go, and she would be left with this feeling she wanted so badly not to have. This desperate desire to be comforted.

Adam loosened his grip on her. "Can you stand up?" he asked quietly.

Hold me. I'm so sad.

"Go away," she sniffled.

"Sera, what happened?"

What happened? Of all the bloody goddamned questions. Suppose she actually answered him?

Well, Adam, my baby died. I was thrown away like rubbish by everyone I loved without a bloody backward glance. It cost me everything and it cost him nothing and I'm still not safe from it and it's not fair that I'm so ravaged and so angry, and that you're looking at me like that, like you finally see *how hopelessly* ruined *I am.*

"Stop looking at me like that! Why won't you leave?" she shouted. "Go away."

He did not even flinch. "Because you need to sleep and I am not going to let you do so in a heap on the floor."

She bounded angrily onto her feet. She may be weaving, but by God, she was standing. She dropped her bodice to the ground, and her skirt after it. She ripped off her stays and shift and threw them across the room.

She walked toward him, naked except for her stockings. "If you must stay and gape at me, then fuck me like I asked. Properly this time. Throw me down and choke me until I come."

She said these words to make him go away, but she wanted it all the same. Sex. The brutal kind. Fingers in her hair, around her throat. Her body used so hard she didn't have to be inside it. She could retreat to a place somewhere above the headboard and simply watch.

Adam shook his head. "My God, Sera, can you see yourself?"

He took her shoulders and turned her to face the dressing table, where even in the dim light her outline was ragged. Her hair was in knots, her stockings were torn and her knees were red and skinned from where she'd fallen. But the worst bit was her face, crumpled and puffy from the wine and spirits and red with her tears.

The sight of herself was strangely calming.

"Yes, I do see myself, Adam. I've always seen myself. Do *you* see me? Finally?"

He closed his eyes like the sight of her made him sick. "This is not who you are unless you want it to be," he said. "You're drunk."

"Yes, I *am* drunk," she hissed. "But you're pious and I'm bored of you."

His mouth formed a tight line. She could see him, wishing to snap at her, controlling himself. Being ever so reasonable. How she hated it.

"Fine," he said in a defeated voice, "I won't continue with you in this state. And if you wish to drink this much, if you can't see how you're hurting yourself—"

"I'm not the one who hurts me!" she cried. "If you only knew the things that have happened to me—"

"Things happen," he said in that terribly calm voice. "Life is full of painful things that happen. We have a choice in whether we try to heal ourselves or wallow in despair and right now you are choosing to destroy yourself and I refuse to watch you do it."

"Wise Adam Anderson," she sneered.

He shook his head, picked his coat up from the back of her chair, and walked out of the room without another word.

She threw herself on top of the coverlet and sobbed, noisily, hoping he would hear her, take pity, and come back. She wanted him to hold her and comfort her just as badly as she wanted the abrading feeling of his scorn.

But he didn't come back.

She cried until her eyes hurt so badly that she closed them.

When she opened them, it was morning.

She was splayed out in only her stockings on the counterpane. Her mouth was full of cotton and her head throbbed with a percussive insistence that made her feel like someone was inside it, beating her brains with a skillet. Her chest felt hot, her knees and hands burned with the cuts and scratches from her fall, her hip was mottled black and purple.

But what was worse was the memory of what she'd done. She blinked, the sun in her eyes burning brighter with every sliver that came back.

All that wine. She'd missed Golowan. The children.

Oh God, and Adam. Pushing him away when he'd tried to comfort her.

Insulting him.

Falling.

Ripping off her clothes, demanding to be fucked.

She lay in her bed and held herself and wept. She wept for him—for what he must have felt, for how he must have suffered. She wept in shame for having taken pains to hurt him, to lash the kindness out of him. She wept for herself, for her unbearable sadness, her own capacity for cruelty, the terrible force of her rage. She wept for Elinor and Jack, for her father. She wept for her poor baby.

She wept until she was a husk, her head aching, her eyes painful in their sockets.

And then, finally, she stopped crying.

And she knew.

If the drinking did not kill her, the despair would.

She had to stop this.

ADAM TRUDGED UP the coastal path wincing at the cheerful wildflowers that drifted in the lazy wind. Had it only been yesterday that he'd picked a bunch for Seraphina, anticipating the sweetness of making up after their first quarrel? Had he really stood here smiling to himself, imagining a few weeks of luxuriating in her bed?

To think how much hope one could lose in a single night was gutting.

There would be no more luxuriating.

Adam had spent enough time with people in the grips of drink to know that an unquenchable thirst could not be reasoned with. When one loved a drunkard, one's love went unrequited; one could not compete with the pull at the bottom of their glass.

He had watched his mother lose this battle, convincing herself she could change his father with arguments and ultimatums, only to be shattered anew each time his thirst proved more powerful than her pleas.

He ached for Seraphina. But he could not subject his children—or himself—to the ravages her thirst would leave on any hearts that got too close to hers.

And he was much too close.

Whether she called him a friend or a lover, he was falling for her. She was in his dreams, in his thoughts. He felt more alive—more daring, more thoughtful, more himself—in her presence. And he craved the moments when he coaxed her brittle shell open for a second, and the kind and tender woman inside shone out.

He'd entertained the idea that if he could wear that crack into a deeper fissure, he could perhaps lodge himself inside her heart and heal it.

But was this not what his mother had imagined of his father, when she remained his mistress, welcoming him back to her bed whenever he visited his Scottish holdings, no matter how dreadful he'd been the time before?

He wouldn't repeat the past. The price was too high, and the things he had to protect were too precious to pay it.

But he wanted a proper end.

He did not want to remember Seraphina Arden stumbling after wine or weeping naked on the floor. He wanted to remember what had drawn him to her—her fearlessness, her beauty, her wit. He wanted to wish her peace.

He knew she would be sick when she awoke so he waited until well after the luncheon hour before walking to her home.

Her house looked odd as he drew near it. All the windows, usually open to catch the ocean breeze, were closed, and the shutters along the terrace were locked, save for the single loose one, which he had forgotten to have fixed. It clattered desolately in the wind.

He walked around the front of the house and knocked. No one answered.

Perhaps Sera was upstairs resting in the dark and had ordered the house closed to visitors.

He was just about to leave when the door opened and the maid, Maria, greeted him.

"Is Miss Arden up to a visit?" he asked.

Maria shook her head. "She left. Early this morning."

"When do you expect her back?"

Maria shook her head. "No, sir. She went back to London with Miss Tompkins. I'm to close the house and return by coach."

She was gone? Impossible.

Maria looked at him expectantly. He realized he was standing with his mouth hanging open.

But how could she have left? What about her book? Curse her bloody book, what about *him*? Did he mean so little she could not be bothered to say farewell?

"Er, she didn't leave anything for me, did she?" he asked. "A note?"

Even as he said the words, he knew they were preposterous. The pitying look that came over Maria's face confirmed it.

"No, sir. I can give you her address in London if you wish to write."

"No. No, that's quite all right." He reached into his pocket for the Celtic amulet that his children had purchased for Seraphina at the Golowan market, and handed it to Maria.

"Would you give her this? Tell her it's from the Anderson children. A farewell gift in thanks for a memorable few weeks."

Weeks their father would no doubt remember all his life.

Part Two

❦

The act of committing my history to paper transformed it from the haze of the long-buried past into gruesome detail.

I couldn't live with it that close to me.

I tried to drown it, one final time, in drink. A pint of brandy, a liter of wine. Enough to be surprised that I'd woken up alive.

When I did wake up, I felt poisoned. From the wine I had consumed, from the pain that was undoing me, from the vicious things I'd said to a man who'd tried to soothe me.

I was becoming utterly undone. I was terrified that in the face of what was coming—the scandal my memoirs would provoke, the threat of prosecution by Lord Bell—I would lose control entirely.

To meet the vow I had sworn the night that Elinor went missing, I had to save myself.

But I did not know how.

I only knew that I could not do it alone, in Cornwall.

I returned to St. Martin's Lane, to my Sirens, and asked their help. That I am alive three decades later is to the credit of Cornelia and Thaïs and my faithful secretary, Jane Tompkins.

They emptied out my wine cellar. They called a physician when I swore that I was dying. They fed me cleansing herbs and broth.

I quickly changed my mind and fought them bitterly. Bless them, they didn't listen.

They took me for brisk walks through the park to exhaust my nervous energy and sat up with me at night when the thirst to drown my memories became so overpowering that I begged them to relent, to bring me just a sip to calm me.

They would not let me ignore my pain, or numb it. Expel it, they ordered me, night after night. Treat it like an exorcism.

I roamed my house in a tattered shift drinking endless cups of tea, writing memories I'd never told another soul on strips of paper that I promptly threw into the fire. Four years of Jonathan Trewlnany's words, his touch, his laughter, his promises, his secrets—all torched. Tamsin. My father. The wretched planter they tried to marry me to. From memory to ink to ash.

The only ones I kept were my memories of my baby girl. I still have them, in the bottom of my jewel box.

None of it helped. Until, somehow, it did.

I was as shocked as anyone when one morning I woke up feeling calmer than I had in weeks and read a newspaper. The peaceful feeling did not last. But it gave me hope that I might not always feel so dreadfully. I took more walks. Drank my herbal tinctures. Slept more than I had in years.

I returned to myself in dribs.

I began to crave sunshine, to bathe and dress myself with regularity, to eat meals without being forced by my friends.

I began to think about the future without dread.

This recovery brought its own kind of despair, for in this state of renewed clarity, I could now see my collapse for what it was. I could see that the life I'd built was no longer enough to sustain me. My ideals were real, but the cause of justice alone was not enough to nourish me. The lovers, the wine, the swirl of parties—I had been using them to distract myself from the part of me that craved softer things I'd always sworn that I despised.

I realized I'd been wrong about soft things; it wasn't that I didn't have a taste for them. It was that possessing such a taste filled me with more terror than dead birds or vile posters.

And now, I was starving.

It was only then that I truly mourned what—who—I had left behind in Cornwall.

I grieved what might have been, had I met him years later instead of on the brink of my collapse. I felt cheated of him.

By then it was August.

Elinor was still in hiding, and Bell was waging war against her in the papers.

My memoirs would be published in a fortnight.

There was no more time to waste in pining for what I'd thrown away.

It was time to gather strength, and celebrate what I did have: my dear, dear friends. Sisters willing to fight for me long after I'd given up the battle. Willing to remind me what I stood to become, not just what I'd lost.

Chapter Twenty-Two

"Oh, the insufferability of nobs," Seraphina sighed, leaning back into the comfortable cushions of Cornelia's carriage as though they might protect her from the tedium of the coming afternoon. The aristocratic guests that attended Lady Westcott's annual exhibition exuded a loftier air than she liked to breathe even *with* the numbing effect of a few glasses of champagne.

She was not sure she could endure it without being slightly stultified.

Giving up one's vices provoked a number of clarities, she had discovered, and one of them was being forced into acute awareness of things one didn't like. Apparently, mingling with aristocrats—a pastime she'd previously engaged in with a gusto fortified by wine—was not among her sober pleasures.

"Now, now," Cornelia said. "Those nobs pay good money for my paintings. And we need to spend the afternoon reminding them your book is about to be published. Anticipation among the liberal set will help the sales. They are like the birds, collecting the seeds of consciousness and dropping them in the far-off land of wealth."

That Cornelia was right did nothing to reduce Seraphina's dread. "My neck already aches at the idea of pretending to be appropriately regal," she muttered.

"Darling, it's time to regain your bearings. Maybe you'll enjoy it."

Sera doubted it.

The carriage stopped before Lady Westcott's extraordinary gardens, which were dotted with sculptures featured in her exhibition. Lady Westcott was a patroness to a number of the members of the Royal Academy, and the exhibitions at her country house outside of London were reliably populated with celebrated artists and the wealthy people who supported their work.

"I need to find Roarkie," Cornelia said. "I promised him a personal viewing of my Sirens series. Will you come?"

"No, I think I'll have a look at the art and see if I can find someone whose conversation doesn't make my head ache."

Cornelia smiled. "That's the spirit."

Sera wandered inside the grand entry of the house. Lady Westcott was positioned below the marble staircase, holding court in a plumed hat of such complexity that Sera could barely find her eyes to greet her.

"Ah, Miss Arden!" she called out. "I haven't seen you in an age! Milton, get the lady some champagne."

Sera shook her head at the servant standing beside Lady Westcott with a tray of glasses. "No, thank you."

Lady Westcott laughed. "Why, Miss Arden, I've never seen you turn down a tipple."

Sera smiled tightly. People were impossible. "Watching my figure."

"Ah, want to look your best for your new book? Everyone is talking about it. When can I get a printing?"

"It's out next week."

"I am salivating with anticipation."

"You are too kind."

"Well, enjoy yourself. Miss Ludgate's work is in the West Gallery. She's showing a portrait of you. Quite a good one."

"Ah. I must go and make certain she didn't sneak any hairs onto my chin."

Sera wandered slowly through the colonnade to the gallery, greeting people with waves and nods but not pausing to talk. She shouldn't have let Cornelia persuade her to come. After a month of isolation, she really was not up to making sparkling conversation.

Oh, Miss Arden, where have you been?

Well, I wrote my memoirs, suffered an emotional collapse, allowed my standard intemperance to fester into mania, and spent a month struggling to leave my bed.

Better not to talk.

She spotted Cornelia's new series. It was called *The Society of Sirens.* Four portraits of Sera, Thaïs, Cornelia, and Elinor, looking intellectual and angry. The proceeds were going to fund Elinor's time in hiding.

A small crowd was gathered before the series, and Sera walked closer.

She caught sight of Adam Anderson among them, staring up at her portrait.

Her breath seized.

What could he be doing here?

She tried to wipe the dampness from her hands, but they felt hot and sticky against her gown.

Oh God. She'd been so awful to him, and when her maid had brought her that little pendant from his children, she'd spent weeks trying to find the words to thank him—and had found herself completely at a loss.

In the end she'd written nothing.

She still felt a surge of guilt whenever she saw the pendant sitting on her dressing table, like a reproach to her rotten character.

Most of the crowd walked on, but Adam lingered, allowing her to get a better look at him. He was smartly dressed but had dark circles beneath his eyes and appeared thinner than he'd been a month ago. But most striking was the way he held himself—hunched, almost like he was in pain.

He turned around and glanced about the room, as if searching for some shoal of a familiar face.

He's uncomfortable here.

Suddenly his eyes locked on hers. He froze, blinking, his face so tense that her own cheeks winced in sympathy.

Should she go to him?

No. She could not imagine he wished to speak to her.

But would it not seem rude if she did not?

She forced herself to lift her hand in a wave, to step forward, to raise the corners of her mouth into some semblance of a smile.

He went stiff as she approached, his shoulders rising subtly, like she was a bear and he didn't want to startle her.

Which, given her behavior at their last meeting, was not unwarranted.

Oh God, oh God. Her heart clamored in her throat like she'd had four cups of tea.

"Adam," she said, forcing herself to affect a tone that did not bespeak her desire to flee from this room and lock herself in Cornelia's carriage where she could not be seen, and cry. She fluttered her lashes at him in mock vanity. "Were you admiring me?"

She meant to be self-deprecating—amusing—but he just looked at her long and hard, completely without humor.

"It's a wonderful portrait," he finally said. "The whole series is remarkable."

"Yes, well, Cornelia did not make me quite as lovely as your sketch in Cornwall, but then, she has had more time to see how unpleasant I can be."

His eyes flashed with something sharp and almost angry. She was trying to be charming, to acknowledge their history with some hint of wryness, but the way she said it made it sound like she was flippant—like she considered his sketch to be a joke. Or worse, that she was making light of her behavior.

She wasn't. She wanted to die of shame.

And she still had his sketch. She'd stashed it in a drawer and tried not to let herself stare at it and feel like the most foolish woman in the world more than once or twice a week.

He turned back to her portrait. "You don't look unpleasant," he said, studying it. "You look intelligent and ferocious." There was a pause. "It's an accurate likeness."

She winced with her entire body.

She deserved that, but she desperately wanted to evade the thrumming of embarrassment that vibrated up her core. She flashed what she hoped looked like an easy smile. "What brings you here? I was not aware you were acquainted with Lady Westcott."

"I wasn't. Your friend Miss Ludgate wrote to me and offered to propose my work for inclusion in her exhibition. Quite kind of her."

Cornelia had invited him? And she hadn't thought to mention it? That utter *rat*.

"Ah," Sera said faintly.

He put his hands in his pockets, and she could tell her presence was making him uneasy, but she couldn't quite bring herself to make an excuse and walk away.

"You are well?" she asked. Her voice was high and nervous.

"I am," he said, in a tone that seemed excruciatingly wary. "And you?"

"Yes, very well."

No, I have been all disorder since I met you. I miss you savagely. What did you pull loose in me?

But she could not say that to a man she'd fled from without a word of apology or goodbye. She felt as if guilt was a lake, and she was treading water in it with bricks tied to her ankles, desperately trying not to drown.

"Well, I shall leave you to enjoy the art," she said.

He sighed darkly. "Is that what one is meant to do? I don't know why I'm bloody here."

She felt a sudden ray of hope. *You know how this works. Help put him at ease. Make introductions.*

She glanced around the room for friendly faces and saw Cornelia walk in with Mr. Roarke, the art collector. Sera waved to them, and they walked over.

"Ah, Mr. Anderson," Cornelia said warmly. "I'm so pleased you came. I was just telling Mr. Roarke how much I like your folio. The aesthetics marry beautifully with the utility of the designs. And such a lively sense of movement."

"Savor the compliment, for Miss Ludgate is not easily impressed," Mr. Roarke said, winking at Adam. "I'd love to see your work, Mr. Anderson. Perhaps you'll show me now?"

Adam led Roarke to his drawings, and Sera grabbed Cornelia's arm and sank her fingernails into the skin beneath the cuff of her sleeve.

"You did not think it worthy of mention that you invited him here?" she hissed.

"I worried you wouldn't come if you knew."

"Yes, *exactly.*"

"I thought it would do you well to speak to him."

"And say what?"

Cornelia pursed her lips. "That you are *sorry.* Excuse me. I must greet my admirers."

Sera stood in the gallery, seething at Cornelia.

Well, of course she was sorry. Did that not go without saying?

Would Adam even *want* to hear an apology? Or would it just be an unpleasant reminder of what had happened?

She glanced over at him. Roarke had left him and he was looking at his fingernails beside a potted plant. Poor man. Clearly he was not a natural mingler.

She caught the eye of Lord Edward Graves, Viscount of Masden, who had recently inherited his title. When he smiled, she pulled him over to Adam, suggesting he might require an architect to consult on improving his estate. She made sure to disappear when the conversation became detailed. But when Masden walked away, she swept in to introduce Adam to Josiah Hewbridge, the ceramics manufacturer who was considering building new factories in London, and Lord Fallenway, a member of the Board of Works.

She was almost disappointed when he seemed to get his bearings and began to circulate through the crowd himself. It meant she no longer had a reason to stand near him.

She went outside and sat in the sunshine to wait for Cornelia.

She saw Adam walk out of the house with another man. He noticed her and paused.

She waved farewell, relieved that he was leaving.

He said something to the man, turned, and walked toward her.

Oh no.

Did he think she had beckoned him? They had already exhausted the usual pleasantries. What more could she say to him? That it worried her he looked so tired? That even so, he was so handsome that she could not look at him without blushing?

That she still missed him?

"Miss Arden," he said "There you are. I looked for you inside to say farewell."

Was that reproach in his voice? Or simple sadness?

"Ah, apologies. I needed air."

He said nothing. She scrambled for something else to say. "I hope you found the afternoon useful."

He gave her a smile that had a note of melancholy in it. She hoped she was not the cause of it.

"Yes, it was," he said. "Thank you for making those introductions. Though I have heard just about enough of my own thoughts on portico design for one day. Never was much good at talking up my work."

She laughed, relieved that he seemed friendlier now than he had when she'd first seen him in the gallery. "I know the feeling. Whenever I speak on lecture tours, I find myself deeply bored of my own opinions by day's end."

He gave her a half-hearted smile. "I doubt your opinions are ever boring, Miss Arden."

Miss Arden. He'd taken care not to use her given name all afternoon. It made her sad, how he addressed her as though they did not know each other intimately.

"You're too kind," she said. She looked up into his eyes. "But then, I suppose you always were."

He swallowed and tore his eyes from hers.

Say it. Now, Seraphina. Before he leaves.

She stood up and let the words come out in a rush before she lost her nerve. "Adam, I want to apologize to you for how I behaved in Cornwall."

Alarm crossed his features. "Oh no, let's not—"

She clasped her hands before her chest, as if in prayer. "Please. Adam, I'm so sorry. I won't ask for absolution nor do I deserve it. Those last few days were difficult for me, but I handled them in a way that . . . I regret that I disappointed your children. I regret the things I said to you. I regret . . . pawing at you like a lecher when you didn't want it. And I am so grateful to you for attending to me with such care that final night. I behaved in a way I hate to remember."

"Sera—"

She shook her head. "And I never thanked your children for the amulet. I was so touched to receive it. I meant to write, but I was . . . ill when I returned, and, well, I suppose I was so humiliated that I . . . just couldn't bring myself to contact you."

He was silent, but his throat was working, like there was some emotion he couldn't, or wouldn't, express.

He'd never held back from her before. *Did I do that to you?*

"Adam, I enjoyed spending time with you, however poor I was at showing it."

He swallowed whatever that lump was in his throat and drew his lips together into the sad etching of a smile. "Me, too."

Why were those words more devastating than his anger?

He was about to bow to her to say farewell, she could see it in the movements of his neck, and she reached out and touched his shoulder.

"I don't know if it's too late, and I know I don't deserve it, but I wonder if you might still wish to be my friend."

He closed his eyes. When they opened, her heart pulsed, for she saw his answer in his eyes.

No.

She dropped her hand and pressed it into her pocket, as if to keep it safe from further injury.

"I'm sorry," he said kindly. "I'm hopelessly busy at the moment with my work. I'm so glad you're well, but I'm afraid I need to depart. We're due back in London by this evening."

She nodded and forced herself to smile. "Of course. Safe journey."

She stood there, alone, reeling.

She deserved to be turned down. She'd succeeded in doing exactly what she'd set out to do the night she'd driven him away: destroyed his regard for her in one fatal hour, so she would not have to suffer losing it, inevitably, in bits.

But it still hurt.

Not least because there had been something stark and firm and *useful* in the fact that Adam had not excused her when she'd fallen apart. That he had drawn a line and told her flat out that he would not continue with her in that state.

She'd needed to hear it. In a way, it had heartened her that he thought she was capable of more.

It was fitting that he now stood by his word.

Fitting that she'd lost him.

But the next time a man who was *nice* wished to do more with her than merely share a bed, she would take care not to sharpen her shale heart into a dagger.

She would *try*.

She had always prided herself on being a woman who lived without regrets.

But she regretted Adam Anderson.

ADAM SAT AT his drafting table, the sketches he urgently needed to correct neglected beneath his copy of the first volume of Seraphina Arden's memoirs. They had been published a week ago, throwing London into a frenzy that he'd tried desperately to ignore. The second volume, which promised to reveal the name of the man who ruined her, was due to come out in a week's time, and London was astir with speculation as to the identity of her dastardly lover. This morning, on the walk from his home to the studio, he'd heard a group of old women speculating in low voices as to whether it was more likely to be George III or William Pitt the Younger.

He'd purchased the volume on the spot, tired of hearing about it secondhand. He'd meant to begin it tonight, before bed, but he'd opened it as soon as he arrived at the studio and read the entire volume in one sitting.

She had said her book would make him weep. She had not mentioned it was because it told a love story. He looked down and reread the passage that had made him ache for her.

> *That first day beneath the bridge, he lay on the bank and spun a future for us from clouds and gold. Marriage. Children. A title. A life far beyond the expectations of my birth, my looks, or my questionable charms. The promises a girl is raised to hope for, to cherish, to live in fear of never having—and which, up to this point, I had been told I would be lucky to have a fraction of. How could I question what he asked of me, when he promised me all that?*
>
> *How could I, the drab, too-tall daughter of a coarse father, deny a man who called me Sorceress, because he said I cast a spell on him and made him magic?*
>
> *Now, you will read these words and smile. Another stupid girl, throwing her life away for*

*flattery and empty promises. More ambition than
virtue. More vanity than sense.*

*But if he had looked at you that way, as if you
were a thing of precious beauty, would you have
found the strength to find the lie?*

*For the desire that he spoke of—the longing for
me in his eyes—that was real.*

And I returned it.

*He was not wrong to see a spark in me that
could be kindled into fire.*

*He said he burned with love for me; instead, he
practiced arson. But never have I questioned that
he was right to see I smoldered.*

*The lie was in pretending that my fire, once lit,
would not burn everything around me.*

He was a fool. All that time, when Sera had insisted
she required a wall between her lovers and her heart,
he'd imagined it was some sophisticated way of living he
was not cultivated enough to understand.

He'd not thought of the simpler explanation: her heart
was broken.

"Anderson, look what's just been delivered."

Adam looked up from the book and tried not to glare
at Mayhew, who was practically dancing a jig in his ea-
gerness to capture Adam's attention.

"What is it?" Adam sighed. He was so tired. Always,
lately, so tired.

With the flourish a bishop might use to crown a newly
minted king, his brother-in-law presented him with a
large, expensive-looking piece of embossed paper.

*The Marquess of Pendrake Hereby Invites Anderson
Mayhew Architects to Present to the Parliamen-*

tary Board of Works Concerning Their Proposed Designs for the Construction of a Naval Armory.

Adam smiled, until he scanned down and saw the invitation came with a long request for amendments to the proposed design to be made and submitted for review before the meeting, which was set for a fortnight hence.

"You cracking genius!" Mayhew said, slapping him on the back. "You bloody did it! We're in!"

Adam grinned at Mayhew, trying to cover his exhaustion at the thought of what this meant. Drafting the proposal had nearly killed him. He'd barely slept in a month. And now he would need to do more work to meet this latest requirement. He didn't know where he'd find the strength.

"Folke is up for it, too—probably others," Mayhew said. "'Twill be a fierce race. But it's a race that we can *win*, Anderson." He pranced around the room. "This is *it*. Everything we've waited for. Aren't you pleased?"

"Very pleased."

He was.

But he'd need to hire a handful of extra draftsmen to revise the plans in time, which would require taking out more loans to pay them, as they were already in arrears on moneys owed to their craftsmen, and he—he was so bloody tired.

"You're fretting," Mayhew said.

"I'm not. I'm calculating. We'll need three more draftsmen for the fortnight. That's—" Adam paused, adding up the figures in his head.

Mayhew threw himself back in a chair. "Spare me, Adam. You'll find the money, you always do. This is what we've worked so hard for. My God, you are morose."

His brother-in-law reached across the table and grabbed the book he'd been reading. *"Memoirs of a Rakess?"* he groaned. "Don't tell me you've caught Seraphilia."

"I was curious to see for myself what the fuss is about. I made her acquaintance in Cornwall. She lives near Tregereth."

Mayhew frowned. "Yes, I noticed you speaking with her at Lady Westcott's. You know, Adam, you must be careful who you're seen with. Pendrake has no patience for Whiggish tendencies, and they say that woman runs with a pack of seditionists."

Adam's feelings on Seraphina Arden were a chaos he could scarcely stand to think about, but he was certain she was not a seditionist. "Surely urging women to know their letters is not an act against the Crown."

Mayhew, indifferent to politics as ever, rolled his eyes. "It's the question of respectability. Wouldn't do to be seen as under the influence of her sort."

"Her sort?" Adam asked. He knew what Mayhew meant, but his brother-in-law's judgment irritated him.

"You know. Jacobin intellectuals," Mayhew said. "They oppose the government, and we need the support of every peer we can find if we're to make us whole." He gave Adam a meaningful look. The debt Adam owed Mayhew for his share of the business was never far from either of their minds. Nor was the tension between them over how they should conduct themselves. The longer they spent in London, with its suspicion of Scots, the more desperate Mayhew was to be seen as more English than an Englishman. Adam understood the impulse, but he disliked the idea that they needed to appear as something other than what they were to move ahead.

Even if it was true.

"Never fear, James. I suspect I can read a book in private without being moved to go give a public speech in support of it to Pendrake."

Mayhew chuckled. "Just have a care you don't corrupt my sister's children with your reading."

He knew his brother-in-law was mostly joking, but even in jest, the comment irritated him. "What is appropriate for my children is my concern, James."

Mayhew looked taken aback at the irritation in his tone. "It's my concern as well, I'd think. I'm their godfather and their uncle."

"And I'm their father."

Mayhew crossed his arms and sighed. They had this conversation at least once a month, over something or other. Mayhew advising Adam to send the children to stay with Mayhew's mother in Edinburgh, to receive a proper upbringing with their cousins. Mayhew suggesting Adam hire a governess lest Marianne spoil the children with her unconventional opinions. It drove Adam mad.

Mayhew's father had never minded that Adam was cut from different cloth, so long as he could support his family. But the elder Mayhew had passed away, and after Catriona's death, the family had developed a way of looking after Adam that seemed suspicious. Like he might somehow turn his children into people more like his parents than their mother. Like he could not be trusted to know what was best for them.

He loved the Mayhews, but he sometimes wished he owed them less, so that he could draw a firmer line without seeming like an ingrate.

Mayhew was staring at him. "You know, you've been intolerable ever since you returned from Cornwall."

"I've been busy, James. You try doing six months' work in as many weeks and see how affable it makes you."

Mayhew shook his head. "Charming. I suppose I just stumble about contributing nothing."

Adam squeezed his eyes together and rubbed his temples. "I'm sorry. I didn't mean it as a criticism. I'm in a low mood. Ignore me."

In truth, his spirits had been low ever since that day that Seraphina had fled from him in Cornwall. He'd spent every night going by her house, angrily ripping posters off her gate.

Trying to understand how she could leave without a single word to him.

Trying not to let his anger leach into his children's consciousness.

Trying to forget her.

"Well, rest up while you can," Mayhew said, patting him heartily on the back. "We've a race to win."

Adam rose. "You're right. I'm going home."

He picked up Seraphina's book, tucked it into his satchel, rolled up his scrolls, and blew out the lamps.

As he walked along the darkened street, he thought about Seraphina's tale. She put great effort into appearing unemotional in Cornwall. It had taken time to see that she was neither as callous nor as impervious to pain as she would have one believe.

But her searing words gave the lie to every bit of that reserve.

It was a testament to youth and longing, an interrogation of the perverse, self-sabotaging yearnings of the heart. To open up such wounds for the betterment of men would require courage from any author. But for a woman like Seraphina—who did not like to indulge in backward glances, did not like to admit when she'd been hurt, who hated to seem vulnerable in any way—the bravery of it was heroic.

Mayhew was wrong about the book's power to corrupt. Her story was a cry in defense of humanity over the expectations of one's station. He felt it powerfully, the injustice of wanting more than what the world believed you were entitled to.

He wished he could tell her.

He couldn't, of course. Not after the terrible awkwardness of that moment when he'd refused her friendship.

He'd felt he had no choice but to decline. She'd been kind at Lady Westcott's, but his father had also been capable of acts of kindness when he was at his best. Trusting it only meant being crushed anew each time the lighter side of the man was swallowed by the darker one.

He was too wary to take the risk.

But perhaps, if he simply wrote to her, expressing his admiration for her work, it would make him miss her less.

His house was dark when he stepped inside. He lit a candle in his study and prepared a quill. And he began to write a letter to Seraphina Arden.

Chapter Twenty-Three

Seraphina awoke to the sound of Thaïs moaning—and not with pleasure.

Ever since Seraphina had returned from Cornwall, Thaïs had taken up residence in her spare bedchamber, hovering protectively. Sera went to Thaïs's door and knocked.

"Sweetling, are you ill?"

The noise that came back in response brought to mind a hedgehog attempting to give birth to a foal.

Sera threw open the door. "Thaïs! What is the matter?"

Thaïs was lying on her bed with a bladder of hot water over her stomach and the soles of her feet pushed up flat against the wall, writhing in pain.

"What in heaven's name are you doing?"

Thaïs grunted. "It's the curse. Twisting through me like the devil himself. Feels like he's wrenching out my innards."

Sera sat down beside her. "Oh dear. Is there anything I can do for you?"

"Take me into the garden and shoot me square between the eyes."

Sera snorted. "Would you settle for a cup of tea?"

"No. Just leave me to die in peace. Bury me at sea."

Sera patted her hand. "I'll go out and get you a remedy at the apothecary."

Thaïs only closed her eyes and groaned. Sera closed

the door, and stood in the dark hallway. Her skin felt tight and sharp and hot.

The curse. Where in the bloody hell was hers?

She had bled in Cornwall. She ticked the weeks on her fingers. That was over two months ago. She fought the desire to collapse onto the floorboards, and instead braced herself up against the wall, took a breath, and walked as calmly as she could to her bedchamber. She dug through her papers and found the journal where she recorded her menses.

No ticks since June.

Well, July had been a blur of emotion. She must have had it and forgot to write it down. But she *never* forgot. And even if she had, should she not have bled this month, by now?

Oh God, if she was—

Breathe.

She was not with child. She'd had none of the symptoms that had gripped her as a girl—no illness in the mornings, no fainting, no fatigue.

And the only man she'd been with was Adam Anderson, and only once, and surely that small failure of their precautions had not been enough to—

No. Her menses would come in the next few days. She would not lose her head with worry over nothing. There was too much work to do.

She dressed and went downstairs to attend to her correspondence. She was hoping for a note from Elinor, letting her know how she was faring in the cottage they'd secured in Surrey. She found a few letters from readers she would answer later, a stack of bills she would leave for Tompkins. At the bottom of the pile was a letter in a hand she recognized.

She hated superstition, but her first thought was that her stepmother would have seen it and crossed herself and said it was a sign. Her fingers trembled as she ripped it open.

Dear Seraphina,

I read the first volume of your memoirs. They are deeply affecting, and to know you were in the midst of writing this story during our time together makes me grieve a bit that I was not able to share the burden with you.

I wish that I had fully known you.

Someday, when they are old enough, I will give this book to Adeline and Jasper, so that they may know that the kind woman with the beautiful dresses of their memory was a philosopher who made a call for what was right, however much it must have cost her.

I regret that I was cold in my reaction to your apology at Lady Westcott's. The truth is that my time in your company made for some of the happiest days I have spent in many years. I cannot think of them without wishing, somehow, that it might have ended differently between us.

The loss of you reduces me.

You may always count me as a friend.

Yours,
Adam Anderson

Seraphina read the letter three more times.

His hand, orderly and masculine and artful on the page, made her feel as though she was back in Cornwall, sitting contentedly in the sun as he sketched her portrait, long fingers dancing capably across the page.

She closed her eyes and imagined how it might have been if that day had ended differently. If their affair had continued lazily apace, a few sun-drenched weeks beside the sea, him kind, her *trying*.

She imagined him in bed beside her on those long, hot summer afternoons, their skin warm as the ocean breeze blew through the open windows. She imagined smelling the salt in the air, lying languid in the heat, with no thought beyond the pleasure of his nearness.

I wish that I had fully known you.

She dipped her quill in ink and began to write.

> *Dear Adam,*
>
> *Thank you for your kind words. They mean a great deal to me.*

But that sentiment, though true, felt laughably insufficient. Should she say she felt the same? That as she had writhed in bed in London, sweating out the poison in her veins, she had soothed herself by imagining his voice? That she could not shake the feeling she had destroyed something tender and alive that had been unfurling like the tiny, delicate shoot of a new fern? That she wished—oh how she *wished*—she had not numbed her senses to its fragile nature?

No. That was far too much.

If she was over-reading the warmth in his letter, it would not do to give the impression she was asking for more than he was prepared to give. His letter, after all, was in past tense.

But if he felt enough to write *the loss of you reduces me,* surely he must—

But no. He did not write *I want you back.*

She had squandered his kindness once. It was generous of him to extend her his forgiveness. She must hold it with care, and not abuse it. She picked up the quill again and jotted out a few more words:

> *I wonder if you would join me for supper Sunday next at eight o'clock, so that we might talk? Please know I will understand if you don't wish to.*

Before she could lose her nerve, she scrawled another line beneath it:

> *But I miss you.*

She dropped the letter in the pile of post for Tompkins to have delivered by the errand boy and went out to the apothecary to buy a tincture for Thaïs. She went back home and gave it to Maria with instructions, then went out again to the milliner to pick up her new hat. She checked her timepiece. It was only eleven. She decided to go to the park for a walk.

She was ignoring her work, but she knew that if she went home she would only pace the halls, waiting for the post. The day was turning wet and chilly, and she didn't have a shawl, so she hailed a hackney home, all the while feeling expectant and low by equal measure.

Oh, she was absurd. She must not go on like this. He would likely not reply. Or if he did, it would be a polite refusal. She could already feel the sting of his rejection. She regretted every word she'd written.

How she hated the disorderly character of emotions.

It made her crave a sturdy, bracing drink. But of course she would not think of *that*, not after all this time and her feeling so much better. When the hackney stopped outside her house she dashed inside. If he had not written, she would shut it from her mind.

She looked for Tompkins or Maria, but no one was about. She paused at the stairs to the basement, panting a bit from her exertion.

"Tompkins?" she called out. "Did I receive any letters?"

"There's a pile of post sent from your publisher," Tompkins called back from the kitchen. "It's on your desk."

Sera went into her study and rifled through the mail. Twenty letters from readers. None from him.

"There was nothing . . . personal?" she called over her shoulder, hating the sound of desperation in her voice.

"No," Tompkins said, walking into the room.

Sera felt like she'd been slapped. The sting of tears hit her eyes and she shut them and turned around to face the wall so Tompkins wouldn't see.

She heard a second set of footsteps.

Tompkins touched her shoulder. "But you do have a visitor."

Sera whirled around.

Adam Anderson was standing behind Tompkins, a pained expression on his face.

"I'm sorry," he said softly. "I couldn't wait for Sunday."

ADAM HAD BEEN fidgeting with a cup of tea in Seraphina Arden's kitchen for the better part of an hour, debating whether it had been a mistake to come here.

That Seraphina took one look at him and started crying made him certain that it wasn't.

The words *I miss you* might have been less devastating in another person's letter. But from Seraphina, who so rarely spoke of what she felt, who had claimed so doggedly not to want any man's affection and certainly not his—it seemed momentous, a confirmation of what he'd sensed beneath all the things she'd never said.

He'd had to see her. But she'd been out when he arrived, and with every minute that ticked by he felt more foolish. He'd been on the verge of leaving. He was so glad—so very, very glad—he had remained.

Tompkins stepped around him and softly closed the door behind her, leaving them alone in Seraphina's study. That was fortunate, as he felt his throat closing with emotion, and he did not wish for Tompkins to look upon him weeping.

"I'm so sorry," Sera said, wiping tears from her eyes with her thumbs. "I'm ridiculous. I don't know what's come over me, I never cry, I'm so embarrassed—"

He stepped forward and gathered her into his arms. "Hush," he got out, burying his face into her hair.

Was it possible her skin was softer now? How had he never noticed that she smelled like citrus? He stepped back, to look at her. Her eyes lingered unsurely on his face, their green made vibrant by her azure dress.

"You're wearing that gown," he murmured.

"What gown?" she asked shakily.

"The one you wore the day you invited me to bed you."

He loved her in that dress. He loved how her chest rose and fell under his gaze. How the thread of her pulse beat in her neck, proof of her emotion. He reached out and brushed his fingers along her exposed collarbone.

She closed her eyes.

He wanted to kiss her there, along the painterly line of that bone and then up to her trembling pulse. He wanted to lick away the shimmer of tears caught in her black lashes. He wanted to taste her salt.

But first he had to say the things he'd promised himself he would tell her if he came here.

"Sera, I know your views on friends and lovers. But observing such a separation is just not how I'm built. I knew it wasn't when I met you."

He glanced at her, because if she objected, there was no use in saying any more. But she was holding her hand to her chest, like it hurt, and nodding.

"I know," she whispered. "I know you're not."

He stepped a bit closer. "I can't *not* care about you."

She closed her eyes, still nodding.

"But Sera, I need to tell you—" He paused, coughed. His throat was sore, raw with all the feeling he'd been harboring as he puttered with his tea.

She shook her head. "You can say anything you wish, Adam. Anything. That you are here at all—it's enough."

"Oh, lass." He did need to say this, desperately, but she looked so raw, like his very presence was lashing at her heart. He couldn't stand to hurt her. He gestured to a small sofa beneath a window. "Will you sit with me?"

She nodded and perched at the edge of the couch, her back stiff and straight, like she was waiting for a blow. The way she moved, accommodating but gingerly, like she was afraid that she might crack—made him understand what he must do.

"Come here," he murmured. He sat beside her, leaned back, and slowly put his arm around her shoulders and drew her toward him. "I want to hold you while I say this. Because I want you to feel that there is no malice in it. I'm saying it because I must, for my sake."

She let out a breath and nodded, braced. He wrapped his other arm around her, pulling her snug against his chest. It felt good to hold her. He took both of her hands in his.

"Sera, my father drank."

She went rigid.

"And when he did, he raged. He'd tear up my mother's cottage, shout dreadful things, frighten the bejesus out of me and Marianne. And then he'd drink himself into a stupor and when he came to, he'd disappear without a word. Come back a few months later as though it hadn't happened."

He felt her trembling. He squeezed her tighter. "Eventually he stopped coming back at all. And I was . . ." he had to collect himself to say the word ". . . glad." He looked down into her eyes. "And I don't want to feel that way about you."

"Adam, forgive me," she whispered.

"I do, Sera. Or, I want to. But that night, in Cornwall, watching you—I haven't felt that way since I was a child, and I won't—I cannot stand—to feel it again. It's too painful." He took a shaky breath. "So, if we are to be friends, or anything else—and I want to, Sera, I do—but you mustn't drink around me. I know it isn't my place to dictate your behavior. But I'm asking, because I miss you so bloody much."

She lifted up their joined hands and pressed his knuckle to her lips. "Adam, I would give up far more to have another chance with you."

He nodded, hoping he could trust her.

She shifted and put her arms around his waist. "I haven't had a drink since that night, with you, in Cornwall. I . . . scared myself. For many reasons, but not the least was how I treated you. I don't want to be that way."

He nodded. Remembering that night was painful even in the abstract. He was glad that it had been enough to shake her. But what if her resolve faded with the memory?

She must have seen his doubts written on his face, because she touched his cheek. "I will be honest, Adam. It has been a fight against temptation. But I want so badly to be strong and so far, I have been. And you have given me another reason to abstain."

He squeezed her, unable to speak.

"Sweet man," she whispered. "I'm so sorry that I hurt you."

"Oh, Sera." He leaned down and caught her lips with his.

Was it possible he'd never really kissed her?

He hadn't. Not like this.

Not the way you kissed a woman when you wanted to say with the brush of your lips, with the lingering of your tongue, with the whisper of your whiskers on her jaw, how much she meant to you.

To print it on her.

To make her understand it in her teeth, her blood, her bones.

Because maybe if she understood it—

Her hand drifted up to his chest, over his heart, and her other hand curled around his nape. Her eyes looked lazy and languid and—dare he even think it—tender.

He traced the curve of her ear. He'd never noticed the delicacy of her ears. They were exquisite, like pink seashells. He leaned in and sucked a lobe into his mouth. She shivered.

"Adam, you will undo me."

"That's not what I want." He pulled back her hair and found her other ear and nibbled it, for symmetry.

Her fingernails bit into his thigh. "What do you want?" she asked in a tremulous voice.

Everything.

"I want to discover where you keep your bed."

Chapter Twenty-Four

The mysterious disappearance of Lady Bell becomes more perplexing. Gentlemen's clubs abound with rumors that Viscount Bell's attempts to help his wife recover from the madness that led to her adultery have been thwarted by the notorious authoress Seraphina Arden. 'Tis heard that the outrageous Arden abducted Lady Bell from the bastion of health where she was so peacefully resting to reunite her with her Jacobin lover, the libel-monger Jack Willow. If the rumors are true, Miss Arden should be prosecuted for this unlawful abduction of a man's wife.

—The London Advocate, 1797

❦

For a woman who made an avocation of erotics, Seraphina Arden had always told herself she wasn't fond of making love.

She was a skilled practitioner of the transgressive midnight bacchanal; the public assignation; the shrieking, desperate fuck.

Making love, she'd thought, was tiresome. The phrase itself was torpid, over-earnest, lacking vigor on the tongue. Historically, when men said those words, she shuddered or took another drink.

And yet.

When Adam Anderson pressed her against her bed-post, his hard cock ridged against her pubic bone and his hand inside her gown, and said the words, "I'm going to make love to you," it made her wet.

Even despite the gentle way he looked at her as he undressed her. The terrifying care with which he removed her hairpins, one by one.

He stripped off his own clothing while she watched, grateful that it was still daylight, so she could see the angles of his form. When he was nude, he lowered her onto the mattress. She lifted her arms, beckoning, but instead he knelt over her and kissed her belly.

And then he kissed lower.

He spread out her legs until she was parted, and gazed down at her quim. He ran his fingers over her hipbones, over her mons. He lowered his face and ran his tongue along her thighs.

"I've got you, lass," he murmured.

She melted down onto her bed, her body already relaxed with instinctive certainty that his words were true. She need not perform for him. She could let herself be taken.

And he was taking her. He was over her, so large and yet gentle, every brush of his skin and mouth a caress her body vibrated with in welcome. *You. More.*

"Ach, Sera," he murmured, lifting himself up on his forearms. He pressed his nose into her womanhood and inhaled her smell.

All at once she felt afraid. His delectation in their intimacy was too much. This was all too fast. She could not remember the last time she'd been with a man without the haze of wine, and she felt her nakedness, she felt his focus, she felt all the ways that she might wrong him, and she wanted to cover up.

She clenched the counterpane, on the verge of telling him to stop, to get up, to get dressed. To leave before she did something terrible they'd both regret.

But he must have felt the rising tension in her, for he looked up, put his hands flat against her stomach, and peered into her eyes. "You're all right, love? This is all right?"

And for some reason, in his sensing that it wasn't all right, it somehow was.

"I'm not accustomed to doing this in daylight. Without wine."

He pressed his face against her belly and kissed her navel. "Let's find out if you like it."

And then his fingers parted her folds, and his tongue pressed down against her clitoris, and his mouth produced a ribbon of pleasure so sudden and surprising that she cried out.

He licked her slowly, making quiet noises of enjoyment, like the quickening he produced in her had an echo in his own loins. He listened to her body with his senses, using her reactions like a map of where to go, and then she could no longer track what he was doing because her only sentient thought was wanting more of it.

You. More.

He lifted her legs and raised them over his shoulders, going deeper, teasing the shallows of her channel with pulses of his tongue. He made love to her with his mouth and hands and breath, and as he did so he began to thrust his hips, grinding his cock into the mattress like her cunt beneath his mouth made him so desperate he had to fuck the bed.

The naked lust of it sent her reeling and she began to shudder and then quake with the intensity. She was keening, soaked, beside herself, and he just moaned into her cunt and lapped at her, guiding her tremors into a shocking crest that rippled on for minutes in staccato little pulses teased out by his tongue.

When she was too spent to endure another second of his delicious torture, she moved her legs. He lifted up his head. "I could do that all day," he murmured, his eyes devilish and gleaming. "I could do it clear until I died."

She dropped her legs and curled onto her side, laughing. He slid up and curved himself against her back, put his hand flat against her trembling belly.

His cock slid against her skin, silky hot and damp.

She rolled over to face him. His eyes were soft and full of light.

He kissed her nose.

And that, that, was *far* too much, this tender nose-kissing. She must distract him with earthly pleasures of her own before the care he took with her made her fall apart.

She reached for his cock and stroked it against her thigh, smearing the wetness at its tip onto her skin. He winced and groaned, and when he reopened his eyes she knew what the expression in them meant. *You. More.*

She did it again, and he threw back his head. She liked watching the muscles of his stomach clench together in response to her. She wanted him to let go.

"Lie back, sweet man. I've got you."

She admired the sight of him supine. Though she worried that he looked so thin, she liked how it made his musculature stand out. She took a moment to run her fingers over the lean lines of his biceps and his forearms, the tight ridges at his navel, the dark hair that trailed down to his belly, the two suggestive lines that made a hollow from his hips down to his cock. She spread his legs and took his bollocks in her hand.

"Wet me," he whispered.

She leaned down to lick his cock but he put his hand on it to stop her. "Not with that."

He looked meaningfully at her quim, his eyes twinkling with lascivious suggestion.

She shimmied up and hovered over him. "Did you mean with my cunt?"

He bit his lip, smiling. "Just a taste."

She opened herself up and placed his shaft against her wetness. It felt so good that another tiny orgasm went through her, and she froze, shocked at her own response to his bare flesh.

"Don't stop," he gasped. She rubbed against him until his cock was slick and coated.

God, she wanted him inside her. But no, she mustn't.

She moved back between his knees to remove the temptation and sank her mouth around his cockhead. He throbbed, tasting of herself and of the sea. She ran her fingers beneath his balls, putting pressure at the strip of skin between them and his arse.

He said something breathy and indecipherable and put his ankles on the bed, opening up his thighs for her so she could reach any part of him she wanted. God, she loved his ease with sex. She wanted to consume him. She wanted to make him come so hard he screamed.

She ventured toward the cleft of his arse and breathed against it, to see if he welcomed that type of pleasure. When he groaned, she put her finger gently to the ring of muscle.

"Christ," he gasped.

She paused. "No?" she asked, glancing up at his face.

His head was thrown back into the pillow, and his chest was rising rapidly. "Christ *yes*," he rasped.

She smiled. "One moment. I have something that might please you."

She leaned over to reach her bedside table and removed a little mushroom made of jade and a vial of oil.

His eyes followed her, glassy with arousal. "What's that?"

"I'm going to tease you with it. Tell me if you like the feeling."

She knelt back between his outstretched thighs, poured oil between her fingers, and smoothed it over his arsehole. Slowly, she dripped some on the plug, then nudged his opening.

"Oh aye," he hissed.

She gently increased the pressure, pouring oil on his cock and belly for good measure. When he began to press himself back against the orb, inviting it to open him, she slid it deeper. He clutched the counterpane, his hips bucking involuntarily, as she lodged it in his channel.

His pleasure sent a stream oozing from his cock.

She lowered her lips and swirled them up and down around his shaft, then sank her mouth around him and drew him deep into her throat. She placed her fingers on the hollow of his belly as she sucked him, so she could feel the clenching of his muscles. He clutched her hair and gave himself to the rhythm of her mouth, and she could feel the tension building, taste his anticipation. It was so arousing that her quim pulsed in sympathy. She reached down and put her fingers to her cunt and moved against her hand.

He spasmed, and she knew that he was at the point beyond return. He scooted back to slide out of her mouth, and his weight sent more pressure to the plug. His eyes bulged, and he shouted as seed erupted from his cock onto his belly, shooting out of him with such force and volume that she came just from the sight of it.

They both stared at each other, panting.

"My God," he rasped. "What have you done to me?"

She reached out and lazily rubbed his seed about his belly, enjoying the way it caught his hairs. "Made love to you?" she asked.

He rose onto his knees and reached behind himself to gingerly remove the plug. "Come here," he said.

She wrinkled her nose. "You're sticky."

He winked at her. "I know."

She laughed. "Sticky men are not one of my perverse pleasures, I'm afraid."

She went to her dressing table to find a cloth. He watched her, smiling faintly.

"Is that—" he said softly. She turned around, not sure what he was looking at. His eyes were fixed on the amulet he'd sent to her, sitting in her open jewel case.

"Oh. Yes," she said, returning to the bed with a linen. She leaned down to wipe his stomach clean.

"You kept it," he murmured.

"Of course I kept it," she said briskly, embarrassed as much by what this revealed about herself as by how much it seemed to move him.

The look on his face nearly broke her heart.

She softened. "I cannot remember a gift that touched me quite so much, Adam."

His face. Oh, his face. "Sweet man, don't look at me like that," she whispered.

But he didn't stop. Instead, he pulled her to him and held her so tight she almost couldn't breathe.

"What are we doing, Sera?" he whispered in her ear.

She wished she knew. This felt different from Cornwall. It felt urgent and searing.

Dangerous.

She looked into his eyes and said the only honest thing she could. "I haven't the slightest idea."

He was quiet for a moment. "It frightens me."

"Why?" she asked, though she did not fully want to hear the answer. She suspected she could provide her own reasons.

He was staring at the ceiling. "Because I want this. I want you. I want . . . more."

You. More. He felt it too. She smiled so hard her face hurt, until she glanced over at him, and saw that he was not happy.

"But I have . . . commitments, Sera," he said softly. "And so do you. And they don't . . . they're not the same, our obligations."

She'd always expected there would be a pivot. But it had taken so long to come that she'd forgotten it lay in wait. He meant his children and her cause, of course. And he was right.

Their lives were not compatible.

But she didn't *want* to give him up. How could she, after this?

"It needn't be more than it is," she said quietly, hoping not to sound like she was pleading. "A discreet arrangement between two friends."

"I think you were right all along, my Sera. We aren't friends."

His voice was far away, like he was already halfway down the corridor, about to walk out the front door. She didn't like it.

"What are we then?" she asked.

He kissed her shoulder and didn't answer.

For a moment, they lay next to each other in silence. He slid his hand down her stomach to her mons and cupped it possessively. "Sera, promise me something."

She held herself still. "Yes."

"I wanted to be inside you, just now. I know you wanted it, too. But don't tempt me, lass. Aye? I can't make you pregnant. 'Twould be a disaster."

Instinctively, she put a hand to her belly, her ribs tightening with a sharp stab of fear about her absent menses. "You're right," she said immediately. "I won't. I promise."

But she felt chilled.

He sat up. "I need to go. I have so much work to do it makes my eyes cross just to think about it." His voice sounded awful—full of dread.

She rose and watched him dress. He was so thin. "You look tired. You can stay and rest, if you like."

He laughed, unhappily. "I'd give anything to, but I've hours of drafting ahead of me."

She wondered if his rush was truly caused by anxiety about his work, or if it was his apprehensions about her. "What is it that you're working on?"

"A proposal for that armory I mentioned in Cornwall. Lots to do."

He didn't seem to wish to elaborate, and she wouldn't press him. Still, she felt tense, watching him dress. Would this be the last time she watched him slide his breeches over his thighs? Tie the laces of his boots?

She hoped not.

He finished arranging his cravat and sat down beside her on the bed. "When can I see you again?"

This question made her feel warm inside. She'd been imagining things. He wanted to come back. She smiled. "I did invite you for supper Sunday."

He kissed her. "Then I shall look forward to it."

So would she.

Far more, she knew, than was remotely sensible.

How was it that you could come your bloody bollocks off with a woman whose very smile made your heartbeat lurch, and leave her townhouse feeling dreadful?

After days holed up in his studio from dawn until late at night, it should feel good to be outside at the scandalously early hour of half past seven, walking through the cool late summer evening, relaxed from a cleansing conversation and sexual release.

He should be elated.

He was, in fact, elated.

And yet, the dying twinges of pleasure mingled with the more nagging ones of guilt.

He had scarcely seen his children in a month. He was already behind in his revisions to the armory plans. Just this morning, Tregereth had written requesting changes to the renovation that would require Adam to return to Cornwall as soon as he was able.

Every minute spent with Seraphina had been stolen. And the theft was tinged with recklessness, for the fervor over her memoirs had only made her more notorious, and rumors of her involvement in kidnapping Lady Bell were adding to the fury.

He should not have come. He should certainly not have slept with her.

And yet he had wanted to linger longer than he had. He had wanted to spend the evening lolling in Seraphina's bed making her laugh. He had wanted to fuck her senseless, then curl up in her arms and fall asleep.

He had wanted to pretend this other life—his real life—was not awaiting him.

He had never been good at limiting his ardor. Catriona called this quality *intensity*. What would she think of him, his Cat, giving short shrift to his work and their children to have a love affair? Would she not tell him to learn his bloody lesson? Focus on his duties before their children suffered for his sins again?

He walked back to the studio, determined to work long into the night to make up for the time he'd spent away. With every step closer, he felt lower.

He despised this work. Despised it. He had never realized until now.

For so long he'd thought that if he could only win projects of greater scale and public value, he'd be happy. He'd stop yearning for a different life. But doing Pendrake's bidding made him feel worse, not better. It was impossible to separate the work from the politics. Adam felt like his soul was shrinking, day by day.

Perhaps if he had not met Seraphina, had not read her memoirs, he would not have noticed. But he could not unsee what Pendrake represented. He felt rotten by association.

More rotten, because he was already complicit. He needed the work. He needed the money. He'd made his choice.

And when Seraphina found out about Pendrake—it would be the end of them.

He'd almost told her, when she'd asked about his work. He knew she'd solve the dilemma by showing him the door.

The longer he hid it, after all, the worse it would become. Which would only make it more painful, for the more time he spent with her, the harder it would be to pull himself away.

And yet, he bloody wanted her. Every time he saw some sign that one of her carefully tended walls was collapsing—

a glimmer of emotion in her eyes, that pendant on her dressing table—he wanted to rip them down himself.

Enough.

He was in a state. He would work through the night, exhaust himself beyond the point of melancholic stewing. Fretting had never solved a thing.

The door to his studio was unlocked, despite the hour. He found Mayhew inside, rummaging through Adam's files.

"There you are! Where have you been? You've been gone all afternoon." His brother-in-law was clad in formal attire, like he was on his way to some fine function.

"I had to check with a mason about the potential changes to the armory plans," Adam lied. Luckily, Mayhew was too uninterested in architectural matters to sense this was not true. And too excited about whatever had him tearing about the studio.

"Easy with those," Adam said, wincing as Mayhew paged through a book of sketches.

"Where is that folio book with the townhouse designs you drew last year? I have a lead on something very promising."

"It should be in the bottom drawer of my desk." Adam walked over to find it and noticed he had left Seraphina's letter sitting out where anyone could see it. The last thing he needed was Mayhew discovering Adam had been to see her and raising a tantrum.

He slipped it into the drawer and handed Mayhew the book. "Here you are."

Mayhew took it and saluted. "I'm off to present our services to Viscount Bell."

Adam stiffened. "Bell?"

"Aye. A fellow at my investment club introduced us, and he told me he is looking to invest in a new square in

Mayfair," Mayhew prattled on, not noticing that Adam had stopped breathing. "Needs an architect. I'm meeting him at his club tonight to discuss it."

Adam tried to remember if he'd introduced himself to Bell the day the man had stormed inside Seraphina's house. No, there would not have been an opportunity. But Bell would surely recognize Adam's face.

"Ah, fortunate," Adam said, trying not to betray any concern.

With any luck, Mayhew's meeting would come to nothing, and Adam would not have to explain to his brother-in-law why it would be impossible for him to work for Bell.

"Well, good luck," Adam said, trying not to betray any concern.

"Yes, could be very good for us to win his favor. I understand he's close with Pendrake. If he likes us, could be helpful with the armory. You know how those lordly types are." Mayhew winked.

Christ.

Adam did know how such men were. They exchanged information, favors, influence. The good opinion of one could lead to a host of opportunities. And a bad opinion would cause them to close ranks without a second thought.

Fuck.

"Right," Adam said faintly, unable to push past his dread to summon enthusiasm.

Mayhew looked up at him and frowned. "You look pallid," he observed.

"Just tired. Busy day. Nothing a little sleep won't help."

Not that he would get much anytime soon. Adam sat down at a drafting table and picked up a pencil.

Mayhew thumped him on the back. "Don't stay too late. We need you sharp. It's all happening, Anderson. Bloody finally."

Adam nodded and watched Mayhew stride out the door.

As soon as he heard the front door close, he put his head down on the table.

Damnation. Was this a punishment? Was divine justice so swift that an afternoon's infraction could be met with retribution in a single evening?

But no, he wasn't being punished. He was merely reaping the consequences of a situation he'd made himself. One could not be the lover of a radical on Monday and the commissioned builder to the Royal Navy on a Tuesday and not expect one to cause problems with the other.

He'd never thought that it was possible to avoid this conflict altogether. He'd just hoped he might avoid it until he'd had his fill.

It was selfish.

He had to stop pretending he could divide his life into separate realms.

On Sunday, he would have to say farewell to Seraphina.

He just didn't know how he'd find the strength.

Chapter Twenty-Five

Marriage was invented by mankind, but childbearing was invented by God. The custom of damning babies born outside of wedlock and the mothers who bear them is the ill of society, not nature.

—*An Essay in Defense of Ruined Women*
by Seraphina Arden, 1793

Sera stood stark naked before her dressing table in the bright morning sunlight, inspecting her body like a treasure map for clues.

She'd gained a bit of weight since July, but only enough to make up for what she'd lost before that, when she'd had no appetite. The smell of breakfast wafting from downstairs was making her feel ill, but her queasiness could be from worry. Her breasts were tender, but then, they usually were before her menses.

Which she had not had in ten weeks.

Ten weeks.

She lurched across the room to a chamber pot and was sick.

When she was finished, she did not feel better. She felt exactly like she had when she'd been seventeen, when no amount of retching had soothed her illness.

She sat down on her bed.

Ten weeks could not be the product of a restless imagination. She was with child.

She was carrying *Adam Anderson's* child.

She lay flat on the bed.

She wanted to weep.

She wanted to smile.

She wanted to scream—though with joy or terror she could not precisely say.

A child. A baby. *Her* baby?

It felt foreign to imagine her possessing such a creature. Almost perverse.

So why did she not feel more upset? She pressed her hands over her abdomen and recalled making the same discovery as a girl. She'd been so ashamed. She'd walked around for a week feeling like she was already dead.

But this felt nothing like that.

It was like she was an observer of her own perambulation down the path of fortune and had just watched a heretofore unseen route unfold, opening up a new direction that would take her to a place she could not yet glimpse.

She could see the possibility for heartbreak.

But at the thought of a tiny being awakening inside her, she felt the strangest tug of tenderness. Not fierce, but soft and persistent, like the mewling of a kitten. She wanted to protect it. To make her strong and keep her safe.

She took a deep breath. Very well then.

She would. By God, she simply would.

To bear and raise a child out of wedlock was within her capabilities. She would give her baby her name and raise her to know that she was wanted and loved as much as any child. She would show women that this was their right, that they needn't be ashamed of the rhythms of nature they were part of, whatever their circumstances.

She could be that most ennobled and powerful of things; that loving figure she'd always wanted for herself, and never had: a mother.

She rubbed her stomach, and this time she did smile.

Very well, little one. Welcome. You are going to have an interesting life.

But, oh dear. What are we going to do about your father?

What had Adam said about making her pregnant? That it would be a disaster?

He hadn't clarified exactly what he meant by that, but it would unquestionably take a toll on his ambitions if it were known he was the father of Seraphina Arden's bastard child.

He was a bastard himself. Would he make demands on her? Try to insist on marriage to give the baby his name?

Or would he do the opposite—deny paternity or insist on secrecy?

After all, there was his own family to think about. Jasper and Adeline would be affected if he acknowledged another child, especially if that child belonged to Seraphina Arden.

She tried to imagine what he might choose, how he would react—but she couldn't bring herself to do it.

Telling Jonathan all those years ago had been the most chilling moment of her life. She still remembered how he'd looked at her. As though she'd done it on purpose, and he knew her game.

It made her want to avoid telling Adam altogether. After all, she'd laughed at him when he'd called bedsport risky. She'd preached to him the security of her methods of prevention. She'd done it in good faith, of course, but that would not change the truth of their predicament.

That would not change the fact that he'd been right.

But no. She was being childish. She would tell him, of course. Tonight, at supper.

That was what the woman she was trying to become would do. A woman who addressed her fears head-on, instead of burying them in a bottle of claret.

A woman who *tried*.

ADAM KNOCKED ON Seraphina's door like a man arriving for a funeral, not supper.

"Mr. Anderson," Maria said, greeting him with a smile. "Miss Arden asked me to show you to the parlor."

He followed her to a sitting room he had not seen on his last visit, a cheerful nook upholstered in the striking fabrics Seraphina favored for her gowns—a coral silk for the sofa, turquoise for the armchairs.

He sat down, feeling like he had been allowed one final night in a summer garden before exiling himself to permanent winter. He did not want to leave this house for good; he wanted to move into it.

Seraphina's laugh entered the room before she did. "Why, Mr. Anderson, don't you look morose."

He rose and bowed as she floated in like a creature from some other, better world. He tried to smile. "Less morose now that I see you. You look beautiful."

Her gown was a color he recalled from a painting of the Adriatic Sea—a crystalline blue, bright, with hints of green. A long gold chain fell down her neck between her breasts and her ears were hung with ruby drops that glimmered in the candlelight.

Her skin against those ruby drops was so creamy he wanted to taste it.

She smiled at him. "Come and kiss me before supper."

It was a struggle to remain standing at a respectful distance, his face hurting from the smile on it, and not move to embrace her. But he was determined to exercise restraint. To get right to the point.

"Before we eat, there's something I need to discuss with you," he said.

She closed the distance herself, taking his hand. "Discuss? Sounds serious." Her tone was playful, flirtatious, welcoming. "Maybe it can wait until I . . ."

She leaned in, threaded her fingers through his hair, and softly kissed him. He could not resist kissing her back.

One last time.

He pulled her closer, gave her his tongue. She laughed softly in the back of her throat, pleased at this show of enthusiasm.

He growled and lifted her off her feet. They went stumbling back against the wall, grasping and entwined, and it brought to mind that night in the rainstorm, when she'd lifted her arms to the gale and it had seemed like she was summoning the thunder, summoning the lightning, summoning something in him that drenched him as mysteriously and undeniably as rain.

She gripped his lower back, then slid a hand down into his breeches and clenched his buttocks, pressing his body against hers.

"Oh God, I've needed this," she whispered. He blindly fumbled for her skirts, lifting them up and out of the way as best he could without breaking their kiss.

Fuck restraint. He needed this, too. One last time.

She hooked her foot behind his calf and he groped down for her cunt until he found it, slick and swollen beneath his palm. He cupped her, dragged a finger through the seam.

She arched back against the wall to open herself and he leaned with her, penetrating her mouth with his tongue and her quim with his fingers the way he wanted to do with his cock.

His groin spasmed with the rhythm, as though he actually *was* fucking her. She broke from his lips and put her head on his shoulder, her hips rocking to take more of his fingers inside her. He felt the heat and muscles of her cunt. He felt with his entire body her desire for him.

She let out a high-pitched cry and clenched around his fingers. He found her mouth again and kissed her as she came, and came, and came. Each wave that took her echoed in his balls, and he realized he was going to come, too, in his smalls, without her even touching him.

"Fuck," he cried, as his legs buckled with the shock of it.

She kissed him hungrily, pulling him toward her by the buttocks as his hips frantically sought hers. He fumbled for the wall to steady himself but he was not able, for he was buckling with an orgasm that felt like it was radiating down to his cock from the middle of his spine. She gripped his shoulders to keep him from collapsing as she shuddered and made some unholy, anguished sound.

They slid down the wall together until they were a puddle on the floor, panting in each other's arms.

He did not know how much time passed in that position. A minute. An hour. A year.

All he could feel was the goodness of it, this small, unlikely peace amidst the loneliness of life.

Sera smoothed a lock of hair that had fallen in his eyes. "There really is supper. I did not entice you here strictly to molest you. I am reformed, you see." Her eyes sparkled with amusement.

In the light, the gold chain between her breasts glimmered. He touched it idly, lifting it to see what dangled at its end.

It was the amulet from his children.

Tears welled in his eyes. She saw, immediately, and her face tensed, like she was embarrassed to be caught.

"I suppose I was feeling sentimental. I never expected this to become . . ." She shook her head.

A great, wracking sob burst from him before he could swallow it back. He clutched her shoulders and pressed his face into her warm, sweet-smelling skin.

She held him, running her fingers over his hair. "Darling, why are you so sad?"

Darling? Had she ever called him something so sweet?

Why did she have to do it now?

Why did she have to wear that necklace, like proof she felt this thing between them, too?

When he lifted his head to look at her, her skin glistened with his tears, and a terrible fear was in her eyes, like he'd already said the words. But he hadn't, and if he did not now he never would, and so he choked out what he'd come tonight to say.

"I can't do this anymore, Seraphina."

Chapter Twenty-Six

My story is not an indictment of desire; it is an indictment of inequality.

If you believe our act in conceiving a child was sinful, we both sinned. If you believe, as I do, that our act was natural, we both took our pleasure.

But I was judged, sentenced, and punished; my lover was not. And I am one of nameless thousands.

Is it coincidence, that the men who enact the laws of the kingdom are the same ones who are spared? None of us is guiltless. Yet half of us bear the consequence and the other half walk free.

—*Memoirs of a Rakess, Volume II*

❧

What was it about a man's tears that made even the most shale-hearted woman feel like she would rather die than watch him cry?

Adam sobbed like he was grieving something.

"Darling, slow down," she said, trying to keep the fear out of her voice. "What can't you do? Tell me what's the matter."

He sat back, put his head in his hands and gathered his breath. Then he looked up at her with shattered, red-rimmed eyes. "I have to end this."

She froze.

Her arms stung. She looked down at her wrists and saw the fine hairs on her skin were standing straight up in the air.

Her body understood before her mind did.

He was grieving *her.*

"What's happened?" she asked faintly.

He closed his eyes and shook his head.

"Every hour of the day I'm a breath away from coming here. I want to live with you, I want to fuck you, I want—"

It was difficult to divorce the meaning of these words from the horrible way he said them, his accent as thick as she had ever heard it, his breath harsh, like he was confessing he had a fatal illness.

"And it's a fantasy," he said. "It's a juvenile, reckless bloody fantasy because every shred of that's impossible."

"Why is it impossible?" she asked, taking care to speak to him gently, as she might address a child. "Slow down. Help me understand."

"Because of who you are, and who I'm not able to be."

This explained nothing, but when he opened his eyes, there was not a question in them but a certainty.

No.

She wrapped her arms around herself. She felt so cold.

He kept those awful, anguished eyes on her. "I have two children with no mother who I've scarcely seen in weeks, and every moment I can steal, I'm contriving ways to be with you. I owe six thousand pounds to Mayhew, and he wants it back. I'm days away from landing a commission that will set me for life, and I can't focus on winning it because my head is here."

He was just exhausted. People said things they didn't mean when they were overwrought.

"Adam, darling, you're tired. Let's get you home, or you can sleep here if you like, and we'll sort this out in a week or two, when you've finished your work."

He shook his head. "Even if I win the commission, if people found about us—"

No.

He looked at the floor and did not finish his sentence.

He didn't have to.

She sank back against the wall. "I see. You're worried for your reputation."

He nodded with such heaviness it was like the movement pained his neck. "The selection is made by the Royal Board of Works. Lord Pendrake is the ultimate decision maker."

No.

Adam was watching her closely, as if to see if she understood the implication. But of course she bloody understood. Of course she did.

"*Lord Pendrake* will decide your fate? And you have known this and said nothing of it at all?"

He nodded with that same weariness, as though he could no more believe it than she. "I know how it must look. I didn't mention it because I was sure you must despise his politics." He paused and looked down at his lap, wincing. "I don't admire the man's views, but I can't afford to be precious about them. I thought I could keep my work separate from . . . this. You. But my partner learned Pendrake is close with Lord Bell. And the risk of association is just . . . it's more than we can afford."

We. How chilling those words were when used to define a group one was outside of.

"I see," she said faintly.

She wondered how long he'd been plotting to give her up over Pendrake's good opinion. Had he decided this afternoon, while she'd allowed herself to daydream that he might smile when she told him her news? Last week, when they'd made love? And for *Pendrake*, of all the ironies.

God, she'd been so stupid.

Adam knelt before her and took her hands. "Sera, don't look at me like that. Please. My every instinct says to blow it up to hell. But you see, my instincts can't be trusted. When I follow them, when I take what I want and damn the consequences, I destroy things. I've done it before. And I cannot live with myself if I do it again."

She wrested away her hands and pressed her fingers to her temples. His emotional display was far less moving with every second he knelt on her polished floorboards lamenting his decision to betray her. "Destroy things?" she repeated sharply. "What do you mean?"

He looked up at the ceiling, pained. "Catriona nearly died giving birth to Adeline," he said quietly. "The physician said that another pregnancy would likely kill her. He took me aside and told me in no uncertain terms not to 'bother' my wife."

His lips curled around the word *bother*.

"I'd been in love with Cat since I was twelve years old. I should have treated those words like gospel. I should have protected her, put her safety above my . . . needs. My children's mother. But I loved her so much, and coupling had always been . . . a part of that. A part of *us*. To not be together, ever, at all was like—" He clenched his eyes shut.

She was remembering all the times he'd flinched at the idea of penetration. She'd thought his concern had been abstract.

The anguish on his face said something very different.

"We did try to be cautious. But we were not careful enough and she conceived. Her third pregnancy was much easier than Addie's, and we both took that as a sign that the doctor had been wrong. And then when her time came the delivery was . . ."

He shook his head.

She did not want to hear the rest of this story.

She could fill in the gaps from her own life.

That animal fear. The mysterious rhythm, the primal pain, all of it absolutely beyond anyone's control.

Stop, she wanted to say, *I can't listen to this. Not now.*

But he was no longer looking at her. His eyes were fixed in the middle of the room, surveying his own grief.

"The labor went on for days and by the end the baby was not living and there was a problem with the afterbirth—an infection. She wasn't strong enough. We lost them both."

His hands were shaking. He needed comfort, she could see that.

He was telling her this not because it brought him any pleasure to recount it but because he needed her to understand, to forgive him.

He could not know that every word he said injured her twice over. Salt rubbed into the gashes of her past. An extra lashing for her future.

Get through this, she commanded herself.

She forced herself to reach out and take his hand. His skin was too hot and she wanted to recoil, but he squeezed her gratefully.

"Afterward," he said haltingly, "the doctor would barely look at me. He acted like I'd killed her. Her mother acted like I'd killed her. That's why I left Scotland. I couldn't stand to be there, with them all looking at me like I'd wanted her to die."

He sat up and looked into her eyes, and she had never seen more misery.

He looked the way she felt.

"So you see, I cannot trust myself. I want something there is every rational reason not to take, and my heart says to take it anyway. Which is why I know that I simply can't. I'm so sorry."

He unclasped her hand and wiped the tears from around his eyes.

She sat fixed against the wall, shivering. She was so, so cold.

He rose to his feet, and she was glad.

Go. Please go.

"Sera," he said softly, looking down at her. "Say that you forgive me."

"Yes," she whispered. She couldn't say more. She hugged herself, freezing.

"Lass," he said in a tone so miserably tender that she could hear the pity seeping out of him, hear how pathetic she must look crouched here, shaking. "Please understand it isn't about you."

Her neck snapped up so forcefully it hurt.

"Not about *me*?"

But wasn't it?

Wasn't this moment, this decision he was making, *precisely* about her?

About the kind of woman she was?

A dangerous temptation one must guard against, lest one's real concerns be threatened?

How elegantly this moment would have fit into the pages of her memoirs. Just today, she had wondered how the story of her girlhood might have gone if she'd met a man like Adam when she was young.

But Adam Anderson was not a happy ending to her story. He was a recurring theme.

And the story was *entirely* about her.

Adam reached down and tilted up her chin. "Sera, lass, know this—" he said in that ragged voice. "I am *reduced* by the loss of you."

She shut her eyes tight and said nothing.

She heard him leave the room and walk slowly down the hall. She heard him open the front door, close it.

She ripped the gold chain off her neck and threw the amulet across the room so forcefully it hit the window glass and then clattered against the wooden floor.

Maria walked into the room, drawn by the sound, and yelped at the sight of Sera curled up on the floor with her face pressed into her knees. "Miss? Supper's ready."

"Throw it out," she said.

Maria came forward, anxious. "Are you ill?"

"Yes. I think I am." Sera stood up, walked to the sofa, and sat down heavily, feeling tired enough to sleep for a year. "Bring me a bottle of claret, Maria."

Maria looked down at her shoes. "We haven't any wine, miss."

Sera closed her eyes. "Then go buy some."

"Miss Magdalene said that we're not to stock any—"

"Maria, does Miss Magdalene pay your wages?"

"No, but—"

"Go buy the wine."

Maria nodded, ashen, and fled the room.

Sera sank her face into the upholstery, letting the fibers scratch her cheeks. She would not weep. She clenched her eyes shut to make sure of it.

She lay in silence, tired to her bones.

What had been the use of all of this? Why try to be better, why try to fight, when it all came back to the same unbearable truth: she was expendable.

She would lie here and wait for her wine and when it came, she would drink so much of it that—

"Sera?"

She opened her eyes. She must have fallen asleep.

A soft hand cradled her head. Elinor was perched beside her on the arm of the sofa, stroking her hair.

But that was impossible. Elinor was in Surrey, hiding. She must be dreaming.

She tried to shake herself awake, but the vision remained. "Elinor?"

Elinor smiled at her sadly. "Dear, what's wrong?"

"Why are you here? Bell will find you—"

"Don't worry about him. I came for you. For your speech tomorrow. I wanted to surprise you."

Her speech tomorrow. She'd forgotten. She was giving a lecture at Jack Willow's shop to mark the publication of her second volume.

She must collect herself. She had to be clearheaded in the morning, so she could finish drafting her remarks. She must ward off this terrible episode of emotion and return to herself.

"Sera!" Cornelia called from the corridor. She and Thaïs rushed into the room. They were both short of breath, like they'd been running.

"Maria came to find us," Thaïs wheezed. "She said you were asking for wine."

"Oh bloody hell," she whispered.

Thank God for Maria. She would have to raise her wages.

"What's happened, darling?" Elinor asked, smoothing her hair. All three of them were looking at her like she might flee.

"I'm pregnant," she whispered.

Elinor wordlessly gathered her up in her arms and held her. Thaïs and Cornelia moved closer, too, until she was shrouded in a fortress made by her friends' limbs.

She never wanted to leave.

"Oh, child," Elinor breathed. She squeezed her shoulders.

For a moment, none of them spoke. No one needed to.

"It won't be like last time," Elinor finally said, her voice firm. "You have us now. And you're so strong."

"Whatever you need, Sera," Cornelia uttered, like a vassal swearing fealty to a feudal lord. "Whatever you need."

"And think, a baby," Thaïs said softly, a smile in her voice.

They were trying to soothe her—they thought she was upset about the baby. But she wasn't.

"The trouble is not that I'm with child," she said tightly. "It's that it's Adam's."

Thaïs's expression darkened. "Maria said he was here. What's he done?"

Sera shook her head. "Nothing. I couldn't tell him." She covered her face in her hands.

"Why not, darling?" Elinor asked.

"Because he came here to end things. To tell me that he must end things because his entire future, his children's future, depends on the patronage of Lord Pendrake."

She paused, waiting for their faces to twist in horror. When they did, she nodded bitterly.

"Association with me is too great a risk, you see. He has to think of his family, his work. And he's right. If only he knew how great a risk it was."

"No," Cornelia pronounced, shaking her head decisively. "Adam strikes me as a principled man. Surely if he knew you were going to have his child, he would find some other way to get ahead, without relying on Pendrake."

Certainly, anything was possible. But that did not mean it was likely. Or worth the cost to herself of asking him and being refused.

"I can't go through that again. Asking someone to choose me, when I know they won't."

They were quiet. They knew that she did not say this lightly.

"I can't imagine, Seraphina, that Adam will not find out about the child eventually," Elinor said. "Pregnancy is not an easy thing to hide, and news of yours will be a scandal. He will have to make the same choice once he learns. Keeping it a secret now will only prolong your fear, without sparing either of you."

This was making her angry. Did they not see that by asking him to make any choice at all, she was setting herself up for something excruciating? Rejection for Pendrake's sake if Adam chose one way, being responsible for his shattered dreams if he chose the other.

"And if he decides he is so moved by the prospect of my pregnancy that he will sacrifice his entire future for me, what then? Am I to *let* him? Am I to carry that? Become his most regrettable mistake?"

Thaïs sank down and put her head on Sera's knee. "Ah, I see. You love him."

"What?" Sera sputtered.

She most fervently did not. If she had allowed herself to become attached, it was only out of some misplaced desire to receive redemption from a male. It was the catechism all women were raised with, after all, to see their value as a reflection of what man would choose them.

She knew better. She had argued for better in her books. But some lessons ran so deep that one had to be vigilant, lest the rotten thinking creep back in.

"I do not love him," she said. "It is a question of respect. Of how he sees me."

Elinor, always the arbiter when it came to wisdom of the heart, cleared her throat.

"Dear, if you didn't care for him, his future wouldn't matter to you. You would demand he think of his responsibility to your child, or you would cut him for choosing his reputation above you. *His* feelings would not factor. Your lovers' feelings never have."

"No, that isn't true," Sera shouted. She had never raised her voice to Elinor before, but this sentiment erased the girl she'd been before she'd known these women. "They *did* once. And what did that get me other than a broken heart?"

"But, Sera, Adam isn't Trewlnany," Cornelia said cautiously. "He's not Pendrake or Bell or any of their lot. He's nothing like them."

Wasn't he though? Had he not chosen their values, by attesting that their power meant more to him than her life?

"You've had a shock," Elinor said gently. "You needn't decide tonight. You'll think about it more and get some rest. And we will support you no matter what you choose to do."

"Thank you," Sera said.

"But, Sera?" Elinor added, looking intently into her eyes. "If you *do* care for him . . . I've never known you to give anything up without a fight."

ADAM HAD ALREADY been in the studio working for hours by the time Mayhew stomped in, looking cross and disheveled. His face was as red as his hair.

"Something the matter?" Adam asked, barely looking up. Mayhew had always been a sensitive, temperamental creature, and today Adam didn't have the patience for dealing with someone *else's* turbulent emotions. He had more than enough of his own.

James pulled a slim pamphlet from under his arm and smacked it down on top of Adam's plans. "This is what's the matter."

The book was embossed with *Memoirs of a Rakess, Volume II*.

"That slut Seraphina Arden is going to be the ruin of us," James said. He slammed his fist on the book so hard it shook the drafting table, sending Adam's pencils clattering to the floor.

The draftsmen in the room looked up in alarm. Feeling their stares, Adam took care to remain calm, though he felt like knocking Mayhew into the wall.

Adam lowered his voice to a growl. "James, with respect, don't you *ever* let me hear words like that out of your mouth again."

"No? Read it," Mayhew shouted at him, not at all chastened. He picked up the book and riffled violently, jamming his finger against a page toward the back. "*Read it. Right now.*"

Adam picked up the book.

The world pulses with the sad stories of women like myself. Ladies who felt a hunger or a flash of vanity or a tenderness—a mad desire to indulge in a transcendent moment of pleasure with someone who made them feel like they were loved. We are no different from men who act impulsively, out of lust or passion. Yet we are the ones punished for our transgressions.

    The blood appeared on my linen three months before the child's term was due.

The child. That was how I thought of her.

I resented her for springing up inside of me, a living embodiment of my shame.

He stared at those words, trying to make sense of them. She'd lost a child? When?

The tale went on, harrowing. A betrayal. A birth. A death.

She'd borne all this and said nothing? She'd listened to him tell his own story, patted his hand, and been silent on the fact that they had this loss in common.

"Adam!" Mayhew barked.

He looked up, dazed.

"You're reading the wrong bloody page," James barked. He pointed at the opposite page of the book.

I did not value my daughter's life until I lost the chance.

And so I thought, as I grieved her, of how I might make it up to her. For she was not a nameless bastard conceived by a foolish girl. She had a mother and a father. A father who whispered vile things about me around town, lest anyone suspect. Who never replied when I wrote to tell him of his baby's death. Who allowed his own father to offer mine a sum equal to the price of three cows to compensate me for the loss of my future.

To this day I've never seen another message in his hand.

But you can find his signature on bills in Parliament.

Jonathan Marcham, Baron Trewlnany. Heir to the Marquess of Pendrake.

Adam let out a breath. "Pendrake. Dear God."

Trewlnany was Pendrake's heir. Suddenly it all made sense.

The posters strung up by Trewlnany's groundskeeper.

The expression on Seraphina's face when he'd said Pendrake's name the night before.

He'd sat in her parlor and told her he was leaving her for her betrayer.

And she hadn't said a word.

He felt like vomiting.

"It gets worse," Mayhew said.

Adam put his hands to his face. "I don't know how it could."

Mayhew took the book and riffled the pages. "She calls for females to be educated and trained to work in trades only fit for men and lists a slew of people who've agreed to take apprentices. You won't believe who she includes."

He smashed the book on the table, his finger jammed so hard at the page it turned white beneath the nail.

Anderson Mayhew, Architects

"Surely, Adam," Mayhew said, his voice vivid with sarcasm, "this must be a terrible misunderstanding."

Adam closed his eyes.

He'd forgotten all about this.

"Tell me, Adam, that it is a mistake," Mayhew said quietly.

"I agreed to hire a female apprentice when I met her in Cornwall. I didn't see the harm in it. I'd forgotten."

"You bloody forgot you pledged our firm to a radical? You bloody forgot you'd destroyed us in her book?"

Adam took a deep breath. "I wasn't aware she intended to publish our firm's name. She didn't mention it."

That was the least of what she hadn't told him.

Did she think he wouldn't care? That her past would mean nothing to him?

"It's slander," Mayhew seethed. "It's bloody slander."

"It isn't slander," Adam bit out. "I agreed. I just didn't know it would be published."

"And you would not have agreed if you had. You were tricked."

"No, not tricked. I'm sure she didn't—"

"Don't defend her!" Mayhew sputtered. "We must undo this. Pendrake's supporters are planning to show up at her lecture tonight to rally against this libel of his son and show their support. Bell's organizing it. You'll come with me and make a speech revoking this pledge and avowing our support for Pendrake and public decency."

Adam shook his head. "No. She is a friend, James, and this is a misunderstanding. You can speak to Pendrake privately to explain we have changed our minds. I will not renounce her publicly."

"Renounce her publicly? Have you gone mad? We *will not* have any chance at the armory if we are viewed to be her conspirators. You do not have a choice. You must disown any connection with her. Think of my sister's children. How will we find a husband for Adeline if she's marked as a daughter of a radical sympathizer? How will we find a place in school for Jasper?"

The unavoidable, ill-making fact was that Mayhew was not wrong.

Adam did not believe Seraphina had meant harm to him. But after naming Pendrake as an enemy, she would be a target.

If he wanted any kind of future, he had no choice but to do what Mayhew asked.

"The rally is at seven o'clock at Jack Willow's bookshop. I had better see you there, Adam. Now is not the time to moon around indulging your Whiggish principles. If we are to save this business, you will join me in the crowd condemning Miss Arden."

The crowd condemning Miss Arden.

He thought of the four dead birds carefully left in a basket at her door.

The posters nailed to her gates and around the town where she had been a child, likely at the direction of the very man who had abandoned her.

The fact was that Pendrake and Trewlnany *deserved* this harm to their reputations.

If they lost a bit of their good name, she had lost everything.

He would not join a crowd in condemning her.

He would not let her show up at Jack Willow's without knowing what awaited her there.

The right thing to do was obvious, and he no longer had the capacity to pretend otherwise.

He had to warn her.

Chapter Twenty-Seven

Seraphina was no longer a flesh-and-blood woman. She was made entirely of nausea.

She had meant to spend the day refining her lecture but instead had spent the better part of it reclining on the sofa, trying not to vomit.

"Jack is here to collect you," Tompkins said, popping her head into Seraphina's bedchamber. "He's waiting downstairs with the ladies. But I don't think you should leave the house. You look positively green."

"I have no choice. Help me down the stairs, would you?"

Tompkins offered a sturdy shoulder, to which Sera clung unsteadily as she walked down the staircase. The effort of putting one foot in front of the other seemed to be taking six times as much effort as usual. Suddenly, her stomach was in her throat. "Wait," she cried. Tompkins paused just in time for her to brace herself on the wall of the landing in front of them, to regain her balance.

Tompkins gripped her arm more tightly. "Back upstairs with you. I'm sending for a physician."

"No, no. I just need a moment."

She did not need a physician. The nausea had been just as bad the first time she was pregnant, making her so ill she could barely get out of bed. There was no cure for childbearing. One simply had to get on with it and hope for the best.

As soon as she finished this lecture, she could take to her bed for a few days, in hopes that rest would soothe her stomach. But if she canceled tonight for so-called reasons of illness, her opponents would see it as fear and cast it as a victory.

Jack was waiting in her parlor, along with Thaïs, Cornelia, and Elinor.

"Christ, you look terrible," he said. "March yourself right back upstairs to bed."

"Absolutely not. If I don't appear, they'll say I'm hiding. Now is the time to show exactly how steadfast we are."

"Steadfast. Seraphina, you look like you might collapse at any second and the crowd won't help. The street is already packed with protesters—Bell's men arranged such a mob I'm half inclined to think they've paid them to show up."

"Then they are fools. The size of the crowd will attract even more press, all of whom will report my ideas." She looked worriedly at Elinor. "But if Bell is involved, surely Elinor should not come with us. It's dangerous enough that she's in London at all."

Elinor winked at the girls. "Shall I tell her my plan?"

"What is your plan?" Sera asked. Something about Elinor seemed different since she'd been away. Sprightlier.

"I'm going to provoke Bell into petitioning for divorce. It's the only way of being free of him."

Jack looked grim. "Elinor, he'll never do it."

Elinor smiled. "Unless he is so enraged . . . he does."

Sera could think of a hundred ways this could go wrong. "And what if he recaptures you tonight?"

"Then I shall resist, and the press will see him taking his wife hostage like a criminal. He'll look like a brute. You know he hates to seem less than gentlemanly."

Cornelia winced. "If his vanity is all that protects your freedom, I might wait for more reliable armor."

"I'll have a carriage waiting behind the arcade, so I can run out the back and flee through the alley if he tries to apprehend me. It may not work, but what choice do I have? Hide forever? I want to *live*."

Thaïs clapped her hands. "That's the spirit. It's better to fight. We promised each other that we would fight."

Cornelia slowly nodded. "I suppose there is a kind of advantage to be won, if we are clever. We can use the outrage over Elinor's divorce to stir up interest for the next phase of our plan. I could paint Elinor as a whore for my Jezebels series. Nude."

Elinor threw back her head and laughed. "Me, posing nude! Oh, what a scandal. Can you imagine?"

Jack had a strange look on his face, like he was imagining. He cleared his throat. "Sera, we need to leave. But before we go—I suppose you saw the afternoon papers? You should be prepared to answer all the latest attacks."

She glanced at the pile of newspapers sitting untouched on the table in front of them. "To be honest, I've been in bed trying not to cast my accounts. What have I missed?"

Jack rummaged through the papers and held up one to show her. *Baron Trewlnany Denies Claims.* "He's vowed to take you to court for libel."

She nodded. "Nothing we did not expect or prepare for."

She had letters between Pendrake and her father proving the substance of her claims. If they went through with a lawsuit it would not succeed in court, but any trial would do much for the celebrity of her cause.

Jack held up another paper. "Three other women have come forward saying that Trewlnany injured their virtue."

She winced. She had suspected she was not the only one. "Poor girls. Bring that one for me, will you? I'll read it in the carriage."

"And this was printed in the *Advocate* this afternoon," Jack added.

He handed her a newspaper.

Tradesmen Unite Against Female Apprentices, the headline read.

She scanned the page. Several prominent business owners had come together to decry her call for female training, and vowed not to hire women.

She sighed. "I fail to see how this constitutes news when none of them hired women in the first place."

She folded the paper and handed it back, but a name toward the end of the article grabbed her eye. She paused and read it more closely.

London architecture firm Anderson Mayhew said it would disavow its support of Miss Arden. "We're horrified by the libelous and immoral accusations in Miss Arden's memoirs," said the owners. "We intend to notify Miss Arden that our pledge was made under false pretenses, and we publicly withdraw as sponsors of her institute."

A fresh wave of nausea rose up from her gut. He hadn't even had the courtesy to denounce her to her face.

She had long made the argument that men took what they wanted until the taking became inconvenient. That their public notions of morality became important to their personal behavior only insofar as it affected their ambitions.

But she'd never for a moment considered *Adam* might be made of such craven stuff. The message was clear: *We men protect each other. You can never out-maneuver our power.*

"Sera, what is it?" Cornelia asked, reaching for the paper.

Sera handed it to her and clamped a hand over her mouth, rushed to a waste bin, and was sick.

Jack came to her with a handkerchief and put his hand on her shoulder. "Sera, I think the best place for you is here. I'll cancel the event."

"Darling, perhaps it's for the best," Elinor said. "You need rest and some ginger for your stomach."

"Nonsense," she said, wiping her mouth. "If women let the small matter of reproduction stop them from their work, I daresay the human race would die out in a single generation. Besides, I find I have quite a bit I want to say."

ADAM STOOD ON Seraphina Arden's doorstep, panting. He'd run here, all the way from Cheapside, skirting past the throngs along the market and the procession of solicitors winding in and out of the Inns of Court and the snarl of traffic along Paternoster. He felt like his heart might burst inside his chest.

The door swung open, revealing Tompkins. Her face turned hostile at the sight of him. "Miss Arden is not here," she said. "And I doubt she'd wish to see you even if she were."

"I . . . has she already left for Willow's?" he asked, baffled at her tone. He and Tompkins had always been friendly, yet now she looked at him like he had stepped in something foul.

She crossed her arms over her chest. "Where she is is her affair. Good day to you. Not that you deserve it."

"Pardon me, Miss Tompkins?" he asked. "Have I done something to upset you?"

She puffed out her lips in disgust. "Miss Arden gets enough grief from her enemies, Mr. Anderson. She does not need added upset from her supposed friends. One would think you owe her common decency."

He was now utterly confused. "I came here to warn her that a crowd of protesters is planning to amass at Jack Willow's bookshop. A gang of Tories is going to denounce her and accuse her of sedition."

Tompkins looked at him as though he was dim. "Of course they are. She would be disappointed if they were not. Their reaction will fan the flames and her memoirs will sell all the better. She does not do these things *accidentally*. And though she provokes this reaction, she is not immune to the toll that it takes. Having seen this yourself, I would think you would already understand as much. I'm disappointed in you. And Miss Arden will likely never say it herself, but so is she."

Tompkins reached for the door to shut it. He grabbed it, stopping it from closing. Tompkins looked at him in shock.

"Don't be a brute," she hissed.

"I'm sorry," he said, shaking his head, trying to piece together what was happening. "You are angry because of what I said last night? That I hurt her?"

Tompkins glared at him. "I am angry about what you printed in the paper this afternoon. *Is there more you did last night?*"

He hadn't printed anything. "Miss Tompkins," he said, not bothering to hide his desperation. "I'm lost. Please, what is it that you think I've done?"

Tompkins turned on her heel and disappeared inside the house, leaving him on the steps. She came back holding a newspaper by two fingers, like it was doused in excrement. The headline read *Tradesmen Unite Against Female Apprentices*.

He took the article and scanned it. "Bastard," he whispered when he saw the quotation at the bottom.

"Precisely," Tompkins sneered.

He was going to throttle Mayhew. "Tompkins, I had no idea. My partner must have done this. I would never have allowed it."

"Well, the damage is done all the same, isn't it?" she said. "You should have seen her face when she saw it. She had to be sick."

He closed his eyes. "I'll explain. I'll make it up to her."

"Can't fathom how," Tompkins muttered.

"She's gone to Willow's shop?" he asked.

Tompkins nodded warily.

He didn't pause to say goodbye, just went running. He could barely see as he elbowed his way through the winding streets to Covent Garden. His mind was fixed with a vision of Seraphina reading that article and thinking he'd said those things *after* he'd learned who Pendrake was to her.

She must think he was the most perfidious, empty-hearted bastard. He hated the idea she would think she'd been drawn in by such a callous person. That she'd let herself care for another man who would toss her aside to save himself.

But then, what reason had he given her to think that he would not?

He'd said as much with his decision last night. And for what?

Mayhew, money, architectural prestige, what did it matter, when the thought of hurting her made him feel like he was being chased by rabid dogs?

He'd known his two lives were not compatible. He'd thought he had to choose the safer path. But that was foolish.

He could not pretend to have a different kind of heart than he possessed. He'd betrayed his own principles. He'd chosen wrong.

He'd protected the less precious thing.

And now he'd hurt her, in the same way she'd been hurt before.

God, this must have caused her so much pain.

His lungs burned from running, but he could not slow down. He had to get to her, had to explain himself, had to apologize and fix this. He reached Willow's bookstore in a lather, stinking with his own anxious perspiration.

A crowd of men was thick in front of the store, blocking the entry. Mayhew stood with a group of them who were passing around signs covered in crude words. He waved and beckoned Adam over.

"Ah, I'm pleased you made it. Was beginning to question your commitment. Here, take this." He held out a vulgar poster.

Adam snatched it from Mayhew's hands and crumpled it.

"You bleedin' dobber," Adam hissed. He threw the poster into the gutter. "I saw your article. Don't you ever speak on my behalf again."

Mayhew's eyes grew wide. Adam had not cursed at him since they were children. "Look here—" James said, puffing himself up.

"Get out of my way," Adam snarled, barreling past. He shouldered and elbowed his way through the crowd of men until he had edged his way inside the shop. Seraphina was on a dais, already addressing the crowd.

The audience, made up almost entirely of women, gazed on with a rapt admiration. He leaned in to hear over the din of the men shouting outside.

"The moral of my tale should not be overlooked amidst the scandal of my naming Baron Trewlnany. In publicly identifying him, I wanted to illustrate the stark difference in the outcomes of our lives. He is a titled heir to a peer. He holds an elected seat in the House of Commons and will someday ascend to the Lords. His family—four children, I believe—live in comfort on an estate. Compare that to me. A woman who cannot attend the celebration of her own book without being jeered by crowds of screaming men."

There was a trickle of vulgar cries from the back of the room, near Adam, where the men in question had begun fighting their way inside the crowded shop.

Sera looked out at the back of the room and chuckled. "Thank you, gentlemen. You illustrate my point handsomely." She smiled out into the crowd. And then she saw him, and the smile left her face.

He held up a hand, a silent greeting. *I'm here for you, not them*, he tried to tell her with his eyes. *I'm sorry.*

For a second she seemed to falter, staring at him mute. She looked back at the women in the front. "I did not tell this story to earn your pity. I am very fortunate; with the freedom my ignominy has given me I may be luckier than many men."

And then she looked directly into his eyes and added, "Including the cowards standing in the back of this room."

He felt like he'd been slapped.

The ladies cheered again as the protesters rumbled more loudly.

"My friends," Sera said above the din, "our struggle is going to be a long one, as these men here demonstrate. Unfortunately, those in possession of unfair advantages see equality as a danger. They believe we want to take *their* power. They cannot see that we simply ask for parity. Power of our own."

There was a scuffle at the door and a crowd of men the room could ill accommodate came bounding inside, chanting.

"Stop the liar!" they shouted. "Stop the whore! Silence her forevermore!"

The ladies looked up in alarm at the commotion. Willow and several men came rushing from near the dais to the back of the room to confront the intruders.

Sera looked out to address them directly. "May I help you, sirs?" she asked pleasantly.

Her voice was clear and strong but he noticed she gripped the podium in a way that seemed unnatural, and sweat glittered on her brow. Tompkins's words echoed in Adam's mind: *she is not immune to the toll it takes.*

"Slanderer!" a bald man shouted, charging closer to the stage. "Lying whore!"

Even from behind, Adam recognized his egg-shaped build.

"Lord Bell," Sera said, smiling. "How kind of you to come to my talk. Which of my words do you find dishonest? That ladies suffer injustice? Or that society would benefit from the equality of all people?"

"Miss Arden is an inveterate liar and a criminal," Bell intoned to the room. "Her filthy book is full of slander and her crimes are not limited to her words. This woman has abducted my wife, and I will be taking her to the magistrate."

Seraphina glanced at someone near her in the audience, as if amused. The lady rose and climbed up to the dais beside Sera.

It was Lady Bell.

The room exploded into pandemonium.

"Good day, my lord," Lady Bell called to her husband over the noise. "As you can see, Miss Arden has not abducted me. I merely found I did not enjoy being locked in an insane asylum, and contrived to leave at my earliest convenience. Through a window, as it were."

The men erupted into a frenzy. Lady Bell smiled knowingly at the women. Standing there so calmly, she looked poised, matronly, sane. She shook her head wryly at the rioting men, as if to say—*can you imagine, them, thinking* we're *the mad ones?*

Lady Bell held up her hand, demanding quiet. "That my husband was and is perfectly within his rights to imprison me and take away my children is a testament to exactly the injustice Miss Arden's book denounces."

Bell was fighting his way to the stage, like he intended to pull his wife off of it, but Jack Willow and his men formed a barrier, protecting her. Lady Bell kept talking, clear and serene.

"Everything you've read about my supposed adultery is untrue. The source of my husband's ire is that I disobeyed him. I disagreed with him politically, and I had the audacity to write down my views." She leaned forward, and addressed Lord Bell directly. "My lord, if marriage to me is so unpleasant, you needn't take the trouble of locking me up—being married to you is already like prison. Why don't you just divorce me?"

"Divorce the whore," a man behind Adam shouted. The men in the crowd raised their fists. "Divorce her!" they began to chant.

Lady Bell smiled. "Finally, something on which we all agree."

She curtsied to the crowd, walked behind a curtain, and disappeared, leaving a chaos of screaming men behind her. The room throbbed with shouting.

"Apologize!" "Recant!" "Kidnapper!" "Adulteress!" "Whore!"

Bell threw himself toward the dais, attempting to shove past Willow's men.

"Lord Bell," Seraphina chided, looking bored. "The stage is mine tonight. If you have an argument to make, do as I have done and publish a book of your own."

"If you haven't committed kidnapping, you've certainly committed libel," Bell shouted, shoving his way past Willow. "I'm taking you in to have you arrested. Submit, or we shall take you by force."

Adam stepped into the skirmish and went running for the dais.

Chapter Twenty-Eight

Seraphina was accustomed to being jeered.

When one made a life's work of speaking on inflammatory topics in public, one learned to see derisive shouts and the occasional piece of lobbed fruit as atmosphere that added gravity to one's message. If you were offensive enough to be harassed, you were being heard.

But she was not accustomed to being charged by an aristocrat like he was a bull.

Don't show fear, Sera commanded herself as Bell hurtled toward the stage and the bookstore erupted into a mass of violent bodies. She would not run. She had done nothing wrong. If he wanted to drag her to a magistrate, she would go in peace.

But as he stormed toward her, a small woman emerged from the front row and stepped in front of him. As she stood, her hat fell to the floor.

It was *Tamsin Rowe*. And she was squaring off against Bell like she was twice his size.

"My lord, you have no case against Miss Arden," Tamsin said in a loud but quaking voice, marching toward him. "What she wrote is true."

"And who are you to slander the Baron Trewlnany?" a tall man beside Bell sneered, stepping in her way, like the portly lord required protection from a woman not five feet tall.

"I am his wife, the Baroness Trewlnany," Tamsin sneered back. "And as such I know for a fact that the story Miss Arden printed was not slander. Every word of it is true."

Sera stared at Tamsin, the girl who had been her dearest friend and closest confidante before she'd married Jonathan, in wonder. *Where have you been, all this time? And why are you saying this now?*

"That is quite enough, Lady Trewlnany," Bell sputtered, grabbing Tamsin's arm. Before Sera could think how to react, Adam Anderson threw himself on top of Bell, pulling him away from Tamsin. And then the crowd flew into such chaos she could not tell who was what.

Her heart pounded in her chest so hard that it was painful. *Breathe*, she ordered herself. *Stand strong.* But in the sea of thrown fists, shouting men, and scared women rushing for the doors, she felt her knees go unsteady. She clenched her forearms on the podium to steady herself.

Cornelia and Thaïs rushed toward her. "I need to get off this stage," Sera whispered. "Right now."

Cornelia took Sera's arm. "Let's get her upstairs to Jack's rooms."

Sera let them guide her behind the curtain, trying to remain tall and steady even as the room went black and started spinning.

Thaïs grabbed her by the waist with both arms. "Can you climb the stairs?"

"I think so," Sera gasped. "Bloody hell, they are going to think I was afraid and ran."

"They are in too great a disarray to think anything. Jack will clear the whole place out before he gets arrested for inciting a mob."

Sera focused on climbing, one foot in front of the next, trying not to think of the cramping in her gut. A decade passed as she climbed two flights of stairs. An eternity. An eon.

When they were finally above the shop she staggered into Jack's rooms.

"Where's Elinor?" Sera asked, looking about.

"She made it out the back," Cornelia said. "She's safe for now. She'll stay in Surrey until this quiets down."

At least there was that. She sat down, trying to get ahead of the nausea that wanted to send her to the floor knees first. But she could not catch her breath. Her shoulders began to shake. She felt like she had when—

No. No. No.

"I need Hawksmoor," she gasped. She could scarcely form words for the fear settling in her throat, making it difficult to swallow air. "Something is wrong."

ADAM DID NOT know how many hands tugged at him as he made his body a barrier between Bell and Lady Trewlnany. He looked out behind him, to see if Sera was caught in the fray, but she had disappeared from stage. He prayed that meant she was safe.

"Come with me," he said to the baroness. "I'll get you to safety."

A man reached out and tried to drag her back toward Bell. "Let go of her," Adam shouted, tossing the pest aside with one hand as he clamped the baroness to his chest with the other.

"She's in defiance of her husband," another man shouted.

"I reckon her husband has bigger problems at the moment than a defiant wife," Adam snarled back, pushing him aside. He was grateful for his height and strength as he struggled through the shouting throng toward the street, Lady Trewlnany huddled under one arm.

"Thank you," she gasped when they reached the pavement. She was ashen.

He nodded, releasing her gently to make sure she was steady on her feet. "You were brave in there. Can I hail you a hackney cab?"

"No, I have a carriage waiting." She pointed, and he saw the vehicle had Pendrake's family's seal.

"It's my mother-in-law's," she said, gesturing at the seal with a laugh that sounded somewhat hysterical. "She thinks I'm at a gown fitting."

He bowed, eager to get back inside to find Sera, but Lady Trewlnany kept speaking.

"You're Seraphina's friend, are you not? The one I saw with her at the inn in Cornwall?"

Adam nodded. He hoped Sera would still count him as a friend.

"I was once lucky enough to call her a friend myself," the baroness said, her voice heavy with emotion. "If you see her, please tell her I have read her book, and am so sorry for everything that happened."

Whatever her husband's failings, this woman seemed to genuinely care for Seraphina.

"Baroness, may I ask you a question?" he said. "Did your husband leave birds at Seraphina's house? In Cornwall?"

Lady Trewlnany stared at him blankly. "Birds?" she asked.

"Aye," he said. "A basket of them. Dead. With a threatening note."

She inhaled sharply. "Were they kingfishers?"

"Aye."

"Oh good heavens," she whispered. "My children keep them as pets. A few went missing over the summer and we didn't . . . Oh, good heavens. Please tell her I'm sorry."

She rushed tearfully to her carriage before Adam could reply.

"Oh, Mr. Anderson, thank God," a cockney voice cried out from behind him. He turned around to see Miss Magdalene rushing out of the shop in his direction. Her pale skin was so white her freckles looked lurid.

"What's the matter?" he asked.

She held out a slip of paper. "I need a favor, urgently. Please can you deliver this note to Alison Hawksmoor at Candlelighter Mews. If she is not at home, find the nearest physician."

Dread pulsed in his chest. "Has someone been injured?" *Don't let it be Seraphina.*

Miss Magdalene looked him dead in the eyes. "I'm not sure, but it's serious. Hawksmoor will understand. Go, right away."

He nodded and went racing through the crowded streets. The address wasn't far. He frantically shouted to a groom for the right door. A middle-aged woman answered when he knocked.

"Are you Mrs. Hawksmoor?"

"I am," she said cheerfully.

"A note for you. It's urgent." He handed her the paper and watched her face intently as she read it.

The woman frowned. "Miss Arden? I didn't know she was breeding."

Breeding?

But did that mean—could it be—fucking *hellfire*.

"What is the nature of her complaint, do you know?" Mrs. Hawksmoor asked.

He tried to find his voice.

"Sir?" she pressed.

"I'm sorry. I don't know. She was giving a speech, and a great mob appeared and interrupted her."

"She must have had a fright. Shock can be bad for a babe. Though Miss Arden is a steady type. You though, sir, do not look steady at all. Is the child yours?"

He ran his hand through his hair. "I don't know. Yes. Probably. God bedamn me."

The woman patted his back. "Don't fret, sir. Whatever happens, she's strong. And you must be strong for her. Wait here while I gather my things."

She ducked into an alcove and reemerged with a satchel, wearing a cloak. He led her briskly through the narrow streets back to Jack Willow's. The crowd had thinned outside of the shop, and they were able to get inside without a fight. Willow and another man were in their shirtsleeves, sweeping up the mess left by the throng.

"You're the midwife?" Jack asked Mrs. Hawksmoor.

"I am."

"Thank God. She's upstairs, in quite a bit of distress. Go quickly." His eyes fell on Adam, nothing short of murder in them. "But *you* are not welcome here."

"I know how it must look, and you are good to protect her, but I need to be here," Adam said, without stopping. He did not wait to be granted permission, just went bounding up the stairs.

Miss Magdalene rushed out to greet them. "Thank you for coming so quickly, Mrs. Hawksmoor. She's resting in here."

Mrs. Hawksmoor followed, leaving Adam gasping for breath in the door.

"She's with child," Miss Magdalene said over her shoulder to Hawksmoor, her voice pitched low. "Early, about two and a half months. Terrible sickness all week, and just now she nearly fainted. You know she lost—"

Mrs. Hawksmoor nodded as they disappeared into

another room. Adam tried to follow them, but Mrs. Hawksmoor stopped him. "It's best she has some privacy." She closed the door behind her.

He slumped back against the wall, unsure of what to do. He heard a cry and rushed to the door and knocked at it.

Miss Ludgate opened the door and glared at him. "You should leave. If she wishes to speak to you, she'll write."

He didn't move. "I need to see her. Please. I'll wait."

She stepped out of the room and pointedly closed the door behind her, as if his merely looking at Seraphina might worsen her condition. "Mr. Anderson, I won't have you upsetting her worse than she's already—"

"It is not your affair," he said, trying not to raise his voice. "If she's carrying my child—if she's lost it—I need to bloody be here for her."

Miss Ludgate let out a breath. "Listen to me. This is very delicate, she's upset—"

"I lost a wife in childbirth," he interrupted, unable to control his tone. "I know exactly how bloody delicate it is and I'm not leaving."

Cornelia paused, looking torn. "Fine, wait here. But if you do the slightest thing to cause her pain—"

"I have no intention of hurting her," he shouted. *"I would never hurt her."*

But even as he said it, he knew he already had.

He collapsed onto a chair. "Fuck. *Fuck.*"

Miss Magdalene came out of the room with tears streaming down her face.

Catriona's lifeless form flashed before his eyes. He jumped to his feet. "What is it?" he rasped. "What happened to her?"

"She's fine," she said, wiping her eyes. "She's fine. Just a scare. She just needs rest."

"And the baby?" he got out.

Thaïs's face looked strained. "All fine, for now. Too soon to say."

He strode to the door, shaking. "Sera? Love, it's Adam. May I come in?"

The midwife opened the door for him. Behind her, Sera sat on a bed wearing only a shift. Her hair fell around her shoulders. She was pale, damp with sweat.

Mrs. Hawksmoor wrapped a blanket around her. "See that she rests. Plenty of sleep. No intercourse."

He shuddered. Like he would try it. Ever again.

"Summon me if there's any bleeding," Mrs. Hawksmoor continued. "I'll check on her in a few days."

"I'll take care of her," he said. "Thank you."

And then they were alone.

Except they weren't, because she was pregnant.

Pregnant.

He repeated the word to himself a few more times, waiting to be awoken from a dream.

But it was only him and her in the small, dark room. Him and her and their baby.

Their baby.

His baby.

His, like Adeline was his and Jasper was his and the little one he couldn't bear to name had been his, the one he'd buried in the same coffin as her mother beneath a gravestone marked Catriona Anderson and Baby, Much Beloved.

Tears pricked in his eyes and he ignored them, for the more urgent feeling than this surge of emotion was ferocity. Ferocity.

He wanted to *kill* the men outside. Rip them *limb from bloody limb* and sling them maimed and bleeding in the streets, the cowards, for trying to intimidate this woman who was braver than all of them. And braver than him.

He was going to be braver for her.

He had to be, for the family they would make. The family that—leaving aside he didn't know how, that it turned all his careful plans to rot, that he could not even slightly afford it—the family they *would* make because he knew that he must and would bloody find a way.

"Why are you here?" Seraphina asked weakly.

He knelt down next to her, grasping her hands so tight he worried he would hurt her, but unable to loosen his grip because he knew now that the dream he'd had in Cornwall had been a premonition. He was a superstitious bloody Scotsman who believed in the prickle in the neck and he would not close his eyes and let her go.

"Why are you weeping?" she asked flatly. "Get up."

"Oh, Sera, I know it's mad," he said, wiping away his tears with both hands. "I know it is, love. I'm just unstrung."

And what he meant was that he was strangely, radiantly happy.

And terrified. And so full of love and hope and joy and bloody certainty that it felt like madness.

It had been a lifetime since he'd been as sure as he was about what was in this room, and it scared the very marrow in him, and he was grateful.

"Marry me," he whispered. "Be my wife."

"Collect yourself," she said again. "You're raving." Her expression was as dull as her voice. Her eyes were almost vacant.

He held her face, willing her to see that he was sincere.

"Sera, darling, I didn't know about any of it. Had I known about Pendrake hurting you or about the baby— I didn't even know about the article. I'll fix it, all of it, just let me hold you."

Her chest rose in a long, long, damning breath that sent the joy washing out of him and left him feeling chilled. "No."

"But, love—"

"Collect yourself," she said again in that dreadful voice, "and be sensible. Nothing has changed about your circumstances. And I'm almost certainly going to lose this baby, if I have not yet."

"But the midwife said—"

"She said there is no certainty until it quickens."

"But if there is even the slightest possibility, we must—"

"No!" she whispered. "No. I cannot hope."

The pain in her voice shattered him. "Darling—"

"No, Adam. Do not continue this. I will go *mad*. I want you to leave, and I do not wish to see you. In the event there is a child, I will write you and you can make arrangements as you wish. You can count on my discretion if you do not wish to be associated with me, as I would not harm your children's futures. But now you must leave, because I cannot bear looking at you."

Could not bear *looking* at him?

He tried again. "Sera, I'm trying to tell you that I love you. I'll do anything to fix this."

She laughed a low, terrible laugh. "Then *go*."

He stood, but could not bring himself to turn around. He could only look at her, taking in the contempt on her face and the fear.

"Thaïs," she called, with a strength of voice that belied her pallor and the sweat on her brow. "Please see Mr. Anderson out."

Chapter Twenty-Nine

And so, Cornelia and Thaïs took Seraphina home.

She let them wash her, brush out her hair, and build a nest for her of blankets on the sofa. She let them order beef broth and chamomile tea from the cook.

The midwife had not been alarmed. *It's only a fright. Avoid too much excitement, my girl, and stay off your feet until the sickness eases.*

But Sera would not let herself focus on what that meant or didn't mean, because pregnancy was perilous, and hoping for joy only set one up for heartbreak. It had been a mistake to hope.

She would inure herself. She would not feel that fear again.

She was too tired.

Tired of wanting things she shouldn't have and of not wanting things she should. Tired of wondering which was which and what it said about her soul. Tired, so bloody tired, of being a champion and a firebrand and a metaphor and a picture in the paper.

She wanted to be Seraphina, a woman in a tired body, who had nothing more to say.

She wanted to stay in her house, under the blankets, and mourn.

Thaïs and Cornelia did not suggest it would all be fine or offer platitudes that were patently untrue. They let her simply sit in her tiredness and sadness until she fell asleep.

It was a half-waking sleep. She flickered through a dream in which she was her mother, and nursed a child that was herself. She woke up filled with terror, soaked once again with a sense of loss that seemed far out of proportion to what she'd thought she'd wanted.

She wanted her baby to live. She wanted to be held. She wanted Adam.

She banished the thought. She hated his dishonest, empty promise that he could ever fix this. That he loved her. Of all the treacherous things to say.

Cornelia reached out and smoothed her hair. "You're awake. What is it?"

"I dreamt of a baby. Of my mother."

"Oh, darling," Cornelia murmured.

"I'm terrified that I will lose her," Sera whispered. "I feel trapped in my own body. I can't stand not knowing."

Thaïs kissed her hand. "You'll get through it, love, whatever happens. How do you feel?"

Sera knew Thaïs was asking about her body, which in fact felt better now that she'd slept.

"I feel stupid," Seraphina said.

"Why?" Cornelia asked.

"Because of Adam."

Thaïs came and nestled up beside her. "What do you mean?"

"Letting myself care about him, when I knew better. I suppose I believed that he *saw* me. As I am. The good and the bad. I thought he was growing to care for me despite what he saw—because of what he saw. But it was just a fancy, no different from when I was a girl. And if I can still be so foolish, what was the point of all that pain? Have I learned nothing?"

Cornelia shook her head. "No. I won't let you entertain such thoughts."

Good. A bracing dose of Cornelia Ludgate's famed intolerance of sentimentality was just what she needed to return to clear-headedness.

"Sera," Cornelia continued, "there is no question in my mind that the distraught man who was in Jack Willow's house today cares about you deeply. Whatever he has done, however misguided, surely you cannot think he is unfeeling. You are not blind."

Sera closed her eyes. This was not what she was expecting from Cornelia, of all people.

"He cares now that he knows I am pregnant with his child," Sera protested. "It is not the same as caring for me. He asked me to marry him. Which, if he understood me, he would know is—"

"Oh, Sera," Thaïs sighed. "Do you hear yourself?"

"What do you mean?" she asked, stung.

"You know I cower before your terrifying brain. But Adam is a man, not some theory you can prove with words. You need to talk to him."

Cornelia smiled faintly. "Thaïs is right."

Thaïs tossed her hair with pleasure and stretched her toes toward the fire. "Finally, she admits to my wisdom."

"I don't want to talk to Adam," Sera muttered. "I'm scared of what he'll say."

"And that is why you must," Cornelia said gently.

Sera considered this. Perhaps they were right. It could not be good for her health to lie here circling the possibilities.

She wanted clarity.

She wanted it right now.

"Fine." She rose. "Help me dress."

Neither of her friends moved.

"The only place you are going is to bed," Thaïs said firmly. "It's late, and you've been ill."

"I feel better now. The sickness will be worse in the morning. You said I must talk to him and you are correct. I must."

"I didn't mean *now*. Hawksmoor said to rest."

But she could not rest feeling this way. She would be up all night. "I'm going to see him. Can you ask Tompkins to summon my carriage?"

ADAM WALKED THROUGH the dreary streets of London and raged at himself for failing Seraphina.

He understood her pain. He understood her desire not to see him. And yet he wanted to pound on her door and plead with her to see that sometimes people became capable of more when life gave them an opportunity to stretch.

He wanted to stretch for her.

He wanted to be the kind of man worthy of a woman who could stare down a crowd of screaming men and firmly tell them, "No, you're wrong."

He had never been an outspoken man. His life was built on things Seraphina rejected.

But he was an architect. If he had one true skill, it was renovation.

He wanted to renovate his life for her.

Baby or no, wife or no.

He simply wanted *her*.

He went home, to his quiet rooms, where his family was already sleeping.

At his desk, he prepared a quill. He wrote a letter to the newspaper, retracting Mayhew's denunciation and reconfirming his personal support for Miss Arden's institute.

He began a second, longer, letter to Mayhew. Pages began to stack up on his desk. The clock struck midnight and he looked over them.

They were good. In fact, they were very good.

He could do this. He really could.

He heard something outside in the street and looked out the window. A carriage was pulling up in front of his house. Odd, for this street never had much traffic, much less so late at night. A hooded figure stood out and walked to his front door. Underneath the hem of her cloak, he saw the frilly laces of a nightdress.

He rushed down the stairs.

Chapter Thirty

Adam pulled open the door before Sera had even finished knocking.

His face broke open as he looked on her, light emanating from his eyes like the glow from a paper lantern.

"Sera," he said, like her name was a poem.

He opened his arms.

She walked into them.

They closed around her, and she felt such a rush of warmth and pleasure. This, at least, had always been lovely between them. He held her like no one ever had.

"You came to me," he whispered, his voice muffled in her hair.

She made herself pull back. "Yes. We need to talk."

He nodded. "I'm afraid we're on the second floor," he said. "Can you climb up?"

She knew there was more to this question, and she felt guilty. He must have been worrying all night.

"Yes," she said. "I'm feeling much better. No more fainting, no blood."

He let out a breath and nodded.

"Come in," he said in a whisper. "Welcome."

She followed him up the stairs into the parlor of a small, dark, pleasant suite of rooms. There were flowers in a vase on a table and plants hanging from the windows. The walls were lined with books and framed drawings of Adam's children. She saw their toys scattered here and there.

"Would you like anything? Tea?" he asked.

"No," she said quickly. She felt odd being in his home, with his family's things all about. She supposed she'd thought of him as a lover who melted into the ether when he left her realm. She had not pictured the quotidian part of him, the man who paid a landlord every month and owned chairs and tables and watched his children play with blocks as he read books.

"Let's talk in my study," he said in a low voice. "I don't wish to wake the children."

She followed him to a small room strewn with papers.

"Sorry, wasn't expecting company," he said, moving piles of architectural drawings and design books from the chairs in front of his desk. "Here you are. Sit, please."

He addressed her with a courteous formality that made her certain he was nervous, but even despite it there was an authoritative grace to him as he moved about his home. Like he was more himself here.

She wondered why she had never thought to visit him. Well, he had never asked her to. But then, why would he, when she'd have certainly declined?

"Did I wake you?" she asked.

"No, I was up, working." He gestured at papers scattered across his desk. She noticed a copy of her second volume sitting beside them.

"So you've read it," she said, pointing at her book.

He nodded. "Twice."

His voice was gentle. Kind but reticent. Like he did not wish to say too much until he'd given her space to tell him what she'd come to say. Which she supposed she should get around to doing, given it was a quarter past twelve.

"I had forgotten that your firm's name would be printed in my book. I was shaken when you left my house and it did not occur to me to warn you when you told me about Pendrake. I'm sorry that it came as a surprise. And that it caused trouble for you."

He shook his head. "It's all right." He shuffled some papers on top of his desk and held one up. "I wrote a letter to the newspaper tonight reaffirming my commitment to the apprenticeship scheme. I'll deliver it in the morning."

"Won't that . . . cause more trouble?" she asked.

"Of course," he said calmly.

She looked at his face for signs of bitterness or resentment, but his mouth was relaxed.

"Then would it not be . . . unwise?" she prodded.

"It would be utterly reckless," he affirmed.

He was so, so very calm that it was making her uneasy.

He reached out and picked up her book and turned through the pages. He held up the page containing her account of the day she lost her child.

"This passage broke my heart for you."

She swallowed. "Thank you. It was a difficult time."

He nodded slowly. "I wish you had told me about it when I came to see you. I know what it's like, you know. That pain. How it never goes away."

She shook her head. "No. It doesn't."

"And I wish you had told me about Pendrake. Who he was to you." His voice held no reproach. He said it like he might have said *I wish I had worn a warmer coat.*

She suspected he sensed she wanted to leap out the window and fly out of this room, that she would rather suffocate than talk openly about these topics. That he was calibrating his words to ease her, like he would address a skittish kitten.

"It did not seem relevant," was all she could force herself to say.

Why was it so hard to put her feelings into words? She could feel them, churning inside her, wanting to be said, and yet . . . she could not articulate them through the rush of fear. It was so much easier to say nothing.

Adam was quiet for a minute. He got out of the chair and knelt down before her and took her hands in his. "How could you think I would not find it relevant?" he asked softly.

This, she could answer.

"Because you explained very clearly why you could not be associated with me, and your reasons were . . . sound. It seemed to me that you had made your decision. And that knowing my story would only make it more difficult for you, without changing your circumstances."

"So you were protecting me?"

Protecting him? Was that what she had done? He made it sound noble and brave. But really she'd been scared. She'd been protecting herself.

"I have lost people I've cared about to Pendrake before. I did not want to face that again. I suppose I thought it easier for both of us if you did not have to make such a choice."

"I would have chosen you," he said fiercely. "I *do* choose you."

She looked down at the floor. "But, Adam, you can't."

He tipped up her chin. "Actually, I can."

"But everything you said, about your work and debts—"

He nodded. "Those things are true. But did you hear any of the other things I said? That I am in love with you, Sera? Had I known about Pendrake, about the baby, I would have—"

Done the stupid thing. For her. And resented her later.

"But, Adam, that's just it. I can have a baby on my own. You can come to visit if you like but you don't need to destroy your future over it. The baby should not change—"

"I was talking about your daughter," he said. "The babe you lost."

She looked away, but his eyes searched for hers insistently.

"I could never choose Pendrake knowing that he caused such pain to a person that I love," he said quietly. "Full stop. I simply won't."

"And what of your family, Adam? Your responsibilities?"

"I'll take care of them, Sera. I'm rather capable of managing my own affairs. You don't have to look after me. I'm not asking you to."

She weaved her fingers together beneath his hand, trying to understand. "What are you asking me?"

"I'm asking you to try to accept that I made a mistake. That I didn't have all the information and I hurt you. I want you to try to trust that if I had known the full picture, it would have changed the calculation I was making. And the baby—our baby—would have changed that calculation, too."

"Adam, you can't destroy your life over a child I may lose."

His face went grim, but it had to be said.

He was quiet for a moment. "Here's the truth, Sera. I know there is no certainty. But when I found out about the bairn, it made me happy. Absolutely, foolishly happy."

She bit her lip. Oh God, what was happening? Why did she feel like the room was swirling? She tried not to smile, but she couldn't stop. And when he saw her smile, he smiled too.

"What I'm realizing, lass, is that there's never any certainty, and I've been naïve to think there ever was. I can try to live my life the safest, most dreadfully dull way, and still have no idea what's in store. I'd rather feel this, Sera. Joy and terror. I'd rather have you." He paused and took a breath. "But what do *you* want?"

The swirl of doubts and hopes and hesitations rose in her again, inchoate, impossible to voice. "I want to believe you," she whispered. "But I'm so frightened."

His handsome face softened in such a way that she wanted to climb into his arms and never leave. "Oh, lass. Of what?"

"Of becoming who I was before. I loved Trewlnany, Adam. I loved him the way only a girl can love. And after everything that happened, I swore to myself I would never ever feel that way again. And I've kept my word. I've made sure that any time I felt so much as the faintest trace of fondness for someone, I cut them out of my life or drove them away. I'm very good at it."

He chuckled ruefully. "Oh, I think I believe you on that score, Miss Arden."

His quip made her feel a little better. But he said nothing more, waiting for her to tell him more.

"I had very nearly convinced myself that you were different, or maybe that I was, when you told me of your ties with Pendrake. And it . . . Do you recall when you told me of your father's drinking, and said you couldn't bear to be around spirits because it brought everything back? Well, that's how I felt, I suppose. Like it brought that terrible time right back. Asking a man to choose me over his own interests. Fearing that he won't."

Adam's eyes were boundless pools of sympathy. "Lass," he whispered.

His kindness broke something open in her. Suddenly, she had the words. "I thought if I could only ignore those birds and posters, if I could simply resist the urge to be hurt by them and write my book, I'd finally get justice. Even if that justice was just exposure, even if it was only embarrassment, it would make them see that they could not simply get away with it. That there was a larger morality outside their power. But when I learned of your ties to Pendrake, his influence over you—it made me feel like a fool. After everything, he could still hurt me. He and Jonathan had already taken so much, and now they were back just when I thought I had my vindication, taking you."

He looked like he wanted to say something, or snatch her up into his arms, but she needed to say all of it, all the things she'd scarcely admitted to herself.

"And then today, Adam, I was certain I would miscarry. And I have tried very hard not to think about my daughter since I lost her but . . . I can't stand the fear that it might happen again. I can't want something and know it will be taken from me. It's too much like . . . before."

She felt childish and weepy and she squirmed in her chair, dying to get up and pace the room. But she stayed still. It seemed important to endure this conversation.

Because somehow, despite making her feel worse, it was also making her feel better.

Adam came and knelt beside her chair. Slowly, like he was leaving time for her to tell him not to, he threaded his arms around her waist. "I'm scared, too. But whatever happens, I am here for you. I'll share it with you. If you'll let me take some of the burden."

Perhaps what he meant is that the pain would ease if it was shared between them. The way she already felt better, leaning against his heat, breathing in his woody smell. She could believe that it might be so, when he touched her. But what of the larger world outside this room?

"But how can we, Adam? You have your family, and I am not accustomed to sharing my life with anyone, besides my friends. I wouldn't know how to begin."

He smoothed back her hair. "I suppose we will just have to try, and find our way."

Try. That word again. Could she?

She closed her eyes and imagined going home knowing she had severed her connection to this man. She thought of the words he'd said to her before: *I am reduced by the loss of you.* She felt the truth of them keenly. She wanted to be with him the way she wanted all her limbs.

"I would like to try," she said. "But I can't promise I am capable. You would have to teach me how."

A smile curled slowly across his features. He let out a breath. "I would be honored."

He paused, his face suddenly going tense. "But there is a complication, Sera. I have to go back to Cornwall. Tregereth has made changes to his plans, and I need to make them in order to get the fee, which I must, as Mayhew will be after me for money. I'll likely need to be there for at least a month."

"Oh. I see." Already, the grand sentiment was tarnished by the finer details.

"I know it's a difficult place for you, but if you came with me, we might have some time to be together. To try."

She did not know what to say. On the one hand, it could be lovely to be with Adam outside of the pressures of London, where they could see each other daily without traveling back and forth across the city.

On the other hand, she was not exactly the type to abandon her work in favor of experimenting with domestic bliss.

And if Pendrake and Trewlnany caught wind, would they persecute her and Adam both? And should it matter if they did? She owned her house and land, after all, and had every right to return. For all the painful memories there, it was also the place of her childhood. The place where she'd met Adam.

And lost him.

What if she risked it, and it was a failure? What if she came back more unhappy than before?

She didn't know the right answer.

"May I think about it?" she asked Adam.

He smiled. "Of course. I want you any way I can have you, Sera. Wherever suits you. As much as you wish to give me. Take all the time you need."

"Sweet man." She leaned forward, and kissed him on the cheek.

And then, before she could help it, she yawned. She was so tired she felt like she might fall asleep in this chair. "It's late. I should leave you."

"Can I steal a good-night kiss?"

She smiled. "You needn't steal it."

He embraced her again, and his lips fell softly on hers. It was a sweet kiss, almost chaste, but once again she had that feeling.

You. More.

In his arms, fine details didn't seem so complicated. In his arms, she wanted to believe that they might find their way.

"I love you," he whispered in her ear.

She did not return the words.

But she weighed what it might be like to say them back.

I love *you*, too? *I* love you? I love *you*.

I love you.

She kissed his cheek. "Good night."

ADAM DID NOT sleep. As soon as Seraphina left, he bundled up his papers and went to the studio. He worked feverishly, putting all the pieces of his plan together, preparing it for Mayhew.

He heard his brother-in-law walking up the stairs at half past eight.

He held himself stiff, feeling like they were strangers after their interaction outside of Willow's bookshop.

And yet, they weren't strangers.

Mayhew looked same as always, impeccably dressed with bouncing steps, exuding the scent of his expensive shaving oil. He took in the sight of Adam's loose white shirt and unshaven face and scoffed, same as he might on any morning. "Good Christ, Anderson. You look like a grave-digger."

For all Adam's anger at Mayhew, he had to smile. Mayhew, ever piquant-tongued, had been taking issue with Adam's lack of elegance since before they could read.

"You look distinguished enough for the both of us."

Mayhew rolled his eyes. "That may well be, but you cannot go about looking like a tramp when we are being considered by the Board of Works. Go home and make yourself into a gentleman."

This was also like James. A determined insistence on seeing the world the way he wanted it to be, no matter how unrealistic his vision was.

"Mayhew, I don't have a chance with the Board of Works. Not after yesterday."

Mayhew sighed. "I had a word with Bell after the dust-up at the printer's. Explained you're a victim of the Scot's enlightenment and briefly lost your head. You know, seduced by the Rakess." Mayhew paused. "And I mentioned who your father was."

They had long disagreed on the merits of letting Adam's background be known. Mayhew argued that Adam's connection to a Duke—even if he was a bastard—would open doors for them. Adam forbade him from mentioning it, not wanting to be associated with a man he despised. "Mayhew, I told you not to—"

"Yes, you did, but the thing is, it worked. Bell is angry but allowed that he won't expose you to Pendrake, provided you sever your ties with the Arden woman and publicly renounce her before the hearing."

"I can't do that."

Mayhew's good cheer instantly evaporated. He threw up his hands. "I'm not asking. You *must*."

Adam stood and walked to the long, flat drawer where the leather portfolio containing the revised plans was stored. He handed Mayhew the sketches. They were some of the best work he'd ever done. Grand but functional. No detail overlooked. He'd sent clerks out to interview naval officers on the flaws in the current armory. He'd studied the topography to improve the use of space. He'd even been sure to incorporate some of the stonework he'd seen Pendrake was partial to in previous commissions.

If Pendrake did not choose their plans, it would not be the fault of Adam's design. He had made sure of that.

"These sketches should win the commission. That other book I gave you contains everything you need to say to the board. It explains the reasoning behind the design and sets out a plan for building it with maximum speed and reasonable costs."

"I'm not a bloody architect, Adam," Mayhew cried.

"No, but you're an excellent talker, and you have a few days to study. You can convince them. Tell them you've run me off after my display of low morals. Tell them you are solely responsible for the efficiency for which we're known—tell them I'm a glorified builder. Tell them anything you want. If you get the commission, you'll hire an architect to replace me. I've left a list of all our laborers and suppliers, to ensure you continue to get preferential pricing, so that my leaving does not impact our contracts."

Mayhew stopped pacing and spun around. "Leaving? Where are you going? This firm is your life."

Not anymore.

"I'm giving you my stake in it. I had Clark write to the solicitor this morning to draw up the papers. The only piece I'm keeping is the Tregereth commission, and only because I need to personally see to it. I'll sign over my equity in return for the forgiveness of my debt. The armory commission should repay you triply if you land it. And if you don't . . . I'll find some other way."

Mayhew gave him a long, probing look. "This is madness. And you look like hell. Are you ill?"

Adam smiled. He was exhausted, but he felt better than he had in months. "Not at all."

"You can't just quit. We're partners. We're *family*." Mayhew's eyes held stark, genuine concern. Adam was touched by it.

"I'm sorry, James. I want this for you. I want to give back to your family what you've given to me. That's why I've done all this. But I can't be part of it."

Mayhew rubbed his eyes. "This is about the Arden woman."

"Aye."

"What does she have over you that your own wife's family does not?"

"James," Adam said quietly, "you know that Catriona meant the world to me. I still mourn her every day. But the truth is that I've fallen in love with Seraphina Arden. And even if nothing comes of it, I want to do what's right by her."

"What's right for *her*? What of your children? Marianne? What will you do for a living?"

"I have my sights set on a new commission. I'll find my way. You needn't worry."

"At the very least take the children to my mother's. If you're going to spin off in some wild—"

"My children are happy and clever and well looked after. And they adore you. For their sake, I'd like to part in peace, with your blessing. But I understand if you can't give it."

Mayhew folded his arms over his chest. "Adam, you're like a brother to me. I won't stop you. I will tell you that you are making a decision it will not be easy to come back from."

Adam set a hand on Mayhew's shoulder and looked at him sadly. "You're right. Some things you simply can't come back from. Some things you don't want to."

Chapter Thirty-One

Seraphina Arden had received many letters in her lifetime.

Letters mocking her appearance. Letters decrying her low morals. Letters wishing ill upon her health.

But never had she received so many letters of support as she did in the week following her speech at Jack Willow's. And never had they been so full of that blessed, useful thing: banknotes.

"I have news!" Sera called as she stepped inside Cornelia's painting studio, having come straight from meeting with the solicitor who handled her accounts.

She lifted up the canvas cloth that shielded the inner sanctum of the studio from the drafty vestibule, and stopped short. Lady Elinor Bell was sprawled atop a dining table in the center of the room, surrounded by cakes, fruit, and jellies.

Nude.

"Good morning, dear," Elinor said blandly.

Seraphina clapped her hand over her mouth.

"I'm surprised to see you out," Elinor went on, as though nothing about her naked form surrounded by sweets was amiss. "The girls assured me you've been resting."

Sera had indeed spent most of the week in bed, answering her piles of correspondence, sipping ginger broth, and sleeping. Though she still had bouts of nausea, she felt more like herself.

Well enough, perhaps, to finally confront the decision before her.

"I'm feeling much better," she assured Elinor. "But what are you doing here, and not in Surrey?"

Elinor gestured at the feast laid out around her. Her ample breasts were just barely disguised by a towering layer cake, and a bowl of succulent grapes hid her womanhood.

"I should think it is obvious, dear," Elinor said. "I've become a dessert."

Sera laughed. This was the Elinor she remembered. Voluptuous, dry-witted, and steady-tempered as a church warden.

"May I present the first of my Jezebels," Cornelia said, stepping back to show Seraphina the large painting of Elinor on her easel. "It isn't finished, of course. But you can see how thoroughly dissolute our Elinor shall be."

"She is going to sell for a fortune," Seraphina said, taking in the rich colors, the seductive pose, and the handkerchief embroidered with Bell's family crest discarded on the floor beside the feast. "And it will make Bell apoplectic."

"Yes," Elinor drawled. "If this doesn't provoke him to divorce me, I don't know what will."

"Oh, I wouldn't be so sure," said Thaïs, who was lounging on a sofa in a corner, eating a tart clearly stolen from the heaping tray at Elinor's feet. "Once he sees you posed like this, he might want you back."

"He can't have me," Elinor said with a rather mysterious smile. "I've decided to declare myself to another."

Sera glanced at Cornelia and Thaïs, wondering if she had missed something during her week of convalescence, but they both looked equally confused.

"You don't mean——" Sera ventured, and Elinor nodded before she could finish the thought.

"I have decided that if I'm going to be publicly condemned for having a love affair with Jack Willow, there is no reason not to actually have one. I've sent my maid out to invite him to visit me in Surrey. If he comes, I shall tell him how I feel about him. 'Tis up to him, of course, but hopefully he is fond enough of me to give weight to Lord Bell's suspicions."

She beamed at them. Sera could not remember her looking so happy in months.

"You love him," Sera said softly.

Elinor blushed in a way that made her look years younger. "Yes. I think I always have."

"I think you are very brave," Thaïs said solemnly.

"And very reckless," Cornelia added, her face decidedly less enthusiastic. "If Bell finds out . . ."

Elinor sighed. "Girls, there is a time for caution, but sometimes we must take a risk for the heart. It's a lesson I wish I had learned much earlier in life. One I hope you will not have to learn at my age, looking back at what might have been."

She looked meaningfully at Seraphina.

Sera glared at Thaïs and Cornelia. All week, they had pestered her to tell them what she had discussed with Adam. All week, she had resisted saying much at all.

It was not that she did not welcome their opinions. But her own feelings on the matter felt so new and unfamiliar that it made her hesitant to air them. Like if she named the fears she had, or the hopes that blossomed up in her better moments, she might discover that the whole thing had been a dream.

She didn't want to ruin it.

"Well, I do have some news. I had a meeting with my solicitor this morning. He's done the accounts. We've raised ten thousand pounds."

Cornelia stopped painting. "You're joking."

Sera shook her head. "I'm not. I looked at the statements myself. We have made a real start on the institute."

"More than a start," Thaïs cried. "Why, that's a fortune! We can buy a piece of land, with funds left over!"

"And commission an architectural design," Cornelia said pointedly, looking at Sera. "I don't suppose you know any good architects?"

Well, perhaps Elinor was right. Perhaps if she waited too long, she would find she had run out of time.

"I'm considering asking Adam for his help," she said, feeling as though she was abandoning herself to fate. "But you see, there is another matter between us, so before I raise the matter . . . well, I'm considering taking a trip."

Thaïs wrinkled her nose. "A holiday? But you despise holidays."

"It would not be a holiday so much as an experiment. You see, Adam has gone to Cornwall to finish his work there. He wants me to join him."

Cornelia dropped her paintbrush. Thaïs stopped chewing. Elinor popped up from behind the cake, realized she was indecent, and rushed to fetch a dressing gown off a hook.

"And what did you say?" Cornelia prodded.

"I said I would consider it. And I have spent days thinking of it from every angle, and I still have no idea what to do."

"Ah, philosophers and their thinking," Thaïs said, rolling her eyes. "Allow a lowly, uneducated woman of the night to help you with the riddle—go."

"Why?" Sera asked.

"Because the mere fact that you would consider going *there* means you want to be with *him*," Thaïs said.

"Part of me does want to . . . well, try, I suppose. But I don't want to leave our work. Not when we've made so much progress."

Elinor cleared her throat. "Darling, you have had an extraordinary few months. You've written a book, you've fought for me, you've stood up to Pendrake and Bell and Trewlnany. You've raised an incredible sum of money for our institute, solicited so many pledges of support. You deserve time to yourself. Leave the rest to us."

"The portraits will take months," Cornelia added. "And we'll have to arrange a showing, solicit more models, drum up interest. We can do all that while you're away. And when things are in order, we'll write and demand that you stop lazing about and come home to watch us have our moment."

They made it sound so much simpler than it was. "There is also his family to consider," Sera said. "If I spend time with him, openly, it becomes harder to leave them out of the scandal."

"Too late," Thaïs drawled. "You are going to have a baby together."

"Well, yes, but his family—"

Thaïs held up a finger. "That makes *you* his family."

She had never thought of it like that. She'd been framing the question in terms of the impact she would have on him, and he would have on her. Not how they might move through the world *together*. Looking after each other's interests, like a team.

Thaïs was wearing an impossibly smug smile. "I have out-reasoned her. Huzzah!"

Sera gave her a level stare. "What if I go, and it's terrible?"

"Then you will come back to me and say, Thaïs, you jackal, you tricked me with your feeble logic of the slums. And we will gather together, the Society of Sirens, and curse the wicked men and this cruel life. And then we will dry our tears and find our next adventure."

"I think," Cornelia mused, "Thaïs is right."

Thaïs clapped her hands. "I am always right. It has taken you a decade to make your peace with it."

Cornelia groaned. "My apologies, oh wise one. But, Sera, the worst that could happen if you go is that it doesn't feel right, and you come back. But what if you go, and it's wonderful?"

It felt dangerous to even consider such a thing. Dangerous and tempting.

"Darling?" Elinor said. "Do you miss him?"

Tears rose in Sera's eyes. "So much," she whispered.

So much that there wasn't really any choice to make at all.

She shrugged. "Very well."

"Very well what?" Cornelia asked.

Sera laughed softly, scarcely believing what she was about to say. "I'm going to go."

Thaïs ran up and grabbed her by the shoulders and kissed her on both cheeks. "Brave girl," she said.

Cornelia wrapped her arms around them both. "We'll miss you."

Elinor joined them in the hug. "I'm so proud of you, darling. You've fought so hard for us. Now go there and fight for the happiness you deserve. And remember— nothing would be a better revenge than you being madly in love with a man who adores you."

ADAM STOOD ON Tregereth's freshly renovated belvedere, pulled his sketchbook from his pocket, and began to draw the cliffs.

He'd come here every afternoon since returning to Cornwall. He told himself he did it because it gave him a clear view of Tregereth's property from which to survey the fruits of the day's work. But really, he did it to hope.

To hope. For a letter, tattered after a week lost in the post. A light, burning from the window of her shuttered house. His daughter's voice, squealing Seraphina's name as she looked out at the coastal path.

And yet, with every day that passed without word, the possibility she might not come grew more akin to fact: she hadn't.

He turned a new page in his sketchbook, and began to draw her, the way she'd looked that day that he'd first met her here. Long limbs beneath a billowing, sheer dress. Green eyes sparkling with intrigue. Lips turned out in a smile that seemed to say *I already know*.

Something brushed his shoulder—his cravat in the wind. He adjusted it and kept on sketching—absorbed in the detail of her hair, the shadow of her lashes.

"Adam."

He turned around.

"I wanted to surprise you," Seraphina Arden said, looking at him like she'd never seen a finer thing in all her life.

His sketchbook clattered to the floor.

He lost sight of what he did then. He might have kissed her with all the longing he'd been afraid to feel since he'd left London. He might have ripped her hair out of its pins. He might have growled, *Get closer, woman*. He could not attest to what passed in those five minutes except that when he came to something like his senses they were in such a state that chance passersby would be witness to obscenity.

He pulled himself away and looked at her, his Sera.

"I was so afraid you wouldn't come," he whispered.

She took a shaky breath. "So was I."

He took her hand and brought her palm to his lips. "This time, let's try not to be afraid."

"Oh, Adam," she said, with liquid eyes. "It's a promise."

She leaned in and kissed him, and he was lost again, and then her hands were on his hipbones and he realized that if he did not stop this here and now there would be no stopping it at all.

"Not here," he gasped, dragging himself away from her, though the loss of every inch of her flesh against his stung him.

She groaned. "Don't torment me. It's been too long. I am . . ." she shivered despite the unseasonal warmth of the autumn afternoon ". . . *wanting.*"

She looked wanting. He felt the hunger of her gaze in the hollow of his sacrum.

"Come." He grabbed her hand. "Tregereth's the only client I have left. Can't get myself dismissed for having my way with his neighbor on his belvedere."

"Wait," she said. Her eyes were playful. "It's low tide. We can reach the caves under the cliffs. They are private and can be quite . . . inspiring. Would you like me to show you?"

Cave. Private. Seraphina.

He looked at her gravely. "I suspect I would like that very much."

She led him to a scraggly footpath that wound through the jagged rocks down to the shoreline. She stopped to remove her slippers, wriggling her toes in the wet sand.

He stripped off his boots and stockings and followed her between twin pillars of rock that protected a little opening beneath the jetty. The floor was lined with clumps of seaweed and bright yellow sponges. A shaft of sunlight lit up the cave, making the water lapping at their ankles twinkle a thousand pastel shades, and dappling the rocks with veins of gold and copper.

Sera draped her cloak over a large, sea-smoothed rock in the center of the cave. "Come here."

He let her remove his coat, and then his shirt. It was cool and damp inside the cave, and his skin prickled with gooseflesh. She ran her hands along his waist and up to his nipples.

"You're cold," she observed. She raised her shift over her head and pulled him against her bare skin, rubbing his arms to warm him up.

"Ah," he sighed. "That's better."

"Back to the matter we were discussing," she said. Her hands drifted down to the trail of hair that led from his navel to his groin, and she followed it until her hand was inside his breeches, caressing his cock.

He closed his eyes and let the feeling overwhelm him. He felt like he was in one of his dreams in which they frolicked in the surf.

A large wave crashed against the rocks, stinging his calves and ankles with cold water. His eyes shot open.

In those dreams he always lost her.

"Adam," she murmured.

He looked down at her, and she was smiling up at him, her eyes tender and alive in a way he'd never seen before.

"I'm here," she said, drawing him closer. "I've got you."

Chapter Thirty-Two

The tide is coming in. We should go," Sera said.

Adam's arms tightened around her. "I don't want to let go of you."

"I don't want that either," she murmured. "I would not suggest it were it not that we will drown."

He squeezed her one last time before sitting up. Every time he did that, another bolt of certainty went through her.

She was so glad she'd come.

They helped each other collect their things and dress and climbed up to the coastal path. Adam took her hand. "I have to go see the children for their supper. But I'll walk you home."

She smiled at the thought of Jasper and Adeline, waiting in the window for him. "Are they happy to be back at the seaside?"

"Yes. They have been asking me if you will come."

Oh, Adam. He said it so lightly, but she wished she had not caused him a fortnight of uncertainty.

"What did you tell them?"

He looked at her from the side of his eye. "I said I hoped so."

Her heart.

"I'm sorry if I unnerved you. I had to be sure. And then once I was, I figured I'd get here as quickly as a letter."

"The only thing that matters," he said softly, "is that you're here."

Her throat felt tight. She cleared it, lest she become unstrung again. To think she'd spent years—years—without shedding a single tear only to become a faucet at the age of thirty-three.

"Would you bring the children over for luncheon tomorrow? And Marianne? I'd like to see them." She paused. "Actually, on second thought, the house might be a mess. There wasn't time to send Maria in advance to open it up and I haven't been inside yet."

He quirked his mouth. "You came directly to find me without going inside?"

She nodded.

He raised a brow lasciviously. "Eager of you."

She rewarded him with a coy smirk. "Quite."

"Let's have a look," he said, as they climbed up her terrace stairs.

"Maria's managed to open all the shutters. That's a good sign." Sera paused to inspect the one that was always loose and banging at the window. Someone had fixed it.

She looked over at Adam. His face seemed curiously innocent, as though he didn't notice.

She opened the terrace doors and found the hinges no longer creaked. When she stepped inside, the loose floorboard did not squeal beneath her shoe.

In fact, everywhere she looked she noticed little changes. Broken spindles along the staircase had been replaced with new ones. Damp spots had been filled with new plaster. Peeling paint had been sanded away and replaced with a fresh, white coat.

But the most striking change was the sound. All she heard was their footsteps. The room no longer moaned with the wind, like it was haunted.

"Welcome home," Adam said quietly.

"Did you do all this?"

His face was tentative again, like he was not sure how she would react. "I hope you don't mind. I had a few men with some spare time, and I wanted you to be comfortable. And the babe. If you, ergh, came."

Sweet man. She walked over and brushed his hair out of his pretty eyes. "Thank you."

"I also left something on your desk. A gift."

"Shall I look now?"

"If you wish."

She took his hand and walked through the door to her study. On the desk was a scroll of architectural plans. *An Institute for the Equality of Women* was written in the margin.

She smoothed it out over her desk, revealing a drawing of a building, tall and elegant, with graceful lines and a classical symmetry and enough height to leave no mistake as to the importance of its purpose. The pages that followed showed a pretty garden, a lecture hall, a large central lobby that looked like a gentleman's club crossed with a lady's boudoir. The design showed respect for the occupants, and awareness of their needs and comforts—a little mirrored dressing table built into each wall of the residence, desks that folded down for practicing lessons, a nursery for children.

Every fanciful idea she'd told him that day he'd sketched here was accounted for. It was as though he'd absorbed the vision from her mind's eye and translated it to pencil and paper.

She was so touched she could barely speak.

"It's perfect," she said.

"You don't have to use these, of course, if you prefer to consult another architect. I just wanted to do something. To help your cause."

"Don't be ridiculous. You'll build it for me," she said decisively. "We've already raised enough to buy a parcel of land. Once Cornelia's series begins to sell, we'll have enough for construction."

"I've broken with Mayhew," he said, "so I'd have to take on new apprentices. Perhaps you might direct me to some eligible female candidates."

She grinned at him. "Now you are just trying to impress me."

He considered this. "I *am* trying to impress you. I suppose I hope you will become attached to me."

She went over and scooped him into her arms. "I already am," she whispered.

He rested his chin on her head, and they stood there for a minute, just enjoying each other's nearness. Finally, she kissed his cheek and stepped away. "Go home to your children before it's dark. I'll see you all tomorrow."

He kissed her tenderly before he went.

She watched him through the window as he walked up the coastal path. She pressed her hand over her womb. "That's your father," she told her baby. "I think that you will love him very much."

Tompkins poked her head inside the door. "Ah, you're back. You have a visitor. I told her you were out but she insisted on waiting."

Sera winced. Trust Kestrel Bay to be abuzz with word of her arrival an hour after her carriage drove past the village square.

"Oh dear," she sighed. "Who is it?"

Tompkins handed her a card. *The Baroness Trewlnany.* "She's waiting in the parlor."

Sera rushed out of the room, not sure if she was excited or afraid.

She found Tamsin perched on the sofa, her posture bracingly straight. On her lap, she held a brass cage. Inside it were two kingfishers.

The sight of them knocked the wind out of her.

Tamsin stood up and put the cage on the ground. "Sera. I'm so sorry to call without notice, and I hope it's not too great an imposition."

Sera sat down in a chair opposite, trying not to betray her nerves at the sight of those birds. "No imposition. Though I suspect your husband would not approve of you paying me a call."

Tamsin sucked in her lips. "There is much about my behavior that fails to meet his approval of late." She paused and narrowed her eyes. "And the feeling is decidedly mutual."

Sera had always loved Tamsin's tart, efficient way with words. Their barbed tongues had been the basis of their affection for each other back when they'd spent every day roaming the cliffs and reading books in Seraphina's attic room.

Tamsin had not spoken to her like this in so many years she'd almost forgotten how it used to be between them.

"I can't imagine why," Sera quipped.

Tamsin nodded, but the smile fell off her face.

"I was grateful to you for standing up to Bell at my lecture," Sera said. "It was a courageous thing to do and I'm sure it cost you more than I know. Thank you."

"Oh, Sera, I don't desire nor deserve any thanks. I read your book, you see. And it made me understand how badly I have behaved. You can't know how sorry I am."

Sera felt her throat becoming unpleasantly tight.

Tamsin's betrayal of her all those years—marrying Trewlnany after Sera told her of her pregnancy and his responsibility—had never been something she'd understood.

They had been such close friends that the loss of Tamsin had been almost worse than the loss of Jonathan. It had always seemed like Tamsin might have broken the engagement, knowing the man to whom she was promised had strayed so wildly. Knowing that he was the father of Seraphina's child.

But she hadn't. She had simply disappeared from Sera's life without another word.

But she was here now. And Sera was glad to see her.

"I blamed you then, perhaps, but not now," she said. "I recognize you were in a difficult position, Tamsin. You were only a girl. Your father had expectations of you, just as mine did."

"Sera, I knew I should call it off when I learned he'd been courting you in secret," Tamsin said. "But you see . . . I didn't feel I could. I had been with him, too."

Sera's head shot up. *"Pardon?"*

Tamsin nodded, her face aggrieved. "Before our engagement was announced, before I knew about you and him, he . . . had his way with me."

"The bastard."

"No, I don't mean it like that. I wanted to. I was in love with him, and he was so handsome, and . . . well, *you* know. Everything you wrote in your book. Exactly that. It was impossible with him, wasn't it?"

Sera felt like she might not be able to draw another breath so long as she lived. "Oh, Tamsin."

Tamsin nodded. "I know. So when you told me about him and the baby . . . Sera, it pains me to say it but I believed him when he said you seduced him. He assured me the scandal would go away, that his father would pay for the child and some other man would marry you. And then, when you threw that fellow off and fled . . . I began to suspect I had made a terrible mistake. But by then it was too late for me to reconsider. I was married."

Tamsin lost her composure on the word *married*.

"Oh, Tamsin. I'm so sorry."

"Do you know the worst of it? He's never changed. He's just as charming and amusing as he was when we were girls, and just as liberal in seducing anyone he fancies. God help me, even I still succumb to his charms, from time to time, because it's so much easier than despising him." She patted her stomach, which had a slight swell. "As you can see. Our fifth. Oh, Sera, what is wrong with me?"

Sera took her hand. "Tamsin, nothing is wrong with you. What could you do differently? Were our situations reversed, would I be any different?"

Tamsin wiped her eyes. "I'm so proud of you, Sera. I've read all your books at least twice. And when I saw you speak, I felt, in a perverse way, pride. Because perhaps if it were not for my cruelty to you, you might not have had the chance to lead." She took a banknote from her pocket and held it out. "I wanted to offer you this, for your institute. Trewlnany pays no attention to his accounts."

Sera looked at the note. "Five hundred pounds. Why, that's a fortune."

"He'll only spend it on women and horses."

"Thank you, Tamsin."

One of the kingfishers chirped, and both of them looked down at it flitting about. Tamsin picked up the birdcage. "I brought you these. I always loved how you had them as a girl. I was envious of them. So when I had children, I gave them kingfishers as pets. We have a lovely atrium for them at Gwennol Bluff. But over the summer, several went missing. And then Mr. Anderson mentioned . . ."

Tamsin shivered. "I'm so sorry, Sera. I wanted to bring you two sweet ones, as a gesture of apology. I'll take them back if you'd rather not look after them but I remember how much you loved them and it just made me so *enraged* that Jonathan would be so cruel."

Sera drew in a breath. "I suspected it was him, but I could not figure out *why.*"

Tamsin craned her neck. "Surely you know. He's terrified of you."

"*Him*, terrified of me?"

"Because you know about his mother. That he's not Pendrake's legitimate son. He thought that's what you intended to expose in your book."

He'd told her this secret once, on one of their dreamy afternoons. His mother had been barren, and Pendrake had sired a son with a mistress with her blessing, so he might have an heir. But Sera had never said a word of it to anyone.

"Why would he think I would expose it, when I never have, even back then?"

Tamsin frowned. "He didn't understand why you would stop at merely embarrassing him, when you could utterly destroy him."

Trust a man like Jonathan Trewlnany to miss the bloody point.

"My purpose was not revenge. It was to show the world that men like him aren't held to the same standards. I wanted people to know how it feels to be the woman in the story, to imagine the anger and the unfairness and the loss."

"Well, in this case you could see how he might worry otherwise. My dear husband does, after all, deserve a bit of revenge." Tamsin smiled sadly.

"Well, I'll allow I did take a bit of pleasure in using his name after all this time. But mostly because without the scandal, no one's interested in the story."

Tamsin smiled sadly. "No. They never are."

"Well, they are beginning to see it now. Eventually there will be enough of us who see. And that's how we will change things."

"I hope so, Sera. I hope so." Tamsin rose. "Well, I won't keep you. I know you've just arrived back and are surely tired. Shall I leave the birds?"

Sera looked over at the little creatures. "Yes, thank you. I know two children who might enjoy helping me look after them."

Tamsin nodded. She turned to go, but then paused and turned back. "Sera, may I embrace you?"

Sera walked forward and wrapped her arms around her friend. "Oh, Tamsin. You're still a gem, you know?"

Tamsin inhaled deeply. "I'm not. But I've missed you. All these years, I've looked at this house and wished you were still in it."

"Well, I'm back for a spell. Visit whenever you like."

ADAM LIFTED ADELINE onto his shoulders and Marianne took Jasper's hand as they walked from the cottage to Seraphina's house.

"I'm glad Miss Arden's back," Addie chirped. "I think she has missed me very much."

Adam laughed. "I reckon she will be very pleased to see you."

He hoped this was the case. He knew there were no guarantees that this happiness he felt would last. He would protect these two, no matter what. But he hoped.

He hoped.

Seraphina was waiting for them on her terrace with a beautiful lunch laid on the table. When she spotted them, she rose, her eyes shining. "Jasper! Addie! How I've looked forward to seeing you!"

They smiled at her shyly as she climbed down the steps to greet them.

"May I have a hug?" she asked. When they nodded, she came down to her knees and gave each of them a long, tight embrace.

Jasper reached out and touched the necklace she was wearing. "It's our amulet!" he said to Addie.

Marianne caught Adam's eye and bit her lip.

"It's my favorite jewel in my entire collection," Seraphina said. "I have something for you, to say thank you."

Sera led them to a small table, where she had made a stack of flower crowns. She put one on Addie's head and one on Jasper's.

Adam met her eye over their heads and touched two fingers to his heart.

Sera blushed bright red.

It made him look down and smile into the knot of his cravat.

"I am very sorry I missed going to Golowan with you," Sera said to the children. "But I thought we could have our own celebration today. I had cook make pasties just for the occasion."

"I am very hungry. I shall have two," Addie pronounced.

"Very wise. That's how you'll grow strong and mighty."

"Addie is already mighty," Jasper supplied. "She can lift a boulder. She helped me make a fort at the beach."

"It was huge!" Addie said.

"Very impressive. Are you going to be architects like your papa?"

Jasper considered this. "Perhaps. When I'm older." He glanced at Adam, as if to check that this hesitation might hurt his feelings.

Adam reached out and ruffled his hair. "You can be whatever you like, my boy."

Jasper perked up. "Maybe I will write books, like Miss Arden."

Sera beamed at him. "What a sound ambition."

"I'm going to be a princess," Adeline said loftily.

Seraphina and Marianne exchanged identical mordant glances. "Well, no rush to decide just yet, Miss Adeline," Sera laughed.

A little chirp caught Jasper's attention. "I hear a bird!" he cried.

Seraphina smiled. "I seem to have made some new friends. Would you like to meet them?"

The children nodded. She took them by the hands and led them to a table where two pretty turquoise kingfishers were perched in a brass cage.

Addie squealed in delight. "Parrots!"

Sera laughed. "They are called kingfishers. I kept them when I was a girl."

"They are very pretty," Jasper said. He moved forward to look at them, then paused a foot from the cage. "Do they bite?"

"No, these two were born inside. They trust people."

The children leaned in to look at the birds. "I thought you might help me take care of them," Sera said. "Birds get very lonely and I'm so very busy. Perhaps, you could come from time to time and help me keep them company."

It touched Adam deeply that she'd thought of this.

Sera had said she needed him to show her how to build a life with someone else. But he suspected she did not need his help at all.

Jasper looked at Adam. "May we?"

Adam smiled. "Of course."

As the children chattered to each other about what they would name the birds, Adam caught Seraphina's eyes.

She smiled at him. Long and calm and happy.

"Shall we have lunch?" she asked the children. "I am very keen to hear of your adventures on the way from London." She came and draped an arm over Marianne's shoulders. "I hope you have not exhausted your dear auntie."

And as his family gathered outside in the sunshine, he looked into Seraphina's eyes across the table.

"I love you," he mouthed to her.

Her eyes filled.

She pressed two fingers over her heart and mouthed the words back.

Epilogue

FROM
The Society of Sirens
A MEMOIR
BY SERAPHINA ARDEN, 1827

❧

If you had told me the night that Elinor went missing that our rebellion would lead to my falling in love with a man, having a child with him, and gaining his family as my own, I would have scoffed at you that that was not the kind of ending I considered happy.

I would have said that the domestication of the female sex was tantamount to her imprisonment. That the burden of motherhood would diminish my powers, distract me from my fight.

I would have argued that I was more effective as a voice for women who'd been denied such things, or who'd rejected them.

But I continue to recall a romantic thing that Adam Anderson first said to me in a letter: I am reduced by the loss of you.

And I have thought often, over our years together, of the corollary: your love increases me.

You see, he was always wise, my Adam.

It turned out the more I began to love, the more I became.

I did not lose myself by loving Adam, nor our children. I became fuller. Richer. I discovered I could be a Rakess, an Intellectual, a Mother, a Renegade, a Helpmeet, and a Siren, all at once.

I never married Adam Anderson, but he stands across the room from me most days as I write these memoirs, painting.

Is it too earnest to confess I still can't take my eyes off him? That he's still the kindest man I've ever known? That even in our worst moments, and of course, there have been many—he was always nice—except in bed?

He would go on to build the institute, and many other things beside it, and to help arrange our life so that I could be all the versions of myself I wanted to. I like to think that, in my way, I did the same for him.

But that is getting ahead of the rest of the story.

That winter, as I prepared to leave the happy little nest I'd been enjoying with Adam and return to London to prepare for Cornelia's exhibition, I received the news that Lord Bell had finally filed a petition to Parliament for a divorce.

I rushed back to London to be with Elinor.

And what I found there made me question all the progress we had made.

For that was not all Lord Bell had done.

He'd taken Jack.

Acknowledgments

Thank you to the entire team at Avon for helping me bring the Society of Sirens into the world, and particularly Nicole Fischer for championing this book and Carrie Feron for helping find a place for my work. Thank you to the indefatigable and heroic Sarah Younger, without whom I would be a speck of dust floating in the wind. Thank you to the team at Tessera Editorial and especially Dee Hudson for her editorial consulting and research, and Trisha Tobias for her sensitivity read. Thank you to my cover models, Lori-anna Izrailova and Keithen Hergott, for bringing Seraphina and Adam to life in a style that can only truly be captured with the flame emoji.

Thank you to my writer friends, who are also my real friends, including (and sometimes especially) the ones who live in my pocket. Thank you to the women in my life, all over the world, who fill me up with joy, conversation, delicious food, Pilates, small business advice, crocheted trivets, and pool days, as required. Thank you as always to my editorial assistant, who remains devoted to and yet terrible at her job, because she is a cat. And thank you to my beautiful, beloved husband.

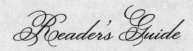
Reader's Guide

1. The "rake" character is a beloved trope in romance novels—but the character is almost always a cis-gendered man. What does Seraphina Arden have in common with the traditional male romance rake? How is she different?

2. Seraphina makes her name challenging the conventional beliefs of the eighteenth century, which held that women were to be wives and mothers, should refrain from sex outside of marriage, and were not entitled to the same education, voting, or property rights as men. What aspects of her struggle still seem pertinent today?

3. Seraphina, Thaïs, and Cornelia have all become notorious because of their sexual histories, and use their celebrity to raise money and force issues that matter to them into the spotlight. What are the risks and benefits of this decision? Can you think of parallels in modern time?

4. Both Adam and Seraphina have had their lives severely impacted by child loss and maternal mortality. How do the risks of pregnancy and childbearing impact both characters' relationships to sexual freedom and pleasure? How do you think the high rate

of infant and maternal mortality in the eighteenth century impacted daily life?

5. When we meet Seraphina, she is using alcohol to dull her pain. Do you view her as an alcoholic? How does her drinking (and sobriety) affect the people she is close to?

6. In the romance genre, the point at which the characters are forced to confront their most painful vulnerabilities in the relationship is often called "the black moment." What is the black moment for Adam and Seraphina? Is it the same for both of them?

7. Complete this sentence: Adam Anderson is a _____ hero.

8. Why is Seraphina opposed to marriage? Do you agree with her reasoning? What will be the impact of her and Adam choosing to make an untraditional family? What do you think would be the consequence if the alternative happened, and they married?

9. Why does Adam decide to sever his ties with Lord Pendrake, knowing what he will have to sacrifice professionally and personally? Do you agree with his decision?

10. Lord Bell sues Jack Willow for criminal conversation, in which a husband can ask for damages from another man who has committed adultery with his wife. Does it surprise you to learn that this practice is still legal in several U.S. states, even though

women are no longer considered their husband's property under law?

11. Lord Bell is able to commit his wife to an asylum for disobeying his edicts as her husband. What were the implications for women of losing their rights when they married? How do you think this has shaped women's roles in society?

12. Seraphina Arden was "ruined" as a young woman and now calls herself "the Rakess" and argues against double standards in how men and women are treated when it comes to sexual morality. How does the trope of the rake in romance novels contrast with the trope of a ruined woman? Is there a parallel in our modern times?

13. What does Seraphina wish to accomplish by naming Baron Trewlnany in her memoir? Why does she hold back damning information about his past? Do you agree with her decisions? How does this relate to modern issues, like "cancel culture" and the #metoo movement?

Don't miss Cornelia's story, and
the next phase of the fight!

SOCIETY OF SIRENS, VOLUME II

Coming 2021